Legacy

www.daniellesteel.com

Also by Danielle Steel

* Published outside the UK under the title PASSION'S PROMISE

For more information on Danielle Steel and her books, see her
website at www.daniellesteel.com

DANIELLE STEEL

Legacy

CORGI BOOKS

TRANSWORLD PUBLISHERS
61–63 Uxbridge Road, London W5 5SA
A Random House Group Company
www.transworldbooks.co.uk

LEGACY
A CORGI BOOK: 9780552158978

First published in Great Britain
in 2010 by Bantam Press
an imprint of Transworld Publishers
Corgi edition published 2011

Addresses for Random House Group Ltd companies outside the UK
can be found at: www.randomhouse.co.uk
The Random House Group Ltd Reg. No. 954009

The Random House Group Limited supports The Forest Stewardship
Council (FSC®), the leading international forest certification organisation.
Our books carrying the FSC label are printed on FSC® certified paper. FSC
is the only forest certification scheme endorsed by the leading environmental
organisations, including Greenpeace. Our paper procurement policy can be
found at www.randomhouse.co.uk/environment

Typeset in AGaramond by Falcon Oast Graphic Art Ltd.
Printed and bound by CPI Group (UK) Ltd, Croydon, CR0 4YY

2 4 6 8 10 9 7 5 3 1

To my beloved children:
Beatrix, Trevor, Todd, Nick,
Sam, Victoria, Vanessa, Maxx,
and Zara,

May the paths you travel always
lead you to your dreams, to
courage, to freedom, and to peace.
And may you find a kindred spirit,
like Wachiwi, to inspire you.

With all my heart and love,
Mommy/d.s.

Legacy

Chapter 1

Brigitte

There was a heavy snowfall that had started the night before as Brigitte Nicholson sat at her desk in the admissions office of Boston University, meticulously going over applications. Other staffers had checked them before her, but she always liked to take a last look at the files herself to make sure that each one was complete. They were in the midst of making their decisions, and in six weeks acceptances and denials would be going out to the applicants. Inevitably, there would be some ecstatic prospective students and more often many broken hearts. It was difficult knowing that they had the lives and futures of earnest young people in their hands. Sifting through the applications was Brigitte's busiest time of year, and although the ultimate choices were made by committee, her job was vetting applications, and conducting individual interviews when students requested them. In those cases, she would submit her notes and comments with the application. But essentially, grades, test scores, teachers' recommendations, extracurricular activities, and sports contributed heavily to the final result. A candidate either looked like an asset to the school or not. Brigitte always felt the weight of those decisions heavily on her shoulders. She was meticulous about going over all the materials they submitted. Ultimately, she had to think about what was best for the school, not for the students. She was used to the dozens of calls and e-mails she got from anxious high school counselors, doing all they could to help their candidates. Brigitte was proud to be associated with BU, and much to her own amazement, had worked in the admissions office for ten years. The years had flown by, seemingly in an instant. She was number three in the department and had turned down opportunities for promotion many times. She was content where she was and had never been terribly ambitious.

At twenty-eight, Brigitte had come to BU as a graduate student, to get a master's in anthropology after assorted minor jobs post-college, followed by two years of working at a women's shelter in Peru and another one in Guatemala, and a year of traveling in India and Europe. She had a bachelor's degree in anthropology with a minor in women's and gender studies from Columbia. The plight of women in underdeveloped countries had always been a primary concern to her. Brigitte had taken a job in the admissions office just until she could complete her degree. She had wanted to go to Afghanistan for a year after that, but like so many other graduate students who took jobs at the university while they were there, she stayed. It was comfortable, safe, and a protected atmosphere she came to love. And as soon as she got her master's, she started working on her Ph.D. The academic world was addictive and womb-like, along with its intellectual challenges and pursuit of knowledge and degrees. And it was easy to hide from the real world and its demands. It was a haven of scholars and youth. She didn't *love* her job in admissions, but she really, really liked it. She felt productive and useful, and she was dedicated to helping the right students get into the school.

They had more than sixteen thousand undergraduate students, and over thirty thousand applications every year. Some were eliminated summarily, for inadequate test scores or grades, but as the number of eligible applicants got whittled down, Brigitte became more and more focused on the process. She was meticulous about detail in everything she did. She didn't have her doctorate yet, but was still working on it, taking a class or two every semester. At thirty-eight, she was satisfied with her life. And for the last seven years, she had been working on a book. She wanted it to be the definitive work on the subject of voting and women's rights around the world. While getting her master's, Brigitte had written countless papers about the topic.

Her thesis argued that how countries handled the voting rights of women defined *who* they were as a nation. She felt that the vote was crucial to women's rights. Her colleagues who had read what she'd written so far were impressed by her eloquence but not surprised by her thoroughness and diligence. One criticism of her work was that she sometimes got so involved in the minutiae of what she was studying that she neglected the big picture. She tended to get caught up in the details.

She was friendly and kind, trustworthy and responsible. She was a deeply caring person and extremely hard-working, and thorough about everything she did. The only complaint that her best friend, Amy Lewis, made of her, to her face as a rule, was that she lacked passion. She intellectualized everything, and followed her brain more than her heart. Brigitte thought *passion,* as Amy referred to it, was a flaw, not a quality, a dangerous thing. It made you lose perspective and direction. Brigitte liked staying on course, and keeping her goals in plain view.

She didn't like rocking the boat or taking chances, on anything. Risk-taking was not her style. She was someone you could count on, not someone who would act impulsively, or without a great deal of thought. And she herself readily admitted that she was slow to make decisions while she weighed all the pros and cons.

Brigitte estimated that she was halfway through her book. She planned to speed up the process and finish it in five years, around the time she got her Ph.D. Twelve years spent on a book covering such an important subject seemed reasonable to her, since she was also working full-time and taking classes toward her doctorate. She was not in any rush. She had decided that if she completed both her doctoral degree and her book by the time she was forty-three, she'd be pleased. Her steady, relentless, unruffled way of dealing with things sometimes drove her friend Amy crazy. Brigitte was not a fast-track kind of person and hated change. Amy thought Brigitte should live life to the fullest, and leap into things more spontaneously. Amy was a trained marriage and family counselor and social worker. She ran the university's counseling office, and liberally offered Brigitte her advice and opinions. They were total opposites and yet best friends. Amy dealt with everything – emotional, intellectual, and professional – at full speed.

Brigitte was tall, thin, almost angular, with jet-black hair, dark eyes, high cheekbones, and olive skin. She looked almost Middle Eastern or Italian, although her heritage was Irish and French. The Irish heritage of her father accounted for her jet-black hair. Amy was small and blond with a tendency to put on weight if she didn't exercise, and she had all the passion about life that she claimed Brigitte didn't. Brigitte liked to accuse her friend of being 'hyper,' with the attention span of a flea, which they both knew wasn't true. But Amy took on new projects constantly, and handled multitasking with ease. While Brigitte had struggled with one epic tome, Amy had published three nonfiction books about dealing with kids. She had two children of her own although she wasn't married. On her fortieth birthday, after years of unsuccessful affairs with graduate students younger than she was or with married professors, she had gone to a sperm bank. And at forty-four, she had two boys, now one and three, who drove her happily crazy. She regularly nagged Brigitte to start having babies of her own. She told Brigitte that at thirty-eight she had no time to waste, her 'eggs were getting older by the minute.' Brigitte was far more casual about it, and wasn't worried. Modern science made it possible to conceive far older than in her mother's day, and she felt confident about it, despite Amy's dire warnings that she was putting motherhood off for too long.

Brigitte knew she'd have children one day, and more than likely marry Ted, although they never discussed it. There was something about living in the protected atmosphere of academia that made you feel, or Brigitte anyway, that she was going to be young forever. Amy always snapped her back to reality by saying they were middle-aged. It was impossible to believe by looking at either of them. Neither one looked her age, nor felt it, and Ted Weiss, Brigitte's boyfriend of six years, was three years younger. At thirty-five, he looked, felt, and acted like a kid. He had studied archaeology at Harvard, got his doctorate at BU, and had worked in the department of archaeology at BU for the last six years. His dream was to have his own dig. BU had many around the world, in Egypt, Turkey, Pakistan, China, Greece, Spain, and Guatemala. He had visited each of them at least once during his time at BU. Brigitte had never gone with him to see them. She used the time he was away to continue doing research on her book. She was a lot less interested in traveling than she had been right after college. Now she was happy at home.

Brigitte's relationship with Ted was a happy one. They lived in their own apartments quite near to each other, and spent the weekends together, usually at his place because it was bigger. He cooked, she didn't. They often socialized with his graduate students, particularly those in the doctoral program, like her. They also saw a lot of the other professors in their respective departments. They both loved the academic life, although Brigitte's work in the admissions office wasn't scholarly, but the life they led and shared suited them to perfection. It was an atmosphere filled with intense dedication to higher learning, and both of them admitted that most of the time they felt no different from their students. They were thirsty for all they could learn, and loved the intellectual world. Like all universities, there were the usual minor scandals, affairs, and petty jealousies, but on the whole, they both enjoyed the life they led, and had much in common.

Brigitte could see herself married to Ted, although she couldn't figure out when. And she assumed Ted would ask her one day. They had no reason to get married for the moment, since neither of them was anxious for children. Eventually, but not yet. They both felt too young for any life other than the one they were living. Brigitte's mother often voiced the same concerns as Amy, and reminded her that she wasn't getting any younger. Brigitte just laughed at them both and said she had no need to nail Ted to the floor, he wasn't going anywhere, to which Amy always responded cynically, 'You never know.' But her own bad experiences with men colored her view of the situation. She was always somewhat convinced that, given half a chance, most men would disappoint you, although even she had to admit that Ted was a really sweet guy, without a mean bone in his body.

Brigitte said openly that she loved him, but it wasn't something they talked about much, nor did they talk about the future. They lived in the present. Each one was perfectly content living alone during the work week, and their weekends together were always relaxing and fun. They never argued, and disagreed about few things. It was a totally comfortable arrangement. Everything about Brigitte's life was steady, her job, her relationship with Ted, and her slow but steady pace on her book, which would eventually be published by the academic press.

According to Amy, Brigitte's life wasn't exciting, but she liked everything about it, and it worked well for her. She didn't need or want excitement in her life, and looking far ahead to the future, she could see where it was going. Her life had direction and forward motion, even if not with great speed. Just like her studies for her Ph.D., and her book. That was enough for her. It was a journey. She was in no hurry to reach her destination or make any snap decisions. Despite her mother's and Amy's cynicism, concerns, and dire warnings, Brigitte wasn't worried about it all.

'So whose life are you ruining today?' Amy asked her with an impish grin as she bounced into the doorway of Brigitte's office.

'That's a terrible thing to say!' Brigitte said, pretending to look stern. 'On the contrary, I'm checking to make sure the applicants sent us all the right stuff.'

'Yeah, so you can turn them down. Poor kids, I still remember getting those awful letters. "Although we were very impressed by the work you've done during your senior year, we can't figure out what the hell you were doing all through junior year. Were you drunk or on drugs or just lazy beyond belief? We wish you the best of luck in your future endeavors, but not at our school . . ." Shit, I cried every time I got one of those letters, and so did my mother. She figured I'd wind up working at McDonald's, not a bad job, but she wanted me to be a doctor. It took her years to forgive me for being "just" a social worker.' Amy's grades for junior year couldn't have been that bad, Brigitte knew, since she had gone to Brown, and eventually got a master's of science degree at Stanford before getting her social worker's degree at the Columbia School of Social Work in New York.

They were all academic snobs at BU. In the academic world, where you got your degrees really mattered, just as how often you published did later. If Brigitte had been teaching at BU, she couldn't have lingered over her book for the past seven years without publishing it sooner. There would have been a lot more pressure on her, which was why she was happier working in the admissions office. She didn't have the competitive spirit you needed to survive as a professor. Amy taught an undergraduate psych class and ran the counseling office, and did both well. She left her kids at the campus day care center while she worked. And she had a profound love for young people generally, and her students. She set up the first suicide hotline at BU after losing too many students in her early years of counseling. It was a common occurrence at all universities, and an epidemic that worried them all. Brigitte didn't like the implication that by turning down applicants to BU she was ruining their lives. She hated to think of it that way. As usual, Amy's opinions went right to the heart of the matter, and were bluntly expressed. She didn't mince words, whereas Brigitte was always more careful and more diplomatic about what she said, and how she said it. Amy used a more frontal and confrontational approach, with colleagues or friends.

'So what are you doing tonight?' Amy asked her pointedly, curling up in the chair on the other side of Brigitte's desk.

'Tonight? Why? Is it something special?' Brigitte looked blank, and Amy rolled her eyes.

'It should be, if you've been dating a guy for six years. You're hopeless. It's Valentine's Day, for chrissake! You know, hearts, flowers, candy, engagement rings, marriage proposals, great sex, soft music, candlelight. Aren't you going out with Ted?' She looked disappointed for Brigitte. Despite her own failed relationships, Amy still loved the notion of romance, and although they were adorable together, she always felt that Brigitte and Ted had far too little of it. They were still like high school kids dating, not like people in their thirties planning their future. And Amy worried about her friend, fearing that the important things in life were sliding past her. Like commitment, marriage, and having kids.

'I think we both forgot,' Brigitte admitted sheepishly about Valentine's Day. 'Ted's working on a paper, and I've been buried in applications. We only have six weeks left to process them. And I have two papers due for my class. Besides, it's snowing, and a crappy night to go out.'

'So stay home and celebrate it in bed. Maybe he'll propose to you tonight,' Amy said hopefully, and Brigitte laughed out loud.

'Yeah, right, with a paper due on Friday. He'll probably

call me later and we'll figure out something. Chinese take-out or sushi. It's not a big deal.'

'It should be,' Amy scolded her. 'I don't want you to be an old maid like me.'

'I'm not, and neither are you. We're unmarried women. That's a highly respected category these days. It's considered a choice, not an affliction, and people who are older than we are still get married and have kids.'

'Yeah, Sarah in the Bible maybe. How old was she? Ninety-seven, I think, when she had a kid. Generally, these days, that's considered a little beyond the usual statistics. I think it was then too. And she was married.' Amy looked meaningfully at her friend, and Brigitte laughed.

'You're obsessed, for me anyway. You're not running around crazily trying to get married. Why should I? Besides, Ted and I are perfectly happy the way we are. No one rushes to get married anymore. Why is it such a big deal?' Brigitte looked unconcerned.

'After six years, it would hardly be considered rushing. It would be more like normal. And in about ten minutes you'll be forty-five or fifty, and it'll be all over for you. Your eggs will be prehistoric, and he can write an archaeology paper about them.' She was being funny, but she meant it. 'Maybe you should propose to him.'

'Don't be silly. We have lots of time to think about all

that. Besides, I want to finish my book first, and my Ph.D. I want to be a doctor when I get married.'

'Then hurry up. You two are the slowest people on the planet. You think you're going to be young forever. Well, I've got bad news for you. Your body knows better. You need to at least think about getting married and having kids.'

'I will, in a few years. What are you doing tonight, by the way?' She knew Amy hadn't even had a date since she got pregnant with her first child four years before. She was totally involved with them and had had almost no social life since. She was too busy working and having fun with her boys. She wanted Brigitte to experience that kind of fulfillment and happiness too. And Ted would make a great father, they both agreed. His students adored him. He was warm, kind, and smart, everything a woman could want in a man, which was why Brigitte loved him, and so did everyone else. He was a totally nice guy.

'I have a hot date with my sons,' Amy confessed. 'We're going to have pizza for dinner, and they'll be sound asleep by seven o'clock, so I can watch TV and pass out by ten. Not exactly the perfect Valentine's Day, but it works for me.' Amy smiled happily as she stood up. She had an appointment in her office with a student who'd been referred by his freshman adviser. He was a foreign student, away from home for the first time, and seriously depressed. Amy suspected she would be referring him to the student health office for meds from what the adviser had said. But Amy wanted to talk to the boy first. She saw kids like him all day and was diligent about her work, just as Brigitte was about hers.

'That sounds like a good plan,' Brigitte commented. 'I'll figure out something with Ted later, and remind him if he forgot. Maybe he just assumed we'd have dinner together.' He did that sometimes, they both did, what they shared was a relationship that worked without any need for definition. After six years, she assumed they would be together forever. They had no reason not to be. It didn't need to be said or written in stone. They were both happy the way things were, no matter what Amy said, or Brigitte's mother. This worked for them. *Comfortable* was the word that defined what they shared, even if Amy thought they needed more romance or passion. Brigitte didn't, and neither did Ted. They were both laid-back people who had no need to make plans set in stone for the future, or spell everything out.

By sheer coincidence, Ted called her ten minutes after Amy left Brigitte's office. He sounded harried and in a rush and slightly breathless, which was unusual for him. He was an easygoing guy who rarely got rattled.

'Are you okay?' Brigitte asked him, sounding worried. 'Something wrong?'

'No, just a little crazy. There's a lot going on here today. Can I see you for dinner?' When he said it that way, he meant at home. He wanted to stop by her place after work. Brigitte knew the shorthand of their conversations, and what Ted meant.

'Of course.' She smiled in response to his dinner suggestion. He had remembered. 'Amy just reminded me that it's Valentine's Day. I had totally forgotten.'

'Oh shit, so did I. I'm sorry, Brig. Do you want to go out?'

'Whatever you want. I'm just as happy staying home, especially in this weather.' The snowfall had increased, and now there was a foot of snow on the ground. Driving wouldn't be easy.

'There's something I want to celebrate with you tonight. How about an early dinner at Luigi's? You can stay at my place tonight if you want.' It was an offer he rarely made during the week, nor did she. They both liked getting an early start to their day in their own familiar settings. They usually only spent weekend nights together.

'What are we celebrating?' Brigitte asked, slightly mystified. She could hear the excitement in his voice, although he was trying to sound calmer than he felt, but she could sense that too.

'I'm not going to spoil the surprise. I want to say it in person. We'll talk about it over dinner.'

'You got a promotion in the department?' She couldn't stand the suspense, and he laughed in answer, and sounded like a man with a secret, or a plan. This was all very unlike him, and it made Brigitte a little nervous. What if Amy was right, and he was going to use Valentine's Day to propose? Suddenly her heart and mind were racing, and she was scared.

'It's much more important than that. Do you mind taking a cab? I'll meet you at Luigi's. I know that's not a very romantic way to start Valentine's Day, but I'm going to be stuck in the office till dinner.' He sounded apologetic.

'That's fine. I'll meet you there,' she said with a quaver in her voice.

'I love you, Brig,' he breathed into the phone before he hung up, and she looked stunned. He rarely said that, except in bed, and suddenly she wondered if Amy's wishes for her were coming true. Thinking about it, she felt panicked. She wasn't at all sure she was ready for a proposal. She was almost sure she wasn't, but it sounded like a distinct possibility to her, and half an hour later she wandered down to Amy's office with a worried look. She stood in the doorway and glared at her friend. Amy's meeting with the homesick freshman had just ended, and she had referred him to see a psychiatrist for meds.

'I think you jinxed me,' Brigitte said with a look of angst as she walked into Amy's office and sat down.

'About what?' Amy looked confused.

'Ted just called and invited me to dinner. He said he has a surprise, bigger than a promotion, and he sounded as nervous as I feel now. Omigod, I think he's going to propose. I think I'm going to be sick.'

'Hallelujah, it's about goddamn time! At least one of you is making some sense here. Listen, six years of practically living together is long enough. You two get along better than any of the married couples I know. This will be great!'

'We don't live together,' Brigitte corrected her. 'We spend weekends together.'

'And how long do you want to do that? Another six years maybe? Ten? If Ted is planning to propose, he has the right idea. Life is short. You can't spend it in a holding pattern forever.'

'Why not? It works for us.'

'Maybe not. It sounds like he wants more, and he should. So should you.'

'I do. I just don't know if I want it right now. Why rock

the boat? "Don't fix what ain't broke," as the saying goes. Our arrangement is perfect as it is.'

'It'll be more perfect if you make a real commitment to each other. You can build something, a life, a family. You can't pretend to be students forever. That's what too many people in the academic world do. We all delude ourselves that we're kids too, and we're not. One day you wake up and realize that you're old, and life passed you by. Don't let that happen to you. You both deserve better than that. It may sound scary to you now, but it'll be great. Trust me. You need to take the next step.' Amy had always thought that Brigitte should do that with her work too. She thought Brigitte should be head of admissions, and could have been, but she didn't want that. She was content to be number three – she said it gave her more time to work on her book and degree and do more research.

Brigitte had never had a need to lead the pack. She was always content to be in an easy space, not the more stressful one of leader. She had never liked to take risks. Amy was sure it had to do with Brigitte's childhood. She had said to Amy once that her father had been a risk-taker. He had gambled all their money in the stock market, lost everything, and committed suicide. Her mother had struggled for years afterward, and worked hard to keep them afloat. What Brigitte hated most in life was risk, of any kind. If she was comfortable, she wouldn't budge. And Ted seemed to be content with that. But at some point, no matter how scary it was for her, Brigitte had to move forward. She couldn't stay rooted to one spot forever. Without risk, there was no growth. Amy ardently hoped that Ted would propose to her friend that night, no matter how scared she was.

'Try not to worry about it,' Amy reassured her. 'You love each other. It will be fine.'

'What if I marry him and he dies?' She was thinking of her father, and her eyes filled with tears as she looked at her friend.

Amy spoke to her gently and could see how frightened she was. 'Sooner or later, if you stay together until you're old, one of you is going to die. I don't think you need to worry about that for a hell of a long time,' she said to reassure her, but her fears were deeper than that.

'I just think about it sometimes. I know what my mom went through when my dad died.' She had been eleven, and she remembered her mother crying all the time, and then going out to find a job to support them. She had been a book editor in a publishing house for years, and had retired only the year before. She had time now to do things she had wanted to do for years and had never had time for: see her friends, play bridge, exercise, take cooking lessons, play golf. For several years now, she had been working on a history of their family genealogy, which she found fascinating and Brigitte didn't. But Brigitte never wanted to end up a widow, with a young child, like her mother. She'd rather stay single, just the way she was, forever.

Brigitte had dealt with her father's suicide in therapy when she was younger. She had forgiven him, but she had never gotten over her fear of change and taking risks. And she was feeling badly shaken at the prospect of Ted's possible proposal that night. So much so that she called her mother after work, before she went out to dinner, and her mother could hear the worry in her voice, and without explanation, Brigitte started talking about her father. It had been a long time since she'd done that, and her mother was puzzled. Brigitte didn't explain why.

'Are you sorry you married him, Mom?' Brigitte had never asked her mother that before, although she had often wondered, and her mother sounded startled.

'Of course not. I had you.'

'Aside from that. Was it worth everything you went through?' Her mother was quiet for a long moment before she answered. She had always been honest with her daughter, which was one of the reasons why their relationship was strong. And they had survived tragedy together, which made them even closer. They shared a special bond.

'Yes, it was worth it. I never regretted marrying him, even with everything that happened. I loved him very much. All you can do is your best in life. What happens after that is the luck of the draw. You hope it comes out right, but you just have to take the chance. And I meant what I said before, you were my reward for the hard times. My life would have been nothing without you.'

'Thanks, Mom,' Brigitte said with tears in her eyes. A few minutes later they hung up. Her mother had given Brigitte the answer she needed without knowing it. Even after the disaster her father had created for them, and his suicide, she had no regrets. It was what Brigitte had hoped to hear. She didn't know if she was ready for marriage at this point in time, and maybe she never would be, but if he asked her that night, she was going to take the chance and say yes. And maybe one day she'd be as sure as her mother had been. Maybe someday she'd have a daughter too. She was willing to believe that it was possible that Amy and her mother were both right. Even though the thought of it unnerved her, she was ready to accept Ted's proposal, if that's what he had in mind. She felt very brave as she got into the cab to meet him at Luigi's.

As Brigitte thought about Ted in the cab on the way to the restaurant, her terror was slowly becoming mixed with excitement. She loved him, and maybe being married to him would be a good thing. It might even be wonderful, she told herself. He was nothing like her father. Ted was solid. She was smiling when she sat down at the table where Ted was waiting for her. He stood up to kiss her before she sat down, and he looked happy and more excited than she had ever seen him. His mood was contagious and she felt more romantic than she had in years. She was ready. It was an important moment. He ordered champagne for her as he smiled into her eyes, and they clinked glasses and each took a sip of the bubbly wine. Despite the wintry weather outside, the atmosphere at the table was decidedly festive.

He said nothing unusual to her all through dinner, and she waited politely without asking questions, trying to calm her mind. She figured he would pop the question when he was ready. There was no doubt in her mind now that he would, given his expansive behavior all evening. Amy was right. Everything about the evening suggested to her that something important was about to happen, and then finally when dessert came, a heart-shaped chocolate cake offered as a gift by the restaurant, he looked at her and smiled broadly. He could hardly contain himself, and she could feel her earlier fears disappearing. Everything about this felt right. She remembered what Amy had said to her, that they needed more romance in their lives.

Brigitte realized now that they did, even though neither of them was passionate or overly demonstrative. But they had loved each other for six years. Their relationship was excellent and suited them. They shared the same interests. They both loved the academic life. He had minored in anthropology, and was supportive of her career and her work. She knew he was someone she could rely on. Ted Weiss was a good man, and when she let herself think about it, a lifetime with him felt right. She was feeling very sure tonight, and waited patiently while he beat around the bush for a few minutes and told her how wonderful she was to him, how much he respected and admired her, and that what he was about to tell her was his dream come true. His lifetime dream. It was the most romantic thing he had ever said to her, and she knew she would remember this moment forever.

She was feeling a little giddy from the champagne. But by then, she knew with total certainty what was coming next. It was easy to predict. She had always known it would happen at some point, in the distant future. And suddenly the future was now, sooner than she expected. All he had to do was ask the question, and her answer was going to be yes. She assumed he knew that too, just as she had guessed he was going to propose to her that night. The predictability of their life made her feel safe.

'This is the most exciting thing that's ever happened to me, Brig,' he said, looking deeply moved, 'and I know it won't be easy, but I hope you'll be happy about it too.' He looked a little more nervous as he said it, and she was touched.

'Of course I will,' she reassured him, waiting for him to ask her the question.

'I know you will, because you're such a kind, generous person, and you've always supported me in my work.'

'Just the way you support me in mine,' she praised him. 'That's part of the deal.'

'I think it's what made the relationship work for both of us. I know how important your work is to you too, and your book.' It wasn't as important to her as archaeology was to him, but she appreciated his respect. He always said good things about her writing, and liked what she had written so far. He agreed with her about women's rights, and had a profound respect for women. 'I'll always be grateful to you,' Ted said quietly as he looked into her eyes, nostalgic for a moment. It was an important moment for them both. 'I can't believe this is happening,' he said with a shaking voice. 'I've been waiting all night to tell you.' She could hear a drum roll in her head as he went on. 'They gave me my own dig today. My own. I'll run it. In Egypt. I know this will be rough on you. I leave in three weeks.'

He spat it all out at once and sat back in his chair then, smiling at her, and Brigitte felt as though she had been hit in the chest with a club. It took her a full minute to catch her breath and be able to speak again. This was not what she had expected to hear from him that night.

'Your own dig? In Egypt? You're leaving in three weeks? How the hell did that happen?' She looked stunned.

'You knew I applied every year. I just kind of gave up hope after a while, but they always said that sooner or later I'd get one. And now I did. They're having me open up a newly discovered cave site. It's incredible. It's my dream come true.' And for a minute, several minutes, she actually had thought she was his dream.

She waited a few more minutes, staring at her untouched chocolate cake before looking up at him again. She was fighting to stay calm, and suddenly wanted to howl in disappointment. After all this time, she had actually been ready to accept his proposal. And there was none. 'What does this mean for us?' The possibilities were obvious, but she needed them spelled out. She didn't want to guess again about something this important, nor assume. This time she wanted to hear his plan for them, if there was one, and what he planned to do about them.

'I guess we always knew that this would happen sooner or later,' Ted said soberly. 'I can't take you along. There's no job for you on the dig, and I don't know if you could get a visa just as a hanger-on. Besides, what would you do there, Brig? I know that your work is important to you here. I think the inevitable has happened. We had a good run for six years, Brig. I love you. We've had a great time. But with me in Egypt for three to five years, or longer if the dig goes well or they give me another one after this, I won't be back for a long time, and I don't expect you to wait around for me. We both have to go on with our lives. Mine will be there, and yours is here. We're both reasonable people, and we knew this would happen one day.' He sounded perfectly calm about it. He was leaving in three weeks, and that was it. Bye, thanks for a fun six years, see ya.

'I didn't know this would happen,' she said, still looking shocked. 'I thought we'd wind up together,' she objected as tears stung her eyes. She couldn't hold them back. He had broadsided her so completely, she could hardly think straight.

'We never said that,' Ted reminded her. 'We talked about it theoretically, but we never made any plans. You know that. Maybe if I never got a dig. But to be honest with you, in the last year or two, whenever I've thought about it, I realize I'm not really a commitment kind of guy. Not in the classical sense. I like what we've had, but I don't need more than that, nor want it. I never thought you really did either. You're not one of those women desperate to get married and have kids, which is why it worked so well for us.'

'I thought it worked because we love each other,' Brigitte said bleakly. 'And I wasn't "desperate" to get married and have kids, but I thought we would.' She had assumed it, which made her feel incredibly stupid now. It was painfully obvious that he could hardly wait to leave and start his dig. Without her. He clearly didn't want to take her with him. She could see it in his eyes.

'You still can get married and have kids,' he reassured her quietly. She was a free woman now. 'Just not with me. I won't be here, for a long time. Who knows, if the excavation sites are rich, I could wind up staying there for ten years, or longer. I've waited for this all my life. I'm in no rush to come back, and I don't want to have any obligations here complicating things for me.' Now all she was was a complication. It sliced right through her aching heart to hear it. 'I thought we had an unspoken agreement, Brig, that this was great for now, with no future plans.'

'That's the trouble with unspoken agreements, everyone interprets them the way they want. I thought we had a commitment, apparently you didn't.' She sounded both angry and sad all at once.

'My primary commitment has always been to my work. You knew that,' he reproached her quietly. He didn't want to be made to feel guilty. His mother always did that to him and he hated it. Brigitte never had. He wanted to celebrate his dig, and his departure, not feel like a bad guy for leaving, which was more than a little simplistic, since it meant the end of their romance. But that was a price he was prepared to pay, and she had never expected. She realized now that she had been blind. And now he was, to everything but his dig. 'I'm sorry, Brig. I know this is sudden. It's hard for me too, but it's pretty clean actually. We don't even share an apartment. In fact, I was going to ask you if you want some of my stuff. I'm going to donate the rest. I don't have a decent piece of furniture in the place, except the couch.' They had bought it together the year before, and now he was getting rid of that too, as easily as he was getting rid of her. She hadn't felt this shocked or abandoned since her father's death, and that came to mind as she sat and stared at Ted.

'What about my eggs?' she asked, as tears rolled down her cheeks. She was slowly losing control of her emotions and feeling panicked. This was not the Valentine's Day dinner she had planned, nor that Amy had hoped for her.

'What eggs?' Ted looked blank.

'My eggs. The babies we'll never have, and I may never

have at all now. I'm thirty-eight years old, we've been together for six years. What am I supposed to do, put a notice on the bulletin board for some guy to marry and have kids with?'

'Is that all I was?' He looked insulted.

'No. You were the man I love, you still are. It was just so simple the way it was, I never asked the pertinent questions, I didn't think I had to. Why can't I go with you?' She looked at him pointedly, and he looked instantly uncomfortable.

'I can't think about a wife and kids with a job this important to do. I don't want the responsibility or the distraction. Besides, I just don't want that kind of commitment. This is the right time for both of us to move on, and see what life has in store for each of us on our own.' She felt her heart ache as he said it. 'I'm not even sure I'll ever want marriage, or not for a long, long time.' Way too late for her by then, as Amy would have reminded her. Her eggs were of no interest to him, and apparently never had been. She felt stupid now for having assumed so much and understood so little. She never thought she had to ask him. It was all so comfortable for so long, she had just drifted down the river with him, and now he was kicking her out of the boat, and paddling on alone. He had made it clear that he didn't want her in Egypt, now or later. She couldn't even blame him for it, she was as responsible as he was for the misunderstanding, and she knew it. He hadn't misled her. They had just lived from day to day and weekend to weekend for six years. And now she was thirty-eight years old, and he was leaving to live his dream, without her. Hearing him say it was the loneliest feeling she'd ever had.

'How do you want to handle this before I go?' he asked her gently. He felt sorry for her – she looked devastated by what he had told her. There was none of the joy for him that he had hoped for, and he realized now that that had been unrealistic. He had never fully understood how far-reaching her hopes were. She hadn't shared those hopes with him. And now all her broken dreams and incorrect assumptions were crashing down around her. She looked like she'd just been hit by a semi and run over. She felt even worse than she looked.

'What do you mean?' She blew her nose into a tissue and couldn't stop crying.

'I don't want to make this any harder for you than it has to be. I'm leaving in three weeks. Do you want to stay with me till then, or would you rather see less of me before I go?'

'If I'm understanding you correctly, you consider our relationship over when you leave, you want to move on, is that right?' He nodded, and she blew her nose again and looked at him miserably.

'I can't maintain a relationship with you here and live in Egypt. And your coming with me makes no sense. I think we would have ended it sooner or later.' That was news to her. But she was beyond arguing with him. She had taken too hard a hit.

'Then I think it's better if we end it now,' she said with dignity. 'I'd rather not see you again, Ted. It'll just make it worse. It was over for us as soon as you got the dig.' Or maybe even before that since he wanted no commitment between them.

'It has nothing to do with you, Brig. It's just life and how things work out sometimes.' But it was his life, not hers, that he was concerned with. She had never before realized how selfish he was. It was all about him, and now his dig.

'Yeah, I understand,' she said, slipping into her coat and standing up. She looked him straight in the eye. 'Congratulations, Ted. I'm happy for you. I'm sad for us, and for me, but I'm happy for you.' She was trying valiantly to be gracious and he was touched, although still disappointed that she hadn't been more enthusiastic and supportive of him. But he also understood that telling her he wanted to move on was a blow. He had wanted to do that for a while, but hadn't had the guts. But now that he was leaving for Egypt, it seemed like the perfect time. To him.

'Thank you, Brig. I'll take you home,' he offered.

She started crying copiously again and shook her head. 'No . . . I'll take a cab. Thanks for dinner. Goodnight.' And with that, she hurried out of the restaurant, hoping that no one would see her crying. Thanks for dinner, and for six years. Have a nice life. All she could think about as she stumbled out into the snow and hailed a cab was everything she had done wrong for six years. She wondered how she could have been so stupid. He wasn't a 'commitment kind of guy,' he didn't know if he wanted a wife and kids, now or ever. It had been easy for both of them. Comfortable. That was the operative word and all she ever wanted in life, and now look what she wound up with. A man she had been 'comfortable' with for six years, and now on a moment's notice, he had dumped her and was leaving for Egypt and the dig he had always dreamed of. He had said goodbye to her the way you would to a student or an assistant, not a woman you were in love with. She realized then that he wasn't in love with her. And maybe she wasn't with him either. She had settled for easy, and comfortable, instead of commitment and passion. It had seemed like enough for six years, and look where it got her. She sat crying in the cab all the way back to her apartment. It was a terrible feeling knowing she would never see him again and it was over. Even worse since she had thought he would ask her to marry him that night. What a fool she had been, she kept telling herself over and over. Her cell phone rang as she walked into her apartment. She glanced at it and saw that it was Ted. She didn't answer. What was the point? He wasn't going to change his mind. It was over. And all that was left now were pity and regret instead of love.

Chapter 2

It snowed all night and there was another foot of snow on the ground by morning. It was now officially a blizzard, and gave Brigitte the perfect excuse not to go in to work. She lay in bed crying when she woke up, and just couldn't face getting up and getting dressed. She felt as though her life was over, and she was overwhelmed by sadness and disappointment. And on top of that, she felt stupid. She had always known Ted wanted a dig of his own, she had just never understood how much he wanted it, or that he would dump her and run if he got one. She thought she had meant more to him than that, but apparently she didn't. She had been a stopgap, a time-passer, until his career panned out the way he wanted.

Meanwhile she had done nothing about her own career,

and had dawdled for seven years over her book. She felt like an utter failure as she read a text message from Ted. All it said was 'I'm sorry.' She knew he probably was. He wasn't a mean person, but he had his own goals in mind, and she wasn't part of his master plan, which made her easy to leave behind. She wouldn't have done it to him, but she also realized now that he was more ambitious than she had thought him. This dig meant everything to him, and she didn't. It was a terrible feeling.

She got another text message about ten that morning. Brigitte was still in bed, and cried as she read it. It was from Amy. 'Where are you? In bed, celebrating? Are you engaged? Tell me, tell me!' For a minute, Brigitte didn't know what to answer, and then realized that she had no choice but to tell her. She'd have to sooner or later anyway. She texted back, 'Not engaged. Dumped. It's over. He got his own dig in Egypt, and leaves in 3 weeks. We ended it last night. Am taking the day off.' It was amazing how you could reduce major life events, and even tragedies, to text messages. She had learned it from the students, who conducted their relationships, and all vital communications, by text.

Amy let out a low whistle in her office when she read it. That was not what she had expected at all, and she knew Brigitte hadn't either. She felt terrible for her. Ted wasn't even a bad guy, he just had his own agenda, which apparently didn't include Brigitte long term. And at thirty-five, he could afford to have wasted six years of his life. Brigitte couldn't. Amy tried to call her then, and she didn't answer, so she texted back.

'Can I come over?'

The response was quick. 'No, I feel like shit.'

'I'm sorry.'

She left her alone for a few hours then, and started calling her repeatedly that afternoon, and finally Brigitte answered. She sounded awful.

'It's not his fault.' Brigitte was quick to defend him. 'I was stupid not to ask him what his plans were for us. He says he's not a commitment kind of guy. How did I manage to miss that?'

'You didn't ask,' Amy said honestly, 'and you were both content the way things were. And maybe too scared to ask.' She knew that Ted's parents had had a bitter divorce that had blown their family apart, and he was skittish about marriage. Amy had figured he'd get over it, and so had Brigitte. And now he didn't have to. Destiny had intervened and given him a dig in Egypt. 'What are you going to do now?'

'I don't know. Cry for a year or two. I'm going to miss him.' But even she had noticed in her misery that as sad as she was, she wasn't as devastated as she thought she should be. So what had she done? Wasted six years of her life because she was afraid of taking a risk and making a commitment? And what happened now? What if she never had kids because of the time she had wasted? Thinking about that depressed her. She didn't want to end up like Amy, going to a sperm bank, and she knew she wouldn't. That was a risk that Brigitte knew she would never take. If she had kids, she wanted the real deal, a husband, a family life, or nothing. She didn't want to bring up children on her own. She had seen her mother, always struggling, always carrying everything alone, all the responsibilities and problems, all the joys and heartaches, and no one with whom to share them. She didn't feel as brave as Amy or her mother, and she didn't want to do it alone. She'd rather not have kids, which was beginning to seem like what might happen. It certainly looked like that now. Her whole outlook on the world and her future had changed in the past twenty-four hours, and not for the better. In spite of everything that had happened, her mother had never been bitter. Brigitte didn't want to be either. It would only poison her own life if so.

'Can I come over after work?' Amy offered. 'I can leave the boys in day care till seven, and I can be out of here by five.'

'I'm okay. I'll be back at work tomorrow,' Brigitte said sadly. 'I can't stay in bed and cry forever.' She had been trying to decide if she wanted to see Ted before he left, but realized that she didn't. It would just be too hard, knowing that it was over and she might never see him again. She was ready to bury it now. She sent him a text that night, telling him she was okay and wishing him well, and thanking him for six great years together. After she sent it, she felt strange. Crazy even. Six years, and all wrapped up in a single text. That seemed much too easy. And how quickly those six years had ended, in one night. One turn of fate, and it was over.

The snow had stopped the next morning when she went to work. The streets had been cleared by the snowplows. It was bitter cold as she pulled her collar around her neck, and her hands were icy when she got to her office. She had forgotten her gloves. She felt as though she had been gone for a lifetime, not just a day, to mourn the end of her relationship to Ted. She was wearing an old gray sweater, which was the one she wore when she was sad or upset. It was a time for comfort foods, cozy clothes, and all the things that would ease the pain she was in. It was a time of sadness and mourning for her.

She had been in her office for half an hour, going over applications, when the head of admissions, Greg Matson, asked her to come into his office. He had only been there for a year, but had been pleasant to work for so far. He had come to BU from Boston College, and had often relied on Brigitte's advice and experience about their policies. It had startled her to realize when he arrived that he was younger than she was, as was the woman next in line for his job. Brigitte had been there longer than either of them, but had never wanted the burdens that went with his job. She had always told herself that it was easier for her to continue working on her book if she was in a lesser position, and she had no need or desire to be 'the boss.'

Greg invited her to sit down with the same collegial smile he always wore. He said she looked tired and asked if she'd been sick. She said she'd had the flu the day before. They chatted for a while about current applications, and he praised her for her diligence and said she did a remarkable job. He explained to her then about the new computer system they were installing in the next few weeks. He said it would make everyone's job easier, and allow them to streamline the department, which was always a concern now with tighter money. He said that their main goal was efficiency and staying ahead of budget cuts, and the new computer system had been a great investment. And then, with a small look of apology, he explained that the new computer system meant that they would be reducing the size of the staff in the admissions office. They hated to do it, particularly after she had been there for ten years. It wasn't personal, he insisted, but she and six other people were being laid off. He said generously that because of her long years of employment at BU, they were giving her a six-month severance package. He said he hoped it would give her the time and money she needed to finish her book. And he said he was really sorry she had to go. He stood up then, shook her hand, gave her a hug, and gently propelled her out of his office and back to her own. He said that arrangements would be made to complete their admissions process for the current applications without her input, and she could leave that day, and get on with her new life.

Brigitte stood in her office, looking stunned. New life? What new life? What happened to the old one? In two days she had lost her boyfriend to a dig in Egypt, and her job of ten years to a computer. She was dispensed with, obsolete, canceled. She hadn't done anything wrong, everyone explained to her, but she hadn't done anything right either. She hadn't wanted to be head of admissions, so she had settled for a mediocre job for ten years. She had been working on a book for seven years that she'd never finished. And she'd spent six years with a man she thought she loved, but who had never made a commitment to her, and that had been good enough for her. In her pursuit of what was easy and without stress, she had rendered herself essential to no one, accomplished nothing, never married, never had kids. She was thirty-eight years old, childless, unmarried, unemployed, with nothing to show for the last decade of her life. It was a stunning blow to her ego, her heart, her self-esteem, her confidence, and her faith in the future.

She got a box from the supply room, put her few belongings into it, and at noon, after saying goodbye to her co-workers, still in a state of shock, she was walking down the hall, feeling dazed, unable to absorb what had happened. It was the weirdest feeling of her life. She felt like a woman without a country, a man, a job. In two days, her whole life had totally fallen apart. She had six months of salary coming to her from BU. And then what? What was she going to do now? Where would she go? She had absolutely no idea.

There were over one hundred colleges in the Boston area, more than in any other U.S. city, and she had ten years' experience in admissions, but she wasn't even sure that was what she wanted to do. She had done it because it was easy and undemanding. But was that all she wanted out of life? No demands? She stood in the doorway to Amy's office, holding the box with her possessions, with a dead look in her eyes.

'What's that?' Amy asked her. She didn't like the way Brigitte looked at all. Her olive skin was so pale that it almost shimmered green, and she wondered what was in the box.

'I just got canned. They're putting in a new computer system. I knew about it. I just didn't know it was replacing me. Seven of us got fired. Or I think the term is "laid off." Dumped. Canned. Whatever. It's been quite a week.' She sounded calm and felt dead.

'Oh, Jesus.' Amy ran around her desk and took the box from Brigitte's arms. 'I'll drive you home. I don't have to be back here for two hours.' Brigitte nodded and didn't protest, as Amy put on her coat, carried the box, and they walked outside. Brigitte felt like she was in shock. She said nothing until they were halfway to her house.

'I feel sick,' was all she said, and she looked it.

'I'm really sorry,' Amy said quietly, as they waited for a light to change. Ted had called Amy that morning to see how Brigitte was. He was worried about her, but ecstatic over his new job. It was painful to hear, and Amy felt even sorrier for her and didn't mention Ted's call. What was the point? He was as good as gone. And now so was her job. It was a lot to absorb at once. 'Sometimes it happens like this, Brig. Everything goes to shit at the same time. It's rotten luck and worse timing.'

'Yeah, I know,' Brigitte said softly, and sighed. 'It's my fault. I always take the easy way out. I'm so busy trying not to rock the boat and take risks that I wind up going down with the ship. I'd never have the guts to do what Ted is doing. I never wanted to be head of admissions. I never pushed myself about the book. I just want to disappear into the crowd. And now look at me, no job, no guy, no kids, maybe ever, a book ten academics may read one day or use as a doorstop, if I ever finish it.' She turned to Amy with tears bright in her eyes. 'What the hell am I going to do with my life?' It was a hard time for her, of taking stock, and facing the mistakes she'd made. She'd paid a high price for them in the last two days. 'I never even asked Ted if he wanted to marry me one day. I just assumed he would. It was easier that way. And the answer would have been no. It would have been better to hear it then than find out now. I feel like life has passed me by, and I did it to myself.' She had, but Amy didn't want to rub salt in her wounds, there were too many of them at the moment. Her man and her job. And all in two days. It was a hell of a blow.

'Don't beat yourself up. You can't change the past. There are a gazillion colleges here, you can get another job in admissions if you want. You can even teach. You have the degrees for it,' but she knew Brigitte had never wanted to. She didn't want the commitment. 'You have a great track record. If you send your résumé around, someone will offer you a job.'

'Everyone is cutting back. I don't know what to do. Maybe I should try to finish the book.' Amy nodded, at least it would keep her busy and from getting too depressed, until her wounds started to heal. She had to do something to get through this. She was blaming herself more than Ted. Amy blamed them both, Brigitte for what she hadn't done, and Ted for what he just had.

'Maybe you should go away for a while. Get a change of scene,' Amy suggested kindly, trying to lift her spirits.

'Where would I go all by myself?' Brigitte was crying as she asked. Traveling alone sounded awful to her.

'Lots of places. Hawaii, the Caribbean, Florida. Go lie on a beach somewhere.'

'That's no fun alone. Maybe I should go see my mother in New York. I haven't seen her since Christmas. Wait till I tell her Ted dumped me and I'm out of a job.' Her mother had so much faith in her, and she felt like an utter failure now.

'Maybe that's not such a great idea at the moment. I think a beach somewhere is a better idea.'

'Yeah. Maybe,' Brigitte said, looking unconvinced. Brigitte and Amy carried her things into the apartment, and then Brigitte turned to her friend with a worried expression. 'Don't tell Ted I got fired, if he calls. I don't want him to feel sorry for me. It's so pathetic. I feel like a total loser.' He had been promoted, and she had gotten laid off. She would have felt humiliated if he knew.

'You're not, and he called me this morning. He wanted to know how you are. I think he's worried about you.'

'Tell him I'm fine. He didn't change his mind about the dig, did he?' she asked with a hopeful look, and Amy shook her head. He was leaving, as planned, just concerned about her, but not enough to take her with him or to stay. It was over. Amy was convinced, and Brigitte was too.

They sat in Brigitte's living room for a while, and then Amy had to go back to work. She suggested that Brigitte come to her house during the weekend, and Brigitte said she was going to try and work on her book. And for the rest of the afternoon, she just sat and stared into space, trying to absorb everything that had happened to her. No man. No job. It was a lot to take in all at once, and on Saturday, after hesitating for a full minute, she answered the phone when her mother called. Ted hadn't called her, or texted her again since the day after their Valentine's Day dinner. He was entirely willing to let her go and cut off communication. It was easier for him than dealing with how upset she was. He hated crying women. He always said they reminded him of his mother. He was allergic to guilt and blame, and being made to feel like the bad guy. So he disappeared. It seemed cowardly to her.

Her mother was startled when she heard her daughter. 'You sound awful. Are you sick?' She was instantly worried. Brigitte was her only child.

'I . . . no . . . yes . . . well, sort of. I'm not feeling great.'

'What do you have, darling? A flu or a cold?' Actually neither, a broken heart.

'Maybe a little of both,' Brigitte said vaguely, wondering how to tell her what had happened that week. She couldn't bring herself to say the words.

'How's Ted? Anything new?' Brigitte's mother always acted as though she expected him to propose at any minute, and couldn't understand why he hadn't. Brigitte hated to admit to her what a mess her life was at the moment, or whine about it. Her mother was always so strong and positive and energetic about life. Brigitte admired her a great deal, and had since she was a child.

Brigitte decided to bite the bullet and start with Ted. 'Actually, he had some big news this week. Great news for him. He got his own dig in Egypt. He's leaving in three weeks.' There was silence at the other end of the phone.

'What does that translate to for you? Are you going to Egypt with him?' Her mother sounded worried when she asked. Having her only child in Boston was hard enough. Egypt was nowhere on her map.

'No, I'm not. This is what he's always wanted, and he's going to be there for a long time. At least three years, maybe five. And who knows, if he does a good job of it, maybe ten. That pretty much lets me out of the plan.' She tried to sound calm and philosophical about it, more than she felt.

'Did you know about this?' Her mother sounded disapproving and shocked.

'Sort of. I knew it was what he wanted. I guess I never really thought it would happen, but it did, and things are moving pretty fast. So we kind of decided to end it between us this week and move on. He needs to be free to pursue his dream.' She tried to sound up about it, but she was way down, in a dark pit of self-pity and grief.

'What about your dreams? You've been with him for six years.' Her mother sounded stern. She wasn't angry at her daughter, but at Ted. The trouble was that Brigitte had never identified her dream, neither to Ted nor to herself. So now he had his dream, and she had none. 'That's pretty selfish of him to just go off and do his thing,' her mother said bluntly. She sounded angry, in defense of her daughter.

'It's what he's wanted since he started working at BU,

Mom. I can't blame him for that. I just somehow forgot that along the way. Anyway, that's the way it is.' She swallowed hard then, and decided to tell her mother the rest. 'It's been kind of a crazy week actually. I got laid off yesterday, replaced by a computer.'

'You got *fired*?' Her mother sounded stunned.

'Yeah, that's pretty much the way it is, with six months' severance, so I'm okay financially, but it was sort of a surprise. I knew about the computer, I just didn't know it would replace me. So it's been kind of a clean sweep. Ted and BU. Maybe it's easier that way.'

'For whom?' Her mother sounded irate on her behalf. 'Not for you certainly. Ted walks out after six years and waltzes off to Egypt, and BU dumps you after ten. I think that's shocking, on both counts. Do you want me to come up?' Brigitte smiled when she asked. She felt like such a loser, but it was nice to have her mother's support. Even though she was outspoken and opinionated, she was devoted, good-hearted, and kind, and had always championed her daughter in all things.

'I'm fine, Mom. I'm going to work on the book and see how that goes. This might be a good chance to finish it in record time. I have nothing else I want to do right now.' She still had the class she was taking toward her doctorate that semester, but after what had happened, she was thinking of dropping it and taking a semester off. She wasn't in the mood for studying and term papers. Working on her book would be more than enough, given how upset she was.

'Why don't you come down and visit me in New York?' Her mother was seriously worried about her.

'I have nothing to do there, Mom.' Brigitte hadn't lived in New York since college, and a lot of her friends had moved away. 'I want to send my résumé out to some of the schools here, to see what jobs turn up. Six months will go by pretty fast. I could start somewhere else next fall. And work on the book between now and then.' Her mother didn't sound convinced and was upset for her.

'I hate to see this happen to you, Brigitte, especially with Ted. You can always find another job. But you invested a lot in the relationship with him. It's not easy to find someone at your age, and if you want children, you have no time to waste.'

'What do you suggest? Leaflets or billboards? Or full-page ads? It's my fault too, Mom. I never pressed the point about children and marriage, I didn't want to. I wasn't ready either, I always thought I had time. And I figured it was a sure thing with him. I assumed. Well, it wasn't as sure as I thought. In fact, not at all. He's not even sure he ever wants to get married or have kids. I guess I missed that message, and I never really asked, not as seriously as I should have. So this is what I get. Maybe no kids.' She felt sad as she said it, and her mother was sad for her.

'He should have said that to you plainly if that was how he felt, and not wasted your time.'

'Maybe. I didn't think we were in a rush. I wasn't ready to commit either.' Neither of them said it, but they both knew that now it might be too late. At thirty-eight, she had been suffering from a delusion of youth. Until now. And suddenly her whole world had crashed, both job and man.

'All you girls today think you have forever to get married and have babies. Women have first babies at forty-five and fifty now, with all kinds of crazy medical help. They don't get married at all. Sixty-year-old women get pregnant, with astounding interventions. It's not as easy as you all think, and sometimes all these modern techno ideas boomerang and give women a false sense of time. Nature is still on the same schedule it always was, no matter what men have invented to trick her. I hope you'll be serious about who you get involved with now. You don't have time to waste anymore.' It was a stern speech and hard to hear, but Brigitte knew she was right.

'I was serious about Ted,' Brigitte said quietly.

'Not as serious as you needed to be, nor was he. You

both thought you were still kids.' Brigitte knew she was right about that too. Her mother usually was. It had been easy living that way, but it had all blown up in her face. 'Now he's going off to Egypt, and you're all alone. That's very sad.' She sounded sympathetic. She felt terrible for her.

'Yes, it is. But maybe it's destiny or something. Maybe it wasn't meant to be.' Brigitte was trying to be philosophical about it.

'I wish he'd made that clear earlier.'

'Yeah, me too.' But Brigitte also realized that they had both been emotionally lazy, cavalier, and immature. They were grown-ups, not kids.

'Let me know if you want to come down. Your room is here for you anytime, and I'd love to see you. I've been making some real progress on the genealogy. I want to show you what I've found recently. If you get tired of working on your book, you can help me with it.' Brigitte couldn't think of anything she less wanted to do right now. The history of her mother's family all the way back to the Dark Ages in France had always been more interesting to her mother than to Brigitte, although she admired her mother's hard work on it. It had been her mother's hobby and passion for years. Their family history was a legacy she had always wanted to give her daughter. Brigitte preferred historical mysteries, and their very proper ancestors always seemed too tame and mundane to her.

Brigitte visited Amy and her boys later that afternoon, and on Sunday she got started again on her book. And for the first time ever, she found the material she had gathered and the whole issue of women's suffrage tedious and dry. It no longer seemed as important to her as it once had. Everything in her life seemed lackluster and dull now, and without meaning. Without Ted and her job, she even hated her book. She felt as though she'd reached a dead end in every aspect of her life. What was the point?

By Tuesday, she was bored stiff with what she'd written. And she had heard nothing from Ted since the week before. She pressed on with the book, but by the following weekend she was ready to scream and felt like throwing it all away. She was getting nowhere with it. She was too depressed about Ted and losing her job. She had sent her résumé out to other colleges, and it was too soon to hear anything back. She realized that this time, if they offered her a job, she'd have to be willing to take more responsibility than she had before. Her unwillingness to take on greater challenges had made her easy to replace with a computer and had done her out of a job. But she didn't expect to hear from the schools for a while.

And after working on the book for a week, it finally

ground to a stop. She had nothing left to say, no energy to say it, and too little interest in her subject. She was blocked. She was beginning to think about Amy's suggestion to go to a beach, just to get away for a while. It started to snow again and everything about Boston depressed her. She hated knowing that Ted was getting ready to leave, and suddenly in the space of ten days, she felt as though she no longer had a life. Without a job or a man, she felt like she didn't have much to keep her in Boston at the moment, and on the spur of the moment, she decided to fly to New York. She needed a break from everything, and her mother was delighted when she called her from the Boston airport.

Brigitte looked out the window on the brief commuter flight. She felt childish doing it, but with everything in her life topsy-turvy, it felt good to be going home. She knew that she needed to start over, but for now, she had no idea where to start, and a few days in New York would do her good. Her mother had suggested that she send her résumé to NYU and Columbia too, but Brigitte didn't want to live in New York again. It was raining, and as the plane landed, she had no idea where her life was going. She wanted to spend a few days with her mother in the cozy apartment she had grown up in. And after that Brigitte planned to go back to Boston, although she had no idea where her life would lead. All she knew now, after the recent changes in her life, was that she wanted it to be different from before. Settling for 'easy and comfortable' no longer seemed like enough.

Chapter 3

Marguerite Nicholson looked relieved and delighted when she opened the door to her daughter. It was pouring rain in New York, and Brigitte was soaked just getting from the cab into the building. Her mother hurried to hang up her wet raincoat, told her to take off her shoes, and a few minutes later handed her a cup of tea as they sat in front of the fire. There was something immensely reassuring about being there for Brigitte, like sinking into a down comforter, or a feather bed, with a sigh of relief. Her mother was a capable, intelligent woman Brigitte could always count on. Marguerite had saved them from disaster and turned tragedy into a good life for both of them. She had built a respectable career in publishing. When she retired the year before, she left as a senior editor, with many well-known books to her credit, and respected in her field. She had put her daughter all through school, for both degrees, and taught Brigitte the importance of an education, and she'd been proud of Brigitte's accomplishments and plan to get a Ph.D. She was only disappointed when Brigitte settled for an uninspiring job in the admissions office at BU, and even more so when Brigitte's seemingly endless years of research never produced her long-promised book. She was as disappointed by that as by Brigitte's failure to marry and have kids. She wanted her to challenge herself and take life by the horns, but so far Brigitte never had. Marguerite knew she was conscientious and worked hard, but she wanted so much more for her. She was well aware of Brigitte's aversion to risk-taking and she knew where it came from. All Brigitte had ever wanted was to be safe. Her mother had always wanted a more adventuresome, inspiring life for her. Marguerite knew she was capable of it, but something always seemed to hold Brigitte back. She was still haunted by the traumas of her childhood and her father's death.

They sat in the cheerful living room of the apartment, and the two women couldn't have looked more different. Marguerite was as fair as her daughter was dark, although both were tall, with good figures, and whereas Brigitte's eyes were nearly as dark as her hair, her mother's were an almost sky blue. They had similar smiles, but different features. Brigitte's looks and bone structure were far more exotic.

The room was warm and pleasantly decorated, there were a few well-worn antiques, and Marguerite had lit a fire in the fireplace before Brigitte arrived. They sat in front of it in worn but elegant old velvet chairs, drinking tea from the Limoges cups her mother was so proud of, which had been her grandmother's. Marguerite looked aristocratic and genteel, although nothing in the apartment was of great value, but she had good taste, and had lived there for years. Their home had the patina of time. On every wall, there were bookcases filled with books. It was a home where learning, literature, and education were revered, and anything about their family history fascinated Marguerite, and always had.

'So tell me what's happening with your book?' Brigitte's mother asked with interest, not wanting to bring up the painful subjects of Ted and her job.

'I don't know. I think I'm too distracted. It's stalling, I'm completely blocked. The research is good, but I can't seem to get it off the ground. I guess I'm upset about Ted. Maybe it'll go better after I take a break. That's why I came down to see you.'

'I'm glad you did. Do you want me to have a look at it?

I have to admit, anthropology isn't my usual subject, and your material is a little lofty, but maybe I can help you give it some zip.' Brigitte smiled at the offer, typical of her mother. And Brigitte was grateful that her mother hadn't made any harsh comments about Ted. She was just sad for Brigitte.

'I think it needs more than zip, Mom. I've already got six hundred and fifty pages on it, and if I follow my outline, through history and in all the countries I want to cover, it will run well over a thousand. I wanted it to be the definitive book on women's right to vote. But all of a sudden, I wonder if anyone will care. Maybe women's freedom is about a lot more than their right to participate in the democratic process,' Brigitte said sadly.

'Sounds like a real page turner to me,' her mother teased, but she was sure it would be a thorough, extensive, impeccably competent book. She knew Brigitte's ability to write, even if the subject seemed dry to her. Brigitte smiled at the comment. It was after all an academic and not a commercial book. 'I've been busy too. I've been back at my research at the local branch of the Mormon library for the last three weeks. It's incredible the documentation they've collected. Do you realize they have more than two hundred camera operators in forty-five countries around the world, taking photographs of local records, for people to use in genealogical research? Their real purpose is to help people baptize their relatives into the Church, even posthumously, but anyone is free to use the records for ancestral purposes. They're incredibly generous with the information they've gathered, and very helpful. Thanks to them I've traced the de Margeracs all the way back to New Orleans in 1850, and I know they came to the States from Brittany around that time. Some of them were there long before that, from another branch of the family, but of the same name. Our direct descendants came from Brittany in the late 1840s.' She said it like a news bulletin, and Brigitte smiled. It was her mother's passion. 'That would be my great-grandfather, and your great-great-grandfather, who came over then,' she went on. 'What I want to know now is the history of the family before they got to America. I know that both a Philippe and Tristan de Margerac came to America, and there were several counts and a marquis in the group, but I don't know much about them, or anything actually, before they left France.'

'Wouldn't you need to research it there, Mom?' Brigitte asked her, attempting to be interested in it. For some reason, although anthropology fascinated her, her mother's tireless genealogical search for family history had always bored her to tears. She had never developed her mother's curiosity about their ancestors. It seemed like such ancient history to her, and so irrelevant today. And their ancestors all seemed so dull. None of them seemed exceptional to her.

'The Mormons probably have more of that history than any library in France. They've photographed local records there. The European countries are the easiest to research. One of these days I'm going to go to Salt Lake City and pursue it, but I've gotten a lot of good material from their library here.' Brigitte nodded politely as she always did, but her mother knew how little the subject interested her, and they moved on to other things – the theater, opera, ballet, which were passions of Marguerite's too, and the current novel she was reading. Eventually, they talked about Ted, inevitably, and his dig in Egypt. The subject couldn't be avoided any longer. Marguerite was still sorry about what had happened, and sad for her daughter. She knew it was a huge disappointment, and Marguerite was impressed by how philosophical Brigitte was about it. She wouldn't have been, in her shoes, to be abandoned after six years. Brigitte was taking a lot of the responsibility on her shoulders, although Marguerite didn't entirely agree with her. She thought he should have invited Brigitte to go to Egypt with him, and instead he was using it as an opportunity to end the relationship and move on.

They talked about the schools Brigitte had sent her

résumé to. She was still determined to stay in the Boston area, but it was too soon for them to have responded to the résumés she sent out. Brigitte knew that the colleges were all busy processing applications, and after that they'd be dealing with acceptances, and their wait list. She doubted that she'd get any response to her letters until May or June. She wasn't panicking, and she was willing to wait until then. She just needed to find something to do in the meantime, but her mother's never-ending ancestral project wasn't it. She wanted to be helpful to her mother, but cataloguing generation after generation of similarly respectable people seemed as dry and predictable to her as her own book. She wished at times that they would turn up a criminal or a creative scoundrel in their background, someone to bring more life to their family tree than what was there.

Both women turned off the lights and went to bed at midnight. The fire was out by then. And Brigitte slept, as she always did, in her childhood room. It was still decorated in flowered pink chintzes, which had been her choice as a young girl. She liked coming home to the familiar fabric and old room, and her long intelligent conversations with her mother. They got on well.

The next morning, they had breakfast together in the kitchen, and then Marguerite went out to do errands, buy groceries, and play bridge with friends. She had a pleasant life, and had been involved with someone for several years. He had died a few years earlier, right before she retired and there had been no one since. She had a wide circle of friends, and went to lunches, dinners, museums and cultural events, mostly with other women, and a few couples. She lived alone but was never bored. And her genealogical project kept her busy on weekends and on nights when she didn't go out. She had learned to put inquiries out through the Internet, but most of the information she had, she'd gotten from the Mormons. She dreamed of putting it all in a book one day, for Brigitte, and in the meantime, she loved the search, and the hunt for history and relatives of centuries past, even if Brigitte found them tedious and unexciting.

She showed Brigitte her latest notes that afternoon when she came home. Brigitte had done some shopping, and then went up to Columbia, to visit a friend who was a professor there, who promised to keep an ear out for any openings in admissions. He suggested that she might consider teaching instead of admissions, but she didn't think she had a knack for it, and wanted an administrative job, which gave her more time to write and take classes toward her doctorate. Brigitte looked in better spirits than she had the day she arrived. Her mother had been right, and it was good for her being in New York. Everything seemed electric and alive, although she liked the academic world around Boston. The atmosphere was more casual and younger. But being in New York gave her a nice change of scene. There was a lot more to do here, which was why Marguerite loved it.

When she looked at her mother's recent research, Brigitte was impressed by the information Marguerite had gathered. She seemed to have the birth and death dates of all her direct ancestors, and many cousins. She knew the counties and parishes in New Orleans where they had lived and died, the names of their homes and plantations, the towns they had migrated to in New York and Connecticut after the Civil War. And she knew the name of the ship one of them had arrived on from Brittany, in 1846. The family seemed to have stayed in the South until just after the Civil War, and then migrated North in the 1860s and 1870s, where they had lived ever since. But what had happened in France before that remained a mystery to her. If anything, Brigitte thought that segment of their history might be more interesting than what her mother knew so far.

'It's not that long ago, Mom. You ought to be able to get that from the Mormon library too, or a trip to France.'

'I really have to go to Salt Lake to do that. They have more of the European records there and a much larger facility. I just haven't had time. And libraries that size terrify me. You're much better at all that than I am.' Her eyes begged Brigitte to help her with the project, and her daughter smiled. Her mother's enthusiasm touched her heart.

'You know, you have enough here for a book, if you ever want to write one,' Brigitte said encouragingly. She was always impressed by her mother's diligence and perseverance.

'I don't think anyone would care about it except our family, and that's mainly me and you, and a few cousins scattered here and there, unless we still have relatives I don't know about in France. But I doubt that we do. I've found no recent de Margeracs in France. And everyone here has pretty much died out. There's no one left in the South, and hasn't been in a hundred years. Your grandfather was born in New York at the turn of the century. There's really just us now.' It was a labor of love that had fascinated her for years.

'You work so hard on it, Mom,' Brigitte said admiringly.

'I love knowing who we're related to, where they lived, and what they did there. It's your legacy too. Maybe one day it will seem more important to you than it does now. There are some very interesting people perched in our family tree,' Marguerite said with a smile, but Brigitte hadn't found that to be so. They were aristocratic, but there was nothing unusual about them.

In the end, Brigitte spent the rest of the week in New York. She had no pressing reason to go back to Boston. She and her mother went to the theater together, the movies, several small, casual restaurants for dinner, and took long walks in Central Park. They enjoyed each other's company and her mother tried to stay off painful subjects. There was nothing left to be said about Ted, except that in Marguerite's opinion Brigitte had wasted six years. And she suspected now that Brigitte thought so too. Ted had proven himself to be totally selfish in the end. Brigitte hadn't heard from him since his text the morning after they broke up.

On Saturday afternoon they spent a lazy day at home, reading the early edition of the Sunday *Times*. Her mother chortled when she found an article about genealogies in the magazine section. Predictably, it extolled the virtues of the Mormons and their libraries, and her mother looked at her wistfully again.

'I wish you'd go out to Salt Lake City for me, Brigitte,' she pleaded with her. 'You do so much better research than I do. That's not my forte, but it is yours, and I can't go any further back now, until I trace the family back to France. I'm pretty much stuck around 1850. Any chance that you'd go there for me?' She didn't want to add 'now that you don't have a job or a man,' but it was true. Brigitte had time on her hands, and she was feeling restless, while she waited to hear about a job.

She started to say no and then thought about it. There was no reason for her not to go, and from what she'd just read in the *Times* about the Mormon Family History Library, she had to admit that it sounded interesting, and it was something she could do for her mother, who was always volunteering to do things for her, and was so supportive of her and always had been. It was a small favor she could do for her and Brigitte had nothing else to do now.

'Maybe. I'll see,' she said noncommittally, not wanting to promise to do it, but she also realized that it was a great way to avoid the book that she was suddenly so disenchanted with. And she thought about it again on Sunday when they were having breakfast in the kitchen and sharing the rest of the Sunday *Times*. Brigitte was supposed to go back to Boston that afternoon. The weather report said it was snowing there with no end in sight. Two hours later they closed the airport in Boston. The weather was fine in New York; the storm currently in Boston wasn't due to hit New York until the next day.

'Maybe I could go out to Salt Lake for you for a couple

of days,' Brigitte said thoughtfully. 'I have a friend from school there, or at least I used to. She has about ten kids and is married to a Mormon. I could look them up and do research for you. It might be fun.' Brigitte smiled at her mother, and Marguerite's face lit up at the prospect.

'I'd be so grateful if you did. I can't do another thing until I trace them back through Brittany. The Mormons have incredible records on microfiche and disks, with assistants to help you find it.' She was selling hard, and Brigitte laughed.

'Okay, okay, Mom,' Brigitte answered, and a few minutes later she called the airline and booked a flight to Salt Lake for later that afternoon. It felt good to help her mother, and it was beginning to sound like a more intriguing project. Brigitte was suddenly fascinated to see the Mormon library in Salt Lake, and she wondered if she'd find something there she could use for her book too, although it was unlikely.

Her mother thanked her profusely when she left, and Brigitte promised to call and report her findings. She had booked a reservation at the Carlton Hotel and Suites, which she saw on the Internet was within walking distance of Temple Square where the Family History Library was located. Now that she had agreed to go, Brigitte could hardly wait to see it. She was vastly impressed by what she had seen on the Internet about it. They apparently had hundreds of volunteers to help, and all their records and resources were without charge, except for photocopying documents and photos. It was a remarkable service to the public that they had been providing for decades. The Mormons had a gigantic organization and the most thorough research operation in the world.

Brigitte was thinking about it when she boarded the flight to Salt Lake, and hoped she'd find something of interest to her mother. She didn't really expect to find anything exceptional in her family history. Everything her mother had come up with so far was both circumspect and benign. They were respectable aristocrats who, for some reason, had chosen to come to the United States in the mid-nineteenth century, long after the reign of Napoleon. Perhaps they had come to purchase land, or discover new territories – and they stayed. But Brigitte wondered now too what they had done in France before they'd come to America, what had happened to them during the Napoleonic reign, and the French Revolution fifteen years before that. She was on a mission of discovery now that suddenly seemed a lot more interesting than chronicling women's rights to vote around the world. Maybe her mother was right after all, and the subject she was researching now was far more worthwhile than what she had been doing for the last seven years. Brigitte was about to find out in Salt Lake.

The flight to Salt Lake City took five and a half hours, and she went straight to the hotel from the airport. It was a European-style inn built in the 1920s, and was a short walk to Temple Square, which was her destination the next day. To orient herself and get some air, she went for a walk before dinner. She found Temple Square easily, a few blocks away, and immediately spotted the enormous Family History Library on the west side of the square, on the same side as the history museum of the Church, and Osmyn Deuel's cabin, which had been preserved since 1847 and was the oldest in the city. She walked past the Mormon Temple with its impressive six spires, and the domed Tabernacle next to it, which was open to the public for rehearsals and concerts of the famed Mormon Tabernacle Choir. Both structures were impressive to see, even from the outside. She saw the capitol, and walked past the Beehive House and the Lion House, both built in the mid-1850s, which had been the official residences of Brigham Young, who had been the president of the Church and the first governor of Utah.

Brigitte was startled to see how many people were walking around the square, despite the chilly weather, and all of them were looking at the buildings with both awe and interest, which suggested that they weren't locals but tourists. There seemed to be a huge number of people in town, many of them congregated around the square. And people looked pleasant and happy, and were obviously excited to be there. The atmosphere was contagious, and Brigitte was in good spirits when she went back to her room at the hotel. She was beginning to enjoy her mother's project more than she ever had before. With the time to explore it now, it was adding a new dimension to her life.

She called her mother from her room, after she ordered dinner, and reported on everything she'd seen so far, and she was sorry her mother hadn't come with her. Marguerite was grateful that Brigitte had made the trip on her behalf. 'I couldn't have gone anyway,' Marguerite said practically. 'I have a bridge tournament tomorrow.' For a woman who had worked hard for twenty-five years and had never expected to before that, she enjoyed her leisure days, and Brigitte was glad she did. She had earned them. And if their genealogy was so important to her, Brigitte was happy to use her own research skills to help the project along. She had a feeling the Mormons were going to advance the project considerably. With two billion names in databases, two and a half million rolls of microfilm, and 300,000 books with information gathered from all over the world, Brigitte was sure that she would find records of some of their relatives in France. Her mother wanted to go back as far as she could. It would have been a thrill for her if the de Margeracs turned out to be important players in the history of France. She had been a history buff since college. There was certainly no harm in that, and it was coming to mean more to Brigitte than women's suffrage, which had seemed so vital to her before. This was far more personal, and she felt as though she was just blocks away now from where the history of her family lay.

She ate dinner in her room, and wished she could share what she was doing with Ted. She knew he hadn't left Boston yet, and thought about calling him, but she realized that hearing his voice when he was already lost to her would upset her too much. He would be leaving for Egypt soon, for the excavation that had replaced her.

She tried to look up her old friend from school that night, and discovered that finding her was hopeless. Her husband was a direct descendant of Brigham Young, she had said, and Brigitte found page after page of Youngs in the telephone book. His first name was John, and there were hundreds of those too. She was sorry not to see her, and wished she had kept track of her over the years. All she knew of her before they lost sight of each other was that her friend had ten kids. It was hard for Brigitte to imagine, but it seemed to be a fairly normal occurrence here, where large families were common.

Brigitte slept well that night in the big comfortable bed. She had asked to be woken at eight o'clock, and when they called her, she was dreaming of Ted. He was still much on her mind, and it was hard to believe he had left her life forever, but it was obvious that he had. Six years gone up in smoke, and now she had hundreds of years of her family history to pursue for her mother. She was suddenly grateful for the distraction. She felt the thrill of the hunt as she got up, showered and dressed, and ate a quick breakfast of oatmeal, tea, and toast before she left the room.

She knew the way to Temple Square now after her reconnaissance mission the night before. She saw the familiar buildings, and walked into the Family History Library, and then followed the signs to the orientation that would help her find her way around. There were hundreds of library assistants throughout the building, just waiting to offer their expertise and help. After seeing the brief presentation, Brigitte knew exactly where to go, and went upstairs to a desk, where she knew she could find records for Europe. She explained to the young woman at the desk that she was looking for a family in France.

'Paris?' the young woman asked her, grabbing a notepad.

'No, Brittany, I think.' Brigitte wrote down her mother's maiden name, de Margerac, which was her own middle name. 'They came to New Orleans sometime around 1850.' It had already been an American territory by then, having been sold by Napoleon to the Americans sometime during his reign, for fifteen million dollars. 'I don't know anything before that. That's why I'm here.' She smiled at the librarian, who was helpful and pleasant. She was wearing a name tag that said her name was Margaret Smith. She introduced herself as 'Meg.'

'And that's why we're here, to help you,' the woman said warmly. 'Let's see what we have in our records. Give me a few minutes.' She indicated a sitting area where Brigitte could wait, in front of one of the film reader stations, where later they would look at microfilm together, poring over lists and records and birth and death certificates from the region, photographed by the researchers who traveled around the world to film them.

It took about twenty minutes for her to return, carrying the film, and she and Brigitte sat down together. She turned on the machine and they began looking at what she had found. It was a full ten minutes before Brigitte saw anything that looked familiar to her, and then suddenly there it was, de Margerac, Louise, born in 1819, followed by Philippe, Edmond, and Tristan, all born within a few years of each other, and in 1825, Christian, who died a few months later, as an infant. The records were from a county in Brittany. It led them to look back further to the previous generation. It took another half hour, and there were three of them, boys, born between 1786 and 1789, right before the French Revolution: Jean, Gabriel, and Paul, brothers born of the same parents. This time, searching forward again, there were records of their deaths in Quimper and Carnac, in Brittany. All three of them had died between 1837 and 1845. Brigitte made careful note of their names in a notepad she had brought for that purpose, and the years they had been born and died. And by moving farther forward on the microfilm, they found the deaths of Louise and Edmond de Margerac, sister and brother, in the 1860s. But nowhere could they find records of the deaths of Philippe and Tristan. The young library assistant suggested they might have moved away and died elsewhere, and Brigitte knew they were the de Margeracs who had come to New Orleans circa 1850 and eventually died there. She knew that was the part of the research her mother had already gathered. Brigitte had written down everything so far to share with her, although she was planning to buy copies of the microfilm documents for her mother as well.

They went back to an earlier generation, and found the

births of both Tristan and Jean de Margerac, names that had been used again in later generations. Jean had been born in 1760, and Tristan a decade before that. There was no record of Jean's death, but it showed that Tristan, Marquis de Margerac, had died in 1817, after the abdication of Napoleon, and the Marquise de Margerac a few months later, but there was no record of her birth in the area before that. Brigitte wondered if she had come from another part of France, and as they checked the date of her death again, only two months after her husband, Brigitte scribbled the information down and was struck by her name. It didn't sound French to her.

'What kind of name is that?' she asked the librarian. 'Is that French?'

'I don't think so.' The woman smiled at Brigitte. Like all families, or most of those she helped research, they had uncovered a mystery in hers. The first name of the Marquise de Margerac was listed as Wachiwi, in the careful scrolled hand of the county clerk at the time of her death in 1817. 'It's a Native American name actually. I've seen it before. I can look it up for you, but as far as I know, it's Sioux.'

'How weird to give a French girl a Sioux name.' Brigitte looked intrigued.

The librarian left the reading station and looked it up

while Brigitte checked her notes again, and then returned to confirm what she had said. 'It's Sioux. It means "dancer." It's such a pretty name.'

'How odd that a French noblewoman would have a Sioux name.' It sounded a little eccentric to Brigitte, although who knew what the fashions had been then, or where Wachiwi's mother had heard the name?

'Not really,' the librarian explained. 'I've heard that Louis XVI was fascinated by Native Americans before the Revolution. I've read stories about how he invited Indian chiefs to France, and presented them to court as honored guests. Probably a few of them stayed, and the most common ports of entry then were in Brittany. So perhaps a Sioux chief and his daughter remained in France, and she married the marquis, your relative. She wouldn't have come alone, and most likely one of the chiefs brought to court was accompanied by his daughter. The Revolution was in 1789, and if she came to France before that in the 1780s, that would make her about the right age. Assuming she was somewhere in her teens when she came into France in the 1780s, she would have been in her fifties when she died in 1817, which was considered a great age for a woman then. The three boys born between 1786 and 1789 were undoubtedly hers. More than likely she was a Sioux woman who came to Brittany from the States, and captured the heart of the marquis. I've never come across a Frenchwoman called Wachiwi – all of the women I've read about with that name were Dakota Sioux.

'There were definitely Sioux in France in those days, and some just never left. It's a little-known piece of history, but it has always fascinated me. They weren't brought in as slaves or prisoners, they were brought over as guests, and several were presented at court.'

Brigitte was enthralled by what she said. She had found a piece of history in her own family that had sparked her interest. Somehow, somewhere, for some reason, the Marquis de Margerac, who would have been the grand-father of her mother's great-grandfather, had married a young Sioux woman and made her a marquise, and she had borne him three sons, the eldest of whom was named for the marquis's younger brother, who had died some-where along the way. They found a record a few minutes later of two other of the marquis's children, born earlier than Wachiwi's three sons. Their names were Agathe and Matthieu. The marquise listed as their mother had a different name than Wachiwi, and she died in 1778, on the same date their youngest child was born. She had obviously died in childbirth, and Wachiwi had been a second wife to him. It was fascinating piecing it all together from the ledgers the Mormons had photographed in Brittany.

'How would I find out more information about Wachiwi?' Brigitte asked Meg with a look of delight over the information she'd been given and that they had unearthed together. It had far exceeded her expectations and surely even her mother's. She had gone back another hundred years from what her mother had been able to learn, and now they had some really interesting things to work with, like a young Sioux woman married to a marquis in Brittany.

'You'd have to go to the Sioux for that information. They keep records, not as detailed as ours, or as varied geographically obviously. But they've transcribed a lot of the oral histories. It's not as easy to find people, but sometimes you do. It's worth a look.'

'Where would I go to find that? To the Bureau of Indian Affairs?' Brigitte asked her.

'No, I think to the Sioux historical office in South Dakota. Most of the material is there. It might be hard to find a record of a young woman, unless she was the daughter of an important chief, or had done something illustrious herself, like Sacajawea, but the Lewis and Clark expedition was about twenty years later than our dates for Wachiwi,' Meg said thoughtfully. They both felt as though they had a new friend, and Brigitte felt suddenly bonded to the ancestor who had married the marquis. 'You look a little Sioux yourself,' the librarian said cautiously, not sure how Brigitte would react to that information, and she looked wistful as the librarian said it.

'My father was Irish. I always thought that accounted for my black hair, but maybe it's not him at all. Maybe it's some kind of throwback to Wachiwi.' She suddenly loved that idea, and wanted to know everything she could find out about her. They pored over the records at the Family History Library for another hour, but for now there was nothing more. She had discovered three generations of relatives, all descended from Tristan and Wachiwi de Margerac, and a mystery she had never known of before that felt like a gift. She thanked Meg profusely and it was midafternoon when she got back to her room at the hotel and called her mother. Marguerite sounded in good spirits and said that she and her partner had won at bridge.

'Have I got a fascinating piece of family history for you!' Brigitte said victoriously, in a voice of excitement that delighted her mother.

'You found something?' Her mother sounded thrilled at the news.

'Lots of somethings. Three generations of de Margeracs in Brittany, and two who have no death dates, Philippe and Tristan, and since Philippe was the eldest, he would have been the marquis at that time. I was able to trace back three generations.'

'Those are the two who went to New Orleans in 1848 and 1850!' Marguerite said excitedly. 'Ohmigod, you found them, Brig! Who else was there? I know all about those two. Philippe was my great-grandfather, my father's grandfather. His brother Tristan moved to New York after the Civil War, but Philippe died in New Orleans before that. I'm so excited you found their birth records. Who else did you find? The Mormons are amazing, aren't they?'

'They're incredible. I found their sister or cousin Louise and brother Edmond, who died in France, and a baby brother Christian, who died as an infant. And in the generation before that, Jean, Gabriel, and Paul de Margerac, whose father was the Marquis Tristan de Margerac, and I found his two earlier children as well, and both his wives, one who died in childbirth, and the other who died around the same time he did. We should probably go to France and look at records there to discover exactly who was married to whom. Sometimes it's a little hard to figure out who are siblings and who are cousins, unless they make it very clear. They don't always, but the really exciting piece of history I discovered was the second wife of the marquis at the time of Louis XVI.'

'That's amazing for one day's research!' The two women

sounded elated, especially Brigitte's mother, who that day had acquired another hundred years of her family history that she had been pursuing for years. What was available at the local branch of the Mormon library wasn't as extensive as what Brigitte had access to in Salt Lake.

'The librarian was incredibly helpful, the records are all there, and I was lucky. Maybe I was destined to find it.' She was beginning to feel that way. There was something almost mystical about it. She had come across more anthropology in the last three hours than she had in the last ten years. 'The name of the marquis's second wife was Wachiwi,' Brigitte said as though she were handing her mother a gift.

'Wachiwi? Is that French?' Marguerite sounded confused. 'I don't think it is. What nationality was she?'

'She was Sioux. Can you imagine? In Brittany. Apparently, Louis XVI invited several Sioux chiefs to the court as honored guests. Some of them stayed. She must have been related to one of them, or got to France herself somehow. But the librarian at the Family History Library said there's no question. She's Sioux. Wachiwi means "dancer" in Sioux. So we have a Sioux woman in our family history, Mom, way, way back through the generations. And she married the marquis, and had three sons. One of them must have been the father of the Philippe and

Tristan who went to New Orleans, and the older Tristan and Wachiwi were their grandparents. That means she was the grandmother of your great-grandfather, Mom. I want to find out more about her. Apparently I have to go to the Sioux nation to find that. I think I might fly to South Dakota from here. I want to see what I can find.' Brigitte hadn't been on a hunt like this since school, but it was what she loved about anthropology. And finally she had come across one of their ancestors who truly grabbed her interest. Suddenly both women's passions had converged, brought to light by this one Sioux woman in their ancestry. Brigitte hadn't had this much fun in years. Even her name was romantic. Wachiwi. The dancer. Just thinking about it made her dream.

'It's hard to believe that a young Sioux girl could get all the way to Brittany, and marry a marquis. That was an incredibly long way in those days. It must have taken months to get there, on some little tiny ship.'

'Imagine what it must have been like to be a Sioux woman at the court of Louis XVI. That's pretty amazing,' Brigitte added. 'I hope I can find something about her in the oral histories. The woman at the Family History Library said it was unlikely, unless she was the daughter of an important chief. But she might have been. She must have been someone important to get all the way to France, and to be presented at the court of the king – if that's how she met the marquis.'

'We might never know, dear,' her mother said reasonably, but Brigitte was on a mission. She wanted to discover whatever she could find about a Sioux girl called Wachiwi, who was part of her history. Brigitte suddenly felt a bond to her like no other, and she was going to do all she could to find out about her. Wachiwi, the Marquise de Margerac, wife of the Marquis Tristan de Margerac. Brigitte felt a powerful pull to find out who she was, as though Wachiwi herself was calling to her, taunting her with the mystery. It was a challenge Brigitte found impossible to resist.

Chapter 4

The trip from Salt Lake to Sioux Falls, South Dakota, was long. Brigitte had to fly to Minneapolis first, kill time in the airport, and then finally get a flight to Sioux Falls. She arrived there six hours after she left Salt Lake. She could hardly wait to go to the university the next morning to begin her research. The university itself was in Vermillion, South Dakota, sixty-five miles from Sioux Falls, but she had decided to spend the night in Sioux Falls, and travel the rest of the distance in the morning. And the only accommodation she could find was at a clean, brightly lit motel, located across the street from a park. The town was situated on the bluffs above the Big Sioux River. And after settling into her motel room, Brigitte went outside for a walk. She found an appealing-looking diner while she was walking and stopped for something to eat. She loved watching the people come and go as she ate.

She noticed that there was snow on the ground when she left the diner. The temperature was freezing, and she was anxious to get back to her motel. She wanted to get up early to drive to Vermillion the next morning. Brigitte's destination was the University of South Dakota, where the Institute of American Indian Studies housed the Dr. Joseph Harper Cash Memorial Library. There books, photographs, films, and videos referred to the oral histories Brigitte was seeking. The Sioux referred to their myths and legends as 'lessons.' She hoped that the mystery of Wachiwi would be solved there.

If not, she had no idea where else to go. The Institute of American Indian Studies was the definitive resting place for oral histories about the Sioux, with nearly six thousand recorded interviews in their archives. But the woman she was seeking had lived more than two hundred years ago, closer to 230, and she wouldn't be easy to find. She was the proverbial needle in the haystack, and it was only with great good fortune that some story about her would have been passed on from generation to generation and been preserved. Maybe the fact that Wachiwi or her father had gone to France had made them noteworthy. She must have been remarkable in some way to have gone so far from her Dakota home.

The artifacts at the institute were ancient and fragile, and had been carefully preserved, and once again Brigitte was able to find a librarian, who in this case was not just helpful, but fascinated by the story Brigitte told. As Brigitte did, the librarian at the institute loved the idea that Wachiwi had wound up at the court of the King of France, or close enough if she had stayed in Brittany and married a marquis. It seemed more than likely to both of them that she had been one of those rare, early Americans who had been guests at the French court, like Benjamin Franklin and Thomas Jefferson. And maybe Wachiwi de Margerac. Why else would she have gone to France? How had she gotten there? Who had invited her? Who had gone with her? And how had she stayed on another continent so far from home? Brigitte wondered if her relatives had traveled with her, her parents, maybe siblings. It was inconceivable that she had journeyed to France alone, particularly as a young Sioux girl.

The librarian introduced herself as Jan and explained to Brigitte that the mores that applied to young Sioux maidens had been extremely strict for a long time. They were kept secluded, their virginity was essential, and they could not look the men in their tribe directly in the eyes. One could only assume that Wachiwi had been carefully surrounded and protected when she went to France. It was hard to imagine her family's reaction to her marrying a French marquis, or that of the French marquis's family to her. It was hardly an ordinary match. Finally, Brigitte had found an ancestor who not only excited her imagination but captured her heart. It made the whole project come alive for her at last.

The woman in charge of the library showed Brigitte countless photographs of young Sioux girls, and this time they both noticed that Brigitte bore a faint resemblance to some of them. Brigitte was older and modern in style, her features were less pronounced, but in more than one of the photographs, there was a similarity between her and some of the young girls. And her long black hair made the resemblance easier to discern. If so, Wachiwi's genes had been strong, or perhaps it was only coincidence, but Brigitte loved the idea. She couldn't wait to tell Amy about it when she went home. It suddenly made her feel more exotic, and she felt an even stronger tie with this young girl, who had ventured into a whole other world.

Jan showed Brigitte the records of the oral histories then, and it was hard to know where to start, there were so many of them. But the librarian knew her resources well. They pored through them all afternoon until they closed. But nothing about Wachiwi had turned up, or even anything about a chief going to the French court, although

Brigitte knew now that several had, and the librarian said she had read of it too, mostly in books about eighteenth-century France. She had even seen drawings of Sioux chiefs in a combination of native and French court garb.

Brigitte was discouraged when she drove back to the motel in Sioux Falls. She had hoped to find something, anything that led Wachiwi from the mists of the distant past. She called her mother and told her they had found nothing so far, and Brigitte dreamed of Wachiwi that night. She was a beautiful young girl.

They found nothing on the second day either, and on the third day, Brigitte was about to give up, when they came across a series of histories that had been taken from old Sioux men of the Dakota tribe. The accounts had been recorded in 1812, and in one case were recollections an old chief had from when he was a boy. He had spoken of a Dakota chief named Matoskah, White Bear, who had had five brave sons from his first wife who died. His second wife had been a beautiful young girl, who also died when their infant girl was born. The child became the song of her father's soul. She grew up protected by her brothers and father and refused to marry until she was older than the other girls in the village. Chief Matoskah thought no brave was worthy of her, and he and his daughter refused all the suitors who came for her hand. The man who had given the oral history said she was a proud, beautiful girl. And then he talked of their wars with the Crow, the many braves who had died fighting to protect the village, the war parties, the raids, and then he mentioned the girl again. He said that on one of their raids, the Crow had killed two of her brothers who were trying to protect her, and a young boy, and the Crow had taken her to give to their chief as a slave. The Sioux braves tried to bring her back but never could, and her father, the great chief Matoskah, had died of a broken heart later that year. The man giving the history said when the girl left, her father's spirit left with her. He had been young himself then, but he remembered it well. He said they heard stories of her later, that she had been given to the Crow chief, and she had killed him and run away. They never found her, and she was never seen again. She never came back to her father's tribe. A French trapper said he had seen her once, traveling with a white man, but trappers were known for their lies to Indians, so no one believed him. The girl was gone. The man telling the story said he didn't know. Maybe she had been taken by a great spirit for killing the chief of the Crow. He said her name was Wachiwi, the most beautiful girl he'd ever seen, and her father, Chief Matoskah, had been the wisest chief he'd ever known.

There she was, Brigitte thought to herself, as he moved

on to another story of his youth and the buffalo hunts on the Great Plains. Wachiwi. She had been taken from her tribe, and given to a Crow chief. They said she killed him, and ran away. Who was the white man the trapper said he saw with her? Brigitte had the feeling that she was following a ghost. Elusive, beautiful, mysterious, brave. She wondered if this was the same Wachiwi who had turned up in France. It was hard to know. More than two hundred years later, the trail was cold. And maybe it didn't matter. They knew enough. But Brigitte was like a dog with a bone. She couldn't let go.

For the next week, she and Jan, the librarian, combed the oral histories of the Crow, who were part of the Sioux nation too, even though frequently at war with the Dakota Sioux. At lunchtime, Brigitte and Jan went to a nearby restaurant, and they talked endlessly of the collections of histories that Brigitte was discovering day by day. The stories were totally absorbing and Brigitte was falling in love with the people she was reading about. Talking to Jan about it brought it more and more to life. It was like traveling back in time.

They found nothing for days, and then finally, there she was again, and the earlier story was confirmed.

The man telling this story sang the praises of the Crow chief Napayshni, whom he had known as a boy. He said the chief had two wives and was given a beautiful girl they had taken from the Sioux. He called her a bad spirit and said she had bewitched their chief, lured him into the woods, and killed him. They never found her again. He thought she might have been taken by another tribe, and a trapper said she had been taken by a Frenchman, but she was long gone. The man telling the story was convinced that she was a spirit and not a girl, and she had simply vanished after killing their chief. As she read it, Brigitte knew it was Wachiwi, and she was mesmerized by the mention of the Frenchman. Brigitte knew in her bones that someone had saved this girl. And whatever had happened, she had clearly been very brave, to kill her captor and run away. She knew in her gut that it was the same Wachiwi who had gone to France, and whoever the Frenchman was in the second story, somehow he had taken her home. The rest of the story might never be told. But it was enough. Brigitte knew what she needed to of Wachiwi, the young Indian girl who had been adored by her father and brothers, taken by the Crow in a war raid, and given to their chief; she had killed him to escape, and then a mysterious Frenchman had found her and took her back to France. She must have been a beguiling woman. The second narrator had called her bewitching. But she was no witch, she sounded like a beautiful, fiercely brave young girl, and from there she became a marquise in Brittany. It was an extraordinary story, and a remarkable history to share.

Brigitte hated to leave, but she had accomplished what she had come to South Dakota to do. She had found the traces of Wachiwi she needed to confirm what she believed. She thanked Jan profusely when she left, and felt as though she had made a friend. After saying goodbye, she drove back to Sioux Falls, and caught a flight that would connect her to Boston. She felt at peace, as though a missing part of her had slipped into place. Wachiwi. The dancer. Brigitte wondered what more she could discover about her if she delved deeper into her family history in France. A girl as remarkable as that would have been talked about there too – a young Indian girl of the Dakota Sioux, who captured the heart of a marquis, and spent the rest of her days in France. Surely someone would have written of her there. It had become Brigitte's mission to follow her trail.

Chapter 5

Brigitte had a lot to think about on the flights from South Dakota to Boston. She had only been gone for ten days, but she felt as though her life had been changed forever by one Dakota Sioux Indian woman. Wachiwi was all she had thought about for days, while she tried to find her in the oral histories. There were still so many mysteries about her. How had she come to leave the Crows who had kidnapped her? Was she the same girl as the Wachiwi who had married the marquis in Brittany? Was she really the one who had killed the Crow chief and disappeared? Had someone rescued her? Who was the white man with her that one of the oral histories talked about? And the Frenchman with her in another? And how had she gotten from South Dakota to France? Brigitte was convinced it was the same girl, and it was frustrating beyond belief not to have all the pieces of the story and all the missing links. She felt like one of Ted's fellow archaeologists finding bone fragments and trying to build an entire dinosaur out of them, to discover everything about him, including where he lived, how he died, who his enemies were, and what he ate. But sooner or later, most of the time, the pieces came together. And she hoped they would about Wachiwi too. It had been such an exciting time for her. She was so glad her mother had convinced her to go to Salt Lake. She had picked up the trail where her mother left off, and had discovered something entirely new. Wachiwi. Brigitte thought she was more interesting than all the rest of their relatives put together, except maybe the marquis.

As exciting as the trip had been, because it had taken her mind off all her problems and failures, coming home to her apartment in Boston sank her into a depression that took her breath away. The apartment looked dark and dusty. It hadn't been cleaned in two weeks, or more since she'd been depressed when she left. The first thing she saw when she looked at the bookcase was a shelf of Ted's books that she had forgotten to return and he had forgotten to reclaim. It reminded her that he was gone forever, that she didn't have a boyfriend – or a job. There was not a single response by mail, or e-mail, to all the résumés she had sent out. No one had offered her a job, or even wanted to see her for an interview. And she didn't have a man in her life. And if she wanted one, she had to start to date again. How was she supposed to do that? Computer dating? Blind dates through friends? Pick-ups in bars? None of those solutions appealed to her, and the thought of starting to date after six years sank her spirits to rock bottom.

When she checked her messages, she found that Ted had called to say goodbye. He hadn't called her cell phone where he knew he would almost surely get her, he had called her at her apartment, at an hour when he'd been almost sure that she was out, so he wouldn't have to talk to her. It was a cowardly thing to do. He didn't want to talk to her, and his voice on the message said he was leaving for Egypt the next day. When she had been flying in from South Dakota, he was flying out. He was gone. Forever. Following his dream. And what was hers? Another job in a college admissions office, checking applications? Finishing a deadly boring book about women's voting that no one would ever read? For ten days she had been totally excited about what she was doing. And hours later, if that, she felt dead again. As dead as her life. But she couldn't spend the rest of her days chasing Wachiwi either. She had lived more than two centuries ago, and many of the mysteries about her would never be solved, the questions never answered.

Brigitte had to go back to trying to finish a book she no longer cared about, find a job she didn't want, and look for a replacement for a man she no longer thought she really loved and who hadn't loved her. What was she doing with her life? And what had she been doing for the last ten years? Damned if she knew. And she knew even less what she wanted to do now. It was a miserable place to be in. And finally, not knowing what else to do, she went to bed.

She got up early the next morning, and organized all the notes she had taken in South Dakota and Salt Lake. She wanted to put them in some kind of chronological order for her mother, and hand them over to her. She had it all in perfect sequence by noon, and then she faxed it to her mother. Late that afternoon her mother called her after she had read it all and digested it.

'That's fantastic, Brig. I'm sure it's the same woman who married the marquis.'

'I can't prove it, but so do I. She must have been quite a woman. It's nice to know we're related to her. She must have been one gutsy kid.' Her mother smiled at what she said. Brigitte sounded better again, but Marguerite was worried about the direction her life was going to take.

'So what's *my* gutsy kid going to do?' her mother asked her. 'Are you going to stay in Boston, or move back to New

York? This might be a good time to do it. You'd probably earn more money here.'

'There are more colleges in Boston,' Brigitte said reasonably. 'I'm just going to wait and see who responds, and try to finish my book.'

But it was easier said than done. She felt as though she had a cement block on her head, when she got back to her book about the vote the next day. Compared to her exciting research about Wachiwi, her book about the vote was like swimming through glue. She just couldn't do it, and she could no longer remember why she thought the definitive work about women's suffrage was such a good idea. She called Amy in her office that afternoon.

'I think I'm schizophrenic,' she announced when her friend answered.

'Why? Are you hearing voices?'

'Not yet, but maybe I should. The only voice I'm hearing is my own, and it's boring me to death. I think I have writer's block. Maybe I'm traumatized over Ted. I hate my book.'

'You're just in a slump. It happens to me too. Go for a walk, or a swim, play tennis. Do some exercise. You'll feel better when you get back.'

'I've just had the most fun I've had in years, for the past ten days.' Brigitte even sounded excited when she said it, and Amy was thrilled to hear it.

'Ohmigod! What? A guy?'

'No, a Sioux Indian girl I discovered in my family tree in Salt Lake. If she's the right one, she was kidnapped from her village by the Crow Indians, ran away from them, may have killed the chief on her way out, possibly ran off with a Frenchman, or a white man anyway, and somehow got from South Dakota to France, where she married a marquis, and may have gone to the court of Louis XVI. Now how exciting is that?'

'Very. But there are a lot of "may haves" and "possiblies" in the story. How much do you know for sure, and how much are you wishing is true?'

'I'm wishing all of it is true. And some of the oral histories are a little vague. But she turns up in several of them, by name. And she definitely married the marquis, and my mother is descended from her, and so am I. She wound up in Brittany, married to a marquis, and she definitely is Sioux. That I know for sure. I fell in love with her, following her life. It's the most exciting stuff I've read about or researched in years, and I come back here, my apartment is dirty, my boyfriend is history, and left me a stupid message before he flew off to Egypt forever. No one is offering me a job and maybe never will, and even if they do, I'm not even sure I care about the job, and I'm trying to finish the dullest book in history, which I hate. Now what do I do?'

'Sounds like you need a fresh start. What if you shelve the book for now and write about something else? Why don't you write about this intriguing relative of yours? That might be a lot more interesting than the women's vote.'

'She probably is, but then I'm throwing away seven years. I threw away six with Ted. And ten working for BU, and they deep-sixed me on two hours' notice. That's a lot of years to have spent and wind up with nothing on all fronts.'

'Sometimes you just have to let go. Like a bad investment, at some point you have to cut your losses and start over again.' It was good advice, and Brigitte knew it.

'Yeah. But on what?'

'You'll know. I think you need a break. Why don't you take a trip? I mean a real trip. Not Salt Lake and South Dakota. Why don't you go to Europe or something? There are a lot of cheap tickets on the Internet if you look for them.'

'Yeah. Maybe.' Brigitte didn't sound convinced. 'Do you want to have dinner tonight?'

Amy sounded apologetic. 'I can't. I'm writing another article, and my deadline is next week. Both of my kids have been sick, and I haven't done a thing. If I don't stay home and work, I'm screwed.'

Brigitte felt better when she hung up, but not enough

so, she still felt antsy and bored and as though her life had no direction, and that night she thought about what Amy had said. Maybe she was right. Maybe she should do something totally crazy, like go to Europe, even though she didn't have a job. In fact, maybe it was a good time to do it. Maybe she could go to Brittany and Paris, and look for history on Wachiwi there. By midnight, she had decided to do it, somewhat nervously. And by the next morning, she was looking for tickets on the Internet, as Amy had suggested.

She found one for the following weekend. March wasn't a great month to go to Europe weather-wise, but she told herself there was no time like the present, she had nothing else planned, and it would give her something fun to do. She called her mother that afternoon and told her what she was doing, and her mother sounded amazed. Wachiwi had given Brigitte a whole new lease on life. She was obsessed with finding her. Her mother thought her trip to Brittany and Paris was a great idea. Suddenly she'd been bitten by the genealogical bug, just like her mother. But what fascinated Brigitte was Wachiwi, not their long aristocratic history, which meant nothing to her. Wachiwi. The young Sioux girl who had defied all odds, survived the unthinkable, accomplished the impossible, wound up in France, and married a marquis. It didn't get more interesting than that, as an anthropologist or a woman. What she was doing was even more exciting to her than Ted's long-awaited dig in Egypt was to him. This was so much more recent, Wachiwi was so real and seemed so alive in everything Brigitte read about her. She couldn't wait to get to France now and continue her research.

With a sigh, she put all her material on the suffrage book in two cardboard boxes, and stuck them under her desk. Like Scarlett O'Hara, she was going to think about that tomorrow. For now, all she cared about was Wachiwi. Everything else could wait.

Chapter 6

Wachiwi
Spring 1784

It was springtime, and the camp that Chief Matoskah had chosen for his tribe was a good one. There was a river nearby, and the women were already at work repairing the tipis from the hardships of winter – the linings had been washed and set out to dry in the sun. There were small groups making clothing for the summer months and following winter, and the children were running and laughing and playing all around them. Chief Matoskah's tribe was one of the largest of the Dakota Sioux, and he was thought to be the wisest chief in their nation. Stories of his youth, bravery in battle, victories against their enemies, and his prowess on horseback and hunting buffalo were legion. His five sons were all equally respected, all were proud men, married, and had children of their own. Two would be leading the first buffalo hunt of the season the following morning. Chief Matoskah, White Bear, was old now, but still ruled his tribe with wisdom, strength, and when necessary an iron fist.

His one weakness, and the joy and light of his life, was Wachiwi, the daughter born to him by his second wife. His first wife had died of an illness in a winter camp, during a war with the Pawnee. He had come home from a raid, and found her already wrapped in a buffalo robe, on a funeral scaffold, her still form covered with snow. He had grieved for a long time. She had been a good woman, and given him five brave sons.

It was many winters before White Bear married again, and the girl he chose was the most beautiful in their village. She was younger than his sons. He could have had many women, several wives at one time, as many of the men did, but he had always preferred to live with one. The bride he chose finally, giving her father twenty of his best horses for her, as a gesture of respect for her family, was barely more than a child, but she was wise and strong, and so beautiful that his heart sang each time he saw her. Her name was Hotah Takwachee, White Doe, and she looked like one to him.

They had only three seasons together when she bore
him their first child, his only daughter. Her mother came
to help her when the child was born in the early days of
autumn. The baby was born, bright and beautiful and
perfect, at dawn. Her mother was dead by nightfall. White
Bear was alone again, with White Doe's tiny girl child.
Other women in the village nursed her and cared for her,
and she lived in the tipi with her father. But White Bear
took no wife again. He hunted with his sons, and sat in the
lodge with them late into the night, smoking the pipe, and
planning raids on their enemies and hunts. And although
he could not admit it openly because she was a girl, he
took endless pleasure in his daughter, who delighted him
constantly. Sometimes he would walk in the woods with
her, and he taught her to ride himself. She was the most
fearless rider in the village, and rode better than most of
the men. Her skill as a rider was well known throughout
the neighboring tribes. Even their enemies had heard of
the dancing daughter of the chief who had magic powers
over horses. White Bear was proud of her, and as she grew
older, she was always at his side.

White Bear received his first marriage offer for her
shortly after her rites of womanhood, from a distinguished
brave older than her brothers. He was a fierce warrior and
excellent hunter who already had two wives and several

Danielle Steel

children, but Wachiwi had caught his eye. He came to play the flute outside their tipi repeatedly, and Wachiwi never emerged, which was a sign to him that she was not interested in him, and when he began leaving blankets, food, and finally in desperation a hundred horses outside their lodge for her, his offer of marriage was official, and eventually declined by his prospective bride. She insisted to her father that she didn't want to leave him, and remembering only too well what had happened to her mother in childbirth, White Bear couldn't bring himself to part with her either, at least not yet. He knew that she would have to marry eventually. She was too pretty and lively not to, but he wanted her with him for a few more years before she took on the responsibilities of a wife and all that went with it. He wasn't ready to give her up. She was the oldest unmarried girl in the tribe by her seventeenth summer, but she was the daughter of the chief. And by then, finally, she had become interested in a young brave her age. He had no important war raids or hunting parties where he had distinguished himself exceptionally yet, and she and her father both knew that he still had to prove himself further in battle and in the buffalo hunts, but in the next year or two he would. Wachiwi was prepared to wait for him till then, and her father was pleased. He would be a suitable husband for her one day, and in the meantime

Wachiwi could stay with her father. He was in no hurry for young Ohitekah to win her hand, but White Bear knew that day would come. Hopefully, not too soon. And Wachiwi was only too happy to remain at her father's side. She was entirely her father's girl, fussed over and protected not only by him but by her brothers.

As the spring progressed, there were horse races and demonstrations. Wachiwi was allowed to enter them because her father was chief and she rode better, harder, faster, and more dangerously than most of the young men. Her brothers loved to place bets on her and were ecstatic when she won. Their father had taught her well, and her brothers added their own tricks to what she learned, so they could win their bets on her. She was a fearsome rider and rode like the wind. And whenever she finished the races, or rode with her brothers, she noticed Ohitekah nearby, but as propriety demanded of her, she never looked him directly in the eye, nor any man. She was always circumspect and well behaved, although high spirited and brave. Her father always said that if she had been a man, she would have been a great warrior, but he was far happier that she was a girl. She was affectionate with him, took care of him, and served him well as a loving daughter.

She loved to laugh with her brothers and they teased her endlessly. Ohitekah would enter into it sometimes, and obviously admired her, and even in their joking and games with her brothers, he treated her with great respect.

As spring led into summer, the hunting parties formed. Hunts for elk and buffalo helped them lay in the stores for winter, and Wachiwi helped the other women make clothes. She did beautiful beading that some of the older women had taught her, and she carefully added porcupine quills to her clothes in intricate patterns. Because of her status, she was able to wear her clothes as ornately as she chose, and even added beads to her moccasins. And often, she dyed the quills in brilliant colors before she sewed them onto her elkskin dresses.

There were tribal dances as the weather grew warm, and long, pleasant evenings as the men sat around the fires and smoked the pipe. There were always sentries protecting the camp too, since war raids were common in summer, to steal horses and furs, or even women. And occasionally they met with other tribes to trade. Wachiwi got a beautiful new blanket on one of those visits, and a new elkskin dress that one of her brothers traded a buffalo hide for, and he got her a second elkskin dress in the trade, trimmed in fur for the following winter. Everyone agreed that Wachiwi was the luckiest girl in the tribe, with five adoring brothers and a doting father. It was no wonder that she didn't want a husband. But her interest in

Ohitekah seemed to be growing, and on one hot night, he came to play the flute outside their lodge, and this time Wachiwi came outside, which was a clear sign to him that his courtship was welcome, although she kept her eyes riveted to the ground, and her gaze well away from his.

His parents had been rebuilding their lodge recently, which was also an indication that a marriage proposal would be forthcoming, and bride gifts would be left for her outside her father's tipi soon, maybe at the change of seasons, or at their winter camp. And they also knew that their son had to prove himself in the hunt and on the battlefield first. But that time was coming soon. The big buffalo hunts had begun.

White Bear and his sons were returning to camp one warm day after just such a major hunt. Ohitekah had come with them and had done well. The buffalo were plentiful, and they had killed many. There was to be a celebration in camp that night. They were riding back, talking and laughing with each other when one of the young boys in camp rode out to them. He said that a war party of Crow had raided the camp, and were already riding away. They had taken horses, and several of their women, mostly young ones, to give to their chief. Without asking for further details, White Bear and his sons and the other men rode hard for the camp. Most of the Crow were gone by then, except for three stragglers, who turned to shoot at White Bear and his men. White Bear wasn't injured, but two of his sons fell instantly and lay dead, and Ohitekah lay beside them, brothers in death now, and not by marriage as the young boy and Wachiwi had hoped. The Sioux men rode into camp just in time to see the three Crow disappearing, and one of them had Wachiwi, bound and tied, looking wild eyed as she shouted to her father. The Crow took off like lightning, but she had already seen her brothers and Ohitekah killed. She was shouting, and fighting her captors, but even her tribe's fastest horses could not catch them. They rode as fast as they could for hours after her, to bring her back to her father, and they returned late that night, worn out and deeply chagrined. They had not been able to save her. The Crow who had her had ridden like the wind. White Bear had been waiting up for them, and he cried like a child when they returned without her. And as though someone had cast a spell on him, as he keened for his lost child he visibly shrank and became an old man. His soul was broken. He had lost two of his sons to the Crow, and the child of his heart. Nothing could console him.

War parties went out the next day, looking for the Crow encampment, but they had come from far away. They too were part of the Dakota nation, but had a long history of wars and raids on the Sioux, and taking the chief's daughter was a major victory for them. White Bear knew only too well that even if they found them, they would never give her back. Wachiwi was gone forever. And more than likely she would be given to their chief as a slave or wife. Her days of freedom and being adored and protected by her father and brothers were over. She belonged to the Crow now. And no one knew it better than her father. He couldn't bear the thought. He walked slowly into his tipi alone, saw the place where she had slept across from him for her entire life, her elkskin dresses carefully folded, even the new one trimmed in fur. He lay down in the place where he slept, his eyes closed, seeing her in his mind as he knew he would forever, and waited to die. He hoped it wouldn't take long for the Great Spirits to take him. Without Wachiwi at his side, he had nothing more to live for. His spirit died within him the day she left.

Chapter 7

The Crow war party that had taken Wachiwi from her tribe rode hard for two days. Wachiwi fought them as best as she was able to, with her hands and arms tied. She did everything she could to save herself, including throwing herself from the horse into some bushes. After that, they tied her legs as well, and the brave who rode with her carried her slung across his horse in front of him, like a prize from the hunt. She would have killed them if she could. Other women would have been afraid of them, but Wachiwi wasn't. She didn't care if they killed her now, she had seen them murder the boy she loved, and two of her brothers. What they did to her now no longer mattered, if she never got back to her father. But she was going to try to escape. She lay across the horse thinking of it, as the war party traveled for days toward the Crow camp. They stopped to kill two buffalo along the way, which they thought was a promising sign.

Once in a while they would untie her, but only long enough to let her attend to her needs. She tried to run away whenever they did, and they would catch her and tie her up again each time. They laughed at how violently she fought them, and one of them slapped her hard and threw her to the ground when she bit him. She was a wildcat in their midst, and in their dialect, they talked about what a prize she would be for their chief. They were well aware from her clothes that she was the daughter of the Sioux chief. She wore a soft elkskin dress that was carefully beaded and covered with the porcupine quills she had dyed. And even her moccasins were delicately made. And although she was not as young as some of the girls in camp, she was very beautiful, obviously very brave, and very strong. She fought them almost like a man, but they overpowered her anyway. The war party was made up of their camp's fiercest men. Some of them would have liked to keep her for themselves, but they were saving her for their chief. He already had two wives, his own and his brother's wife, whom he had married the previous year when his brother was killed in the hunt. It had been his duty to marry her, and she was already with child. This girl was much younger than the two wives he had, and far more beautiful. He would be pleased. She had a lovely figure, and although she did not look at them, even now, she had enormous eyes. And all of them had noticed how courageous she was, even being kidnapped by a war party, and no matter how much they tried to scare her. Other girls her age, or older, would have been screaming in fright. Wachiwi tried to run away whenever she could, and clearly didn't care if they killed her. But she was too sweet a prize for their chief for them to want to lose her. So they kept her tied up as much as possible, and rode with great speed for their camp. One of the men tried to offer her food, willing to feed her with his hands, and each time she turned her face away and refused. She looked none of them in the eye, but her face was filled with hatred, and in her heart was despair for the father she knew would die of grief without her.

It was the end of the third day when they rode into the Crow camp at last. It was smaller than her own, and she saw the same familiar scenes, of children running, women sitting in groups and talking while they sewed, men coming back into camp after a hunt. Even the layout of the camp was similar to the way her people set up theirs, and the brave who carried her rode up to the chief's tipi, followed by the others who had made up the war party.

The women and children looked up with interest as the brave jumped off his horse, unceremoniously pulled her off, and dumped her on the ground. She lay there in her elkskin dress, tied up like an animal they had killed, unable to move as one of the men went to find the chief. Both his women were sitting near the tipi, sewing, and as they watched, Wachiwi looked up and saw him. He was much younger than her father, and looked proud and strong. He was closer to her brothers' age. She heard one of the men call him Napayshni. It meant 'courageous' in her tongue as well. Their language was close enough to her own that she could understand what they were saying.

They told him that she was the daughter of the chief, and they had brought her back to him as the spoils of war. They reported that they had also taken several good horses, and three other women, but some of the men had ridden ahead with them, so Wachiwi didn't see them on their travels. The men told him that the war party had split up after they left her father's camp, and the other group had taken a different route back. Those who carried her said they had gone a more circuitous way, in case the men of her tribe came after Wachiwi. No one had followed them at all. The Crow who had absconded with her had hidden her well, taking a more remote route. Her people hadn't been able to find her, and her captors were proud of having outsmarted and outridden them with their prize. And she was a beauty.

Chief Napayshni stood looking down at her without expression. 'Untie her,' was all he said, and the man whose horse she had ridden on was quick to object.

'She'll run away. She tried every time we untied her. She's fast as the wind and very clever.'

'I'm faster than she is,' the chief said, looking unconcerned.

Wachiwi said nothing, but her hands and legs were numb when they untied her. Her hair was tangled from the trip, and her face was filthy from the dust. Her elkskin dress was torn in several places from the buffalo-sinew ropes they had used to tie her. It was a few minutes before she was able to stand. She dusted herself off, trying to look proud, and stumbling a little. She turned away so the men who had taken her would not see the tears in her eyes. Life as she had known it, among people she loved, and who loved her, was over forever. She was a slave now. She knew she would run away, but first she had to learn the layout of the camp and be able to take one of their horses. And then she would go home. Nothing could keep her with the Crow.

Chief Napayshni continued to observe her. He saw the torn dress. It was unmistakably the garb of the wife or daughter of a chief. Her moccasins were beaded, and the whole top of her dress was covered in the porcupine quills she was so proud of. These had been dyed a deep blue, with a paste she had learned how to make with berries. It was a skill few of the women in her camp had mastered. And in spite of her matted hair and dirty arms and face, it was still easy to see how beautiful she was.

'What are you called?' the chief asked her directly. She ignored him. But this time, instead of acting according to maidenly tradition in all tribes, she stared him in the eyes with a look of utter hatred. 'You have no name?' he said, looking unimpressed. She was like an angry child, but he knew that other girls in her position would have been terrified, and she wasn't. He admired that in her. Her bravery was perhaps just an act she was putting on, but she didn't seem to be afraid of him at all, and he liked that about her. She had spirit, and courage. 'You are the daughter of a great chief,' he said, knowing exactly who her father was. The raid on her camp had been no accident, only taking her had been a random act by the braves who saw her and grabbed her, as a prize of war for their chief. And although he would never have said it to them, Napayshni felt sorry for her father. It would surely be a grief to him to lose a daughter such as this, for any man for that matter. And his men had reported that they had killed two of the chief's sons, and others. The raid had been a great success for them, and a hard blow for Wachiwi's tribe.

'Then why did you take me?' she asked him, 'if you think my father a great chief?' She continued to look him straight in the eye, pretending not to fear him, or what he could do to her now. She had heard stories of kidnapped women who became slaves in other tribes. They were not happy stories, and this was her lot now.

'We did not plan to. They brought you to me as a gift,' he said gently. She looked hardly older than a child.

'Then send me back to my father. I do not want to be your gift.' She stuck her chin out, and her eyes blazed. She had never looked any man in the eye except her father and brothers.

'You are mine now, you with no name. What shall I name you?' He was playing with her a little, so she wouldn't be frightened of him. Despite his reputation as a warrior and fierce chief, he was a kind man, and her situation touched his heart. He had children too, and he would not have liked his own daughter to be taken by another tribe and given to their chief. The thought of it made him shudder.

'I am Wachiwi,' she said angrily. 'I don't want a Crow name from you.'

'Then I will call you by your own,' he said, signaling to

the two women sitting nearby. His own wife was younger and better looking than the one he had inherited from his brother the year before. Wachiwi could see that the older of the two was heavy with child, and she was the one who came forward when her husband called her. 'Take her to the river to get clean,' he instructed her. 'She needs clothes, until hers can be sewn.'

'Is she our slave now?' the woman asked with interest, and Napayshni said nothing. He owed her no explanation of his plans. He had married her, as was his obligation to his brother, and had now given her his child, that was enough. He did not want Wachiwi as a slave. He wanted her to get used to them so she would not be so hostile with him, and in time, when she had settled into their camp, he was going to make her his wife. She was much prettier and appeared more graceful than the others, and he liked the look of wildfire in her eyes. She was like a wild horse he wanted to tame, and he was sure that he could do it. Like her, he was an outstanding horseman.

Wachiwi followed the pregnant woman and said nothing to her. The woman spoke in the Crow dialect to Napayshni's other wife, and Wachiwi understood all that they said, although she pretended she didn't. The chief had spoken to her in her own tongue. And his women were commenting on the quills on her dress and wondered how she got them that color. They hoped that in time maybe she'd teach them. She vowed to herself as she listened to them that she would do nothing for them. Ever.

She washed at the river and they gave her a dress, it was plain and ill fitting, and one of the women handed her a blanket that she wrapped around herself. That night Wachiwi repaired her elkskin dress with the porcupine quills as best she could. Some of the quills had broken when she was thrown over her captor's horse. She put the dress back on as soon as she had sewn it. It was all she had left of her old life.

Napayshni came into the tipi that night and said nothing to her. He slept at the north side of the tipi, as her father did, and she and the other two women on the south side, with their children. There were seven of them. And the tipi was not as tidy as she had kept her father's. Two of the children kept waking in the night, and for most of it, Wachiwi lay awake, looking up at the sky through the opening at the top, and wondering how soon she could try to escape. It was all she could think of. She had refused to eat with them, and was determined to go hungry until she could stand it no longer. Later she finally ate some cornmeal cakes when she thought she would faint from starvation, but it was all she ate.

Napayshni got up at dawn to oversee the moving of the

camp. Being a smaller village than her own, they moved every few days to follow the buffalo, and find new grazing land for the horses. She had heard that the men were going hunting that day after they set up camp again. Wachiwi was hoping to make a run for it then, if the women were busy, and most of the men were gone. She wanted to check on the three other women from her tribe, but had no opportunity to see them before they broke camp.

They didn't have far to go to find more buffalo that day, and the men took off in the early afternoon, talking and laughing and in good spirits. She wondered how far she was from her father's camp. She knew they had traveled three days to get here, but alone, she could travel in a straight line at great speed. All she needed was a good horse and an opportunity to get out of camp.

She wandered around aimlessly, and no one paid attention to her. She had caught a glimpse of one of the women from her tribe but couldn't speak to her. The other women had each been given to braves at the camp and had no choice in the matter. All Wachiwi wanted to do was run.

There were some horses left after the men rode off, though not the best ones. She spotted one that looked solid and sturdy enough to travel with, though maybe not as fast as she liked. She walked over to pat his neck, looked at his legs, and without making a sound, she untied him, slipped onto his back, lay flat, lying along his side and holding on, and gently urged him out of camp while no one noticed. You couldn't even see her on him, she had concealed herself on his far side, a trick her brothers had taught her when she was a child, and she had often fooled them and her father with it in later years. It had delighted her father and won her brothers many of their bets.

She got the horse moving fast across the plain toward the trees, before she allowed herself to sit up, and then she pushed him harder. She was going at a fast pace, although he wasn't as good as the horses she was used to, and then she heard hoofbeats behind her, going even faster than she was. She didn't dare look back, but only pushed the horse more fiercely. She was nearly at the treeline, going with all the speed she could, when the rider caught up with her, and grabbed her with one powerful arm. It was Napayshni, riding alone. He said nothing to her, but put her in front of him on his own horse, as the one she had been riding slowed, grateful to halt the killing pace she had urged him to, and quietly began to graze. Napayshni slowed his own horse down and reined him in. His was much more lively, and she knew she could have gotten away on it.

'You ride well,' he commented, undisturbed. He liked

her spirit, and he had never seen a woman ride as she did. Her father or her brothers had taught her well.

'I thought you were hunting,' she said, her voice shaking, wondering if she would be punished now, or beaten. Maybe even killed. She had been willing to risk it, and knew she would again.

'I had some things to do in camp. The others went without me.' He had wanted her to think he was gone, to see what would happen if he left her. Now he knew. 'Will you do this again if I leave you?' he asked, looking down at her. He thought she looked lovelier than ever, with her cheeks flushed from the heat and the fast ride. She didn't answer his question, but he knew the answer anyway. She would continue trying to escape until she felt some bond to him, but it would be a long time before that would happen. Maybe not until she was carrying his child. But he didn't want to rush that either. She had been given to him as a gift, and now he wanted to make her one. He didn't want to break her spirit, only to tame her, like a wild horse on the plain. He believed that he could do it. He had tamed wild horses before, but nothing as wild or beautiful as she. She was a prize worth having.

They rode in silence back to the camp, with the horse she'd been riding led on a rope by Napayshni. The horse seemed relieved to be freed from his demanding rider. Napayshni kept her in front of him on his horse. He dropped her at his tipi, where the women were sitting, and then went to tie up the horses with the others. It had been an interesting afternoon for him, and a frustrating one for Wachiwi.

He kept a close eye on her that night, and said nothing to the other men. But he watched her for a long time as she lay sleeping, wondering how long it would take to tame her. He hoped it would be soon – he had a powerful hunger for her growing in him, but he didn't want to make a move too quickly. And for all he knew, if he did, she might try to kill him. She was capable of any-thing, and afraid of nothing. No girl would have dared what she had tried to do that afternoon, and none would have dared to ride the way she had. He had watched her concealing herself along the side of the horse. Only his best riders were able to do that, and there weren't many. And none with the ease with which he had seen her do it. She was quite a rider!

They moved camp again three days later, following the buffalo. The men killed some elk and a mule deer. There was abundant meat at the campfires, and they were already tanning the buffalo, and cutting it up to use it.

The Sun Dance was held around the campfire that night, to celebrate the summer months, and give thanks for their good hunting and the plentiful buffalo. Wachiwi stood to one side, watching the men dance. They did a similar dance in her tribe, and she was discovering that their customs were not so different. But all she could think of as she looked at them was that she wanted to go home. She wondered what her father and brothers were doing, and hoped that her father was well. Tears filled her eyes as she thought of her brothers who had been killed, and Ohitekah, and that she might never see her father again, but she hadn't given up hope yet of making a successful escape. She had been thinking of trying to make a run for it that night, when the men were dancing, but it might be too dangerous to cover rough terrain at night, so she decided to wait. Next time she knew that she had to be sure that Napayshni had left the camp, maybe when they went out in a hunting party that would be away for several days.

She left the campfire early, and ate very little of the meat. She wasn't hungry, and when she walked into their tipi, she was startled to see one of the chief's wives writhing in pain. The other one told her that the baby was coming, signaled to Wachiwi, and told her to help. Wachiwi had never been at a birth in her own camp, and she had no idea what to do.

She sat down next to the two women and watched. The

one giving birth was crying, and an old woman had come in to help them. And what Wachiwi saw looked horrifying to her, and then with utter amazement, a short time later, she watched the old woman help the baby into the world. She wrapped it tightly in a blanket, put it to its mother's breast, delivered the afterbirth, and went to bury it outside, as Wachiwi helped clean the young mother up.

By the time Napayshni came back from the Sun Dance, he had a new son. He observed him with cautious interest, nodded, and went to bed. Wachiwi lay on her own mat that night, hoping that would never happen to her. She had been in love with Ohitekah, and the Crow had killed him as they had her brothers. Now she wanted no man, and surely not Napayshni, or to have his child. She knew her days were numbered before he took her as his wife, and she was more anxious than ever to escape.

Napayshni continued to observe her, as they continued to move camp every few days, and the days melted into weeks. One morning, after she had seen him ride out with the men to hunt buffalo, she tried to escape again. She found a better horse this time, and rode even harder than she had before. This time she was followed out of camp by one of the young boys on a faster horse than hers. He had been guarding the horses, and Napayshni had warned him that Wachiwi might try to escape. In desperation to stop her, he shot an arrow at her, which grazed her shoulder and tore her dress. But she didn't stop for anything, even when she felt it burn. He was almost as good a rider as she, and nearly as fearless, and he was driven by his desire to please his chief.

'You can't stop me!' Wachiwi shouted at him when he drew close to her. Her shoulder was bleeding through her dress.

'I'll kill you if I have to!' he answered. 'Napayshni wants you back.'

'He'll have to kill me first. Or you will,' she said, shouting at him, and pulled ahead. It was a race to the death. He followed her for miles and stayed on her heels, and then destiny betrayed her, her horse stumbled, and she had to stop him, or she knew he'd break a leg. Both horses were in a lather when she stopped, and the boy glared at her.

'You're crazy!' he shouted. Wachiwi looked disheartened, as blood poured down her arm. His arrow hadn't pierced her, but it had sliced her deep. 'Why do you want to run away?'

'I want to go back to my father,' she said, fighting back tears. 'He's old and frail.' The boy was much younger than she was, and he was mystified by her.

'Napayshni will be good to you. You should be married by now anyway, shouldn't you?' She wondered if she should try to make a run for it again, but she knew that if she did, her horse would be lame before they reached the trees. She had been beaten again.

'I don't want to be married,' Wachiwi said, looking sullen. 'I just want to go home.'

'Well, you can't,' the boy said practically. 'I'm sorry I shot you. Napayshni said to stop you any way I could. Does it hurt?'

'Not at all,' she said blithely, unwilling to admit that it did. Quite a lot in fact.

She rode silently back to camp with him, let him lead away her horse, and went to the river alone to bathe her shoulder, wondering if she would ever get home again. She was beginning to lose hope that she would. And she would rather have been dead than be here. She was momentarily sorry that the boy's arrow hadn't killed her, instead of just wounding her. It had stopped bleeding by then, but it was a nasty wound and still hurt. She bathed it with the cool water from the stream and put her dress back on. She was walking back to their tipi when Napayshni rode back into camp. They had killed more buffalo that day than ever before, and he was pleased. He saw her as he rode up and didn't notice the blood on her dress at first. He was about to say something to her, when she looked up at him with a blank expression and fainted dead away at his horse's feet.

Napayshni was off his horse in an instant and picked her up. He had no idea what had happened to her, and then he saw the blood seeping through her elkskin dress. He called out to the women, and sent one of them to get the medicine man. He laid Wachiwi on her pallet as she slowly came around and then fainted again.

She was awake by the time the medicine man and an old woman came into the tent. The women had stripped off her dress, and Napayshni was inspecting her wound. His wives said they had no idea what had happened, but Napayshni suspected that she had tried to run away again, and something had gone wrong. And while the medicine man put powder into the wound, and a paste that almost made Wachiwi scream out, he went to find the boy who had been guarding the horses that afternoon.

'Did she try to escape again?' he asked him bluntly, looking ominous, as the boy trembled under the fierce glance.

'Yes. She did. You told me to stop her any way I could. So I did.'

'I didn't tell you to kill her. You might have, shooting her in the shoulder like that. You could have grazed her leg.'

'I didn't have time. She was going so fast. My horse could hardly keep up with her.'

'I know,' Napayshni answered. 'She rides like the wind. Be more careful next time. What did she say when you brought her back?'

'That she misses her father and he's old and sick. I told her it will be better for her here, with you.' He smiled shyly at his chief.

'Thank you. I won't tell anyone about this, and I don't want you to either.' If anyone had known he was so concerned about his captive, they would have thought he was an old woman, not the chief. He wasn't about to become a laughingstock for her, no matter how beautiful she was. 'You shot a bird and you missed. You're a terrible shot, Chapa. Isn't that right?' He coached him in what he was to say.

'Yes, it is.' He knew better than to argue with his chief. He had shot a bird. And he missed. That was the story, no matter how humiliating it might be for him.

Napayshni went back to the tipi then, and Wachiwi was sleeping with some potion they had given her. The medicine man and the old woman had left, and Wachiwi was dead to the world. She stirred once, and then fell into a deep sleep again as he left the tent.

She slept until the next morning, and she looked groggy when she got up, startled to be wearing only a blanket and not her dress, which was neatly folded next to her. She saw the blood on it and remembered what had happened the day before. Her attempt to escape had failed again. She was overwhelmed with sadness as she got up and put on her dress. She noticed then that there was blood on her moccasins as well.

Napayshni saw her as she came out of the tent. She looked as though she was in no condition to attempt an escape today. She looked tired and sick, and disoriented from the powerful potion they had made her drink.

'How is your shoulder?' he asked, as she stumbled past him and winced in the bright sun. All the men were in camp that day, and the women were tanning hides and curing meat. Their winter stores were almost complete.

'It's fine,' she said, looking unconvinced. It still hurt, but she was too proud to admit that to him.

'Chapa's a bad shot. He was trying to shoot a bird, and hit you instead.'

'No, he didn't. He said you told him to stop me any way he could, so he did.'

'How many times are you going to do this, Wachiwi? This time you got hurt. You could fall off a horse trying to escape, and be killed.'

'Or be shot by one of your men,' she said bluntly. 'I'd rather be dead than here.' It was the truth. She would never give up trying to go home until she was dead.

'Are you so unhappy here?' He looked sorry to hear it, and the truth was that he had been kind to her. He could have made her his own the first night, and she had been there for weeks now, but he wanted her to get used to him, before he made her his wife. She was no friendlier to him now than she had been in the beginning. He didn't want to be rough with her, but she couldn't keep running away forever. And sooner or later, someone would shoot her and kill her, or hurt her badly. He wanted to protect her from that. What had happened the day before was bad enough.

'You killed my brothers,' she said fiercely. And Ohitekah, but she didn't say his name.

'It happens during raids and war parties.' He couldn't change that, and he wanted her to be his. He wanted that very much. 'Can we try and be friends?' He thought that if she could think of him as a friend, the rest would be easier after that, and she would accept him as her husband. She wasn't the first woman to have been taken by a war party and given to a chief. Many of them became slaves. The other three women from her village had accepted it. Wachiwi had seen them with their braves and new families. They looked unhappy but knew they had no choice, and they were younger and more placid than Wachiwi. She had met them several times at the river, but the older women who treated them as slaves did not want them to talk to Wachiwi.

Napayshni wanted to give her more than the life of a slave or captive, and treat her as his wife. Wachiwi would have none of it.

'You're my enemy, not my friend.'

'I want you to be my wife,' he said softly. He was a great chief, humbling himself to a young girl, which was rare. In other tribes and circumstances, it would be an honor. But like the man who had offered her father a hundred horses for her and whom she refused, she didn't want to be Napayshni's wife. He had killed her brothers and the boy she loved, or his men had, which was enough. And they had taken her from her father. She would never forgive Napayshni for that.

'I will never be your wife,' Wachiwi said fiercely. 'You will have to take me with a knife at my throat.'

'I won't do that. I want you to come to me on your own.' She glared at him as he said it, but in spite of herself, something softened in her eyes. He was asking her, not telling her, or forcing her. That wasn't entirely lost on her. Things could have been a lot worse. He was an honorable man, and treated her with respect, although she didn't do the same to him. She had been harsh with him since they met. She didn't want to be his wife or his slave, or his prize of war. 'I won't force you, Wachiwi. I don't want to make you my wife that way. Go where you wish in the camp, do what you want. Be my wife when you are ready, and not before. But if you try to escape again, I will tie you up every day. You're a free woman, within the camp. And when you wish it, you will be my wife, and never my slave.' He was not going to make another chief's daughter his slave, and White Bear was an important chief. His daughter was worthy of respect. 'Stay away from the horses,' he warned. 'Other than that, you are free to go where you choose. On foot.' She didn't answer him, and he walked away. What he was offering her was more than fair. But she wasn't ready to make peace with him, and swore she never would. She was still planning to try to escape, every chance she got.

They were in their summer camp by then, and it was hot. They weren't planning to move for several weeks. There was work to do on the game they had killed, the women were sewing, men were tanning and curing, furs were being prepared for trade. There were good grazing lands for the horses, and plenty of buffalo nearby if they wanted more. It was a relief not to have to move camp every few days, especially in the heat. And Wachiwi's shoulder was healing by then. It didn't hurt anymore. She was still waiting for an opportune moment to escape, but there was none now. There were too many people in camp all the time. She could never take one of the horses and ride away. She had no choice but to do what Napayshni had said, she could walk everywhere, but she couldn't ride.

One day, she heard from some of the men that there was a lake nearby. It was a long walk, but she had nothing else to do. She had no children, no husband, and no official chores in camp. She was being treated like a guest, and Napayshni's two wives did everything, even washed her clothes for her. Napayshni had ordered them to do so. And although they grumbled at first, they did as they were told, and treated her like another child. She had an easy life, except for the fact that she didn't want to be there.

Napayshni was trying a new tack, as with a horse, to win her over. He was ignoring her entirely, and hoping she would come to him. It hadn't borne fruit so far, but she looked less bellicose than she had before. As they stayed in the summer camp, Wachiwi seemed more at ease. She played with the children, and sat with the women sometimes for a few minutes. She did some of her beading, and repaired her torn dress yet again. She even taught two of the young girls how to dye porcupine quills like the ones on her dress. They found the right berries, and they got them the same striking blue and were thrilled. Napayshni was pleased to see her calming down, although he made no comment to her.

And on their second week at the summer camp, she decided to take a long walk, and discovered the lake she had heard about from listening to some of the men. There was no one there. She was all alone in the most beautiful spot she had ever seen. There was a waterfall high up on a hill, and down below, the peaceful lake. There were fish in it, and a little sandy beach. She looked around, saw no one, took off her moccasins and dress, and swam naked in the lake. Her brothers had taught her to swim like a fish.

It was the most perfect afternoon she could remember in years, surely since she had been here. She had hidden her clothes so no one could see them if any of the men came to the lake. But no one did. They were busy in camp and had work to do, and it was too far to walk for the women and children. She felt as though she were in a sacred place. She smiled broadly for the first time since she'd been taken captive, and she stayed all afternoon, lay in the sun, and swam again several times. She was singing to herself when she went back to camp. She had freedom now, because Napayshni knew she could not get far on foot. And they were too far from her own tribe for her to walk.

She looked happy and carefree and young, with her black hair loose down her back. Napayshni saw her walk into camp, and he said nothing, but his heart glowed when he saw the look on her face. She looked peaceful and happy and at ease.

He asked her what she had done that day, as they all ate dinner at their campfire. The new baby had grown strong and healthy since it was born, and his mother looked well. Both women were pregnant again, with babies that would come in the spring. The baby Napayshni wanted was Wachiwi's, but he said nothing to her. He didn't want to frighten her, particularly as it seemed as though she was finally settling in.

'I went to the lake today,' Wachiwi said quietly. She was less hostile to him now since he rarely spoke to her, but she still didn't want to be his wife, or even his friend.

'On foot? That's a great distance to walk.' He was impressed. He knew that some of the men had gone there on horseback at first, but didn't have time these days.

'It's a beautiful place,' she said, looking serene. He nodded, and turned away from her again, pretending to ignore her. She was his beautiful wild horse. He hadn't tamed her yet, but he knew now that he would one day. He could see it in her eyes. The time was coming, and all he wanted was for it to come soon.

Chapter 8

Wachiwi went to the lake every day. It was a long walk in the heat, but it was worth it – the time she spent there was idyllic, and totally peaceful. It reminded her of a lake where she had gone with her brothers. And one day, just to see if she still could, she reached down and caught a fish with her hands, laughed out loud, and then threw it back. She enjoyed the time she spent there by herself. And she was so certain that no one was there that she lay naked in the sun for hours, swam with no clothes on, and even picked berries and wandered around nude in the hot sun. She felt like a child. She felt totally safe here and alone. She wanted these days to last forever, but she knew that in a few weeks, they would break camp and start traveling toward their winter camp. It was then that she planned to try and make a run for it again, but for now, she had nothing to think of, worry about, or plan. And she looked happy and relaxed when she went back to camp every night.

She had turned totally brown, and she had worn a hole in her moccasins from the long walk daily to the lake in the morning and back to camp at dusk. She always got back just in time for dinner, and Napayshni loved what he saw in her eyes. She looked expansive and welcoming and warm, sometimes even to him, when she forgot to look indifferent or angry at him. What he saw when she was open to him warmed his heart, and seemed to be opening hers. It was his fondest hope that perhaps by the time they broke camp and moved on, she would finally be his. He had been patient with her, and it was starting to bear fruit. He could feel it, even in the way she spoke to him now, when she talked about swimming at the lake. He had thought of giving her one of the horses to get there more easily, but he didn't want to tempt her to run away again. She still might. She wasn't his yet. Once she was, and had his baby inside her, he knew she would never try to leave again. But now she still could. He had to make her his own first, and then he would be safe and Wachiwi would be his for the rest of his days. It was all he wanted now, and he thought of it every day as he worked.

Wachiwi was oblivious to his passion and deep feelings for her as she walked to the lake every day with a light step, anxious to get to her private place and spend the day there. She was lucky, she had been given no work to do at the camp, which was Napayshni's gift to her. Instead she could play all day, swim at the lake, lie on the beach, and dream. She still dreamed of her family and her village and her father, but now she had other thoughts too, about the two women she lived with, their children, and Napayshni sometimes. She didn't want to believe it, but she could see he was a decent man. He was good to his men, and his wives, gentle with his children, and kind to her. If he had been a Sioux and hadn't killed her brothers and Ohitekah, she would have liked him and might even have agreed to be his wife. Now she never would. And soon, she would be gone. No matter how kind he was to her, she was more determined than ever to run away. She was biding her time until they broke camp, and enjoying her days at the lake.

She lay sleeping on the beach one particularly hot afternoon. She had tucked her dress and moccasins under a bush, and she had fallen into a deep sleep after swimming for a long time. The children had woken them in the heat the night before, and she was tired. She had been dreaming of her father, when she heard a sound. She thought it was a bird rustling in a bush nearby. She opened an eye, looked around, saw nothing, and then sat up on the warm sand, and as she did she saw something she had never seen before. It was a man in buckskin breeches and an open white shirt, with white skin and dark hair, and he stood staring at her with a mixture of disbelief and terror. He was too paralyzed to move, and so was she. She could hear his horse now, tethered nearby. She didn't know who or what he was, having never seen a white man before, and as she looked at him, she instantly remembered something her father had said about white spirits who had come from far away. They had always sounded mysterious to her, but having never seen one, she had never thought about it again. And she knew instantly when she saw him that this was one. She didn't know if he was an evil spirit or a good one, and she stood naked before him, afraid to move, not sure what he would do. And he looked as frightened as she was. He was not sure if there was a party of braves nearby who would come for her and find him. And as he gazed at the exquisite young girl, her nakedness seemed almost mystical. She was perfect in every way.

To reassure her, he held up both hands and made a sign of peace that she knew was either Iroquois or Huron, but she had seen it before. It wasn't Sioux or Crow, but she understood.

In fact, it was Huron, which he learned as he traveled

with that tribe for two years. He had come west on his own, traveling, exploring, making drawings when he saw something interesting. He had drawn some maps that he thought might be useful for others following the same path, but mostly he was just exploring the New World. The second son, and younger brother to a responsible, adoring older brother in France, he had no obligations at home, and had followed his dream to the New World. He had stayed in New Orleans briefly when he arrived five years before, and ever since, the virgin territories, the Indians, the sheer beauty of it all, had given him endless joy. And he had had no bad experiences so far, with the exception of a few close calls. He had once missed a Pawnee war party by a matter of hours, who had killed the people he had been staying with, and the burning of a fort and the massacre of its occupants, where he had been days before. Other than that, his time discovering the woods and Great Plains, forests, and rivers had been a time of great happiness for him. He had thought the area he was in completely unoccupied, and now this naked girl was rooted to the spot looking at him. He could see that she was Indian, but without clothes, he could not tell what tribe, or if they were warlike or peaceful. And whatever she was, the men of her tribe could not be far away and would not welcome his meeting one of their daughters or wives naked at a lake. They would kill him on the spot. He knew they were both in great danger standing there like this. He indicated his clothes and pointed to her. She nodded and ran into the bushes, and a moment later she emerged like a doe in her elkskin dress and moccasins. The oddest thing about her was that she didn't look frightened by him, but more intrigued and somewhat puzzled, as though she had never seen a white man before. And now that she was dressed, he thought she was a Sioux of some kind, and of obviously high rank, because her dress was beaded and ornate. He suspected she might be a chief's wife or daughter.

He made the sign of peace again and made no move to approach her. He wanted to ask her if she was alone, but didn't know how. He looked around as though searching for someone and then quizzically back at her. She understood and shook her head, wondering if she should admit to him that she was alone. She had a small knife at her waist, but it was for cutting berries and vines. She had never used it on a man. She still didn't know if he was a good spirit or a bad one, but he didn't look menacing to her. In fact, he looked scared and surprised. So much so that she smiled. She said something to him in Sioux that he didn't understand. She pointed in the direction of their camp and made a sign for tipis with her hands. He nodded, grateful for the information so he could stay away. And then wondering if he would stop her, she began to walk away. He didn't move. He just watched her go.

Wachiwi reached the path she walked every day. She turned back several times, and he was still standing there. He hadn't moved, and his eyes were rooted to her. She was the most beautiful girl he had ever seen. And then quietly, he melted into the forest, untied his horse, and rode away. She turned one last time to see if he was still there, and he had disappeared. The first white spirit she had ever seen had evaporated. She wished there were someone she could ask about it, or tell them what she'd seen, but she didn't dare. Something told her that she couldn't.

She looked serious this time when she walked back into the village an hour later. Everyone was busy, and she joined the women outside her tipi, and began to play with the children. She held the baby, which she did sometimes, and made him cackle with laughter. She was laughing with him when Napayshni came home from tanning buffalo hides, and he thought he had never seen a happier sight than Wachiwi playing with his baby. He hoped that the next child she held in her arms would be her own, and his.

Wachiwi said nothing to anyone in camp about the man she had seen at the lake. She knew instinctively that it might put him, or even her, in danger. Perhaps someone would blame her for his presence. She looked for him again the next day, but he didn't come. But the day after that, he came back. She was swimming when he showed up, and she had just popped her head out of the water when she saw him emerge from the woods and approach her. He was wearing the same buckskin breeches and tall black boots. His hair was long, as dark as hers, and pulled back. He made the odd sign of peace again, and came nearly to the water's edge. He smiled at her, and his whole face lit up when he did. He had watched her for a while and saw that she was alone. She was so beautiful it took his breath away. He knew he was being both brave and foolish to come back, but he had been compelled to. He wanted to see her again, and discover more about her if he could. She was the only Indian woman he had ever been alone with. He had spent his five years in America discovering nature, finding himself, growing into manhood in the world he loved that was so different from his own. And now he was mesmerized by this woman who looked to him like an Indian goddess. He realized that her being at the lake alone wasn't just a random occurrence, he had the feeling now that she came here often, maybe even every day. And all he knew once he had seen her was that he had to see her again. He would have liked to paint her portrait and capture the remarkable free spirit and grace he saw in her as she played in the water. And Wachiwi wondered how he knew the Huron signs but couldn't ask him.

He had seen the Crow village by then, from the distance, and had steered a wide berth, and camped far from it, in a cave in the forest. He knew the ways of the woods well and was adept at them. He had been on the lookout for war parties, but there were none. He had seen through a telescope that everyone at the camp appeared to be busy. It was the end of summer, and he suspected they were getting ready for winter. He wondered if this girl in the lake had just slipped away to play instead of working. She looked young enough to do that, and if she was the chief's daughter, perhaps they let her, as a kind of privilege. There was so much he wished he could ask her, so much he wanted to know about her.

He could see as she swam that she was naked again, and she didn't seem to care. He kept his eyes on her face, and not the bits of flesh that emerged as she moved around under the water. She stood up in the water then, and it only reached her waist. Their eyes met and neither of them moved, and then she smiled and ducked under the water again. She was teasing him, like a wood nymph. He almost felt as though he had imagined her, but she was all too real, and such a beautiful woman. He couldn't imagine any wood nymph prettier than she. And the look of innocence in her eyes overwhelmed him. He decided to introduce himself, although it seemed more than a little foolish here.

'Jean de Margerac,' he said, pointing to himself and bowing low. She looked puzzled for an instant, as though she didn't know what he'd said. He said it again, pointed to his chest, and didn't move, and then she got it.

'Wachiwi,' she said softly, and pointed to herself. He didn't know enough about the local tribes to be sure which one she was from, and when he tried a few words, it was clear that she spoke neither English nor French. He spoke both, and had learned English since coming to the New World. He had learned Iroquois and Huron, but she didn't seem to recognize those either. They were tribes far to the east of where they were. They were left with signing to each other and miming, which seemed to be enough.

They now knew each other's names, although nothing of each other's histories. There was a nobility to her that told him that she came of privilege in her world, but was a free spirit, just as he was. In an odd way, their histories were not so different. He had felt too confined in his own world in France. And out of love for him, his older brother, Tristan the marquis, had allowed him to leave France, with his blessing. She was signing something to him then, and it took him a while to understand that she was asking him where he came from, pointing to the sky with a question in her eyes, and then the forest. He pointed to the woods in answer, indicated that he was riding a horse, and tried to convey many, many, many days. Trying to explain to her that beyond was an ocean and an even longer journey was too much to translate into pantomime for her. He had come from France, Brittany, and was the Comte de Margerac. The fact that his older brother Tristan was the marquis, and lord of extensive lands, would have meant nothing to her. All they had to share was who they were at this moment, to each other, with no past and no future. All they had was now, which was a heady feeling for them both.

He took off his boots and waded into the water with her, feeling slightly crazy. If any of the braves had come, he would have been dead, without boots or a weapon. Like her, he wore a knife at his waist, for cutting his way through the woods, but he wouldn't have wanted to engage in hand-to-hand combat with any of the braves from her village, and he had left his gun on his horse, so he didn't frighten her. They were like two children, meeting in a forbidden place, taking an enormous risk, and he could see in her eyes that she knew it. She looked like a girl with a lot of spirit. Most women would have run screaming from him in her situation. Instead she swam naked in the water only a few feet away from him, tempting fate, or trusting him, he wasn't sure which. And she didn't look like a loose woman. There was no hint of invitation in her eyes, just innocence, curiosity, and friendship. She was a most unusual girl. And luckily for her, she was safe with him. And something told him she sensed that. But she was either very foolish or very brave.

She dressed again, while he turned away, and they sat on a log, trying to exchange small bits of information. He asked if she had children and she shook her head. He guessed that she wasn't married then, although she seemed to be of a mature age. Perhaps she was a chief's favorite daughter he couldn't part with. She pantomimed then that she had been taken from her home and ridden many days. She showed him the scars from where she had been bound, since she still had them, and then pointed to the village from whence she came. What she tried to say to him made it sound like she was a prisoner there, but that made no sense to Jean since she was alone at the lake. He went to his horse then and showed her his drawings and sketches, of lakes, forests, a few of people, and she nodded. They were very good. He showed her one of his maps, but she didn't seem to know what it was, having never seen one. She indicated that she liked his drawings better. And then it was time for her to go.

They had managed to form an odd friendship, curious

about each other, from two entirely different worlds. An Indian girl, perhaps of rank, and a French nobleman, both far from home, who had happened on each other in this peaceful place. He stayed after she left and drew the waterfall, and wanted to give it to her the next day.

Jean came the next day, but she didn't. Both of Napayshni's wives were sick from berries they had eaten, and she stayed in the village to take care of the children.

It was two days before Wachiwi came to the lake again, and she was disappointed to find that Jean wasn't there. She wondered if she would ever see him again, or if he had gone back to where he came from. She knew that he hadn't run into any of the Crow braves, because she had heard nothing about it in the village, and she would have if they had found a white man and killed him. They would have brought his scalp back to the village and given it to the chief. He had just vanished as he had appeared. But he seemed like a good spirit to her. He had done her no harm and seemed peaceful and friendly in every way.

She was quiet when she went back to the village that night. The men had a celebration to honor yet another hunt, and some of them got raucous. Napayshni had a lot to drink, which was rare for him, but he was in a festive mood, and he tried to come to her in her bed. She felt him near her after he came back to the tipi, she ignored him and pretended to be asleep, and he went back to his own bed. Before he did, he had touched her face and neck with gentle fingers, hoping she would wake. She was not ready for him, and didn't think she ever would be. She had sensed his mounting passion for her recently, and it reminded her that she needed to get away. She was worried that soon he would force himself on her, frustrated by the long wait. He had been patient so far, but she knew he wouldn't be forever. She knew from other women of the things men did, and in fact, like it or not, she belonged to him. He could do what he wanted with her. It was a miracle that he had never pressed the point.

It would be a long winter sleeping in the same lodge, and both of his wives would be heavily pregnant by mid-winter. It was easy to guess that he would turn to Wachiwi for his needs, and want her to get pregnant too. Having many children was a sign of virility and importance for the chief. And he had wanted Wachiwi since she arrived. He had been restrained with her, but she knew. Soon he would make her his wife. She wanted to be gone before he did. She had vowed never to let him near her. The murder of her brothers and Ohitekah was too much for her ever to forgive.

There was talk of breaking up the camp soon, in the final days of summer. The buffalo were beginning to move on, and the Crow wanted to hunt some more before winter. They had had a long time in their summer camp, and Wachiwi had enjoyed the time she had spent at the lake, especially since she had met Jean. And she had enjoyed her time alone there even before that. The day before they broke camp, she went back to the lake for a last time. She thought he was gone by then, as she hadn't seen him in several days, and she didn't expect to meet him again.

She walked as she always did, at a good pace, so she would have enough time at the lake before she had to get back. The air had gotten a trifle cooler, and she could sense that autumn was coming. A few leaves were starting to fall from the trees, but it was still warm enough for her to swim. She took off her clothes as she always did, and even the water was a little cooler. Afterward, she put her dress and moccasins back on, thinking of Jean, and was startled when he suddenly appeared. It made her wonder if he really was a spirit after all. She hadn't seen him in at least a week. He signed to her that he had gone away and come back. He couldn't express it to her, but he had hoped to see her again, at least once. He felt he had to see her one more time before he left. He handed her the drawing he had done of the waterfall, and she looked pleased. She gave it back to him, because she couldn't take it back to camp with her. And then he showed her a sketch he had done of her, which touched her even more. She smiled at him the moment she saw it.

They sat on their favorite log then, as they had before. She picked berries and handed them to him, and they were sitting there peacefully like two children, when they both heard a sound at the same time, like the stirring of leaves. Wachiwi started, and so did Jean, and before either of them knew what had happened, Napayshni walked into the clearing, looking as stunned as they did. For an instant none of them reacted, and then without a sound Napayshni lunged at Jean. Wachiwi didn't know what to do. She had no idea he had followed her there, he never had before, and she didn't know if he had come alone. What she didn't know was that he was tired of waiting, and had decided to consummate his marriage to her at the place she loved so much, before they broke camp. He thought it was the right thing to do. And as she watched, terrified, Wachiwi saw both men locked in a deadly grip, their faces red, grunting, and their hands around each other's throats. She stood helpless, afraid to interfere, and just as Napayshni seemed about to get the best of Jean, she saw Jean loosen his grip on the Indian's neck, reach for the knife at his belt with one swift movement, and run Napayshni through. The man to whom she belonged stared at her in amazement and made a gurgling sound, as blood exploded from his throat, and he fell slowly backward onto the ground. Jean was choking and trying to catch his breath, as they both looked down at Napayshni. His eyes were open, he lay still, blood was gushing from his chest, he was dead.

'Oh my God,' Jean said, with a look of terror, with no idea what to do next, and Wachiwi moved faster than he did. She took one of Napayshni's legs, pointed to the other and Jean, and pulled him toward a thicket. It was not the way to bury an Indian chief, but there was nothing more they could do. They both knew they had to move quickly. If anyone knew he had come there, or had followed him from camp, Jean and Wachiwi would be killed. Jean had never intended to hurt him, but he had had no other choice. They had been playing with fire when they made friends.

Wachiwi was powerful and swift as they dragged Napayshni into the bushes. The brush was so thick there, she knew he wouldn't be seen or found for a long time, and then she pointed to herself and to Jean, and in the direction of his horse. She was saying clearly that she had to go with him, and he had figured that out too. He cleaned his knife in the water as quickly as he could, replaced it in his belt, and together they ran soundlessly toward his horse, saying not a word. Wachiwi swung herself onto his horse in front of the saddle, as though she belonged there, and Jean mounted, put an arm around her, took the reins, and in an instant they were off at full speed.

She pointed to paths and clearings in the forest that he hadn't noticed and would never have seen. And it was clear to him as he rode with her that she had spent a lifetime on horses. She kept urging the horse faster, and both of them knew that they had to get as far away as quickly as they could. When Napayshni's absence was discovered in the camp, if it hadn't been already, they would come searching for him. Jean had guessed the moment he saw him that he was the chief. What he didn't understand was Wachiwi's lack of emotion at seeing him killed. If anything, she seemed relieved. He couldn't figure out if he was her husband, or what their relation to each other was. But he had no time to ask as they rode. Wachiwi was concentrating on getting them through the forest. They rode on for many hours at full speed until it was dark. His horse was exhausted by then, and Jean just prayed that they wouldn't lame him in the woods. They still had a long way to go. They were riding north and east. She finally let him stop when she noticed a cave. They tied the horse to a tree, and he followed her into the cave. This time he took his weapons with him. He wasn't entirely sure where they were, nor was she, but he had a vague idea. He was trying to get to the home of a trapper he knew, where he had stayed for several days on the way west. He was French, they had met in Canada, and had known each other for years. Jean didn't want to endanger him, but by the time they got there, they would be a long, long way from the Crows.

Jean could see something in Wachiwi's eyes then, as though she wanted to express something to him. For a moment, as they left the lake, she had wanted to take him in the direction of her father's village, but she realized immediately that if she did, she would be bringing danger to them, and maybe even a full-scale war with the Crow. As far as they knew, and would figure out, when she didn't come back either, if they found his body and not hers, they would assume that she had killed their chief and run away. They would be certain of it if she went back to her village, and they would take harsh revenge. She had to stay away from her father's tribe. Maybe the Crow would think she had been kidnapped by another tribe at the lake, when Napayshni was killed. But it was unlikely, since there was no one else around. They would think she did it. All she could do now was travel with the white man, and what would happen to her after that, she didn't know. She had no idea what he would do with her now. He said very little that night, nor did she. They exchanged glances, but no words, and they made no effort at pantomime. Both of them knew what had happened and what the consequences would be if they were caught.

They slept little that night, left before dawn, and rode even harder that day. They had to cover some open terrain, and Jean knew they were in Teton Sioux territory, which was never safe. The Teton Sioux were fiercely hostile even against other Sioux and feared by all. But by sheer luck they saw no one when they covered open ground. They rode like the wind, and then disappeared into the cover of the forest again. It slowed them down, but they met no one on the way. There was no cave to sleep in that night, and they both sat awake, listening to the sounds of the forest, but no humans emerged, and after two days of riding, so far no one was following them. They both wondered if maybe Napayshni's body hadn't been found yet. Jean hoped not. Maybe his disappearance and Wachiwi's was still a mystery to the chief's people.

On the third day, Jean's horse was getting noticeably tired as they pressed on. But Jean knew where they were by then, he had mapped the territory, and thought they were relatively safe. The Crow could still come after them, but the tribe didn't know in which direction they'd gone since they had a long head start. And the tribes in the area they were now traveling through were mostly peaceful and involved in trading and agriculture. They weren't as war-like as the Crow or the Teton Sioux. There were generally no war parties in the vicinity, and Jean hoped that was still true.

They had covered hundreds of miles by then, at full speed, faster than Jean had ever ridden before. Wachiwi was tireless, and she urged his horse on in a way he knew he never could. She was twice the rider he was. She acted as though she had been born on a horse. They rode on after dark that night, and had begun to see farms, a few settlers' homes, and finally Jean recognized the cabin he had been looking for. He brought their horse to a halt in the front yard, and led him into the barn, and then he urged Wachiwi onto the porch and knocked on the door. It was the home of Luc Ferrier. He had been in the New World for years, trapping in Canada, and trading with the Indians. He had been married to an Indian woman who had since died. Jean considered him a good friend, and trusted him. Luc opened the door and gave a shout of delight when he saw him, and they spoke rapidly in French.

'What are you doing back so soon? I didn't expect you for another month. Did you run into trouble or get scared?' He always teased Jean, mostly because he had a title, and Luc didn't. He was from the Pyrenees and a rough mountain man, but he had a kind heart and a lot of ill-disguised respect for Jean, although they liked to tease each other with friendly insults. Luc had seen Jean in some difficult situations, and he always handled himself well.

'A minor incident,' Jean said casually, but Luc could see that they were tired and could guess that they had ridden hard. He didn't know why or for how long, but he could tell that something had happened and he didn't want to pry. Whatever it was, they would be safe with him, which was why Jean had headed for his cabin as soon as they left the lake.

'Who's your friend?' Luc couldn't resist asking. She was lovely.

'Her name is Wachiwi, and that's all I know. I think she's Crow, or maybe Dakota. I can't tell. I don't know these tribes as well. I tried to speak Iroquois and Huron to her, she doesn't speak either. She was living in a Crow village, but she tried to explain to me that she was taken from somewhere else, I think maybe from her father.'

Luc spoke to her in Dakota then, which he spoke fluently since he traded with them at times. He was conversant in many dialects and had an ear for languages, and Wachiwi answered rapidly and talked for quite a long time, explaining her story. She was very impassioned about it, and very expressive, as Jean listened to them both, and understood not a word. But Luc nodded and commented occasionally. Jean wondered if she was telling him that Jean had killed the Crow chief. He hoped not. He didn't want to implicate or involve him in any way, which it might if he had knowledge of it. This was their problem, not his, and Jean fervently hoped that nothing would come of it. He was planning to continue traveling east with Wachiwi to Fort St. Charles, and to St. Louis after that. He wanted to get both of them as far away as possible from the Crow. What he would do with her after that, he had no idea. And he didn't know what she wanted either. He was hoping Luc could find out.

It was a long time before Luc turned to him and explained. They were sitting at his kitchen table by then, and he dished up two big plates of stew that he had made himself. He was a good cook, and they hadn't eaten anything more than berries in three days. Jean was starving, and Wachiwi looked pale. She looked at the food with interest, and gingerly poked it with a finger. Luc handed her a spoon and showed her how to use it. She was quick to learn, and ate politely as Luc explained her situation to Jean.

'She's a Dakota Sioux. Her father is Chief White Bear. He's an important chief. I've heard of him, although I've never met him. They don't trade with the French, but keep their goods among themselves. She said they were attacked by the Crow last spring, in a raid. She and several other women were taken. They killed two of her brothers and several young men, and she was given to the Crow chief as a war prize. She said that he wanted to make her his wife, and she refused. I might point out to you, by the way, that that's very unusual. When you're taken as a slave and refuse to marry the chief you've been given to, which is considered an honor, it doesn't go over very well. He could have killed her. Apparently he chose not to, and she said he treated her decently. She tried to escape several times, by stealing one of their horses. And they caught her and brought her back every time.'

'She's an incredible rider. I can testify to that,' Jean added. 'She can ride anything under any conditions over any terrain. I'm amazed my horse is still standing. She got more out of him in three days than I have in three years. We may find him dead in the barn tonight.' Luc laughed at what his friend said.

'She's a very courageous girl, defying the chief, and trying to run away. She says you rescued her from the Crow, which is an act of insanity on your part, I might add. If they had caught you stealing the chief's slave and future wife, and absconding with her, they would have had your scalp in about two seconds. I don't know how the hell you two got away.'

'We got a head start,' was all Jean said. It was obvious from what Luc said that Wachiwi hadn't told him Jean had killed her captor and left his body hidden in the bushes. Jean couldn't help wondering if they'd found him by then. 'I'm not planning to stay here long,' Jean went on. 'It's still a little too close for comfort. I want to get to Fort St. Charles, and then to St. Louis. We'll be fine once we get to the fort. I'm a little uneasy till then.'

'I think you'll be all right from here on. I'll give you one of my horses. You need a fresh mount if you've been pushing yours hard for three days. She says she wanted to go back to her family, but she can't now. She doesn't want to get them in trouble either, and she thinks the Crow will be very angry at her for running away and succeeding this time. She doesn't want to endanger her father or brothers.' And then he looked at his old friend with a question in his eyes. 'What are you going to do with her, Jean?'

'I have no idea. If she can't go back to her family, which sounds reasonable,' particularly knowing that she would be blamed for killing Napayshni and the Crow would seek revenge if she went back to her village, 'I don't know where to take her.'

'Are you in love with her?' Luc asked him bluntly.

'I don't even know her,' Jean answered. It wasn't entirely true. They had been meeting for several weeks, but he didn't know her well enough to love her. They couldn't even talk to each other. 'I just did her a favor, getting her out.'

'She says she's your slave now,' Luc informed him.

'I don't need a slave,' Jean answered quietly. 'I don't even have a house. All I have is a horse, and a bunch of maps. I suppose I could take her to my cousins in New Orleans and leave her there. Maybe she'll want to stay at Fort St. Charles.'

'There won't be much for her there. And she speaks no French or English, and has never been out of her village, except with the Crow. She's never been to a town or a city. Can you imagine her in New Orleans? What would she do there?'

'I don't know,' Jean said, running a hand through his hair. 'She needed help. I didn't think beyond that.' And in fact, they had had no other choice but to escape, as fast as they could. Both their lives were on the line, not just hers. But he didn't say that to Luc.

'I think you should keep her,' Luc said, smiling at her. She smiled back at him in return, and told him the food had been good.

'She's not a piece of furniture, for heaven's sake, or an

object. I can't just "keep" her. She should have a life, a husband, children, something. I can't drag her around with me on my horse.'

'Maybe you should get a house and leave her there. She's a bright girl, and she's got spirit. You can tell that talking to her. She's very brave to have been taken by the Crow, defying their chief, and trying to run away. And she says she's not worried now. She's with you.'

'Thank her for her faith in me. She's more responsible for getting us here than I am. I would have gotten lost several times. She had an unfailing sense of direction. She knows the forest as though she's been in it all her life. She never looked frightened or complained.'

'If you teach her French, you can talk to her.'

'And then what? I think I'll take her to my cousins. I can buy her some decent clothes in St. Louis.'

'What she's wearing is more than decent. Everything about it says that she's a chief's daughter. The beading, the quills, the beads on her moccasins.'

'I don't think my cousins in New Orleans will understand that. If I take her there, I need to buy her proper gowns. My cousin's wife, Angélique, is extremely proper.' There was a quiet dignity about Wachiwi, and a grace, that anyone would notice and have to respect. Angélique had been born in Paris, and was a distant cousin of the king, and never let anyone forget it. She had been in New Orleans for forty years, but she was still extremely French. He knew he would have to teach Wachiwi a few words of French by then.

Jean had stayed with them for several months when he first arrived, and still did from time to time, when he needed a taste of civilization. But it always rapidly became too much for him, and then he took off again. He enjoyed his wanderings in the wilderness and discovering new territories too much to settle for a life in town. He couldn't imagine Wachiwi happy there for long either. But it would be a good place to take her, until she adjusted to life away from her own culture and people. For some reason, Jean was convinced she could learn. She seemed to be curious about everything. She was now as she explored Luc's kitchen, and quietly washed their dishes in the bucket he kept for that purpose. As Jean had, she devoured the simple meal. It was delicious, and she thanked Luc in Sioux.

He only had one bedroom to give them, and he insisted they take it. He slept in the sitting room on a comfortable old couch. And as soon as they were shown the bedroom, Wachiwi lay down on the floor. She had never seen a proper bed before, but she made no comment, and assumed it was for Jean. Before that, Luc had shown her the outdoor plumbing facilities, which she had never seen before either, and she thanked him. Jean pulled her to her feet when she lay on the floor, and pointed to her and the bed, and indicated that he would sleep on the floor, but she refused and lay down on the floor again. They argued about it in sign language for a few minutes while she insisted. She was his slave now, but as far as Jean was concerned, she was a woman, and had ridden just as hard and as long as he had. In the end, to make the point to her, he lay down beside her on the floor, and she giggled. He was telling her that if she slept on the floor, so would he. She didn't budge an inch, and he was amazed at how stubborn she was. It shouldn't have surprised him from all he knew about her now. He was still amazed by the story Luc had told him, of her courage and all that had happened to her in the past few months. And now she was riding east with him, to an unknown fate, and he was a stranger to her. But it was clear that she trusted him completely. They had survived their trial by fire. Her fate would have been very different if Napayshni had killed him instead. She might have been dead by then, for meeting a white man in secret. In fact, Jean had not only rescued her, but saved her life, and she knew it. And now she believed she belonged to him. He had no idea what to do with her, but he couldn't just abandon her. She had nowhere to go. And in the face of her insistence, he finally gave up and slept in the bed. He got a good night's sleep and so did she. He handed her a blanket, she wrapped herself in it, and was asleep in less than five minutes, as Jean lay in bed and thought about her. It had been an amazing three days, which he suddenly realized had changed his life forever. He had no idea what to do with her, but he now was responsible for this exquisitely beautiful Dakota girl.

Chapter 9

Luc made breakfast for them before they left, and gave them food and fresh water for their journey. He kept Jean's exhausted horse and gave him one of his own, a solid young horse with strong legs that would take them as far as they needed. Jean thanked him for his kindness, and Wachiwi did the same in Sioux. And then they began the two-day trip to Fort St. Charles. It took longer than Jean expected, and they arrived on the afternoon of the third day. The trip had been long and arduous but not dangerous. The fort was familiar to him, because he had stayed there before. It was manned by French soldiers, and no one seemed surprised to see Wachiwi with him. Many men traveled with Indian women, and they directed her to the quarters set aside for Indian women. There wasn't the remotest possibility that she could stay with Jean. She was treated like a servant or a slave. She looked unhappy when Jean came to see her that evening after having dinner with the commandant. It had been a hearty meal of roasted rabbit, prepared by a French chef, with excellent wines, delicious coffee, and a delicate dessert – and afterward the commandant's aide handed out cigars. It was the best meal Jean had had in months.

But when he went out to see Wachiwi, he was embarrassed to see that they had served her slop in a dish like a dog. It upset him to realize she was being badly treated. It had never occurred to him that they would do that to her. And the other Indian women seemed less dignified than she did. He looked at her and tried to express how sorry he was, and she looked as though she understood. She nodded. And when the door to the women's dormitory opened, he noticed that they slept on blankets on the floor. They weren't treated like humans, but more like dogs, and when he saw that, he decided to move on the next day. His goal was St. Louis now, where he could get her a room in a hotel and get her properly dressed. It was another two-day ride from where they were.

He appeared at her dormitory the next day, pointed to the horse Luc had given them so she knew they were leaving, and spoke to her in French. She looked pleased, and Jean had decided that Luc was right. She needed to learn another language other than Sioux, either English or French, or ideally both. If she was going to exist in the civilized world, there were many things she had to learn. She seemed bright, and Jean thought she could. He taught her a few basic words in both languages as they rode.

There was a lot about her that intrigued him and so much more he wanted to know, about how she had grown up, what her ideas were, what she thought. He had been dazzled by her beauty from the first, but even without a common language, he sensed that she was a woman of depth, spirit, and soul.

Their pace was less frenetic, because they weren't escaping from anyone now. They were beyond the reach of the Crow, theoretically, or even practically. Wachiwi could never go back, but she was in no danger now, except from the usual rigors of the road. They camped in the woods that night, but Jean had gotten supplies at the fort, and had brought blankets for both of them. They lay looking up at the stars, and as he thought about all that had happened and how far they had come, she quietly reached for his hand and put it over her heart. He understood that it was her way of thanking him, and he was touched. Her unwavering trust in him moved him a great deal. She was both vulnerable and strong, and she suddenly seemed very young. He was worried about what would become of her now, particularly after the poor treatment he'd seen at the fort.

He slept fitfully, and when he woke, it was still dark, there was a full moon, and he saw that she was awake. He wondered if she was frightened or sad, but there was no way he could ask her, so he gently touched her face and stroked her hair. He wanted to reassure her that everything would be all right. Whatever happened, he wanted to leave her in a safe place. They had come through a lot, and he was going to see her to a good situation somewhere, wherever that was. He was not going to abandon her now. He felt surprisingly responsible for her, a feeling he'd never had before. She was a young girl, and he was going to find a good home for her. He hoped that his cousins would be kind to her in New Orleans, and perhaps let her work for them in some capacity. Perhaps she could help take care of Angélique's daughter's children, or work for them in the house. There had to be somewhere where Wachiwi would fit in. He lay on his side then and smiled at her reassuringly. She lay under the blanket he had given her, smiling at him, and this time she leaned over and touched his face and then kissed him on the mouth. He hadn't expected it, and didn't know what to say. She had startled him totally. So he said not a word, tried to resist the tender feelings he had for her, and then kissed her back. She was all he could think of and he didn't want to take advantage of her in any way. They were totally alone in the forest and in the world. And as they kissed, he was suddenly filled with passion and an electric current passed between them. They had been through so much and been so frightened, and now they were like two shipwrecked people on a beach. They had escaped and survived together, and neither of them was sure where to go next, other than into each other's arms, which seemed to be the only safe place they had. Jean kissed her with a fervor he had never felt before for anyone, and she embraced him with all that she had saved and held back for her whole life. She had never dared to look a man in the eye in her own village, and now she was lost in Jean's arms, swept away by their passion, which ignited like a fuse to which someone had put a match. He moved toward her and under her blanket without thinking, and she had taken off her dress. He saw and felt the same exquisite shape he had seen at the lake, and this time she wasn't a mysterious stranger, she was familiar and warm and entirely his. And when they fell asleep in each other's arms as the sun came up, there was no doubt in either of their minds that they belonged to each other now and this was meant to be. But where they would go now, and how, was still a mystery to both of them, yet to be revealed.

*   *   *

It was late the next day when they woke up and the sun was shining brightly. Jean looked at Wachiwi as she opened her eyes, watching her intensely for signs of remorse, and there were none. She smiled at him and opened her arms to him again, and he lost himself in the wonders of her body with all the passion and relief and joy he felt for her after the night before. This was not what he had expected or planned, and yet it seemed to be a gift they had been given. They were both laughing and smiling when they got up. They couldn't talk about it, but they both understood what had happened. Somewhere along the way, the night before, or days or weeks before, without realizing it they had fallen in love. If he hadn't killed Napayshni, they wouldn't even be together, but destiny had intervened and now they were. He couldn't help wondering if a child would come of the night before. He had seen that she was a virgin when they made love.

And now, the woman who called herself his slave was the woman he wanted to be with, whom he cared about and wanted to protect. In all his twenty-four years, he had never been in love before, but there was no question in his mind now that he was. Youthful passion on both sides had turned to love unexpectedly, and now Jean was totally, madly, passionately in love with Wachiwi, a girl from the Dakota Sioux nation, whom he had met beside a lake. It would be a story to tell their grandchildren, if they had any. He knew what he wanted to do now. He wanted to keep her with him. But first he had to make her suitable to bring into his world.

He redoubled his efforts in speaking to her in both English and French as they rode more sedately toward St. Louis. They stopped often to make love in the forest, and their coupling was pure joy. They got to St. Louis two days later, and by then she had learned several phrases in both languages and many words. She didn't always use them correctly, but she tried ardently to please him, and she was doing surprisingly well. She learned quickly, and she looked fascinated and a little daunted when they reached the hotel, and he led his horse to the barn, and they checked in. She was amazed by their surroundings. He asked for two rooms, which seemed more respectable, and the clerk stared at Wachiwi in disapproval, but he said not a word as he handed Jean both keys. They walked up the stairs, and she followed him, as he led her into the rooms. They were only going to sleep in one; the second one was to protect her reputation. But she had none, to the people in the hotel she was just an Indian girl traveling with him, and they would have thought it a waste of a good room. True to his upbringing, Jean was noble to his core, even with a young Indian girl, and she sensed his respect.

They had dinner in the dining room of an inn that night, and Wachiwi began eating, as Luc Ferrier had taught her, with a spoon. She copied Jean when he put his napkin on his lap, and he showed her how to use a knife and fork. She speared her food with the fork, but the knife made no sense to her, and the food was complicated for her. Jean could only imagine how foreign everything must seem. But that was nothing compared to the adventure they had the next day when he took her to a dry goods store and a dressmaker and outfitted her.

He bought her several simple dresses at the dry goods store, and the dressmaker had three gowns that had never been picked up and fit Wachiwi as though they'd been made for her. There were two dresses that were suitable for dinner at his cousin's house, four demure ones for the day-time, proper shoes that he could tell Wachiwi didn't like, and five bonnets that looked beautiful on her. There were mysterious undergarments that she had no idea how to put on until the saleswoman showed her. She was wearing more clothes at one time than she had ever worn in her life. There were gloves, several shawls, three purses, and a fan. They had it all delivered to the hotel, and Jean was relieved that they were taking a boat to New Orleans. It would have taken several horses or a mule train to carry everything he'd bought her. The boxes were stacked in their rooms. He bought two trunks to put it all in and made arrangements for the horse to be returned to Luc.

By the end of the day, they were both exhausted, and Wachiwi spoke to him in her few words of halting French and thanked him for everything he had given her. She looked more than a little dazed, and when they got back to the hotel, she put her elkskin dress and moccasins on again and looked relieved. At least that was something she knew how to wear. She had insisted on keeping them, and she looked like the little Indian girl he had first met when he saw her in the elkskin dress again, with the deep blue porcupine quills on the front, and she touched his heart again.

He had taught her *jolie robe* and *chaussure* and *chapeau* that day, along with *gown, bonnet, undergarment, shoes,* and *gloves.* She knew the names for everything he had bought for her. She was slowly learning to speak to him, mostly in French, but in English too. When they ordered dinner in their rooms, she ate with a knife and fork to please him, but when he lit a cigar, she wanted to share it with him. He laughed as he let her do it, but explained that she could only do it with him. Her father had let her share his pipe with him from time to time when no one was looking, so she knew what Jean meant, and put her finger to her lips to show that it was a secret . . . like the dead man they had left in the bushes. Neither of them wanted to think of that again, but it was his death that had brought them together.

They made love in Jean's bed that night, with the same passion as they had before. The love that they shared was visceral and sensual and explosive. It was something he had never known before, and that was a mystery to her. She had no words for it, and they didn't need them. What they shared when they made love to each other was magical.

The next day, he helped her dress, and with her new trunks full of the clothes he had bought her, they boarded the keelboat to New Orleans. Wachiwi looked excited and was smiling happily. She knew of this river, but had never expected to see it. She had heard of it in the lodges. Her people called it the Great River. The trip to New Orleans was going to take three weeks, with good winds and fast currents if they were lucky, while the boat made many stops and people got off and on.

There were canoes, flatboats, barges, and other keelboats all along the river, which was teeming with activity. Wachiwi was fascinated by it and beamed at Jean. He had reserved two cabins for them to look respectable once again, as he had at the hotel. They put all her trunks in one, and slept in the other. And when she got confused, he helped her put the undergarments on and laced up her corset. He laughed as he did it, and had never had so much fun. She was horrified by how tight the corset was and made him loosen it. He couldn't expect her to learn everything at once. Only days before she had been swimming naked in the lake where he met her, living in a Crow village, and now she was dressed like a lady, on the way to New Orleans to meet his noble cousins.

He was slightly daunted by the prospect, and mildly unnerved by the stares of people on the keelboat when they saw that he was traveling with an Indian woman. She was so beautiful that the men understood it, but the women didn't, and turned their backs on her the moment they saw her. Jean was startled by it and hoped that people in New Orleans would be more understanding, and captivated by her beauty. She was so innocent, so delicate, and so mesmerizing that he couldn't imagine anyone being able to resist her. He certainly couldn't, and his nights with her for three weeks on the Mississippi were passionate beyond belief. The trip to New Orleans gave them the time they needed to get to know each other, and improve her English and French. She was so bright and eager that she made rapid strides in both.

They had passed Fort Prudhomme and Fort St. Pierre, and finally arrived in New Orleans.

Wachiwi looked particularly beautiful that day. She

wore a pale blue day gown he had bought her that looked like sky next to her skin, and a matching bonnet he tied beneath her chin for her, and gloves that he helped her put on. And her undergarments were in perfect order, thanks to him. She was part child and part woman, and what he loved most about her was that she was entirely his. Not his slave, but his woman. The chieftain's daughter. Wachiwi. The dancer. Luc had translated her name for him. When the boat reached the dock in New Orleans, he helped her off and she walked with silent grace right behind him.

They took a carriage to a guest house Jean knew on Chartres Street, with all their belongings. He wanted them to wait in a comfortable room while he sent a message to his cousins at their plantation just outside of town, explaining that he was back and had a friend with him, a young lady. He didn't want to impose on them and assume that they could stay with them. Within two hours a note was returned to him, from his cousin's wife, Angélique de Margerac, insisting that they come at once and give up their rooms in town. She didn't mention the young lady, but Jean presumed that there would be a room for Wachiwi too, since he had been clear in his note that she was traveling with him. It was an unusual occurrence, but he felt sure that his cousins could accommodate them both, and would be glad to do so. Angélique's note had been welcoming and warm.

She sent her carriage for them, an elegant French-made Berline drawn by four horses, and a separate carriage for their trunks. Jean smiled at Wachiwi as they set out for the long ride to the plantation, thinking how far they had come. He looked at her proudly, and took her hand in his own. He didn't doubt for a moment that his cousins would fall in love with her too. It was the first time he had ever traveled anywhere with a woman, but the New Orleans Margeracs were his family, and had always been wonderfully hospitable to him. He was sure that this time would be no different.

Chapter 10

Angélique de Margerac was actually married to Jean's father's cousin, and she was from an illustrious family of aristocrats in the Dordogne herself, directly related to the king. She had married Armand de Margerac forty years before, and he had brought her to New Orleans under protest. She had been willing to live in Paris, but not the New World. He had fought hard to convince her. New Orleans had been founded by the French thirty-five years before they got there, and her husband had done everything imaginable to make her happy. He had bought her a house in town on Toulouse Street and a splendid plantation with an enormous house in the West Indies style, which he let her fill with all the antiques her family sent her from France. Armand planted cotton and sugarcane, and it became one of the most successful plantations in the region, and Angélique's home the most elegant in the district. Their children were born there, and eventually acquired plantations of their own, and by the time Jean arrived from France, she held a decades-long reputation for being the most gracious hostess in Louisiana.

The Spanish had acquired the colony by then, but Angélique and Armand were close friends with the Spanish governor, and he dined often at their plantation and at the house on Toulouse Street. Angélique had closed the house in town the year Jean arrived, after the great fire that destroyed nearly a thousand buildings on Good Friday. Miraculously, their home had survived, but she said she was too nervous to be there any longer. She was afraid of another fire and preferred staying on the plantation. It was so much more comfortable and infinitely more grand. She loved having houseguests and had convinced Jean to stay with them for several months before he began his travels north to Canada, and eventually toward the Great Plains in the west. She had been extremely hospitable and introduced him to all their friends and several very attractive young ladies. He had shown no particular interest in any of them, but everyone had found their newly arrived French cousin very charming.

The area around New Orleans was very international, there were not only French and Spanish people living there, but a large community of Germans, which, as Angélique said, made their soirées and dinner parties so much more interesting. She was particularly proud of the balls they gave, and the many important people who had stayed there. The plantation itself was situated between Baton Rouge and New Orleans, and it took Jean and Wachiwi two hours to get there in his cousin's elegant horse-drawn carriage, which had come by ship from France. There were two footmen riding behind, and the coachman kept the horses at a brisk pace. Angélique wanted them there in time for dinner, which Jean already knew would be an elegant affair. He had coached Wachiwi for it the night before, and he hoped she would be equal to it. He felt comfortable in the knowledge that the dresses he had bought for her in St. Louis would be perfect, not as elegant as Angélique's of course, who still had her gowns made in Paris and sent to her by ship in the New World twice a year. And she had a clever little dressmaker in New Orleans who could copy anything she saw, even some of the gowns from Paris.

They approached the plantation, which had been named after Angélique when her husband acquired it, along a seemingly endless driveway lined with oaks. The grandeur of the West Indies house came into view fully ten minutes later. Jean smiled at Wachiwi and patted her hand. Her understanding of the language wasn't strong enough yet for him to reassure her as much as he would have liked to.

'It will be fine,' he said quietly, and his tone said as much to her as his words did. He was wearing a beautifully cut dark blue wool coat that he had brought with him from France when he arrived, and seldom had a chance to wear now. He kept it carefully rolled in his bags. Their visit to the plantation was the perfect occasion for it, as well as for the satin coat and knee breeches he would wear at dinner, which he had left at his cousin's home before, for his return. He was grateful that he didn't have to wear a wig or powder his hair as he would have in Europe. Fortunately his cousins were not quite that formal, and his own dark hair would be fine.

Wachiwi was staring at the house as they approached it. Her eyes were huge in her lovely face, framed by the bonnet he had bought her. She glanced at him nervously, and it struck him that she was far less frightened on a horse, going at full speed, which would have terrified almost anyone, than she was in the situation he had put her in here. It had been brave of her to come with him, and he had a strong urge to protect her and shield her from harm as one of the footmen handed them out of the carriage.

There were six liveried servants waiting for them on the front steps, all of them black and perfectly groomed in matching uniforms. They were slaves, Jean knew – hundreds of them worked in the fields on the sugarcane and cotton crops that had made his father's cousin an almost limitless fortune. Before Jean could say anything more to Wachiwi, Angélique de Margerac swept grandly through the front door to greet them. She was smiling warmly at Jean, and for an instant she didn't notice Wachiwi, standing just behind him. After embracing Angélique, he stepped aside and introduced them. The look on his cousin's wife's face was instantly one of shock mixed with horror. She pulled back the hand she had extended, took a step backward, and looked at Jean in amazement.

'Oh . . . I see . . .' she said disdainfully, and walked back into the house without a word to Wachiwi, who followed Jean into the grandeur of the front hall, with a look of terror. 'Why don't we have the young lady taken to her room immediately so she can be comfortable after the drive,' Angélique suggested as she signaled to one of the liveried servants and whispered something to him. He nodded, and then motioned to Wachiwi to follow him.

She disappeared from the room almost before she had entered it, and then Angélique embraced her cousin again with a warm smile, immensely relieved to have dispensed with Wachiwi so quickly. And as she did, her husband Armand appeared from the library where he had been smoking a cigar in peace. He looked delighted to see Jean, and couldn't resist teasing him a little.

'I understand you brought a young lady with you. Is there to be great news soon? Perhaps we can convince you to settle in New Orleans, instead of running around all those uncivilized places you enjoy so much. So where is she?' He looked around, surprised to see Jean talking to Angélique alone. They had both been a little startled that there had been no mention of a chaperone for the young lady traveling with them, an aunt, mother, sister, or cousin. And they hoped she was suitable for him, and of distinguished birth. They knew he wouldn't bring a mistress with him to their home.

Angélique's look of violent disapproval when she saw Wachiwi with him had not been lost on Jean, and he was afraid that even without proficiency in the language, Wachiwi had understood it too. His cousin had made it as clear as possible that she was not welcome in their home. There was no hiding the fact that she was an Indian. It was all Angélique needed to know. For her, at that moment,

Jean's traveling companion ceased to exist. She couldn't believe he'd brought her here. It was a shocking impertinence and insult to them.

'I sent her to her room to rest before dinner after the drive from town,' his wife explained smoothly. Jean hoped that she wasn't going to be difficult about it at dinner. They offered him a glass of champagne, and then sent him to his own room to freshen up. And as he was led to the large guest quarters on the second floor, he couldn't figure out which room they had given Wachiwi, and he was afraid to ask, but he would have liked to see if she was all right.

He knew the house well and had stayed there often before in the past five years, but all of the guest room doors were closed. He hoped she wasn't frightened or upset, and just before he went down to dinner, he began to seriously worry about her. He knew that she would need help getting into her gown, and more than likely would be afraid to ask. He began knocking on doors shortly after, hoping to find her without making a fuss. There was no answer at any door, and when he poked his head in, the rooms were dark and empty. He had no idea where she was. And finally, not knowing what else to do, he rang for one of the servants. An old man named Tobias answered his call. He had worked for years as Armand's valet and had always been kind to Jean before. He had recognized him immediately and greeted him warmly when he and Wachiwi arrived.

'Do you know where the young lady is, Tobias? I can't seem to find her. I'd like to see her for a moment before we go down to dinner. Do you know which room she was given?'

'Yes, I do, sir,' Tobias answered respectfully. It was one of the few plantations where the slaves were treated well. Armand de Margerac had a reputation for being kind to them, and most of the time tried to keep families together, which was rarely the case in other homes, where husbands and wives were often separated, one of them sold to a different owner, and their children sold separately as well. It was a practice that always made Jean feel ill. It was one of the things about the New World that he had never liked. In France, the free trade of human beings like so much cattle was unthinkable. 'Where is her room, then?'

'In the cabin next to mine,' Tobias said quietly, lowering his eyes. He had had a feeling that that circumstance would not go over well with their young cousin from France.

'I beg your pardon?' Jean decided that he must have been mistaken in what he just heard. There were no guest rooms in the cabins, only slaves, and the quarters they were housed in. There were fourteen of those cabins behind the house.

'Your aunt thought she would be more comfortable there.' He had taken her there himself immediately after she arrived. He felt sorry for her, she looked so frightened and lost. He had left her with his wife, who was showing her around.

'Take me to her at once,' Jean said through clenched teeth, and then followed Tobias down the stairs, out a side door into a back garden, and then through a locked gate, to which Tobias had a key. Only a few of those who worked in the house did. The other slaves had no access to the main house. Nor did Wachiwi if she was behind that gate.

Tobias led Jean down a series of paths in a confusing pattern, past several buildings that were the 'cabins.' Each one housed two dozen slaves. There were a few smaller, nicer cabins, where the more trusted house slaves lived, like Tobias, and his children when they were young. He stopped at one of the better cabins, and led Jean inside. There was a narrow hallway, a honeycomb of tiny rooms, and in each of them he could see several people. He found Wachiwi finally, in a back bedroom with four other women. Her trunks filled the room, and she was sitting on one of them, with a look of despair.

'Come with me,' he said quietly, his eyes blazing. He gestured to her to follow him, and she looked terrified that he was angry at her. She was sure she had done something wrong, and she had no idea who these people were or why she was in a house with them. She hadn't seen Jean all afternoon. While he thought she was resting quietly in a guest bedroom, she had been shunted away to stay with the slaves. He turned to Tobias then and told him to have her trunks sent to his room.

He took her back to his own room, took off her bonnet, smoothed her hair, and told her how sorry he was. She didn't understand all the words that he said to her, but she got the idea. She was smiling again by the time her trunks arrived, carried by two of the house slaves. Jean opened one of them and took out one of her dinner gowns.

He dressed her himself, did up her corset, helped her into the underwear. He took out the fan he had bought for her, and when he was finished ten minutes later, she looked dazzling. She had been transformed. He brushed her hair until it shone, and she looked at him gratefully when she saw herself in the mirror. She looked exotic and at the same time elegant, fresh, and young, and totally respectable as he tucked her hand into his arm and led her down the grand staircase to the drawing room.

Angélique and Armand were waiting for him there. They had invited a few friends to dinner, but no one had arrived yet. They had been planning to have a quiet drink with Jean before dinner, and with his friend, before they knew what she was. Angélique had explained the situation to her husband, and he was greatly relieved that she had solved the problem so quickly. They agreed that their cousin had clearly lost his mind and judgment after spending too much time with the natives. It was unthinkable that he had brought one of them to stay with them.

They looked equally horrified when he strode into the room with Wachiwi on his arm. Her gown looked appropriate, although her flowing black hair wasn't, and Angélique sat down looking faint when she saw her walk into the room.

'Jean, what are you thinking?' she asked him, as her husband stared at Wachiwi. He had to admit that she was beautiful and he could see why his young cousin wanted to be with her, but certainly not in anyone's drawing room. The idea that Jean had dared to bring her here thoroughly shocked them both.

'What am I thinking, cousin?' Jean asked, his eyes smoldering dangerously. Wachiwi had never seen him that way before, nor had they. But they were getting a clear picture of what his temper could be like. Normally, it took a great deal to anger him. But now he was enraged, on Wachiwi's behalf. 'I'm thinking you've been extremely rude to my guest. I found her in the slave quarters half an hour ago, in a room with four other women. There seems to be some mistake. I've had her moved to my room,' he announced smoothly. 'I'm sure you understand.'

'No, I don't!' Angélique said, springing to her feet, her eyes every bit as ominous as his. 'I will not have a savage in my house. How *dare* you bring her here! She belongs in the slave quarters where Tobias put her. I will *not* have a black woman at my dinner table. Get her out of here at once!' She wanted Wachiwi to disappear immediately, before her other guests arrived, and her husband was fully in agreement with her. Jean was not.

'She's not a black woman. She's a Dakota Sioux, and her father is a chief.'

'What? One of those savages who run around naked, killing people? Who did she murder before she came here? What white woman's baby did she kill? Are you insane?'

'That's a disgusting thing to say. If you'd like me to, we'll go back to New Orleans immediately. Send your carriage around,' he said firmly as Angélique blustered at him, as furious as he was.

'That's an excellent idea. And where do you think you'll stay in town? No decent boardinghouse will have you

either. You can't bring an Indian girl into a proper estab-
lishment, any more than you could bring one of our
slaves.'

'She's not a slave,' he said sternly. 'She's the woman I
love.'

'You've lost your mind,' Angélique assured him. 'Thank
God your parents aren't alive to hear you say a thing like
that, about *her*.' Wachiwi was watching them battle back
and forth, not entirely sure what the argument was about,
except that she did not feel welcome here. And she could
only assume the argument was about her. She didn't want
to cause problems with his family. But Jean stood next to
her in a reassuring protective way. It was obvious how
angry they all were from the harsh tone of their words. In
the short time she had known him, she had never seen Jean
act that way or heard him speak as fiercely before. He had
always been gentle and kind, with her and everyone else.
But he was clearly furious with his cousins, and they were
equally so with him.

'We'll find a place to stay in town,' he said calmly.

'I doubt you will,' Angélique said shrilly, and as she said
it, they heard carriage wheels on the driveway in front of
the house, and both senior de Margeracs looked panicked.
'Get that woman out of my drawing room immediately,'
she said tersely, and without another word, Jean took

Wachiwi's arm and led her up the stairs. They had just reached the upper landing when the first of the guests walked in. And as soon as he reached his own room with Wachiwi, he explained to her as simply as he could that they were going back to town.

'They are angry for me,' she said clearly, looking sad for him. Tobias walked into the room then, and Jean asked him politely to pack his things. Wachiwi's trunks were all over the room, but very little had been unpacked.

'No, I am angry at them.' He didn't want to hurt her feelings and try to explain it to her. But their reaction had been a revelation to him. Was this what they had to look forward to, if they stayed in New Orleans? He had naïvely expected a warmer reception than this, in a civilized place. And now where were they supposed to go? Where would they live, if they stayed together, which he wanted very much now. But where? In a shack at the edge of Indian territory, like Luc Ferrier, hidden away with his Indian concubine until she died, never to go into the polite world again? Were people so narrow-minded? So mean-spirited? So absurd? And where was he going to take Wachiwi now?

The only relatives he had in America were his cousins in New Orleans. He knew no one else, except travelers and explorers and surveyors and soldiers he had met on the road. And it was one thing to lead a nomadic life alone, it was entirely different doing so with Wachiwi. He had hoped that they could stay there for several months, as he had before, until he figured out their plans. That night his elder cousins had shortened that time considerably.

The Margerac carriage drove them back to town half an hour later, and it was nearly midnight when they arrived at the boardinghouse in the city where they had stopped for a few hours earlier that day. Jean had asked to be taken back there. He had had no problem before, but had said they would only be there for a few hours. This time the desk clerk looked at him strangely, went to consult the manager, although it was the middle of the night, and finally gave them a small room at the back of the house, usually reserved for slightly unsavory people. They hadn't seen Wachiwi when they gave him the room that after-noon. But at least they had a place to stay.

'Will you be staying long, sir?' the clerk asked uncomfortably.

'I don't know,' Jean said honestly. He had no idea where to go. And for the time being at least, he had no desire to see his cousins, nor expose Wachiwi to them again. 'It may be several weeks,' he said solemnly, wondering if he should take her north. For the moment, he had no idea.

Once in the room, he took his coat off and laid it on a chair. He helped Wachiwi out of her gown, and she put it into the trunk, and gratefully took the corset off and the complicated undergarments. He had bought her several nightgowns to sleep in, but she put on the elkskin dress instead. It was more comfortable than anything else she owned, and it was familiar for her. To Wachiwi, it was like the buckskin breeches he wore to ride when he traveled, which were easiest for him.

He talked to her about his own homeland then, as they sat in the small room. He didn't know what else to say to her to distract her. It must have been obvious that something had gone very wrong. And as he talked to her, he had an idea. He was not sure if things would be better there, but they couldn't be much worse than here, and he was beginning to fear that Wachiwi would be treated badly everywhere in the New World, west, north, south, or east. He wanted to take her home with him.

He told her there was a great lake called the Atlantic Ocean, and he lived on the other side. It would take them two full phases of the moon to get there, which seemed like a long time. He told her of the beauty of it once they arrived, the countryside in Brittany, the people she would meet in France, his brother who lived in their family château. He said that their lodge was much bigger than the one she had seen that night. She laughed at him then and said it was called a 'house,' not a lodge, and he laughed back. With her he could face anything, climb any mountain, overcome any obstacle, and he wanted to protect her from the terrible affront and humiliation she had experienced at the de Margerac plantation. He suspected now that others would be as unkind to her as his cousins, and he was convinced that things would be better for them in France. He hoped that there she would be considered a rare and exotic bird, and not someone to be punished and mistreated, and cast away. He knew what he had to do now. He would take her home to Brittany with him.

He planned to write to his brother the next morning, saying that they were coming home on the next ship. His letter would only arrive weeks or days before they did, but it would warn Tristan that they were arriving, and roughly when. Jean was going to book passage for them on the first possible ship going back to France. There was nothing for them here. It would be yet another adventure for them, and a long one, but after all they'd been through so far, being tossed around on the Atlantic Ocean for two months didn't seem so bad. And for the first time in five years in the New World, Jean felt ready to go home. He hadn't seen his brother nor his homeland in all that time. But he had done everything he had come here to do, discovered new places, had astonishing adventures, and now he had met the love of his life, a beautiful Sioux woman he wanted to marry and have children with. He had no idea what his older brother would think of it, but Tristan was a wise, understanding man, and no matter what anyone thought, Jean knew that Wachiwi was the woman for him. They were going home to start a new life together. As he smiled at her, he knew his boyhood days were over. And with his bride, the rest of their life would unfold.

Chapter 11

Just as Jean had decided the night before, after their disastrous visit to his cousins, and as he had told Wachiwi he would, he wrote to his brother Tristan in the morning. It was a long, careful letter that gave him the important points and left out some of the details. He didn't tell him that he had murdered a Crow chief and absconded with the woman he intended to marry, who had been the chief's slave. He said simply that he had met the woman of his life at last, that he was ready to come home and help his brother run their large estate. His wandering days were over now. It was time to settle down, and he had never felt that way before.

He was ten years younger than his brother, who was a widower with two young children, one of whom Jean had never met. When Jean had left Brittany, his brother Tristan had had a beautiful young wife and a year-old baby. A year later Tristan's wife died when their second child was born. As far as Jean knew, his brother had been alone ever since. He hadn't remarried, although Jean had no idea if he had a mistress of some sort, but Tristan was such a serious man that Jean doubted he would engage in anything but marriage and a respectable life.

They had the largest château in the district, and extensive lands. Tristan had always taken his responsibilities seriously, and Jean suspected he would be relieved that his younger brother was coming home to settle down too. At twenty-four, it had taken him time. He rhapsodized about Wachiwi in his letter, but gave Tristan few details, only that he loved her and that they were coming home to Brittany and planned to be married in the family church on their estate. Tristan had inherited the title and everything that went with it when he had been barely more than a boy himself, when their parents died in a terrible epidemic. Tristan had been eighteen, and Jean a child of eight. Tristan had been the head of the family ever since, and as much a father as a brother to Jean. The two men had been close before Jean left France, but he had felt a yearning in his soul to travel, something Tristan had never allowed himself. He had too much on his shoulders with all their properties, landholdings, and their vast estate. They had shipping interests, their parents' enormous house in Paris that they seldom used, and Tristan was a regular presence at court. He was closely tied to the monarchy, and now Jean wanted to be too.

Jean had grown up, and the lovely Indian woman he was bringing home with him had helped him do it. He said everything that was important to him about her in the letter, except one detail. After the fiasco with his cousins, he didn't want Tristan making judgments about Wachiwi before he met her, so he did not tell Tristan that she was a Sioux, nor her name. He wanted his older brother to love and accept her too, and Jean felt sure he would. He told his older brother how lovely she was, how brave and kind and gentle. She was a noble woman and a dignified human being, whatever her origin or race, and worthy of respect. Jean was sure that Tristan would see that immediately. He was that kind of person, and Jean had enormous admiration for him and all that he had carried without complaint for so many years. Everyone in the county adored him, and so did Jean. He could hardly wait to introduce him to Wachiwi now. And he was determined to teach her flawless French on their long journey, so that she could converse with his brother and all their friends in Brittany when they got back. She no longer had to learn

English – their home and their life were going to be in France.

Wachiwi dressed herself carefully, and Jean smiled at her in approval as they left the boardinghouse and walked down to the port. It was a busy city, with a great deal of activity around the harbor. And Jean noticed with displeasure the disapproving glances cast at them as they walked along. He would have had no greater censure if he had been strolling through the port with a naked slave from one of the plantations. Men looked at her lasciviously since she was so beautiful, and women gave him a disgusted look and turned their gaze away. All women, particularly married ones, were aware of the things that men did when out of sight of respectable people, but parading publicly with an Indian woman, no matter how pretty she was, was beyond the pale. It was almost worse because Wachiwi was so lovely – the women who saw her with him seemed to loathe her all the more. Even Wachiwi, in her innocence and ignorance of the customs of his people, couldn't miss the hostile stares. She asked him about it once when one particularly outraged matron gathered up her children around her, said something unpleasant to her husband, and forced them all to cross the street rather than be on the sidewalk with Jean and Wachiwi. People were clearly incensed that he acted as though Wachiwi were a respectable woman, and had dressed her like one, and treated her that way. If he had put his horse in a bonnet and a dress, they would have been less upset. And it was not just the women who ostracized him, the men obviously envied him but were blatant in their disapproval too. If they couldn't do something like that, why could he? New Orleans was very definitely not the place for them, and Jean couldn't wait to leave. He wanted to get Wachiwi away from their ugly stares, audible remarks, and their impression that she was no better than their slaves. He couldn't wait to get back to France now, where he hoped she would be treated like a human being, and addressed with respect.

He spoke to two ship captains that morning, with Wachiwi standing next to him. He thought it best to say that they were married, and he explained that they wanted to book passage on the first ship back to France. The first captain took a long look at Wachiwi, recognized that she was an Indian, and a few minutes later said that all the cabins were booked. He said there was not a bit of room on the boat for them, which Jean did not believe. He felt certain that the captain didn't want to deal with the complaints of other passengers on the ship, particularly the women, who might be outraged by the beautiful young Indian girl in their midst. And even more so that he was claiming she was his wife. Their fury would have been unpleasant for the captain to deal with for the seven or eight weeks it would take to get back to France. He didn't want the headache.

The second captain was mellower and seemed more relaxed. He also recognized easily Wachiwi's origins, but he didn't seem to care. Jean could smell that he'd been drinking whiskey, but he booked their passage, took Jean's money without questions, and said his ship was leaving for Saint Malo in Brittany in two weeks. He glanced at Jean's traveling papers and didn't care that Wachiwi had none. He didn't have to account for the passengers on board nor even list them, and Jean's money was good enough for him. She was neither a Spanish nor a French citizen and had no need of papers to enter France. The young French count said she was his wife, which was possible, although the captain considered it unlikely.

The captain estimated that the trip would take from six to eight weeks. It would be late September when they set sail, hurricane season would be almost over, and with luck and good weather, he hoped to reach the coast of France in November. The seas would be rough by then on the Atlantic, but there was nothing they could do. Jean didn't want to wait a moment longer than he had to. He just hoped that the boardinghouse would let them keep their room until they sailed. If guests complained about Wachiwi's presence, they might be asked to leave. But they had passage on a ship now, in the best cabin, and before they left the port, Jean gave his letter to his brother to another captain, who was sailing for France on a tiny, miserable-looking ship the next day. If the ship didn't sink before it got there, his brother would have the letter announcing Jean's return to France, shortly before they arrived.

Jean was more determined than ever to marry Wachiwi the moment they got back to France. He would have done it before he left, but he was certain that there wasn't a priest or minister in all of New Orleans who would have performed the ceremony. They would have to wait until they reached France.

For the next two weeks, they stayed mostly in their room. They went for long walks at night, strolling through the busy city in the still-balmy night air. It was easier for them to go out at night than brave the disapproving stares of 'respectable' people in the daytime. And in their confined daytime hours in the hotel room, he spent hours teaching Wachiwi French. She was doing surprisingly well, and knew the names for many things now. It was harder expressing abstract concepts and her feelings, but she was managing that too, although awkwardly at times. But they could actually have conversations, share ideas, and laugh a lot. Wachiwi seemed totally happy with him, and they spent a considerable amount of time in bed when they had nothing else to do. It was a universal language, and their passion and deep feelings for each other knew no bounds.

Jean's cousin, Armand de Margerac, came to see him several days after their fateful visit to the plantation. He tried to talk Jean out of taking Wachiwi home with him to France. He said everyone there would be shocked as well, he would turn himself into a pariah, and cause his brother and family profound humiliation and shame.

'Thank you for your concern, cousin,' Jean said politely, digusted by the opinions of the old man, but he was certainly not alone in what he thought. In New Orleans society they would have been outcasts overnight, and already were, just on the streets and in the hotel. Jean had contacted none of the people he knew there, and didn't dare. He had already seen enough when he visited his cousins, and wherever he went out with Wachiwi. 'I'm not sure I agree with you, however. Our monarch has been known for many years to have a great admiration for the Indian tribes in the West. He has invited several chiefs to court, not as curiosities, but as honored guests. My brother wrote me about it once or twice. It sounded quite amazing. They wear their headdresses and moccasins with court clothes that the king sent them so they wouldn't feel out of place. Some even wore full native dress. I've never heard of Indian women at court, but there are certainly men from her tribe who have been to Louis's court.' He was referring to the King of France at the time, Louis XVI, who was known to be fascinated by the Indians from the New World, and the account Jean related to him was true and had been reported by his brother several years before. There was no reason to think that had changed.

'And you're planning to take her to court?' Armand looked horrified at the suggestion. In his mind, it would have been like taking one of their slaves. An unthinkable scandal. There were several women in the slave quarters he had consorted with for years, and two generations of his natural children there, quite a number of them, but he wouldn't have considered for an instant taking any of them out in public, being seen with them in polite society, and he would have died before taking them to court. They were good enough to lie with him and have his babies, but nothing else. What Jean was doing was beyond unthinkable, and Armand could only explain it to himself as the folly of youth. Jean was still a very young man, and he had obviously been living away from 'civilization' for far too long.

'I might take her to court,' Jean said blithely, beginning

to enjoy his cousin's obvious discomfort. It was becoming amusing to shock him, since he was so appalled by the elder's hypocritical ideas. 'I don't go very often myself. My brother goes far more frequently than I do. But then, he's more respectable, and he and the king and some of the ministers are rather close. Perhaps I'll go with him someday and take Wachiwi. I'm sure our revered king will be fascinated by her. She might even meet some of her relatives there. I hear that several have stayed in Brittany, and integrated into society there, rather than going back. It's where they land when they arrive, and where many want to stay.'

'How appalling,' Armand said with a pained look, as though talking about an infestation of some kind, of rodents perhaps. The idea of Indians blending into French society made him feel ill. It only confirmed the decadence of his countrymen to him. At least in the New World, they knew where to keep their slaves. Out of sight, and out of the drawing room certainly, unless they were serving their owners and their guests. 'I think you're making a terrible mistake taking her back to France. You should leave her here where she belongs. She's uneducated, uncivilized, she doesn't speak the language. Think of the embarrassment for your brother. It's one thing to bring savages over as a curiosity if you're the king. What will you do with her

when you get tired of her? Then what will you do?'
Armand couldn't imagine anything worse than what his
young cousin was doing.

'I'm going to marry her, cousin,' Jean said quietly. 'The
uncivilized savage you're referring to will be my wife. She
will be the Comtesse de Margerac just like your wife.' Jean
delivered the blow with a gracious smile, and knew it
would hit his cousin hard. The idea of comparing Wachiwi
to Angélique was more than the older man could bear. He
left a few minutes later, still fuming, offended beyond
words. The two men bade goodbye to each other, bowed
formally, and Jean doubted he would see him again before
he left. He didn't want to anyway, and went back to
Wachiwi in their room afterward, and continued their
lessons. He was confident that by the time they landed in
Brittany, she would speak credible French.

They were on the dock with her trunks and his luggage
several hours before the boat was scheduled to leave. The
weather had been stormy for several days, but hurricane
season seemed to have ended. The other passengers were
gathering on the dock.

People were setting sail on *La Maribelle,* a small merchant
vessel that looked as though it had seen better days. And the
captain looked as though he'd had a rough life.

Jean hoped the trip wouldn't be too hard for Wachiwi, and he had a feeling he wouldn't be returning to the New World again himself. His five years there had served him well, but he felt entirely ready to go home as they settled into their cabin, and the rest of the passengers boarded the ship. There were four other couples, and two men traveling alone. All but two of the passengers were French, as was the captain and all of the crew. Wachiwi would have plenty of opportunity to practice her French. The other women had given her quizzical looks, but Jean had sensed none of the hostility they had experienced on the streets of New Orleans or at the hotel. The rest of the passengers seemed intrigued by her, and their relationship, and wondered how he'd met her, but no one made unpleasant comments when he referred to her as his wife. And the captain politely referred to her as Madame La Comtesse. Jean's traveling papers were in order, although the captain didn't care about them, and Jean had vouched for Wachiwi himself, just in case, with a letter he had provided the captain, sealed with his crest, as Comte de Margerac. He had referred to Wachiwi in the letter as Wachiwi de Margerac. Their destination was Saint Malo, Brittany. Some of the other passengers were going to Paris or other provinces afterward, but Jean and Wachiwi were going home to his family's château, only a short distance from the port in the Breton countryside.

They stood on the deck with the other passengers when they set sail, and watched New Orleans slowly disappear behind them. Jean was relieved to leave the city. It had made such a bad impression on him during this last trip that he would be perfectly happy to never see it again. But there were other things he knew he would miss in the New World, the beautiful countryside, the forests, the terrain he had covered in Canada and out west, the majestic mountains, the incredible plains that went on forever with buffalo grazing, and animals running free in the territory where Wachiwi came from. And he suspected she would miss it too. He put an arm around her as America disappeared on the horizon, and they set out on a rolling sea. Some of the other women had already taken to their cabins, feeling unwell, and one or two of the men, but Wachiwi told Jean in sign language, not knowing the words for it yet, that she liked the movement of the ship. He taught her how to say it in French. She was smiling broadly, her long black hair whipping in the wind, a heavy shawl around her shoulders, and a look of freedom in her eyes. To her, being on the boat felt a little like galloping across the plain. She felt wonderfully free being on the ocean, and she loved being with him. She trusted him completely, and wherever he chose to take her. She was looking forward to the days ahead, and so was he, especially once they got back to France. He was planning to buy horses for her to add to their stables at the château. She was such an extraordinary rider, that he wanted to buy her the finest horses he could find. His brother was an excellent horseman too, and Jean knew he would be impressed by Wachiwi's skill.

By nightfall, the boat was pitching heavily, but Wachiwi wasn't sick. She was proving to be a sturdy sailor, and Jean was relieved. It would be a long two months otherwise. And after a light dinner in the cramped dining room, they went to bed. Wachiwi said the ship felt like a cradle, and it lulled both of them to sleep.

The next day they walked around the small deck. About half of the passengers had remained in their cabins and were feeling sick. Wachiwi stayed out on the deck all day, and Jean sat with her in a sheltered corner. He read, and she did some embroidery with things they'd bought in New Orleans. She was embroidering a shirt for him, with what looked like tiny Indian beads. She explained to him that it was for their wedding day, and he looked pleased. They spent another quiet night, and the next days went well.

They had been at sea for three weeks when Jean began feeling sick, and said he had a sore throat. Wachiwi was feeling fine and brought him some hot tea from the galley. She wished she had the right herbs to put in it, but they had nothing on the ship. She put her blanket around Jean's shoulders. They were outdoors so much of the day that Jean said he had caught a chill. But that night he was worse.

By the next day he had a raging fever, and for the next week he was frighteningly sick, and delirious most of the time. Wachiwi sat beside him quietly and never moved. The captain came to see Jean in his cabin, and said he needed to be bled, but they had no doctor on board. The captain said he had seen something like it before and told Jean he thought he had 'inflammatory quinsy,' which was a severe infection of the throat. Within a week of coming down with it, Jean's throat was so sore and swollen that he could no longer swallow. Wachiwi tried for hours to get him to take a few sips of water or tea, but his throat was almost closed and he could hardly breathe.

He looked worse day by day, and after two weeks of it, Wachiwi sat beside him, chanting softly to the Great Spirits she had prayed to all her life. She begged them to come to him and make him well. She knew that a sweat lodge would have helped him to break the fever, but there was nothing like it on the damp, drafty ship. She covered his shivering form with everything they had to keep him warm, and when he felt chilled to the bone, she lay on him to share her body heat with him. Nothing helped. And she held him in her arms all through the night.

They had been at sea for almost six weeks by then, and the captain estimated that they were another two weeks from shore as Jean continued to get steadily worse. He looked ravaged by whatever disease he had. Wachiwi had a dream about the white buffalo one night as she held him, and thought it was a sign of some kind. But she had no one to tell her what the sign meant, nor any of the herbs or potions or berries that she might have used to help him, or that a medicine man would have given him in her tribe. They were at sea as he got sicker and sicker. She lay holding him and crying seventeen days after he fell ill, and when she fell asleep that night, he died quietly in her arms. She woke and found him, his eyes open, staring at her, as though he had been watching her when he died, his jaw slack, and his arms around her. He already felt cold and stiff. She wrapped him tightly in her blanket and held him gently on their bed. She was thunderstruck by what had happened. It had never occurred to her that he would die and leave her alone. He was so young and strong. She had been sure he would recover, even though he was very, very sick. She silently closed the door of the cabin and went to tell the captain, who looked instantly distressed. He had been worried that there might be an epidemic of quinsy on the ship. He didn't know how contagious it was, and so far no one else had it, so it clearly wasn't as contagious as other diseases that had gone like wildfire through other ships. But there was no question in his mind that they had to bury Jean at sea. He didn't want the body kept on board.

The captain explained that to Wachiwi after they left the cabin where Jean lay wrapped in her blanket and looked like he was asleep. He told her that they couldn't keep his remains on board, they would have to bury him at sea. She nodded, still trying to absorb what had happened. She looked as though she was in shock, and what he described to her was not in her customs, but she was ready to do what he felt best, and they agreed to hold the burial that afternoon. The captain wanted to give her some time with him till then, and she sat next to Jean in the cabin, kissing his cold face and stroking his silky hair. He looked totally at peace. She knew then that that had been the meaning of the white buffalo she had dreamed of. He had come to carry Jean away, and she began a low chant as she sat next to him, praying to the Great Spirits to welcome him and keep him safe.

Wachiwi looked devastated when four sailors came to take his body and put him on a litter, and she followed them upstairs to the deck. All the other passengers were there except two women who had scarcely left their cabins and had been sick for the entire trip. Everyone looked solemn, and one of the male passengers had volunteered to read a passage from the Bible and say a prayer. The captain had offered to wrap Jean in a French flag, but Wachiwi wanted him left in her blanket. She wanted Jean to take it with him, to keep him warm. She looked into the dark, deep waves, and it frightened her to leave him there, but she understood that there was no other choice. She covered her mouth to stifle a cry when two of the sailors tipped the litter, and Jean's body wrapped in her blanket slipped silently into the sea. He disappeared almost instantly, and Wachiwi gave a mournful cry that was the sound of grieving in her tribe.

She stood for a long time at the back of the ship, looking out at the ocean as silent tears poured down her cheeks. Everyone on the ship left her alone, and at nightfall she went back to the cabin where he had died, and lay on the spot where he had lain in the bed, and she cried all night. She had no idea what would happen to her now, and she no longer cared. She knew without a doubt that he had been the only man she would ever love. What happened to her now no longer mattered to her. She would have jumped into the ocean after him, to follow him, but she hadn't dared. It was the first time in her life that her courage had failed.

In the morning, she came back on deck, carrying arm-loads of his belongings, and she explained in her halting French that in her village, one must give away a dead man's things, because he cannot take them with him. And since she had observed none of the other Sioux rites for him, she wanted to honor this one. She gave the sailors his shirts because they were about his size. One of the passengers was grateful for his buckskin pants. The captain took the fine dark blue coat although it was tight for him. There was a musket they could use on board. Another passenger took his boots, and his wife was grateful for Jean's books. One by one they all took something, and the only thing Wachiwi kept was the wedding shirt she was making for him. She would have liked to bury him in it, but there wasn't time. She was going to finish it anyway and put it away, as a memory of him. But the real memories she had of him were far more vivid, of meeting him near the water-fall, their daily encounters at the lake, startled, excited, fascinated by each other, their terrible battle with Napayshni, and riding for days together to escape . . . his kindness to her . . . his gentleness . . . their passion and the way they made love . . . the words he had taught her . . . the beautiful dresses he gave her in St.

Louis . . . the way he looked at her with tenderness and love and respect . . . his promises to her of their life in France . . . it had all left with him when he slipped into the sea, but Wachiwi knew that as long as she lived, she would love him and never forget him.

Chapter 12

With a strong wind that came up behind them unexpectedly, *La Maribelle* sailed into port a few days early.
The journey had taken a little less than eight weeks, and
Wachiwi stood on deck, wondering what would happen
when they came into port. She knew the name of his
family's château, he had mentioned it often, it bore his
name, but she had no idea how to get there, or how to find
his brother, or what he would do when he discovered Jean
was dead. Perhaps he would send her away. And she had
nowhere to go. She had given the captain Jean's money for
safekeeping, but she didn't know how much it was, or how
far it would get her. She knew nothing about white man's
money, all she knew about was trading for furs and horses.
And that would do her no good here.

The captain was pondering the same thing as they docked the ship in Saint Malo. He wondered if someone would come for her, or if they would accept her without her husband. He had been thinking of making her an offer. He had lost his own wife ten years before, and had never remarried. He liked her and she was beautiful and alone now. She had given away all of Jean's possessions except herself. And the captain decided to wait discreetly to see what happened.

People on the quai watched *La Maribelle* come into port, and it took them a while to tie up at the dock. There were sandy beaches and rocky headlands stretched out on either side of the port. It was beautiful and rugged as Wachiwi looked around her while the freight they had carried was unloaded. The passengers anxiously got off the ship, hungry for land and unsteady on their feet after their long confinement at sea. Their trunks were taken off, and arrangements were made to take them to their final destinations. After looking through Jean's papers, the captain sent one of his men to the Château de Margerac nearby on horseback, to tell the marquis that the ship had docked. The sailor came back two hours later without comment. He said he had informed one of the servants, they thanked him, and he left and came back. He never saw the marquis and they had no idea if he was coming.

The sailor did not tell them that the marquis's brother had died, the captain thought it better not to.

All the other passengers had left the ship by then, and the captain very kindly told Wachiwi that she was welcome to stay on board for the two weeks they would be in port, in case no one came for her. They were both beginning to think the marquis might not come. Perhaps there was some quarrel between the two brothers that Wachiwi didn't know about. And the offer the captain made her to stay aboard was a prelude to any other offer he might make her before he left again. He didn't want to speak of it prematurely.

Wachiwi was sitting quietly on deck, looking out to sea sadly, near the spot on the ship where they had slipped Jean's body into the ocean, when the captain saw an enormous black carriage roll toward them, pulled by four white horses, with liveried footmen front and back, and a crest emblazoned on the door. It was an impressive carriage, and the man who descended from it minutes later even more so. He was the image of his younger brother, only broader, taller, and visibly a decade older, but still a very handsome man, and he looked every inch the noble-man he was, although simply and inconspicuously dressed. He was wearing a dark blue coat much like his brother's, which the captain was the proud owner of now. The captain immediately left the ship, went to the dock, and bowed low to the marquis.

'I'm honored, sir, by your presence,' the captain said humbly, his hat rapidly shoved under his arm, as the marquis looked over the ship, stunned by how small it was to make such a long trip. He knew it couldn't have been pleasant for those aboard.

'I'm here to meet my brother. The Comte de Margerac,' he explained, but the captain already knew.

'I'm aware of that, sir, your honor.' He bowed low again as he said it. It wasn't often he saw noblemen like this one, of such obvious distinction. 'I'm afraid I have unfortunate news for you. Your brother fell ill halfway through the trip. Quinsy, I believe it was, sir, a terrible illness of the throat. He succumbed a little more than two weeks ago, and we were obliged to bury him at sea.' The marquis froze where he stood and looked at the captain, as though he had been shot. The prodigal son, or brother in this case, had almost returned to him, and now he was gone, and never would. It was beyond thinking, and tears instantly blinded the older brother's eyes. Without shame, he wiped them away. Although he hadn't seen him in five years, he was deeply attached to Jean and loved him dearly.

'Oh my God, how awful. I just got the letter days ago that he was coming, and this morning your message that you'd docked. How terrible. Did others get the disease?'

'No, no one, sir. Not yet.' He didn't say it, but his own throat had been sore for a few days, but he had no fever and felt otherwise healthy, so he had said nothing. It might have just been a cold, or a draft. He didn't want to panic the passengers before they arrived, so he had kept silent about it. 'I'm very sorry. He seemed like a good man.'

'He was.' Despite his years of absence, Tristan still loved him as he always had. Jean had almost been more like a son to him than a brother, or both, and now he was dead. Tristan was heartbroken at the thought. It was devastating news.

'His wife is still here, sir,' the captain said softly, as though mentioning a forgotten trunk a passenger had left, and he saw that the marquis looked startled, as though he didn't know about her. All Jean had written was that he intended to marry the girl he was bringing home with him, not that he already had. Knowing him, Tristan wondered if what the captain said was true or not. He knew his brother well enough to suspect that he might have claimed to be married to her in order to preserve her reputation until they did marry in France.

'Where is she?' the marquis asked, still overwhelmed by the shocking news, as the captain pointed to the deck, to a solitary figure sitting there with her back to them as she

231

stared out to sea, oblivious to the fact that Jean's brother had arrived.

The marquis nodded, boarded the ship, and walked up a short stairway to where she sat. He wasn't sure what to say to her, except that he was sorry, and knew they both were. Her dark hair hung straight down her back, and he made a sound to warn her that he was behind her. She turned slowly and saw him, and there was no mistaking who he was. He looked so exactly like Jean, only larger, more serious, and more imposing, but he had warm eyes. She almost wanted to throw her arms around him, but didn't dare. Instead she stood up and looked at him, and dropped the low curtsy Jean had taught her, as Tristan looked at her in amazement. Jean had not written to him that she was a Sioux. And the full force of it hit Tristan now. Jean had wanted to come home with an Indian girl, only she had arrived, and he hadn't. He was speechless for a moment as he looked at her, stunned by both her origins and her beauty, and bowed low in answer to her curtsy.

'Countess,' he said, and reached for her hand to kiss it, but she didn't let him.

'We didn't marry,' she said softly. 'We were going to here.' She didn't want to lie to him and was honest immediately.

'I know, that's what he wrote me . . . but the captain

said . . .' She shook her head with a shy smile. She didn't want to pretend to Jean's brother to be something she wasn't. She was not a countess, and never would be now. She didn't mourn the title, only the man.

'I'm so sorry. For both of us,' he said kindly. 'What will you do now?' He had no suggestion to offer, and was completely at a loss himself. What was he going to do with an Indian girl who had nowhere to go in France, and surely no money of her own?

'I don't know. I can't go back to my people.' She had caused a chief to be killed and she and her people would be blamed for it entirely and punished severely by the Crow if she returned. There was no going back for her. Jean had known that. His brother didn't.

'Perhaps you can stay for a while until you decide,' he said gently. He could see how devastated she was about his brother, and so was he. He had been prepared to celebrate, and now he would be in mourning for the brother he hadn't seen in five long years. 'Will you come with me?' he asked politely. She nodded and followed. She had nowhere else to go.

Wachiwi left the boat with Jean's brother. She thanked the captain in the greatly improved French she had learned on the trip. And the marquis handed her into his carriage, and told the captain he would send another shortly for her trunks. Then the impressive carriage took off at a fast clip and left the port, and turned sharply toward the hills. Wachiwi had noticed the beautiful horses and wished that she could ride them. She saw that Jean's brother was looking at her intently, as though studying her face, trying to discover who she was, and why his brother had loved her. For now, it was all a mystery to him. And then he realized something else.

'Jean never told me your name.' He had a kind face, Wachiwi decided, just like his younger brother. His was softer and not as full of fire and passion as Jean's, but he had gentle eyes.

'I am called Wachiwi,' she said simply in French.

'You're Indian, I presume.' There was no judgment in it, just a statement, unlike the people she'd met in New Orleans, who made 'Indian' sound like a curse.

'Sioux,' she answered.

'I've met two of your great chiefs in our king's court,' he said as they drove to the château where both brothers had grown up. 'Perhaps they were related to you,' he said, trying to be pleasant, and still trying to absorb that the brother he loved was dead, and he had brought an Indian girl back to France. It was a lot to digest all at once. And what would he do with her now? Where would she go? He couldn't keep her at the château forever. He would have to help her figure out something, but for now she could stay at the château with him and his children. And then Tristan smiled to himself as he looked out the window of the carriage. It was so like Jean to do something like this, to fall madly in love with an Indian girl, which was bound to shock everyone, and then die and leave Tristan to deal with her. He laughed as he thought about it, and smiled as he turned to Wachiwi. There was something totally absurd about it, and totally outrageous. And wonderful in a way too. He was sure that she was a remarkable girl if Jean had loved her enough to want to marry her. He had yet to discover what Jean had loved in her, and she was certainly very pretty. Tristan looked at her with a fatherly air and smiled. 'Welcome to France, Wachiwi.'

'Thank you, My Lord,' she said politely, just as Jean had taught her, and then they sat silently together, and rode the rest of the way to the château.

Tristan could easily imagine Jean smiling at them, from wherever he was, or even laughing. Wachiwi, lost in her own thoughts, could feel Jean close to her, and had ever since he died. Even more so now that she was here.

Chapter 13

The drive to the Château de Margerac took longer than Wachiwi expected, since Jean had told her it was on the sea and not far from the port, but even with fast horses pulling the carriage, it took them nearly an hour on the narrow winding road.

The château was enormous and sat on a cliff with a magnificent view of the ocean. The terrain looked rugged, and the château was imposing and had been built in the twelfth century, but what softened its appearance were miles and miles of gardens, filled with brilliantly hued flowers and ancient trees that towered above them. Wachiwi had never seen anything so lovely in her life.

As they approached, Tristan told her some of the history of the family and the house. He said that his family had all been warriors in the early days, which was why the château looked so much like a fortress, and was inaccessible, to protect them from their enemies. It had served them well for centuries. She smiled and said that her ancestors had been warriors too, and the men in her tribe still were. Saying it made her think of her brothers and made her look momentarily sad. Tristan couldn't help wondering how she had come to be with his brother, and how he had managed to take her from the Sioux. He wondered if Wachiwi had run away with him, which seemed likely.

'You'll have to tell me sometime how you met my brother,' he said, sounding curious, and she nodded but said nothing. She didn't want to tell him so soon that his brother had killed a man, because of her.

A footman handed her down from the carriage, and the marquis led her inside the château. There were long dark hallways going in all directions, filled with somber paintings of his ancestors. Some of them looked like him and Jean. There was a great hall in the center filled with hunting trophies and heraldic banners, a gigantic ballroom he had not used since his wife died, and several smaller receiving rooms. And all of it was cold and drafty, and looked daunting to Wachiwi. She wondered what it would have been like to discover all this with Jean, and not his more serious older brother. He was telling her about various ancestors as they walked around. She was confused by most of what he said, and overwhelmed. But she tried to look attentive. He spoke quickly in French, not realizing how recently she had learned.

And then he took her upstairs to an enormous living room with large chairs and many couches that looked like some kind of council room to her. She could imagine the warriors in his family meeting there to plan their raids on other tribes, just as the men in hers sat around the camp-fire or came to her father's tipi to discuss similar things. In some ways, their histories and family traditions were not so different. War and hunting. She noticed with interest that there were no buffalo on his walls, mostly deer and antelope and elk. She wondered if they had no buffalo in France, but was too embarrassed to ask him.

A woman in a plain black dress with a lace apron came in and offered to serve them tea. She came back with two other women and a man and a gigantic silver tray almost too heavy to carry, covered with silver teapots and porcelain jars, and plates with small sandwiches and cookies. It all looked very interesting to Wachiwi, and she was starving. She sat down on the chair Tristan indicated, and ate as delicately as she could. It was all new to her still, but Jean had taught her well. He hadn't wanted her to be embarrassed or feel awkward when she came to

France, and thanks to his diligent lessons, she didn't. The food tasted delicious to her.

She noticed that Tristan was watching her carefully, trying to decide what to make of her, and from time to time Wachiwi glanced out at the view of the ocean. And as she looked at the sea, she thought of Jean's spirit, which was there now. And as she thought of him, two children walked in, with a tall serious-looking young woman with a pale face. She was wearing a gray dress, and she looked like an unhappy person, even to Wachiwi. She had plain brown hair, gray eyes, and everything about her seemed drab. The children looked like they couldn't wait to escape her, and referred to her as 'Mademoiselle.' They stopped in their tracks when they saw Wachiwi. The little girl looked to be about four years old, and the boy about six. Although they were beautifully dressed and very different, they reminded Wachiwi of the Indian children she had known. They bounded around the room like puppies, leaped at their father, and ogled the cookies on the tea tray, as Mademoiselle attempted unsuccessfully to dampen their spirits and make them sit down. They would for a minute, and then leap up again to laugh and play with their father, who looked delighted to see them.

Wachiwi didn't like the tall spare-looking woman, and it was obvious the children didn't either. She seemed cold and distant to Wachiwi, and Mademoiselle pointedly ignored her as though she didn't see her in the room. It was the same disdainful attitude she and Jean had met in New Orleans.

'And these are my children,' Tristan said with a broad smile. 'Matthieu and Agathe. Jean saw Matthieu when he was a baby. Agathe was born after he left.' They stared at Wachiwi with interest. Even though she was dressed in ordinary clothes, they could observe easily that there was something different about her, if nothing else the creamy nut color of her skin. 'This is a friend of your Uncle Jean,' Tristan explained to them, trying to contain them, and relenting over the cookies, which they rapidly devoured as Wachiwi giggled. She looked like a child herself. Agathe smiled at her immediately. She thought she was pretty, and looked nice.

'Is this the lady Uncle Jean was going to marry?' Agathe asked, as she hopped onto the couch next to her father, and Mademoiselle scowled her disapproval. She thought they should stand at attention and never sit down in the drawing room when they visited their father. He was far less rigid than that with them, and the governess firmly disapproved.

'Yes, it is,' her father confirmed, surprised that his daughter remembered. But he had told her only a few days before, when he got Jean's letter, and the little girl was excited about a wedding, and wanted to know if she could be in it.

'Where is Uncle Jean?' Matthieu chimed in, and there was a brief silence in the room. And then finally, with a heavy look and sagging shoulders, their father answered. His grief was easy to read.

'He is with Mama now, in Heaven. They are together. His friend came here alone.'

'She did?' Agathe turned to her with wide eyes. 'On a boat?' Wachiwi nodded, smiling at her. The little girl had soft blond curls, a sweet round angelic face, and was impossible to resist. Matthieu had the stamp of Tristan and Jean and was tall for his age. Agathe looked more like her late mother, who had been the light of Tristan's life until she died, and still was. He had mourned her for the past four years.

'Yes, I came on a boat,' Wachiwi said. 'I just arrived today.'

'Was it very scary?' The little girl's eyes were wide.

'No, it was all right. It just took a long time. Nearly two full moons,' she said, and caught herself. 'Almost two months,' she corrected, remembering Jean's words.

'I don't like boats,' Agathe said firmly. 'They make me sick.'

'Me too,' Matthieu added, studying Wachiwi. He wasn't sure what she was, but he knew that she was different and interesting, and he could tell she was nice to children. Both of them had already decided that on their own.

The children chatted animatedly with them for a few minutes, and then Mademoiselle announced that it was time to go. Both Agathe and Matthieu protested, to no avail. She told them to say goodnight to their father, and escorted them firmly from the room.

'They're so wonderful!' Wachiwi said sincerely, 'and your son looks just like you and Jean.' It had warmed her heart to see it, and despite their fancy clothes, they reminded her of the children in her tribe.

Tristan smiled at what she said. 'Yes, he does look like us, poor boy. Agathe looks like her mother. She died when Agathe was born. But the governess is very good with them, we've had her since Matthieu was born. Particularly now, without a mother, they need someone to keep them in line. And I'm not always here.' It felt odd speaking to her about these things but he was curious about the woman his brother had brought home, and intended to marry, and he wanted to get to know her. He wasn't nearly as shocked at her being an Indian as Wachiwi had feared he would be. In fact, he appeared not to be at all. He was an amazingly open-minded and kind-hearted person and made her feel welcome at the château.

'She seems very severe,' Wachiwi said honestly about the governess, surprisingly at ease with him. She had disliked her the moment she saw her, but knew enough not to say that. She didn't want to offend her host. In Indian culture, Mademoiselle would have been a relative of some kind, but she had already learned from Jean that in Europe the people who worked for them were 'servants,' and in New Orleans they were 'slaves.' The slaves had seemed nicer than Mademoiselle, who was painfully austere, and cold as ice. She didn't appear to like children.

'I'll have the housekeeper show you to your room,' Tristan said then. 'You must be tired from the trip. How fortunate that you didn't catch my brother's illness. You're feeling well, aren't you?' He looked concerned. He didn't want her ill or spreading disease, but she looked healthy to him and said she felt fine. And it was obvious to him that she was young and strong.

He rang a long bell pull next to the fireplace, and a woman appeared who looked like an older relative of Mademoiselle's, and Tristan said she would show Wachiwi to her rooms. He said that he had arranged for her dinner to be served in her own suite that night, but he would see her in the morning. He didn't want to sit down to a solitary dinner with a single woman. It didn't seem right to him, and he had no idea what they would do in future. Perhaps she could eat in the nursery with the children. It wasn't proper for him to eat with her every night. Without Jean, their situation was more than a little awkward. Wachiwi taking her meals with the children seemed like the only possible solution to him.

The suite of rooms that Tristan had assigned to her, once he knew that his brother wasn't with her, were a far cry from the slave quarters where his cousin Angélique had put her in New Orleans. She had an enormous sitting room with a view of the ocean, a bedroom with a four-poster canopied bed worthy of a princess, a large bathroom, a dressing room, and a small writing room with an elegant ladies' desk. Wachiwi had no idea what to do with all the space. And she was so sad that Jean wasn't with her. If he had been, although she didn't know it, she would have eventually shared his gigantic suite on the same floor as Tristan's, but under the circumstances, the marquis had put her in another wing of the château. The nursery where the children lived was just above her, up a single flight of stairs. She could hear them, but didn't dare go up and risk Mademoiselle's glacial gaze and stern disapproval.

She wandered around the room, opening drawers and cupboards, in awe of everything she saw, and eventually an enormous silver tray appeared, with meats and vegetables and fruit on it. There was a choice of sauces, a plate with cheese and bread, and a beautifully presented dessert. She cried when she saw it because they were being so kind to her, but all she really wanted here was Jean.

She slept fitfully in the enormous canopied bed, draped in swaths of pink satin, with tassels everywhere, and a wondrous feather bed. She dreamed of the white buffalo again, and didn't know what it meant. The last time it happened, Jean had died, and she wondered if he was coming back to her now in spirit. She wished he would tell her what to do now. She was lost here without him, and Tristan was equally so about what to do with her. He had visions of her living in the attic of the château until she was an old woman, a legacy left to him by his brother. But what else could he do with her? He couldn't send her back to America, since she said she couldn't return to her people. He couldn't turn her away, or refuse her shelter and care. He couldn't really keep her there forever, unless he found something useful for her to do, and he had no idea what she was capable of. Probably not much. None of the women he knew would have been capable of surviving on their own, without the protection of their families and men. And Wachiwi was from an entirely different world and knew nothing of theirs. She was totally alone.

In the morning, Wachiwi dressed carefully in one of the

dresses Jean had given her. She would have liked to go out to the gardens, but had no idea how to get there, so she walked up the stairs to where she guessed the nursery was instead. And she was right. The children's voices grew louder as she approached a room just over her own, and she could hear the governess scolding them. She knocked as Jean had taught her to do and opened the door, and there they were. Agathe was sitting on the floor holding a doll and playing a game, and Matthieu was playing with a hoop, which the governess had just told him to put down at once.

Wachiwi smiled at them, and they bounded over to her the moment they saw her. They looked delighted, and she talked to them for a few minutes. She said she wanted to go to the gardens but didn't know how to get there, and Matthieu instantly begged the governess to let them show her. Looking pained by the whole experience and Wachiwi's visit, she agreed, and a few minutes later, with coats on, they all ran down the stairs, as Wachiwi followed. It was cold outside, but sunny, and there was a stiff November wind, but running through the maze, across the grass and in between the flower beds, both children stayed warm, and chasing them in their games, so did Wachiwi. She was having a wonderful time with them, and looked like a child herself. None of them noticed when the children's father appeared and stood to one side watching them. He had never seen his children have so much fun.

Wachiwi noticed him only when she crashed into him, running away from Matthieu. She was startled when she saw him, and out of breath. She apologized profusely and looked embarrassed.

'Don't let them wear you out!' he warned.

'I love playing with them,' Wachiwi said, breathless from their games, and he could see that she meant it. And with that Mademoiselle used the opportunity to say it was time to wash up before lunch, and spirited them away. 'You have wonderful children!' Wachiwi said admiringly. 'We've had a lovely time together this morning.' She was still smiling as she said it, and sorry they had left.

'How did you sleep?' he asked, looking serious.

'Very well, thank you.' It was one of those standard responses that was one of the first Jean had taught her. But in fact, she hadn't. She had barely slept at all. 'It's a very comfortable bed.' That was true, but her bad dreams and concerns about her future now made it irrelevant how soft the bed was. And she didn't want to seem ungrateful to him. She was well aware that what happened to her now was not his problem, and he was being very kind, out of love and respect for his brother and the woman he had wanted to make his wife.

'I'm glad to hear that. I hope you're warm enough. The house can get a little chilly.' She laughed then.

'So can a tipi.' He looked at her, not sure what to say, and he laughed too. She was so open about everything, and not afraid to be who she was, or say what she thought, without ever being inappropriate or rude. 'Your brother said you have wonderful stables.' She was aching to see them, but she didn't want to push.

'I wouldn't go that far. I was going to buy some new horses in the spring. We have some good ones. I use them mostly for hunting.' She nodded. 'Would you like to see the stables?' He didn't know what else to suggest to her. He was planning to have lunch with her, to be polite, but the stables would provide a welcome distraction before that. He assumed they had very little in common, and conversation would be pretty thin. His brother must have talked to her about something, or maybe their relationship was all about physical attraction and passion. But he had to admit, the French Jean had taught her was excellent. She made few mistakes, and usually corrected them herself when she did. He had taught her well, and she had had two months of constant practice on the boat. Jean had been very diligent with her about it, preparing her for their arrival in France, into his world.

Wachiwi followed him to the stables, and Tristan saw her

face come alive when she entered. She went from stall to stall, checking out his horses, sometimes she went in, and felt their muscles or their legs. She talked to them soothingly in what Tristan assumed was Sioux, and she singled out each of his best horses with a practiced eye.

'You must like to ride,' he said pleasantly, impressed by how at ease she was with them and what she seemed to know.

She laughed at what he said. 'Yes, I do. I have five brothers. I used to ride with them, and sometimes they would have me race against their friends.'

'Horse races?' Tristan looked startled. He had never known a woman who raced horses. But Wachiwi knew he had never known a Sioux, although she had been unusual in her tribe too. None of the young girls raced horses against the men, or at all, except Wachiwi. He was guessing that the horses she had ridden had been very tame. 'Would you like to go for a ride this afternoon?' he suggested. It would be something for her to do. He was treating her like an honored guest, which she was. She had come all the way from New Orleans to marry his brother, and now she had nothing to do and no reason to be here, and he had even less reason to be with her. If riding would help pass the time while he attempted to entertain her, he was game. Her eyes lit up the minute he suggested it.

'You ride sidesaddle, of course?' he questioned, and she shook her head.

'No, I don't.' She had seen women riding sidesaddle in New Orleans, but it looked awkward and uncomfortable to her, and like a very insecure and silly way to ride. She had said as much to Jean at the time, and he laughed and told her she would have to learn. It was the only thing he had ever told her that she refused. Riding was sacred to her.

'What do you prefer?' Tristan asked, looking bemused. He couldn't imagine her riding astride like a man, although perhaps it was a tradition for women to do so among the Sioux.

'No saddle at all. Just bridle and reins.' Jean had told her what they were called. 'I've ridden that way all my life.' She didn't mention her little trick of sometimes riding along the side of the horse. Tristan looked startled at what she had suggested, but he was suddenly curious to see what kind of rider she was. 'Will anyone see us?' she asked, which shocked him even more.

'Just the grooms and stable boys.'

'May I wear whatever I choose?' He was a little frightened by what she was suggesting, and wanting to be polite to his brother's almost-bride, he nodded. 'I'd like to wear one of my old dresses when I ride. I can't ride properly in all this.' She looked down at her voluminous skirt, the gloves, the bonnet, the shoes. It was just too much, and impossible for her to ride that way.

'Do whatever pleases you, my dear,' he said kindly. 'We'll have a nice ride in the hills after lunch. Did you see any particular horse that struck your fancy in the stables?' he asked, as they walked back to the château. The stables were set apart and had been built more recently. She had seen one horse she liked, and described him to Tristan, who looked shocked. 'He's quite dangerous. He's not fully broken yet. I don't want you to get hurt.' His brother would never have forgiven him. He had a responsibility to her now, even if it was different from the custom in her tribe, where a surviving brother had to marry his dead brother's wife, as Napayshni had. She hadn't been Jean's wife. And that wasn't the custom in France. But he did feel somewhat responsible for her, and was still trying to figure out what that meant, how far the obligation went, and what he should do. For now it meant entertaining her civilly, and providing her a home until she figured out somewhere else to go. And he realized that under the circumstances it might take months, so they had to make the best of it for now. He was trying, but that didn't mean getting her killed on an unreliable horse.

They had lunch in the enormous dining room, at the far

end of an endless table. And the cook had made them a very good fish soup. Wachiwi ate it all and the plentiful cheese and fruit they served afterward. And then she went upstairs to get ready for their ride. When she came back, Tristan was more than a little surprised to see her wrapped in a blanket. She had brought it with her, and beneath it she was wearing her elkskin dress with the quills, and the doeskin leggings that went with it. On her feet were the beaded moccasins she had made herself. She was entirely comfortable and at ease and moved with a striking grace. Looking at her, Tristan was mildly embarrassed and hoped that no one but the grooms would see her, but as he followed her to the stables, he noticed that she moved with the lithe agility of a dancer, worthy of her name. And he made no comment about her dress other than to ask her if she was sure she could ride in that. He had already tried to talk her into a different horse, to no avail. When she was pressed, he could see that she was a headstrong girl. He tried not to notice the look on the grooms' faces when she mounted bareback in the elkskin dress. Their eyes bulged in amazement, but they said not a word. Her jet-black hair streamed down her back. The horse began to prance as soon as she was mounted, and instantly he saw something different come over her, and within a second she was one with the horse, and the skittish mount began to calm down. She rode him serenely from the stables with a practiced hand, and Tristan followed her on his own familiar horse, which was spirited and solid, but not as wild or as fast or as racy as the one she was on. Wachiwi looked peaceful and happy, as Tristan watched her, fascinated by her control of the horse. She mastered him with ease.

They said nothing for a few minutes as they followed a path Tristan knew well, and when her horse began to dance again, she startled Tristan by giving him his head and took off like a shot. The horse was so fast and she so glued to it that he couldn't even follow, and suddenly as he watched her, Tristan knew what he was seeing, an incredibly gifted rider with more skill than any man he had ever seen. She flew, she galloped, she jumped over a hedge, she lay flat against the horse, she controlled him totally, and he wasn't sure who was having more fun, Wachiwi or her mount. She was the most incredible rider he had ever seen. She was a joy to watch. And he was laughing when he caught up to her at last. He was breathless. She was not. She looked blissful and totally at ease.

'Remind me never to try and teach you anything about a horse. Good God, you're an amazing rider. Now I can see why your brothers bet on you in races. I imagine they never lost. It's a pity we can't do that here.' And he looked as though he meant it. Watching her on horseback was poetry in motion. He had never had a riding partner anything like her, woman or man.

'Why not?' She was interested in what he said, as they slowly turned back to the château after a two-hour ride in the hills. She hated to go back, and this time so did he.

'Women don't race horses,' he said simply, and she nodded.

'They don't with my people either.' And then she added, 'Your brother was a good rider.' She remembered their long flight from the Crow village to St. Louis. Lesser riders than both of them would have been killed. Their skill and expertise had saved their lives.

'Yes, he was,' Tristan agreed.

'So are you,' she said, smiling at him. 'I had a good time riding with you today.' He was far more circumspect than she, and was astride a slower horse, but she could see that he was an excellent rider too. Just not as wild as she. Few riders were.

'So did I,' he admitted easily. He was enjoying her company. And her conversation was easy and intelligent. 'It's fun riding with you, Wachiwi. Maybe it's the dress,' he teased her. 'It must be a magic dress.'

'I wore it when your brother and I escaped from the village where the Crow had taken me as a slave.' He was shocked to hear it. It made him realize how little he knew about her life, and the customs of her people. Being taken as a slave sounded horrifying to him. 'Your brother saved me. We rode hard for many days to get away.' She didn't tell him about killing Napayshni. He didn't need to know.

'That must have been frightening,' he said in an awed voice, aware of how uninformed he was about her relationship with his brother.

'Yes, it was,' she said calmly. 'I tried to escape many times, but they always caught me and brought me back.' She showed him the mark on her dress where she had been shot with the arrow. She had repaired it, but the mark was still there, as it was on her shoulder as well. She had a nasty scar where she'd been shot, but didn't show him that. Jean knew it well.

'How terrifying. You're a very brave girl.' He was curious about her then. There was more to this young woman than met the eye. She was not just beautiful, pleasant to talk to, and an excellent rider, she had a history and abilities that he knew nothing about, and which he suspected were fascinating. She looked like a child, but she wasn't. Perhaps his brother knew what he was doing after all. Tristan had doubted it for a moment when he first saw her, and thought her only an exotic, pretty girl. But he didn't now. 'Was your father a chief?' She nodded. He had suspected as much from her confidence, dignity, and grace. 'A great one. White Bear. My brothers will be too one day. They are already brave warriors now.' And then she looked at him sadly. She missed them so much and thought of them often. They were so far away now, and she fully realized she would never see them again. It brought tears to her eyes. 'Two of them were killed when I was taken by the Crow. I never saw the others again. And I never will now. If I go back to my father's tribe, the Crow will make war on them, because I ran away from them. I was given to their chief.'

'Remarkable,' Tristan said quietly, wondering what else she had in her history, other than that amazing story and her incredible skill with horses. They led their horses into the stable, and Wachiwi followed him back to the château after they dismounted. It was late by then. They had ridden longer than planned, but they had both enjoyed it. He was tired now, but Wachiwi looked more alive than ever. The ride in the hills at full speed had been good for her soul.

'I'm going to Paris tomorrow for a few days,' Tristan told her before he left her.

'To visit the king's court?' she asked with interest, sounding like Matthieu or Agathe.

'Probably. I have some other things to do as well. When

I come back, we'll have to ride again. Perhaps you can show me some of your tricks.' She laughed openly as he said it, and she turned to smile at him.

'I will teach you to ride like a Sioux.'

'After what I saw today, I think I'd like that. Thank you, Wachiwi.' He smiled back at her, and went up the grand staircase to his rooms.

As Wachiwi found her way back to her own suite, she could hear the children laughing in the nursery. Instead of going straight to her room, she stopped to say hello to them. She forgot that she was still wearing her elkskin dress, and they were fascinated by it. Predictably, their governess looked shocked and turned away from such a disgusting sight.

'I saw you ride with Papa today,' Matthieu commented, 'from the window. You were riding very fast.'

'Yes, I was,' she admitted. 'I like to do that sometimes.'

'I don't like horses,' Agathe interjected, and Wachiwi didn't try to change her mind. In their world, that was probably a good thing, and entirely expected.

'Will you teach me to ride like that?' Matthieu asked her, looking wistful.

'If your father says I may.' She didn't tell him that his father wanted to learn to ride that way too, and had asked. Maybe teaching both of them was something she could do for them in exchange for their kindness and hospitality to her. She felt useless here otherwise. She had not come here to do nothing. She had come to be Jean's wife. And now she had to find something else to do. Teaching the marquis and his son to ride like Sioux warriors was going to be fun for her, and maybe for them too. 'You have to ask your father. I will do whatever he says,' Wachiwi said wisely, as the governess sniffed and glared at her. She had never in her entire life seen anything as shocking as Wachiwi's elk-skin dress, and she said as much to Agathe after she left.

'I liked it!' the little girl said defiantly. 'And the blue things on it are pretty. She said she made them herself with berries.' Agathe was proud of her new friend. It was nice having a young woman around, one who was kind to them, and not a sourpuss like Mademoiselle.

'How disgusting,' the governess said, turned her back, and began putting their toys away.

And in her own room, looking out the window at the ocean, Wachiwi was thinking about them. She knew now that she would never marry. She had refused the suitors in her village, and Napayshni. The only man she had ever loved and wanted to marry was Jean. And now he was gone. A tear crept down her cheek as she thought of it. But at least she could be kind to his nephew and niece and brother, for as long as she could stay. She didn't know what would happen to her now, but she knew that sooner or later she'd have to go. She couldn't stay here without Jean. Of that she was certain.

Wachiwi saw Tristan leave for Paris early the next morning, before dawn. She had awakened early and was looking out the window when she saw him come out of the stables on horseback with his valet and a groom. He didn't bother taking the carriage now that he was alone. And Matthieu had told her that the three men would stop at an inn that night. They would ride for fifteen hours for two days and then stay at his Paris house. Tristan had told her himself that he didn't like going to Paris. He preferred his quiet life in Brittany and had too much to do here on his estate to waste time going to court. He said that since his wife's death he went as seldom as he could, but he didn't want to be disrespectful of the king, so he went from time to time.

Wachiwi wondered what it was like at court, and found it hard to imagine. Jean had described it to her, and all she could envision were women who looked like his cousin Angélique, which seemed daunting to her. He had described millions of candles and mirrors, long tables with enormous feasts, music, dancing, and complicated intrigues that made no sense to her. Jean had said that many people wanted favors from the king and queen and did all kinds of things to obtain them.

She couldn't imagine Tristan as part of all that, or even dancing. He seemed like such a sober, quiet man, and as though he would be happiest on a horse, or with his children. She couldn't envision him in satin breeches and a powdered wig and was glad she didn't have to see it. She liked the person he was here, in Brittany.

She watched him ride away from the château, with his two servants riding behind him. It started to rain softly as they disappeared from sight, and she knew it would be a long ride to Paris. She hoped he wouldn't catch a chill or get sick. Jean's death had reminded her that even strong men could be fragile. And she had already come to like and respect Tristan. He was the older brother she no longer had and still longed for and whom Jean had described with such love and respect. Tristan was someone she already sensed that one could count on. She was embarrassed to be so dependent on him without Jean. But for now, Tristan and his children were all she had. She prayed for his safe return from Paris, for their sake and her own.

Chapter 14

Brigitte

The plane took off for Paris from Kennedy Airport on a Friday night just before midnight, as Brigitte looked out the window, thinking about what she was going to do. She wanted to go to Brittany, but she planned to go to the Bibliothèque Nationale in Paris first. It seemed fairly simple, once she figured out her way around their archives; all she had to do was look up the Marquis de Margerac and see what they had on him. She already knew he had been married to Wachiwi, but she wanted to see what else there was about them. And then she would go down to Brittany by train.

She'd been brushing up on her French for the past week.

It had been fairly decent in college, and she'd written some good papers, but she hadn't spoken it in sixteen years. She'd been listening to Berlitz tapes for the last several days. And the moment the flight attendant spoke to her in French on Air France, she felt paralyzed. She understood what she'd said but couldn't answer. She just hoped they spoke English at the National Archives. She was planning to go there on Monday.

She had booked a reservation at a small hotel on the Left Bank that someone in her office had recommended to her years before. She and Ted had always wanted to go to Paris, and never had. They had gone to the Grand Canyon, and an art fair in Miami instead. That was as far as they got. And now here she was, going there alone, while he started a dig in Egypt. They were on separate paths forever now. But she liked the one she was on better, and felt good about it.

The weather was beautiful when she got to Paris the next morning. It was still chilly and felt like winter, but the sun was shining brightly, and she took a cab from the airport to her hotel. She managed to tell the driver in French where she was going, and he understood her, which was a major victory for her. She was traveling on a new passport, because her old one had expired. She hadn't left the country in that long. But now here she was. She was giddy with excitement as they drove into town. And the driver couldn't have planned his route more perfectly. He drove down the Champs Élysées, where she could see the Arc de Triomphe, across the Place de la Concorde full of Japanese brides having their photographs taken in their wedding gowns, and then they drove across the Seine, onto the Left Bank, and he took her to her hotel. She caught a glimpse of the Eiffel Tower on the way.

The small hotel was clean, and her room was tiny. But there was a bistro across the street, a drugstore down the block, a dry cleaner – everything she could need. After she dropped her suitcase in her room, having managed to check in in French, another victory, she walked across the street and sat down at a sidewalk café and ordered lunch. She was doing great so far, and she felt like the mistress of her own fate as she watched people wandering by. There were a lot of couples kissing, men on motor scooters with girls wrapped around them, or the reverse. Paris looked like a city of couples, but for some reason she didn't feel lonely there. She was happy and excited about what she was doing, and she couldn't wait to go to the archives on Monday. She just hoped she'd find someone who spoke enough English to help her. And if not, she'd manage in her rusty French. Much to her amazement, she wasn't even scared. Everything that she was doing felt right.

After lunch, she wandered through the narrow streets of the Left Bank, and eventually found her way back to her hotel, without asking for directions. And she lay on the bed in her room that night, looking at her notes on Wachiwi again. What she wanted to find now was some mention of her and the marquis somewhere, hopefully at the French court, and maybe then she would discover how she had met him, if it mattered. She had married him and had his children, which was enough. But locating some history of her at court would be the icing on the cake, or what the French called *la cerise sur le gâteau,* the cherry on top of the cake.

Brigitte explored St. Germain des Prés further on Sunday, and went to church. She walked to the Louvre, and strolled along the Seine. And feeling like a tourist, she stood and watched the Eiffel Tower, hoping it would sparkle for ten minutes on the hour, as it did at night. There was no sign of that in the daytime. She had forgotten how much she loved the city – it was beautiful and part of her heritage. So was Ireland, through her father, but she had never had any particular interest in that, nor affinity for it. France was so much more romantic and more fun to read about. She had always been interested in French history, maybe because her mother talked about it so much, and after she was eleven, her father wasn't around, so her link to her Irish ancestors had vanished.

Sunday went by faster than she had expected, and she had dinner at the bistro across the street from her hotel. The food wasn't terrific, but it was good enough, and before she went to bed, she walked back to the Seine again, and watched the Bateaux Mouches drift by, all lit up. She could see Notre Dame in the distance. And the Eiffel Tower did its sparkler act for her at last. She was thrilled by it and felt like a delighted child as she watched. The cab driver had told her on the way in from the airport that it had been doing that since the year 2000 – it sparkled for ten minutes every hour. And even Parisians loved it.

She was excited when she went to bed that night and she woke up early. The hotel served croissants and coffee in the lobby and she helped herself to some and then took a cab to the Bibliothèque Nationale. It was on the Quai François Mauriac, and it was open when she got there. She went to the information desk and explained what she was looking for and the approximate years. They sent her upstairs, where a librarian clearly had no desire to help her. She simply looked annoyed and didn't speak a word of English. It was a far cry from the help she had gotten from the Mormons in Salt Lake.

Brigitte carefully wrote down on a piece of paper what she wanted, what kind of books, and the span of years and subject, and the woman handed it back to her with a stream of hostile French. Brigitte had no idea what to do, and had an overwhelming desire to burst into tears, but she controlled herself, took a breath, and tried again. Eventually, the woman just shrugged, tossed the paper back at her, and walked away. Brigitte stood looking after her, and wanted to hit her, and instead she started to walk away in defeat. She knew she would get nowhere. She wanted to regroup and figure out what she was going to do now. Maybe she had to forget Paris as a resource and go straight to Brittany instead. She turned around to leave the desk, and as she did, she bumped into a man behind her, and expected him to shout at her too. Instead, he smiled.

'Can I help you? They're not very helpful to foreigners here. You have to know what you're looking for very specifically,' he said in excellent English. He had been listening to the exchange. He reached for the paper, and Brigitte handed it to him without a word. He looked as though he was in his early forties. He was French, but spoke English with a British accent, as some educated French people did. But he was obviously fluent. He was wearing jeans and a parka and loafers, and had hair almost as dark as hers. He had warm brown eyes and a nice smile when he looked at her, and he took the piece of paper and approached the desk again. The same woman came up to it, and he explained smoothly in French what he believed Brigitte wanted. The woman nodded, disappeared, came back, and gave him the exact location of the whole section Brigitte was interested in. He hadn't asked for anything different than she did. He had just said it in better French.

'I'm sorry. They're not very nice here. I come here all the time. I can show you where the section is. I did a book on Louis XVI last year. I know where it is.'

'You're a writer?' she asked as he led her to the right section. There were desks and chairs and benches, and endless stacks of books.

'I'm a historian turned novelist because no one buys history unless you lie about it and make it more interesting. The truth is that the real stories are even more intriguing, they're just not as well written. You're a writer too?' He handed her back the piece of paper, with a smile. He was of medium height with slightly tousled hair that gave him a boyish look. And he definitely looked French. He wasn't sexy, he was friendly. She smiled to herself, thinking that Amy would have said he was 'cute.'

'I'm an anthropologist. I'm researching some family history for my mother. Or I was. I fell in love with it, and I guess now I'm doing it for me. I'm hoping to find some diaries about the French court. You wouldn't know of any, would you?' He seemed to be her only hope now of locating anything here.

'There are an enormous number of them. You just have to wade through them. Anything in particular?'

'I'm looking for accounts of the Sioux Indians that Louis XVI invited to the court as guests, and an ancestor of mine who was a marquis.'

'That sounds interesting. You ought to write a novel about it,' he teased.

'I only write academic nonfiction that makes no money and puts people to sleep.'

'So did I, until I started writing historical novels, which is actually a lot of fun. You get to play around with history and add fictional people to the real ones, and they do what you want. Most of the time anyway.' He seemed interested in what she was doing, and he had been very helpful to her.

He went in pursuit of his own research then. Brigitte took down a stack of diaries in the section he had pointed out to her, but she found no mention of Wachiwi or the Margeracs, so it turned out to be a lost day. She ran into him again when she was leaving the archives late that afternoon. She had been there all day, without even stopping for lunch. She had brought an apple in her purse and ate it while she continued reading.

'Did you find anything?' he asked with interest. She shook her head, looking disappointed.

'That's a shame. You have to keep at it. It's here somewhere. Everything is,' he said calmly. But he knew his way around. Brigitte didn't.

'What are you working on?' she asked politely as they left the building together.

'A book about Napoleon and Josephine. It's hardly an unusual subject, but it's fun to write. I teach literature at the Sorbonne, so that pays my rent. But the books help a bit too.'

He was very friendly and open with her, and he introduced himself as they stood on the front steps on the way out. He said his name was Marc Henri. His name sounded familiar, but it was a fairly ordinary French name.

She saw him again the next day as she made her way through the stacks. She still hadn't found anything of interest when he wandered over to her in the late afternoon. And she was exhausted from reading in French. She had to use a dictionary constantly, which made it tedious work.

'What is the name of the ancestor who was the marquis? Perhaps I can find him for you,' he said helpfully, and she wrote it down for him. 'We can cross-reference him in their lists.' And five minutes later Marc had found him.

She was embarrassed by how easy it was for him, and how difficult for her. But the archives were confusing, and it wasn't her language.

They looked up Tristan de Margerac together, and it listed his Paris address in 1785. It was on the Left Bank, and she had a feeling it wasn't far from where she was staying. She wondered what the building was now. But it said nothing about his wife.

'We might find him in some diaries tomorrow,' Marc said hopefully, 'if he went to court often. Did he live in Paris all the time?'

'No, the family seat was in Brittany. I'm planning to go there next week, to visit the château.'

'You have very fancy ancestors,' he teased her, and they both laughed. 'Mine were all either paupers, priests, or in prison. What about the Sioux Indians you're looking for? Are you related to them too?' He was kidding, and didn't expect a positive response when she nodded.

'The marquis married one of them. She was a Sioux Indian, the daughter of a chief in South Dakota. I'm trying to figure out how he met her. I think it must have been at court. But I don't know how she got there, or to France. She's an amazing young girl.'

'She must have been, for a French nobleman to marry her. It would be interesting to know how that happened, wouldn't it?' She told him about her research with the Mormons and at the University of South Dakota then, and he was intrigued. 'That *is* fascinating. I can see why you're pursuing it. I feel that way about Josephine Bonaparte when I read about her. She was a bewitching woman too. And so was Marie Antoinette. I'd give you some books to read about them, but they're all in French.' He casually suggested a drink to her on the way out, and feeling somewhat swept away by their mutual interest in history and research, she agreed. She didn't usually go out with strangers, but there was a café nearby and he seemed like a nice man.

'So tell me, what do you do when you're not chasing your relatives all over France? Do you teach anthropology or only write books?' he asked her, as they sat at a table in the café.

'I worked in the admissions office of Boston University for ten years.' She was about to tell him she had just quit, but decided to tell the truth. 'I got laid off. That means I got fired, and a computer took my job.'

'I'm sorry to hear it. What are you going to do now?'

'This, for a while. And then I'll probably go back to work in the admissions office of another college. There are a lot of them in Boston, that's where I live.'

He smiled as she said it. 'I did a master's in literature at

Harvard, and one at Oxford. I had more fun in Boston. Where do you live?' She told him, and he said he had had an apartment about four blocks from hers. It was a funny coincidence, and then she realized why she had recognized his name. 'You did a book about a little boy who looks for his parents after the war, didn't you? I remember your name now. I read it in translation. It was incredibly touching. They were in the Resistance and had been killed, and another family takes him in, and eventually he married their daughter. It was the sweetest book I ever read, although it was very sad.'

He looked pleased. 'That little boy was my father. My parents actually. My mother is the daughter of the family that took him in. My grandparents were killed in the Resistance. That was my first book. I dedicated it to them.'

'I remember. I cried like crazy when I read it.'

'So did I when I wrote it.' She was impressed that he had written that book. It had been beautifully written even in translation, and very poignant. It had haunted her for weeks after she read it.

'You know, you look a little Indian,' he said, looking at her.

'The woman at the Mormon Family History Library said that too. I think it's just because I have dark hair.'

'I love the idea that you're part Sioux. How exotic. And

how interesting. Most of our histories are so boring, and look at you. An Indian great-great-great-great-whatever-grandmother, who came from America and married a marquis.'

'Better than that, she was kidnapped by another tribe and ran away from her captor. She may have killed him, and then escaped with a Frenchman, or at least a white man, and wound up here. No mean feat for a woman in 1784.'

'Those are powerful genes,' he said admiringly. But so were his, she remembered from the book he'd written. His grandparents had been war heroes and were decorated by de Gaulle posthumously. They had saved countless lives before they lost their own.

'So what about the rest of your life? You write academic books. You worked at a university until recently. Are you married?' He seemed interested in knowing more about her. And so was she, about him. But she was sensible about it too. No matter how appealing he was, she was going home in a few days, and he lived here. So even if they liked each other, all they could ever be was friends. More than that made no sense. She wasn't into casual sex or sleeping with men she'd never see again. And she was still feeling raw after the breakup with Ted. So at best they might be friends. Nothing more.

'No, I'm thirty-eight, I've never been married, and my boyfriend and I just broke up a few weeks ago. He worked at the university too,' she answered simply and honestly.

'Ah,' Marc said with interest, 'both academics. Why did you break up?' He knew it was a little rude to ask her, but he was curious anyway.

'He went to Egypt to run a dig. He's an archaeologist, and he wants to stay there for several years, and he figures it's better like this, going our separate ways. So we broke up.' He was surprised by what she said.

'And you? Were you heartbroken?' He was searching her eyes as he asked, and she shrugged.

'Not really. Disappointed. I thought it was forever. I was wrong.' She tried to sound matter-of-fact about it, more so than she felt. It was still fresh, and not yet healed.

'I had a relationship like that too,' Marc volunteered. 'I went out with a woman for ten years, and we broke up last year. She said she realized she didn't want to be married and have children. I thought she did. I was waiting for her to finish medical school. And when she did, she didn't want me. It feels stupid after ten years. But I realized afterward that we hadn't been in love with each other for a long time. We were in the beginning, for the first few years. After that it was just convenient and easy. Somehow you drift along on the river, and one day you wake up and you're someplace you don't want to be, with someone you realize you don't know. I've never been married either. And after that, I'm not sure I want to be anymore. I gave ten years of my life to that relationship. Now I'm enjoying my freedom and doing what I want. I don't regret the woman, but I'm sorry I stayed in it for so long. I kept thinking it would grow, but it never did.' It was exactly what had happened to her with Ted. Nothing had grown. 'It took me a while to get over it, but I'm fine. We're friends now. I take her to dinner once in a while. She hasn't met anyone else, and I think she'd like to come back, but I won't. I like my life now.'

'I don't think Ted and I will end up friends. Geography, if nothing else. And I was pretty upset about it . . . mostly at myself. I made a lot of assumptions that didn't apply. I missed all the signs.'

'We all do that sometimes. I did it too. Now I'm forty-two and a bachelor. It's not what I expected, but I'm fine like this.' He seemed to have come to terms with it, as she had with Ted.

'Me too,' she said quietly. 'I feel like those posters that say, "Oops, I forgot to have kids," but I did. I was too busy being a kid myself. I think working at a university does that to you. You forget how old you are. You think you're one of them.'

'I agree. I like the class I teach, but I wouldn't want to be there full time. It's a very insular life.' He finished his glass of wine then and smiled at her. 'Shall we take a walk and see where your illustrious ancestor lived?' She had made note of the address at the library that day.

'That would be nice.' She liked his openness and honesty, and he was interesting to talk to. She liked him a lot. She was sorry he didn't live in Boston, he would have made a good friend.

She took the address out of her bag, and he had remembered it himself. It was only a few blocks away from her hotel on the rue du Bac. They found the number easily and looked up at the house when they got there. It was a once-beautiful building that looked somewhat frayed now. The doors to the courtyard were open, and they walked in. Marc explained to her from the signs that were posted that it was occupied by government offices now, as many beautiful old houses on the Left Bank were. But you could see easily what the house had once been, with stalls for the carriages that were garages now, and tall windows, and Marc explained that there was probably a big garden on the other side of the house. It was a handsome place, and as she looked up at it, Brigitte felt the magic of knowing that Tristan de Margerac had once lived there when he was in Paris, and almost certainly Wachiwi had lived there with him. They had no doubt used it when they went to court and stayed in town.

They wandered back out to the sidewalk, and he walked her to her hotel. He asked if she was going back to the archives the next day, and she said she was. He suggested lunch and she agreed. It was fun having someone to talk to about their projects, as she hunted for Wachiwi, and he researched his book.

Marc was waiting for her in the lobby of the library the next day when she arrived. He had looked up some references for her, and she hit pay dirt this time when she checked them out. She almost squealed with delight as soon as she found them, and went running to find him. She had come across a diary where a lady-in-waiting from the court talked about the Marquis de Margerac and his beautiful young Indian bride. She said that she had been at their wedding, in a little church near their house on the rue du Bac. She reported that there had been a small reception at the house afterward, and the next day the new marquise had been presented at court to the king and queen, and she even mentioned Wachiwi by name.

It thrilled Brigitte to realize that their wedding reception had been in the house that she and Marc had looked at the night before. This was incredible, and it was all so real. It still said nothing about how she had come to France. And then, miraculously, later in the afternoon, Brigitte came across another of the same woman's diaries on her own, chronicling court life. She mentioned the birth of Tristan and Wachiwi's first child, and his christening. She said they had named him after the marquis's dead younger brother, who had accompanied Wachiwi from America to France. The woman said that he had saved her, and was planning to marry her, but had died on the trip over. And eventually Wachiwi had married his older brother the marquis instead. So that was how she had come. The younger brother, Jean the count, had rescued her and brought her from New Orleans to Brittany by ship, as the diary explained. The Frenchman mentioned in the oral histories in South Dakota was probably he. Brigitte couldn't help wondering if the Crow chief Wachiwi had supposedly killed when she fled was really killed by Jean who rescued her from them. How he had found her no one would ever know. But now she knew how Wachiwi had come to France. And there were also mentions of the Sioux chiefs who came to court from time to time, but apparently Wachiwi was not related to any of them. The woman who had written the diaries found it a little odd that their king was so obsessed with them. She thought the Indians who visited court an unruly lot, but she had nothing but kind things to say about Wachiwi and said she was a lovely girl, and made the marquis an excellent wife.

Brigitte pored through several more of her diaries, but found no further mention of the marquis and his bride. But now Brigitte had it all.

She was wildly excited when she talked to Marc about it at the end of the day, when they went for a drink again so she could report what she'd found. He said he had had a good day too, and had found some excellent diaries himself, about Josephine, written by her ladies-in-waiting, and one dearest friend.

'And what are you going to do with it now?' Marc asked her with an interested look.

'I don't know, write it up for my mother for her family history. That was the whole purpose of this.'

'That was fine when your ancestors were ordinary people, but they no longer are,' he said with a serious look. 'This girl is remarkable. You have to write a book about her. If you fictionalize it a little, it would make an extraordinary novel. Or even just the way it is. Like my grandparents and parents. Sometimes there is no greater romance than the truth.' Brigitte was unsure, but it was certainly more interesting than the women's vote. That much was sure. But she was scared to tackle Wachiwi's story and not do it justice.

'I'm fascinated by it because I'm related to her. But do

you think other people would be?' Brigitte asked hesitantly. This was way out of her normal realm.

'Of course. You read my book about my father, and he was just a little boy. This girl traveled across continents, oceans, was kidnapped by Indians, married a nobleman. What more do you want? Do you know what happened to them during the Revolution? Were they killed?'

'I don't think so. Their death dates are later than that.'

'Many of the nobles in Brittany resisted, and escaped the guillotine. They held out, and they were a long way from Paris, which helped. But a lot of the Royalists and nobles in Brittany survived. Some even managed to keep their châteaux. The French call those Royalist resistants after the Revolution *Les Chouans*.'

'I'll find out about that when I go to Brittany. I'm going to go down there in a few days.' And then she had a crazy idea, since she hardly knew him, but he had been so helpful so far and they were becoming friends. 'Do you want to come?'

He didn't hesitate for an instant. 'I'd like that very much.' And then she looked nervous. She didn't want him to get the wrong idea. She wasn't propositioning him, she was asking him as a fellow researcher and a friend. He had understood that. He didn't want to spoil their budding friendship either, and he was equally aware that she was going back to the States in a short time, when she finished her research.

'There's no romance involved, by the way,' she clarified, and he laughed. American women were so direct. It had shocked him a little when he went to graduate school in Boston. A Frenchwoman wouldn't have said that in quite that way.

'I understood that. Don't worry. I can help you with your research there.'

'You've been fantastic,' she said, and meant it. He had been invaluable to her, and Providence had brought him to her. If he hadn't turned up, she would never have been able to work the Bibliothèque Nationale on her own. She would be eternally grateful to him for that. She just didn't want to get carried away with him romantically. It didn't make sense, and they'd just get hurt, no matter how appealing she thought he was. They were much better off staying friends, and apparently he agreed.

'I know a nice hotel there, by the way. I'll make the reservations, and yes, I know, *two* rooms, and a chastity belt for the lady.'

'I'm sorry.' She blushed a little. 'Was I rude?'

'No, you were honest, and I like that. We both know where we stand.'

'It would just be silly to start something, and then I go back, and we're both sorry.'

'Are you always so sensible?' He was interested in her as a person, and liked what he knew so far.

She thought about it and then nodded. 'Probably too much so.'

'You don't have to go back, you know. You said you don't have a job. You could work at the American University of Paris, they have an admissions office, and you could write your book here.' He had it all worked out, much to her surprise. He liked organizing people's lives, and helping them get what they wanted. But she didn't want to write a book about her relatives, nor stay in Paris. She was going home.

'I haven't said I would write a book.' She smiled at him. He was looking and sounding very French, and he wanted her to stay. He thought her a very interesting woman, more than anyone he'd met in a while.

'Why don't you talk to them at AUP? You could spend a year here, and see how you like it.' She laughed at the thought. He was crazy. She lived in Boston. And had a book to finish about women's suffrage. But Wachiwi was so much more interesting than the vote. She was what women's freedoms were all about, and had been two hundred years ahead of her time.

He didn't press the point, and they stayed at the bistro and had dinner, and she had an odd feeling as she walked back to the hotel. Tristan and Wachiwi had lived in the house so nearby. They had married, had their wedding reception, had a baby. Their lives had happened so close to where she stood, and hundreds of years later they seemed so alive to her. It was as though they were reaching out to her. She couldn't get them out of her head.

She wondered if Marc was right and she should write a book about them, as a tribute to their love. She was beginning to like the idea. She even liked his suggestion that she work at AUP, but she had a life in Boston she had to go back to, or thought she should. Paris was so seductive, with its sparkling Eiffel Tower, its bistros and cafés, and even Marc, whom she barely knew but liked so far. But she couldn't let herself get seduced by any of it. She was determined to resist the charm of Paris, and even his. They would go to Brittany, she would see what she could find there about her ancestors, and then she was going home. This was real life, not a book. And in real life, people met, nothing happened, and you went home. Or they went off to Egypt and told you that they weren't a commitment kind of guy after six years. That was real life. Not a guy like Marc. Or the marquis.

Chapter 15

Wachiwi
1784–85

The marquis returned from court a week after he had left, and he was happy to see Wachiwi. He came home to find Wachiwi giving Matthieu a riding lesson in the ring. A very sedate one. She wanted to ask Tristan for his permission before she did anything more advanced with his son. She asked him as soon as they met again, and he instantly agreed. He couldn't imagine a riding teacher more competent than Wachiwi, from what he had seen. And she promised not to teach Matthieu any of the wild things she did on her own. But she wanted to teach him to ride bareback and to feel comfortable with their horses.

There was a natural quality to her riding that Tristan wanted to learn from her too, but he suspected it was in her blood, and he would never fully achieve the ease she had. When the governess told him where Matthieu was, and his father went out to the stables to watch, he saw that Matthieu was doing well, and Wachiwi asked Tristan permission to teach him more.

Wachiwi was wearing her elkskin dress and moccasins, and was showing the boy several things about his horse. How to check his muscles, how to feel at one with him. She took the saddle off, and led him bareback around the ring. The boy looked thrilled, and then gave a shout of glee when he saw his father. Wachiwi helped him off so he could run to him, and smiled as Matthieu took off and threw himself into his father's arms.

Wachiwi was planning to give Agathe a short ride on a pony that afternoon, to try and get her over her fears. She had become their new riding mistress while their father was gone. Her methods were unorthodox, by their standards, but her skill was supreme. And Tristan knew that if Matthieu learned from her, he would become an exceptional horseman, and he liked that idea.

He looked over Mathieu's head at Wachiwi and smiled at her. He thanked her for her lessons to his son.

'I enjoy it even more than he does.' She was in the

stables all the time now and rode out in the hills by herself. No other woman in the district did that, but she was totally at ease. There were no dangers here. No war party was going to attack her, or spirit her away. She was safe on his lands. And he suggested they ride together that afternoon. 'How was court?' she asked him politely.

'As it always is. Excessively busy, with too many people and a thousand intrigues. It's very fatiguing, but one has to go. It makes a bad impression to stay away for too long.' But it was a long trip for him from Brittany.

'At least you have a house in Paris to stay at when you're there,' she mentioned, and he nodded.

'Since my wife died, I seldom use it anymore. She enjoyed going to court more than I do, and we went to Paris more often.' Matthieu was running ahead of them as they walked back to the house. He loved his riding lessons with her. And Tristan was excited at the prospect of her teaching the boy more.

'Is your house right in town?'

'Yes, not far from the palace of the Louvre, although the king and queen are more often in Versailles now, which is just outside the city. Perhaps you will go one day,' he said vaguely. He had mentioned her to one of his friends at court, who had said it would be amusing if he brought her. But Tristan felt cautious about his role with her. She had been his late brother's fiancée, and no matter how much he liked her as a person, her presence was still awkward for both of them. She was keeping busy with the riding lessons for the children, and he was grateful to her. He liked the way she was with his children. She was sensible, and warm with them. And he could see how much they liked her. When he went to the nursery to see Agathe after his trip, she threw herself into Wachiwi's arms first, and then her father's. She was hungry for the mother she had never had. Mademoiselle was no substitute for the mother she had lost. Wachiwi wanted only to be her friend, and had hoped to be her aunt.

The riding lessons continued over the next several months. Matthieu became noticeably more proficient, and Wachiwi taught his father a few of her 'tricks' (as he called them). She had taken his breath away one day when she showed him how she could conceal herself along the side of a horse at full speed. He wasn't about to try it, but she seemed to become part of the horse, and hang in space as they flew and she clung to the heavy beast. She had no fear at all. She could stand on the horse's back as it galloped, and leap onto its back from the ground. She had a magic with horses and they did things for her they would do for no one else.

His children adored her, and even Agathe had come to

enjoy her pony rides now. She would never be a horse-woman, her mother hadn't been, but she wasn't frightened anymore, and she loved feeding her pony an apple when she got off.

Another thing they had all noticed about her was how silent Wachiwi was. Particularly in her moccasins, but even in normal shoes, Wachiwi made absolutely no sound when she walked. She seemed to walk on air. Her father had frequently commented on it too. She had the grace of a butterfly and made as little noise. The Dancer was the perfect name for her.

She was able to laugh at herself too, which was a trait that Tristan admired in her. When she did something silly or wrong, she made a joke of it and herself, and they all laughed with her. She had a multitude of good traits, all of which Tristan appreciated and admired in her. He had never been as comfortable with any other woman before.

'I want a dress like Wachiwi's,' Agathe said one day as they went back to the house in a group, and her governess instantly gave her a furious look. She thought Wachiwi's native dress disgraceful as it molded her figure and ended just below her knees. Despite the leggings she wore beneath, the governess thought her native costume shock-ing. It looked well worn now, and Agathe's remark gave Wachiwi an idea. She sewed almost as well as she rode, and had made a little doll for Agathe for Christmas, and a small bear for Matthieu, and they loved them.

It was spring by then and the weather had been unseasonably warm in Brittany. They had a picnic in the garden one day, on a cliff overlooking the sea. The king had been sick that winter, and the queen had given birth to the Duke of Normandy only weeks before. So the marquis had only gone to court once, but he was planning to go again soon. He hated to make the long trip but knew he should. And he wanted to bring a gift to the new royal baby. But he was so much happier in the country, with his children, on his own land. There was always so much to do. This spring they had been busy cutting down trees that had been damaged in storms during the winter. And he loved talking to Wachiwi about what he did on the property. She was always interested and offered him excellent ideas, which sometimes amazed him coming from a young girl.

He surprised her one afternoon after a long ride, when he asked her to have dinner with him that night in the dining room. He had never asked her before. She usually took her meals in the nursery with the children. They loved her company, although their governess still didn't.

Wachiwi accepted his invitation with pleasure. She always enjoyed her conversations with him. They spoke of many things – he was very knowledgeable, and her French was proficient now. The one thing she didn't know, and wished to learn, was how to read. He had promised to teach her, but hadn't had time to do it that winter. She wanted to read the books in his library. They looked fascinating to her.

He told her about some of the current intrigues at court that night at dinner, and why they fatigued him. People had been complaining about the queen and her extravagance for several years. Tristan had always found Marie Antoinette a pleasant woman, even if silly when she was young. But now that she had begun having babies in the past few years, she seemed more serious to him, and more mature. He had no patience with the politics and manipulations of the ministers, the courtesans, and all the opportunists who gravitated to the court. He told Wachiwi that the queen was Austrian, not French, which people tended to forget, and she had become queen as barely more than a child. Her marriage was arranged when she was fourteen. Wachiwi explained that that happened in Indian culture too. Girls married very young, and most marriages were arranged. She was grateful her father hadn't done that to her. Undeniably, the queen had led the court into incredible excesses and people were constantly vying for her favor and her ear. It was a lot of power for a young girl. But it was all too much for him. He was a quiet man who enjoyed managing his vast properties, and spending time in the outdoors. They were still talking about the court at the end of dinner, and Wachiwi found what he told her very interesting, but she could tell that he didn't. Jean had told her that he had never liked court much either, and had been happy to flee to the New World, rather than get caught up in the intrigues of the court. But as head of the family and owner of extensive lands, the marquis couldn't avoid his responsibilities to the king, and couldn't shun going to court. It was even more tedious for him now without his wife. At least he had enjoyed showing her off and dancing with her. Now he stood talking politics with the men all night.

As they left the dining room, Tristan turned to her with a warm smile. Their evenings together were always pleasant, and they had stayed at table that night for a long time. He was lonely at times, and had been since his wife's death, and he envied Wachiwi her nightly dinners in the nursery with his children. He would have enjoyed that too, but it would have seemed odd for him to be there. Something had occurred to him that night during dinner, and he suggested it cautiously to Wachiwi.

'Would you like to come to court with me next time? I have to go in a few weeks. It might be interesting for you to see it, and I'm sure the king and queen would like to meet you.' She was very flattered to be asked. She was worried that she didn't have the proper clothes, but he said he'd see to it that the local dressmaker made something suitable for her, and she thanked him for his kind invitation. She mentioned it to the children the next day, and they were excited for her. Agathe said she thought she should wear her pretty dress with the porcupine quills, and Wachiwi smiled mysteriously when she said it. The child's birthday was a few days away, and Wachiwi had been working on a present for her for months, and it was almost ready.

It had been singularly hard for her to find all the materials she needed for the gift. In her village all of it would have been easy. Here it was a challenge to find each piece she needed. She hadn't been able to find elkskin, but she had been able to buy deerskin in the village, which reminded her of Jean's buckskin trousers that she had given away when he died. The porcupine quills had taken months to find. Tristan's game warden had gotten them for her. And she was delighted to find the right berries to make the paste she needed to dye them. She had taken the beads off the shirt she'd made for Jean. She preferred to give them to his niece now. She had carefully sewn them on the tiny deerskin dress. And she had had enough left over to make a pair of moccasins for her. And on Agathe's birthday she carefully wrapped the gifts in a soft red cloth and tied it, and she gave the package to her in the nursery that morning. The child squealed with glee when she saw them. She insisted on putting them on immediately much to Mademoiselle's horror, and to Wachiwi's delight they fit perfectly. It was an exact replica of her own dress with the porcupine quills, only it was fresh and new and perfectly proportioned for her, and the moccasins fit her small feet exactly. Agathe was so excited that she ran downstairs to show her father, without asking for her governess's permission. And the moment her father saw her, he burst out laughing.

'You look like a little Sioux!' Agathe was beaming and preened proudly for him. And when Wachiwi followed her downstairs, he thanked her. 'Now if you can teach me to ride like one, I will be very happy.' But she had already taught him enough that he had become a far more skilled rider, and so had Matthieu. She had shared many of her talents and customs with them, and it was hard for any of them to believe that she had already been there for five months. Doing little things for them was the only way she could think of to repay them for their kindness. She still had no idea where to go, or what she would do when she left them, but she knew that sooner or later, she had to move on, whether she wanted to or not. She couldn't take advantage of Tristan's kindness and hospitality forever. But in the meantime, the dress and shoes for Agathe were an enormous success.

And the gown Tristan had made for Wachiwi for court was even more so. It arrived the day before they left for Paris. It fit her perfectly, and she looked spectacular in it. It was a heavenly pink satin, and had a deep décolletage and an enormous skirt with huge extensions on either side, beautiful sleeves trimmed with lace, and a lace shawl to wear with it. The color was very flattering to her, and Agathe gasped when Wachiwi tried the dress on, and assured her that she looked like a queen. She showed Tristan and he approved as well. The gown was packed in its own trunk, and she took several of the dresses Jean had given her the year before. All of her things were carried in a separate coach when they left for Paris. They rode in Tristan's elegant carriage.

The children waved goodbye when they left, and Wachiwi looked nervous and excited. She and Tristan chatted easily on the long two-day drive. They had left the château at nearly dawn, drove into the evening, and stopped at an inn along the road. The accommodations were decent but no more than that, and on the second day, they arrived in Paris after midnight. The house in Paris had been prepared for them. There were candles burning everywhere, the furniture had been polished till it gleamed, and one of the bedrooms had been opened and aired for her. She was sleepy when she walked into the house on the rue du Bac, but dazzled when she saw the main hall, the beautiful marble staircase, and her apartment. And it had been exciting just driving through the city late at night. Tristan had gone to his own rooms once he put Wachiwi into the hands of the housekeeper and told her he would see her in the morning.

She could hardly sleep that night she was so excited, and she was up early the next morning. She was surprised to see Tristan already downstairs, finishing his breakfast. He left shortly after, saying he had business to attend to. He told Wachiwi to rest all day, and they would leave for court that afternoon. A hairdresser was coming to do her hair, and would powder it if she wished, but she didn't like the idea, and preferred to leave it her natural color. And since the king was expecting her visit and knew she was a Sioux, he might be disappointed if, like everyone else at court, she had white hair. It was a style that had been set by the young queen, who had a passion for all things white.

She went for a walk that afternoon and took one of the grooms to escort her, as was the custom. She walked for a long time, and found her way to the Seine, where she looked at the water, the bridges, the boats drifting by, and the buildings on the opposite bank. She had never seen anything so lovely as Paris, and it didn't frighten her at all.

She looked invigorated when she got back to the house, and the hairdresser was waiting for her by then. By the time Tristan got home, she was almost ready, and two of the maids and the housekeeper helped to dress her. Her undergarments and corseting were far more complicated now than when Jean had dressed her in St. Louis and New Orleans. And she looked exquisite when she walked down to Tristan, waiting for her at the foot of the grand staircase. He was in pale blue satin knee breeches, and a red brocade coat with a jabot of lace at his neck, and his hair had been powdered. She hardly recognized him. He smiled broadly when he saw her. He had never seen a woman look as lovely as Wachiwi in her new gown.

He complimented her as they got into the carriage, and it seemed like only moments later they were at the palace, as they chatted on the way. He could tell that she was nervous and she admitted it to him shyly. He patted her hand reassuringly, and told her she would be wonderful. He was sure of it.

The royal family had wintered at the Louvre, but they were already at their summer residence in Versailles, and Wachiwi could never have dreamed of anything as opulent as the hall they entered. The grounds and gardens and orchards had already impressed her as they arrived. They were led to where the king and queen were receiving, in a small private room before they joined the others. Tristan whispered to her just before they walked in, to remind her to make a deep curtsy to them both. She executed it to perfection, and the king thought her charming. Marie Antoinette ignored her, as she often did with guests. She was whispering to two of her ladies-in-waiting who were huddled near her. But the king more than made up for his inattentive wife, and eventually Marie Antoinette acknowledged her, and she and Wachiwi ended up giggling like two girls. Tristan was delighted and thought their audience with the king and queen had gone exceptionally well.

The king had asked about her tribe with interest. She told him about her father and five brothers, and Tristan added that she had a warrior's skills with a horse. And then they left the room to join the hundreds waiting for the king and queen to enter. When they did, dinner was served, and there was music and dancing. People were milling about, talking to each other, trying to make deals and exchange information and trading gossip. Tristan introduced her to several of his friends, who were visibly intrigued by her, but neither disapproving of her nor shocked, as they had been in New Orleans. This was a far more sophisticated group and because she was an Indian, she was of greater interest to them. Her shining black hair had been arranged in enormous curls on top of her head, and the fact that it wasn't powdered made her stand out more. Wachiwi was a great success, and Tristan was the envy of all the men who saw her. She couldn't help thinking that this was a long, long way from the slave quarters to which she had been banished in New Orleans. And she looked as elegant as all the other women there in the dress that the marquis had ordered for her.

She was having such a good time she didn't want to leave. She loved watching people dance although she had no idea how to do it, and she thought the music was lovely. It reminded Tristan that he really ought to teach her how to dance, particularly if he brought her to court again, which was beginning to seem likely. She had been far too big a hit not to bring her back, and she enjoyed it so much that he didn't want to deprive her of some fun. It made everything far more pleasant for him as well, and for the first time in years he wasn't bored all evening at court. He had fun watching her be fussed over, talk to people, and make friends.

She was still talking excitedly about everything as the carriage drove them back to the house on the rue du Bac, and he smiled as he listened to her. She looked as animated as Agathe after a birthday party with her friends.

'I'm glad you enjoyed it,' he said to Wachiwi easily, relaxing in the carriage, happy that it was over. Even though he had had a much better time with her there, he always found visits to the court fatiguing and stressful, and the powder in his hair made him sneeze. She teased him about it as they rode along. She felt very important and very special, and she turned with a grateful look at him.

'Thank you for being so kind to me, Tristan. I had a wonderful time.' She only wished that Jean had been there. They both did. She still missed him, and so did his brother. 'It was the most perfect evening of my life.' She expressed it so elegantly that he smiled. He had been very proud of her that night. So many people had approached her, and then afterward praised her to Tristan, he was actually surprised. He had expected at least some of the women to be critical of her, but they weren't. They seemed only too happy to welcome her, and she was so innocent and open with everyone that they willingly embraced her. The king had made a point of telling him to be sure to bring her back.

When they reached the house, they chatted for a few minutes, and then said goodnight and went to their respective rooms, where the housekeeper helped her out of her finery Wachiwi lay awake for most of the night, replaying every moment of the evening in her head, and still unable to believe she'd been to court. It was even better than she had expected, and far more wonderful than anything she'd hoped. And she had been very proud to be at court with Tristan, who as always had been so kind to her. And after a brief sleep, she was up early the next morning, and they met at breakfast again.

Tristan offered to show her some of the sights that day, and she could hardly wait to see them. They visited the gardens at the Palais Royal near the Louvre, and walked in the Tuileries Gardens. They drove to Notre Dame and the Place des Vosges in the Marais. She was bursting with excitement again when they got back to the house, and they had a quiet dinner that night in the dining room before going back to Brittany the next day. She was anxious to tell the children what it had been like to meet the king and queen. She had particularly promised to tell Agathe everything about it. And she was going to tell her how handsome her father had looked in his red brocade coat and blue satin breeches, and his elegant shoes with the buckles.

He looked entirely different when he got into the carriage to leave. He was wearing easy traveling clothes and a long black coat to protect his clothes from the dust on the road, and he covered Wachiwi with a blanket before they left in the cool morning air.

They talked for many hours this time as they rode along, and they stopped at small inns for lunch and dinner, and again for the night at an inn by the side of the road. The trip seemed to go faster on the way back, but it was still late on the second day of traveling when they reached the Château de Margerac, and everyone was sleeping. She thanked him again, and he told her that her trunks would be brought up in the morning. The men were tired from the long trip.

And even before breakfast, Wachiwi ran up the stairs to tell the children all about Paris and their evening at the court. Agathe said she wanted to go too one day, and Wachiwi said that she was sure she would. Her father would take her there and be very proud of her in a beautiful dress that he would have made for her, and she would look like a princess.

'And will you come too?' Agathe asked with dancing eyes, and Wachiwi hesitated before she answered. She didn't know it, but Tristan was waiting for the answer too. He had just walked into the nursery when Agathe asked her the question, and Wachiwi hadn't seen him.

'I don't know if I'll be here,' Wachiwi told her honestly. She never lied to children, or to anyone else. She was unfailingly honest. Her father had taught her that as a child. His wisdom and honesty had made him a great chief, respected by all who knew him. 'That will be a long time from now, you know, and by then I'll be an old woman, and I don't know where I'll be.'

'I want you to be here with us,' Agathe said, looking worried.

'Then she will be,' her father said, stepping forward, and Wachiwi looked startled and bade him good morning.

'By then, you'll know everything there is to know about riding,' she said to him and his children with a smile. It had been an awkward moment for them all. 'And I'll be too old to teach you. I'll have to ride Agathe's pony.' The child giggled when she said it, which lightened the mood again. And the children claimed their father's attention, as Wachiwi quietly slipped away and went back to her rooms.

Tristan found her there a few minutes later, after he left the nursery. 'The children want you to stay, Wachiwi, and so do I.' He addressed the issue immediately. He hadn't liked her answer either, nor had his children. They had brought it up again when she left the room.

'I can't impose on you forever,' she said so elegantly that it was hard for him to believe she had only spoken French for a year, thanks to his brother's foresight.

'You're not imposing. We like having you here. You

make my children happy.' And then he spoke more softly to her in a voice raw with emotion. 'You make me happy too, although I don't say it.' He looked into her eyes, and it was easy for him to see why his brother had loved her. She was at the same time gentle and strong, and always kind to all of them. She was fierce in some ways, and as light as a feather in others. He had come to realize that she was the perfect woman. For him, and his children. And there was no one for him to ask if he could court her. 'Will you stay with us?' he asked solemnly.

'For as long as you want me to,' she reassured him. He nodded gratefully, and with a troubled look, he left the room. She didn't see him again until later that afternoon, when he found her in the garden. He walked with her for a while, and together they sat on a bench and looked out at the sea.

'It feels like you've always been here,' he said quietly.

'Sometimes it does to me too, and then at other times I think of my father and brothers and my village.'

'Do you miss them a great deal?' She nodded and a tear sneaked down her cheek, and he gently wiped it away, and touched her face in a way he never had before, and then without warning, he leaned over and kissed her. He didn't want her to think he was taking advantage of her, and he quickly pulled away. She looked up at him, still surprised.

He had never shown any interest in her in that way before, and she didn't know what it meant that he had kissed her now.

He had wanted to wait a month or two for an opportune moment, but he had made the decision in Paris, and now he wanted to tell her, so that she would know his intentions were honorable toward her. He was not looking for a mistress, he wanted a wife.

'I want you to stay here, Wachiwi, for as long as you live, for as long as we both live.' He looked at her meaningfully, and she still looked puzzled.

'That's very kind of you, Tristan, but if you marry again, your wife won't like that. She won't want an Indian girl staying here.' She smiled shyly at him as she said it. She thought the kiss a moment before had been an aberration of some kind, never to be repeated. With Jean she had known immediately that he was in love with her, but Tristan was different with her. He was quieter, and always courteous, but he didn't show his emotions. He had learned to hide them as a young man and still did.

'I don't think we should worry about how my future wife would feel about you,' he said cryptically.

'Why not?' she asked him with wide innocent eyes that melted his heart. He had realized for a while that he had been in love with her from the first moment he saw her, but with Jean's recent death, and her reason for coming here, the situation had been too awkward to let himself even think about it or say anything to her. But now he felt he had to. He couldn't keep his feelings for her a secret any longer nor did he want to.

'Because you're the only wife I want, Wachiwi.' He got down on one knee then, next to the bench where she was sitting, and took her hand in his own. 'Will you marry me?' And then he added what he had wanted to say for months, and hadn't even allowed himself to feel. 'I love you.'

'I love you too,' she said softly, lowering her eyes. She had known it for months too, and loved every moment she spent with him, and his children, but she had never dared to think that her feelings for him would be returned.

He took her in his arms then and kissed her hard. They sat on the bench talking for a long time, making plans. By the time they walked back to the château, they had agreed to marry in Paris in June, with the children present, and he would present her at court as the Marquise de Margerac the next day.

They told the children when they got back to the house, and Agathe and Matthieu jumped all over the nursery laughing and shouting and they both kissed Wachiwi. The governess slipped quietly out of the room then, and gave her notice the next morning. The children were thrilled about that too. But most of all they were thrilled that Wachiwi would be their mother now, and so was she. They didn't want a governess anymore, they had her. Forever. And Tristan did too.

Chapter 16

For the next two months, Tristan and Wachiwi rode together, walked in the gardens, made plans, had dinner in the dining room every night, and talked endlessly of all the things they hoped to do in the future. He wanted children with her, but he admitted that he was terrified that he would lose her as he had Agathe and Matthieu's mother.

'That won't happen,' she reassured him. 'I am very strong.'

'So was she,' he said sadly. 'Sometimes bad things happen when you least expect them.' She knew that was true, she had learned that with Jean, and all that had happened to her before that. She had never expected to be kidnapped by the Crow. And she always wondered what had become of her father after she left. She didn't know and never would.

'It won't happen to us,' she said quietly. She felt sure of it. She wanted to have his babies. She was surprised that nothing had occurred with Jean in the few months they had been together. She hoped that she wasn't like one of those women in the village who never produced children. They had been looked upon as defective and freaks of nature. And she wanted to have a child of their own soon. She loved Agathe and Matthieu, but she wanted to carry Tristan's children, as many as she could have. 'Perhaps by this time next year, I will be able to give you a son,' she said, looking proud in anticipation of it, and then a cloud passed over her eyes. 'Would you mind if we call him Jean, in honor of your brother?'

'I would like that very much,' he said quietly. He knew that she had loved him, but he wasn't troubled by it. He felt now as though his brother had brought her home for him, that it was what destiny had wished. And although Wachiwi had loved him, she had told Tristan that she loved him more. She had never really known what love was, she said, until him. She had still been a girl when she and Jean met at the lake, innocent and foolish to take such enormous risks. Now she felt like a woman, wise, and strong, and sure of what she felt for Tristan. She was his.

The next two months passed quickly, and in June, Wachiwi and Tristan and the children set out for Paris.

Agathe slept on her lap much of the time, and to keep him entertained on the long trip, Matthieu rode with the coachman. And finally, very late on a warm summer night, they reached their home in Paris. All the servants were waiting for them, the house was filled with flowers, and everything was ready for their wedding the next day. Handwritten invitations had gone out weeks before to Tristan's closest friends in Paris. Because it was his second marriage and his brother had died within the year, they wanted to keep the wedding small.

The children went to the nursery, and the housekeeper stayed with them. Wachiwi couldn't sleep, she was too excited. She kept thinking of how she had gotten here, and how blessed she was to belong to Tristan now. She could hardly wait to become truly his, in the eyes of God, and man, and in his arms as well. She wasn't an innocent girl this time. She was a warm, loving woman and wanted to welcome him into her heart, her body, and her life. She was a passionate woman, and beneath Tristan's cool exterior, his desire had been smoldering for her for months. Only respect for his late brother and Wachiwi had kept him silent for so long. He was standing in his room that night, looking out the window, and thinking that in the morning, the most beautiful girl in the world would be his.

He left for the church before her, and she came a few minutes later with the children in the carriage. He had asked two of his closest friends to serve as witnesses, since Wachiwi had no one in France except Tristan and his children. The ceremony was Catholic in a tiny chapel on the rue du Bac, close to the house. She had asked to become Catholic and had been studying with a priest in Brittany for the past two months. She had been baptized before their wedding. She wanted to do anything to please him.

Their friends attended them at the wedding, and his children stood beside them, and Wachiwi held Agathe's hand as Tristan looked into her eyes in a way no other man had before. Matthieu stood solemnly next to his father. And Agathe held her bouquet of lily of the valley as Tristan took Wachiwi's hand.

They said their vows, and he slipped a narrow diamond band on her finger. He had given her a large emerald ring as well, but this was the one she knew she would always wear. She was wearing a white satin dress that the queen herself had lent her when she heard about the marriage. She said she had so many dresses like it that it was nothing to her to give this one to Wachiwi for her wedding. And she still hadn't lost all the weight from the baby she'd had three months before. And as they walked out of the church together as man and wife, Wachiwi looked as beautiful as any queen. The Marquise de Margerac, a chief's daughter of the Sioux nation, had come home.

They all had lunch at the house together, and that night it was filled with friends and well-wishers dancing and drinking champagne. They stayed until early in the morning, and when Wachiwi and Tristan finally walked upstairs to their bedroom, she felt as though she had belonged to him all her life. She had been born for him, in a Sioux village far from here, and she had come across a continent and an ocean, for this moment in time, and this man. She looked up at him once he closed the door to their bedroom, and gently slipped the white satin dress off her shoulders. It took some doing, but finally it fell to the floor, and a few minutes later he saw her, just as Jean had, when he discovered her at the lake in all her naked beauty. Her skin shimmered in the moonlight, as she reached her arms out to him, and he gently laid her on their bed.

It was the moment they had both waited for and desperately wanted, the moment when they became one body and one soul, when she was truly his. He melted into her as though there had never been another time, another place. They lay together and clung to each other and later knew they had become one forever that night as the sun came up. He was her destiny, and now at last she was his.

They stayed in Paris for three days after that. She was presented at court as the Marquise de Margerac the day after the wedding, and everyone cheered and called when the crier said her name. Rivers of champagne were poured, and she danced with Tristan all night, and once with the king. Tristan had given her dancing lessons in Brittany in preparation for this day.

Her wedding day had been the happiest day of her life, and her presentation at court as his wife completed it. Marie Antoinette had been equally excited for her, and had embraced her warmly, admiring a new dress Wachiwi wore that Tristan had ordered. It was a brilliant red brocade and looked incredible with her skin and hair. And she was wearing a ruby necklace that had been his mother's. They went home together late that night, and discovered the wonders of each other's bodies again.

They took the children all over Paris, and then went back to Brittany. They almost hadn't gone back to court before they left, but Wachiwi thought they should and convinced Tristan to do so. He was in such good spirits after their wedding, he didn't mind. He wanted to do whatever his bride wanted, and knew she was right to pay their respects to the king and queen before they left town again, and they both realized afterward that her impulse to do so had been destiny. There was a Dakota

Sioux chief being presented at court when they arrived.

He was a tall, imposing-looking man, younger than her father, with fierce eyes, but he smiled when he saw her and so did she. He said he had met her once with her father when she was a child, although she didn't remember him. But he knew her father well and she recalled his name. He was Chief Wambleeska, White Eagle, and two of his sons had made the trip with him to France. In a combination of court garb and native dress, the three men were an impressive sight, and Chief White Eagle began speaking to her in Dakota as soon as they were introduced. It made Wachiwi's heart ache to hear it, and long more than ever for her father and brothers. She had to fight back tears as they spoke.

Within a few minutes she asked him if he had news of her father. Chief White Eagle had made reference to her kidnapping by the Crow and said that the death of their chief had become legend among the Dakota Sioux. She was thought to have become a spirit after she vanished, and he was stunned to see her here.

'And my father?' she asked softly, as Tristan watched her face, guessing what she had asked from the look of pain and hope in her eyes. He feared what she would hear, and so did she. She always said her father had been very old and frail and she was born late in his life.

Chief White Eagle spoke for several minutes with a stern look on his face. Wachiwi nodded and a few minutes later, the chief was whisked away to meet other people at the court. He made a sign of peace to her and the marquis, and Tristan looked at his wife with a puzzled expression. It had been startling listening to them speak Dakota here.

'What did he say?' Tristan asked softly, and there were tears swimming in Wachiwi's eyes when she looked at him and answered.

'The Great Spirit took my father before the winter came, before they even got to winter camp.' She had known it in her heart for months. It had been a year since she was kidnapped by the Crow, and her father had been gone for most of it. She would never see him again, but at least she knew now that he was at peace, and so was she. Their destinies had led them on different paths to where they were meant to be. And he had died of a broken heart without her, just as she had feared. It made her hate Napayshni all over again and not regret what had happened in the forest. It was retribution for what he'd done to her brothers, and her father.

'I'm sorry,' Tristan said softly as they left the court, and she nodded and held his arm. It made her heart ache to think of her father dying of grief, but at least she knew now. And they were both free. He had led a good life, and hers was ahead of her, with Tristan, his children, and their own. And she knew that, like Jean, her father would live in a peaceful place in her heart forever. She was sad but felt at peace.

She had asked Chief White Eagle to bring news of her to her brothers and tell them that she was well and happy, and married to a good man. He promised to do so, but said he did not know when he would leave France again.

She leaned her head against Tristan in the carriage on the way home. And they made love again that night. She lay in his arms, thinking of the new life that had begun for them. And when she slept, she dreamed of the white buffalo again, and a white dove flying near its head. She saw her father in the dream and when she woke in the morning, she saw Tristan smiling at her and knew her life was perfect as it was.

They went back to Brittany that day, and once back at the château, she moved into his bedroom, and they went for long walks together every day. They walked along the sea. She thought about her father and felt peaceful about him. And she and Tristan went riding for a few weeks, and then one morning in August, he suggested they go for a ride together in the woods, and she shook her head with a small smile as she looked at him.

'I can't,' she said quietly.

'Why not? Are you ill?' He looked concerned, but she had already understood what was happening, and as he looked at her, he suddenly did too.

'Oh my God, are you sure?' She nodded solemnly. She was certain it had happened on their wedding night, just as it was meant to be. There would be a baby in the spring. They both hoped it would be a boy called Jean, in honor of the man who had brought them together. Jean had brought Wachiwi to Tristan, he had saved her, and brought her home where she belonged, forever, with Tristan and their family. She knew then that the white buffalo in her dream had led her home to him.

Chapter 17

Brigitte

Marc and Brigitte left Paris on a sunny April morning for Brittany, in his ridiculously tiny car that made her laugh when she saw it. She had never seen anything so small, but it made sense for Paris. She wasn't quite as amused to be on the highway in it, but he assured her it was safe. It looked like a toy car to her, and her small overnight bag took up most of the backseat. His even smaller one filled the trunk.

They drove at a reasonable speed for several hours while Marc told her about his new book. He was deeply engaged in the intricacies of Napoleon's relationship with Josephine, and its subtle effects on the politics of France, and it sounded fascinating to her. She smiled as she listened to him. What he said and how he analyzed things were so French. He was passionate about politics, but the love relationship between the two historical figures was crucial to him as well. She loved the combination of the two, the emotional and the analytical, the historical and the political. She was sure it would be a good book. He was a very bright, erudite man.

'So will yours be when you write it, about the little Indian girl,' he said with a knowing smile. He had an intelligent face, and a kind expression, and his eyes lit up when he talked to her. There was so much about him that she liked. She was sorry that geography made anything more than friendship undesirable for both of them, especially for her.

'What makes you think I'll write it?' she asked him, curious why he seemed so certain that she would.

'How can you not? With all that you know, have discovered, and can deduce between the lines, how could you possibly resist a story like that? It's action, adventure, mystery, history, and romance. And think of the time they were living in, the days of slavery in America, the last years before the Revolution in France. And what happened to them afterward? Did he lose his château? Was he a Royalist resistant? What happened to their children? The Indian piece makes it even more fascinating. And from a love angle, she came to France with one brother, and married another. How did she escape the Crow? Did she really kill her captor? Was she dangerous or an innocent girl? You have enough for ten books there, not just one.' He said it almost enviously with a wistful look in his eyes.

'Maybe you should write the book,' she said seriously.

He was quick to shake his head. 'It's your story, not mine. Writers don't respect much, but I do respect that. Honor among thieves,' he said, and laughed as he looked at her, and then grew serious again. 'I truly hope you write it, Brigitte.' He always pronounced her name in French, and she liked it. 'I think you should come back and do more research, and spend a year or two writing it here.' And then he added with a meaningful look, 'I would like that very much. I can help you, if you like.'

'You already have,' she said sincerely. 'I would never have found the court diaries without your help. I wouldn't know as much as I do now if I hadn't found them. I would never have known that the marquis's younger brother brought her here and died on the way. I thought she just got lucky and married a marquis. The real story is so much more interesting than that, and more complicated.' She had to agree with him, it would make a wonderful book. It was more than just family history, it was an important record of the times, in both countries, America and France.

'That's why you have to write it. I'm going to continue annoying you until you do. Besides, I have a vested interest in this.'

'And what's that?' She was teasing him and enjoying their banter. They hardly knew each other, and yet she felt completely at ease with him. She wondered if Wachiwi had felt that way with her marquis, or if he had been daunting. There was nothing daunting about Marc. On the contrary, she felt relaxed and so at ease with him, and she enjoyed their conversations on a variety of subjects.

'My vested interest,' he confessed, 'is that I want you to come to Paris, and stay for a while. Long-distance relationships are too hard, and I don't like them. In the end, they always fall apart. I like Boston, but I've already lived there. I'm too old for the student life, and even the life of an academic, and I'm much too old to be traveling every few weeks. It's too tiring, and I have to write. So do you. You can't commute to Paris either. Long distance won't work.' He spoke as though a relationship were a serious option, for both of them. It seemed premature to her.

'I thought we were just friends,' she said calmly.

'Is that all you want?' he asked her honestly, taking his eyes off the road to look at her, but there was very little traffic.

'I don't know what I want,' she said truthfully. 'Maybe

it's enough for now. And you're right. Long distance doesn't work, which is why my boyfriend and I broke up.'

'Do you miss him?' Marc asked, curious about how she felt. He had asked her that before, and she thought about it again now.

'Sometimes. I miss having someone familiar in my life. I'm not sure how much I really miss him. I'll probably know when I go back to Boston.'

'That's not missing him then. That's just missing having a generic boyfriend. If you missed *him*, as a person, you would miss him here too.' She thought about it and realized he was right. And the odd thing was that after six years of evenings and weekends and dinners and daily phone calls, she didn't miss Ted that much. She missed being able to tell him things, like what she had discovered about Wachiwi, but she didn't long for him like a woman who lost the love of her life. He hadn't been. It had been easy. And she had been too lazy to want more. She thought that was a terrible statement about herself, and she shared it with Marc. He was less critical of her than she was of herself.

She had thought a lot about the relationship with Ted since it had ended. There hadn't been enough there to justify keeping it going for six years, with no future plans between them. She had just 'assumed.' It was so stupid, and yet it was so easy to do. Easier than facing what wasn't there. And now she was thirty-eight years old with no man in her life, no future plans, and no kids. Not even a job now. Because she had assumed that that would last forever too. And the worst of it was that she had been passionate about neither, neither the man nor the job. She had settled for 'good enough,' mediocrity, and no passion. Worst of all, for the last decade, she realized now, she hadn't been honest with herself, or demanded much. She had settled. She didn't want to do that again. Nor did she want to get into something she couldn't handle, or that didn't make sense. Like a long-distance relationship between Paris and Boston. And he didn't seem to want that either. So they would have to be friends.

'What about you?' she asked him. 'Do you miss the woman you were with?'

'Not anymore,' he said, truthful again. 'I did in the beginning. It was convenient, but not enough. I'll never do that again. I'd rather be by myself than settle for so little.' And then he smiled at her, looking very Gallic. 'Or with you.' He was charming, and had been enormously helpful to her, but it was too soon to know if he was sincere. Maybe he was just smooth. But it sounded good when he said it, and she took it at face value. A flirtatious thing to say and nothing more.

They rode on in silence for a while after that, and stopped for lunch at a quaint inn he knew in Fougères. He told her about the region they were in, and its history. He knew a lot about many things – literature, history, politics. He was an intelligent man, and she was grateful she had met him. He had been invaluable to her research, and her mother would be thrilled with all that she'd found. The project seemed to have grown beyond its original purpose, and she now knew so much more than just a list of her ancestors, and when they lived and died. Wachiwi had become a little sister, a symbol of courage and freedom, an inspiration, a best friend.

'Tell me about the Chouans,' Brigitte asked him as they finished lunch. He had referred to them several times now, and she knew it had to do with Royalist resistants in the aftermath of the French Revolution, but she didn't know much more than that, and it was obvious that he did.

'You should read Balzac's book on the subject,' he suggested helpfully. '*Les Chouans* were the nobles and their supporters who refused to give in to the Revolution. In Paris, with rare exceptions, they lost their heads, and whatever they had – their houses, châteaux, lands, money, jewels, and mostly their lives, unless they were able to escape, but few did. The revolutionaries wanted revenge for years of oppression and inequality, and they wanted all the royals and nobles and aristocrats killed, and they made it happen. But the heat of the battle was in Paris. Farther away, particularly in a region called La Vendée, and Brittany, where your ancestors lived, the battle was not so thick, and the resisters were stronger. Many of them refused to surrender their châteaux, and put up a fight. *Les Chouans* are all of those who resisted, and also *les Vendéens*, but the heart of the resistance was in Brittany. Many kept their châteaux, although some were badly burned by the revolutionaries. But they weren't able to kill as many aristocrats in Brittany. They didn't have the forces they did in Paris, so the Royalists held their ground. Many were killed, and some of the châteaux were destroyed, but many survived. It will be interesting to see how your marquis fared when we get to Brittany. He may have been forced to surrender his château. It obviously wasn't entirely destroyed if it's still standing and they have tours there, or it may be nothing more than a burned-out shell. Many of the burned-out châteaux were never restored. It's a great pity.'

And then he added some gratuitous information. 'Many people blamed Marie Antoinette for the excesses of the time, and the direction in which she led the king. One can't put it all at her door, but the nobles in those days, and the royals, certainly created a terrible situation for the poor, and didn't seem to care. They paid for it dearly. *Les Chouans* were the only resisters, and their neighbors in La Vendée. But they weren't as overwhelmed by sheer numbers as they were in Paris. It served them well that they were so far away. They were safer in Brittany, as safe as anyone was during the Revolution.' It shocked her to realize that the Revolution had been barely more than two hundred years before, which didn't seem so long ago. Napoleon had come just after. The monarchy had been replaced by an empire, which wasn't much better. And Napoleon had been just as excessive in his own way.

'It's fascinating the role that women played in all that. Marie Antoinette before the Revolution, and Josephine after. It fits into my women's gender studies. I should write a paper on it one day,' she said, looking pensive. She liked the idea.

'And don't underestimate the courtesans. They were powerful women as well. The intrigues and manipulations at court were tremendous, and in some cases, women held all the power, and the key. Men are always willing to ride into battle. Women are much more clever, and can be very dangerous at times.'

'What a book that would make,' she said, smiling. 'And to think I've spent seven years researching women's right to vote, and I thought that was interesting. It's nothing compared to all this.' But the French were singularly committed to intrigue, and when she said it to Marc, he didn't deny it.

'That's what makes our history so interesting. It's never what it appears to be on the surface. All the important pieces are on the underside of the story, and you have to search for them to know what really happened.' Not unlike the details she had unearthed about Wachiwi. 'How do you feel about having an Indian in your ancestry?' he asked her. He had wondered about it.

'I like it,' she said simply. 'At first I thought my mother might be upset, since she's such a snob about our aristocratic French background, and such a purist. I wasn't sure being part Sioux, even by a fraction, would please her. But she seems to like it too. And I love the idea that there's something more exotic in my DNA than a lot of French nobles with titles, with all due respect,' she said, glancing at him apologetically for the comment.

Marc laughed when she said it. 'Don't worry, I don't have a single aristocrat in my background. My ancestors were all peasants.'

'Whatever they were, they were courageous people, judging by the book about your parents and grandparents.'

'I think going against the tides is in our nature. That's very French too. We never want to do what we're supposed to. It's much more fun to start a revolution, or be in the resistance. We're oppositional people, and we never agree with each other either. That's why we love talking politics here, so we can disagree with everyone.' There were heated debates in cafés constantly, and on campuses, about meaningful subjects. It was one of the things Brigitte had always liked about France.

They talked all the way to Saint Malo, and it was too late to visit the château when they got there. They checked into the hotel where he had booked rooms for them, and they walked around the port. The town was old-fashioned and pretty. He told her it had been a whaling town long ago, and he entertained her with more stories about the region.

They stopped and bought ice cream, and sat down on a bench to eat it, looking out at the ocean.

'Can you imagine the size of the boat Wachiwi must have come here on?' She looked dreamy when she thought about it. What a brave girl she must have been. And the man she loved and was traveling with had died on the trip. It must have been terrifying for her.

'I don't want to think about it,' he said. 'I get seasick.' He finished his ice cream, and they walked back to the hotel. They each had a tiny room barely bigger than the bed, and they shared a bathroom, but it was cheap.

They each paid for their own room. He had offered to pay for hers, and Brigitte wouldn't let him. He had come here to help her with her research, and there was no reason why he should pay for her. And she didn't want to be obligated to him.

They ate dinner at a fish restaurant that night since their hotel served no food. The meal was delicious, and he ordered an excellent bottle of inexpensive wine. And dinner with him was lively and interesting. She always had a good time with him. He was so well educated and knew so many things about history, art, literature. She was astounded at his memory for historical facts and dates. He knew more about some aspects of American history than she did. And he was well informed about politics in the United States too. He was incredibly bright without being pompous, which was rare. So many of the professors she knew in academic life were disconnected from the real world and thought they knew it all. Marc knew a lot but still managed to be humble and make fun of himself. She liked that about him, and he had a good sense of humor. He told her some funny stories about his student days in Boston, and they were laughing when they got back to the hotel, said goodnight, and went to their respective rooms.

She was wearing an old flannel nightgown and brushing her teeth when he walked in on her in the bathroom. She had forgotten to lock the door, and he was wearing boxers and a T-shirt and looked just like any other guy at home. He didn't look sexy and French, he looked human and real, and she liked that about him. He apologized profusely for walking in, although her nightgown covered her from neck to ankles.

'That's a sexy-looking gown,' he said, teasing her. 'My sister used to have a nightgown like that when we were in school.' He had mentioned her to Brigitte before. She lived in the South of France, was married, and had three kids and he was close to her. He referred to himself as her black sheep brother because he had lived with a woman, never married, nor had kids. She was a lawyer, and her husband was a judge in a small provincial town. 'I don't think she caught her husband by wearing it though,' he continued to tease Brigitte.

'I'm not in the market for a husband tonight,' she quipped back. 'I left all my sexy nighties at home.' The truth was that she didn't have any, and hadn't bought sexy lingerie or nightgowns in years. She didn't need them. She'd had Ted.

'What a pity, I was just about to propose.' He put toothpaste on his brush while he chatted with her, and a minute later, they were both brushing their teeth at the sink. It was a funny thing to be doing with a man she hardly knew, but somehow she didn't mind. They were becoming real friends, despite his teasing her about relationships and proposals. For them, there was no risk of either one, she was determined to be friends.

When they finished brushing their teeth, he said goodnight, and they went to their rooms and locked the doors. Or she did. He left his unlocked just in case. He would have been perfectly happy if she had become overwhelmed by a tidal wave of lust during the night. Instead, she slept like a baby, and felt fresh in the morning. He expressed his disappointment over it at breakfast, and was teasing her again. In fact, he would have been startled if she had turned up in his room. She had made her boundaries perfectly clear to him, and despite what he said, he respected them, and her. He thought her a very impressive woman, and Ted a fool for having left her. No royal mummy he found in Egypt, or pharaoh's tomb, would be worth it, in Marc's opinion. Brigitte was a good woman and brighter than anyone he'd met in a long time.

They drove to the center of town after breakfast, and Marc stopped at the town hall. He had told her that marriages, births, deaths, and whatever had happened in the county were recorded here. It would confirm what she already knew, and perhaps unearth some things she didn't. And once again, he was right. After paying a small fee, they spent several hours poring over ledgers. They found the entries for Tristan's birth and his younger brother's, and their parents' births and deaths; both had died relatively young and within days of each other. Marc guessed they had died as a result of some epidemic, and he noted that Tristan had been only eighteen at the time, and his brother ten years younger, so he had inherited the title and everything that went with it when barely more than a boy.

They found the record of the births of Tristan and Wachiwi's children, the first one named after his late brother. She had seen those names and dates already in the photographic records of the Mormons, but here they were, right where they originally came from. It moved Brigitte to see them in the ledgers. She made notes on everything for her mother, and when they walked into the courtyard afterward, there were young couples with bright expectant faces waiting to be married. Marc explained that in France one had to have a civil wedding before a church one, so all of the young couples there were having their civil ceremonies, and then would marry in church a week or two later. They all looked excited and happy, as Brigitte and Marc walked past them in the courtyard. The various sets of parents were chatting with each other. Brigitte smiled as she walked by, and then she and Marc got back in the car and drove to the château. They had timed their day perfectly. The guided tour was starting in less than an hour. She wanted to hear what they had to say, and to finally see what had once been her family's château centuries before.

They drove up the same road that Wachiwi had traveled when she got there, to where the château sat on a cliff, looking out to sea. The Château de Margerac was a government-run monument now. They bought two tickets at the entrance to the gardens, and strolled together. Brigitte was amazed at how enormous it was. It looked like a fortress and had changed very little over hundreds of years. There were still bright flower beds in the garden, a maze, and benches where you could sit and look out at the view. They had no way of knowing that the bench where they sat for a few minutes was the one where Tristan had proposed to Wachiwi. But just being there made Brigitte feel steeped in her own history.

The stables were long empty, and there were a few ancestral portraits but not many, and those had been reclaimed at auction by the Department of Historic Monuments. Brigitte noticed some dusty hunting trophies, as people gathered at the foot of the grand staircase to take the tour, led by a young woman who explained who the Margeracs had been.

She said the château had been built in the twelfth

century, and she reeled off a list of names of the generations who had lived there, and what they had done in the community and county. She said that the château was one of the largest in Brittany, and its owners had successfully fought off their enemies in the Middle Ages. And then she explained that that had been the case after the Revolution as well. They were taking the tour in French, and Marc translated for her as the guide spoke quickly, leading them through the master bedroom on the second floor and through several other grand rooms that were empty. They were told that there were bedrooms on the upper floors, as well as the nursery, but they were empty and closed to the public.

And as she finally led them back to the great hall, she announced almost proudly that the Marquis Tristan de Margerac had joined the forces of the resistance, after the Revolution, *les Chouans*, and had succeeded in keeping the château from being taken from them or invaded. She said that local history showed that he had kept his family sequestered there, despite a fire set in one part of the château by revolutionaries. But the marquis had prevailed and there were local stories that his wife had fought valiantly at his side. Tears sprang to Brigitte's eyes as she said it. She could easily imagine Wachiwi fighting to defend her home, her family, and her man, a Sioux to the end. The guide said that the château had remained in the family until the mid-nineteenth century, when they had migrated to America. And at the turn of the century, after other owners sold it and it changed hands several times, the Department of Historic Monuments had taken it over and restored it. She said that much of what they saw there was as it had originally been, although in the time that the last generations of marquises had lived there, it had been far more grand. There had been antiques, many of which had disappeared, many servants, extensive lands, all of which had been sold off when the château changed hands. She said the stables had been filled with thoroughbred horses, and she mentioned that Marquis Tristan de Margerac's wife had been an exceptional horsewoman of legendary skill in the county. She made a passing comment that she was remarkable in that she was a Native American, believed to be a Sioux, and had come to France to marry him, although she didn't know the details. She said that her name was Wachiwi, and both she and her husband were buried in the family cemetery behind the thirteenth-century chapel on the estate, where members of the family had been buried for hundreds of years. She added that no direct members of the Margerac family still existed in France. They had all emigrated to America during the nineteenth century and possibly died out.

Marc squeezed her hand when the guide said it, and it made Brigitte want to wave her arms and shout, 'Here I am! I'm one of them!' She was still looking deeply moved and vibrant and excited when the tour ended and they walked back outside. She had bought several pamphlets and postcards for her mother, and she looked around feeling a deep tie to her ancestors and their château, and most especially to Wachiwi, who was an inspiration to her now.

She was intrigued to know that Marc had been right. Tristan de Margerac had been a Chouan, and had been able to keep the château, despite the revolutionaries' attempts to capture it and set it on fire. He had held his ground like others in the region, and Wachiwi had helped him, with all her Sioux fierceness and courage. It must have been a frightening time.

Hearing about it made Brigitte want to write about it, but she still didn't know how. Fact or fiction? Historical novel? Anthropology? History? Romance? She didn't know which avenue to pursue, or if she ever would. Maybe it was enough to just know about it, and realize that she was part of it in some way.

She and Marc went down to the small cemetery behind the chapel, although the others didn't. They had no interest in looking at the headstones and vaults of dead Margeracs for centuries of generations. The chapel was

Danielle Steel

empty when they went inside. One side looked as though it had been damaged by fire long ago, but it was still standing. Brigitte couldn't help wondering if it was part of the damage done by the revolutionaries or if it had happened later on.

They wandered out into the garden behind it. There were several somber-looking mausoleums, and many headstones, some of which had been worn smooth by time and the names on them lost. Brigitte knew what she was looking for and what she hoped to find, as Marc followed her into the first two mausoleums, and then a third. All were the names of Margeracs of previous generations, and the carvings of their names were well preserved. They were mostly sixteenth and seventeenth century, and some from the mid- and early 1700s. Tristan and Jean's parents were there. Brigitte was disappointed to find that Tristan and Wachiwi weren't, as they walked back outside.

There were two handsome monuments at the back of the cemetery, under a tree, with smaller headstones around them. She had lost hope of finding Tristan and Wachiwi by then, but there was something soothing about reading the names that were her forebears', and part of the ancestry her mother had been pursuing and chronicling for years.

Marc saw them before she did. He had walked all the way back to the rear of the cemetery to read the names on the last two monuments, and he waved excitedly to Brigitte. She climbed through some tall weeds to get there. The path that meandered through the cemetery was long since overgrown.

He was standing there reverently with tears in his eyes as he silently held out a hand to Brigitte. Their names were clearly marked. They had both died in 1817, within less than three months of each other, twenty-eight years after the revolution, three years after Napoleon's abdication, and two years after the battle of Waterloo. Wachiwi had died thirty-three years after she had come to France, and thirty-two years after she became the marquise. When they searched through the tall grasses, they found many of the others, her children, their spouses, and two of their children who had died in France. Still others had gone to the States. So many of the names she had seen recorded recently in ancient ledgers were there, with Tristan and Wachiwi in their midst. Their monuments sat solemnly in the peaceful garden, side by side just as they had lived. Tristan had died at sixty-seven, which had been a considerable age for those times, and it was hard to know how old Wachiwi had been. If she had been around seventeen when she left her village, and eighteen when she married Tristan in that case, then she must have been fifty when she died, and perhaps had died of grief without him, although it wasn't unusual to die at that age. He was more unusual for having lived much longer. The dates of his birth and death were recorded on Tristan's tombstone; on hers only the date of her death was inscribed. Probably no one had ever known her precise age – nor had she, since there was no record of her age when she left her tribe, and later fled with Jean.

It was deeply moving, standing there. There had been generations of her ancestors that had come later, but it was Wachiwi, the little Sioux girl who had stolen her heart, whose story she loved. The wild girl from the Dakota Sioux had survived being kidnapped, crossed a continent, an ocean, and come to France, found love and stayed, been presented to a king and queen at court, lived through a revolution and defended her home, and had been an important link in a long chain of generations that ultimately connected her to Brigitte, who felt a deep bond to this girl. Standing near Wachiwi's final resting place, and her husband's, made Brigitte feel as though she had come full circle in some way, and found her roots at last. She felt a part of this place, and these people, almost as though she knew them, and in many ways, thanks to what she had read about them, she did. She was suddenly deeply grateful to her own mother for leading her on this path, albeit reluctantly at first.

She and Marc stood holding hands in the cemetery, and then slowly, reluctantly, they walked away, past the chapel and the château. He put an arm around her, and they walked back to where they had left his car. It was an unforgettable afternoon. And she felt sad to leave them, and the château, as they drove away.

'Thank you for letting me come here with you,' Marc said quietly as they drove back to the little town. It had been moving for him too. The story had been so intricate until now, so mysterious, like a puzzle they had been trying to solve, and now it was laid out before them like a stained-glass window, all the pieces fit and the light was shining through it. He was proud to have been a part of it, and grateful to have shared it with her.

'I would never have known all I do about her now, if it weren't for you,' Brigitte said, smiling at him. The court diaries she had found had made a huge difference in her understanding of who Wachiwi was and what had happened to her.

'I think it was destiny that brought us together,' he said with a sigh. He believed that. Stranger things had happened.

'Maybe,' she conceded, but she hadn't done as much for him, and wished she had. She liked listening to his stories about his book.

'Perhaps it's your destiny to stay in France too, like Wachiwi,' he said cryptically, and she laughed. He was definitely taken with her, enjoyed her company, and didn't want her to leave. She had finished everything she had come here to do. And after they got back to Paris, she had to go home.

'I have to look for a job,' she said practically. 'In Boston.'

'You can find one here.' He mentioned the American University of Paris again, and conveniently he had a friend there in the admissions office, whom he offered to call on her behalf.

'And then what would I do? I have no apartment, no friends. I have a dozen years of history in Boston.' And boredom, she thought to herself, but didn't say it.

'You have me,' he said cautiously, but they were both aware that they hardly knew each other. Nothing had happened between them, and maybe never would. She couldn't move to Paris for a man she liked talking to. That wasn't enough, and they both knew it. And Brigitte wasn't an impulsive person. She was sensible, and always had been. 'I think you should write the book here, about your Sioux ancestor,' he insisted, but she wasn't convinced. It was a wonderful story, because it mattered to her, but she wasn't sure if it would make a book, nor if she could write

Legacy

it. She wasn't a novelist or a historian, she was an anthropologist. This was different, it was full of the raw emotion she had no experience writing. 'It might do you good to spend a year in Paris,' he said, still trying to convince her. 'At some point in our lives, we all have to do something crazy that makes no sense but warms our heart.' And he knew that Wachiwi did.

'I don't like taking risks,' Brigitte said quietly, and he turned to look at her.

'I know. I can see that. Maybe you should.' But it wasn't his decision to make, it was hers. And hers was to go home to Boston. It felt like the right thing to do.

They had dinner at a different fish restaurant that evening, and spent the night in the little hotel. And on Sunday morning they drove back to Paris. They chatted occasionally on the drive, and part of the way Brigitte fell asleep. Marc looked over at her with a smile. It was nice having her there next to him, dozing peacefully as he drove. He was glad he had gone to Brittany with her. And he was sad thinking that in a few days she'd be gone. He only hoped that the days since he had met her had convinced her to stay.

Chapter 18

Wachiwi
1793

The months and years after the onset of the Revolution had been frightening for all of them. Fortunately, they had been in Brittany when the first outbursts of violence had erupted in the streets of Paris. The news that came to them from those who fled was impossible to believe. Versailles invaded by armed ruffians and revolutionaries, the entire royal family arrested and imprisoned, the Palais du Louvre thronged with crowds defacing the exquisite rooms. Noble children murdered, adult royals on the guillotine, heads rolling in the streets, blood in the gutters everywhere. And many of Tristan's friends and relatives were dead.

They had no idea what had happened to their house in Paris for many months and finally learned that it had been pillaged and looted. Revolutionary soldiers had camped out in it, and then abandoned it again, taking much of value with them. Wachiwi was grateful that they were in Brittany with their children.

Wachiwi was frightened at first and reminded of when she was kidnapped by the Crow. Tristan understood immediately and assured her that no one would ever take her away again.

'I will kill them first,' he promised her with an unfamiliarly murderous look in his eyes. 'I will protect you.' And she knew he would. She felt safe with him. He turned the château into a fortress, raised the drawbridge, and transformed their home into an armed camp, with other nobles staying with them. They formed a band of more than fifty *resistants* staying there. He taught Wachiwi to fire a musket and load a cannon, and she fought at his side on many nights. She was never afraid when she was with him.

It was Wachiwi who saw the flames first the night the revolutionaries set fire to the north wing of the château. Her babies were inside, with Agathe and Matthieu, and the man she loved, as flaming arrows flew over their walls and set fire to the trees, which spread almost instantly to the château, fanned by a fierce wind. And then suddenly the Sioux in her rose up and took control. She took a powerful bow from one of Tristan's archers and began firing arrows back at them and injured many men, and killed more than a few. She was a Catholic since her marriage, but had no pangs of conscience about what she was doing. She was fighting for their home, and as he watched her, Tristan was proud of her and had never loved her more. She was the only woman fighting beside the men, and she was tireless as she fired muskets, and shot arrows at their attackers.

She was wounded once in the same shoulder that had been injured when she tried to flee from the Crow, but it was only a graze this time too. After that Tristan insisted she stay with her children, but within hours she was back in the fray, alongside him and the other men.

It was an infamous time in France with their country-men turning on each other and killing their own. The damage to the north wing was considerable, but in time the attacks diminished and the revolutionaries left. The other Chouans went home, the countryside was peaceful again, and Tristan put his efforts into rebuilding the château, grateful that they had lost neither their heads nor their home. He hadn't been to Paris to observe the damage there. The house was closed, and he had no desire to leave Wachiwi, their three small boys, and his two children. He wondered if they'd ever feel safe again. And he loved her more than ever. He had discovered a fierceness in her as she fought beside him that made him realize again what an extraordinary woman she was, and how much she meant to him, more even than his country or his home. He had been fighting to protect her and their children, more than anything else. And she felt the same way about him. She lived for Tristan and their three sons and her stepchildren, and would have killed anyone who was a threat to them.

'So, Madame la Marquise,' Tristan said as they walked in the sunlight of the gardens that were still partially burned. The stables had been damaged too, and they had lost some horses in the fire. But the revolutionaries had retreated, when they couldn't take the château. The Chouans in it were too fierce, so they moved on to other locations that were less well defended. Tristan and Wachiwi had saved their home. He looked proud of her as he smiled and sat down on the bench where he had proposed to her, and it showed scars from the fire too. The maze had been destroyed. 'It can all be rebuilt,' he said quietly, and Wachiwi knew he would. He loved his home, and hated the revolutionaries and what they did. She had never realized what a brave warrior he was until then. He was a peaceful man, but no one was going to take his home or hurt them. It reminded her of her brothers who were so far away. She still missed them, but her life was here with Tristan and her children. She felt as much French as Sioux now, although the Sioux in her had come out during their battle to defend their home.

'How is your shoulder?' he asked gently, and she smiled back at him.

'It's fine. You would make a good Sioux warrior,' she said, and he laughed as he put an arm around her as they sat on the bench.

'I don't ride as well as you do.'

'Neither did my brothers,' she teased.

'You'd make a good archer for the king, if we still had one,' he said sadly. Everything had changed. The world was upside down. Too many people he knew were dead. He didn't want to leave Brittany again. They were better off here, in peace, far from Paris. He feared it would be years before the country settled down. 'Are you sorry you came here?' he asked her, meaning France and looking worried. It was such a terrible time.

'Of course not,' she said softly as her eyes looked deep into his. He could see her strength and her love, and was reassured. He hated what they'd been through. 'This is my life. You are my life,' she said firmly, 'and our children. I was born to be with you.' She was certain of it. He was her tribe now, and the only one she needed or wanted. She was not Sioux, she was his, and had been since she got here. 'I want to die with you one day,' she said solemnly, 'a long time from now. When you go, I will come with you.' He looked at her as she said it, and knew she meant it, as he leaned over and kissed her. It was a gentle kiss from a gentle man who loved her with the same fierceness with which she loved him.

'I want to live a long life with you, Wachiwi,' he said quietly, and then looked out to sea. She leaned against him, and smiled up at him peacefully. The war to save their home was over, and they had much to do, and look forward to.

'We will,' she said softly, as they sat looking at the sea together, and then, hand in hand, they wandered back to the château they would repair in the coming months. They walked upstairs to the nursery together to see their children. Agathe and Matthieu were there playing with their younger siblings. They were still shaken by the battles they'd been through and all they'd seen. Tristan looked over their heads at Wachiwi and smiled at her happily. And she smiled back at him. There was nothing to fear as long as she was with him.

When they left the children, they walked downstairs to their bedroom and closed the door softly. She put her arms around him, and this time he kissed her with the same passion he had felt for her since the beginning.

She followed him to the bed where their babies had been conceived and born, and as he held her and she kissed him, he knew he was the luckiest man alive that the chief's daughter named Wachiwi was his, and would be until the end of his days. She was the dancer of his heart and soul and dreams.

Chapter 19

Brigitte

On Monday, Brigitte spent the day doing errands, and a little shopping. She wanted to buy a present for her mother, and something for Amy and her kids. She walked along the Seine again after that, and she went to see an exhibit she had wanted to see since she arrived but hadn't had time for. She figured that she had another day or two of museums and monuments she wanted to see, and then she no longer had an excuse, she had to leave. She had to get on with her life. And her real life was in Boston, not here. But she loved being in Paris anyway.

When Marc dropped her back at her hotel on Sunday, he had said he would call her soon. He knew she was leaving that week. He mentioned that he had a meeting with his editor the next day, and he called her late Monday afternoon and invited her to dinner. He suggested a place she'd never heard of before, in the seventeenth arrondissement, and he said they had excellent food.

He picked her up at eight o'clock and they had a terrific evening together, as always, and at the end of the meal, as they drank *café filtre* and shared ice cream and *macarons,* he looked at her sheepishly and said he had a confession to make. She couldn't imagine what it was, and was stunned when he told her. He had called his friend at the admissions office of AUP and asked him if they would meet with her to see about a job. He admitted readily that it was a presumptuous thing to do, but he insisted that there was no harm in it. If they had nothing, it didn't matter, and if they did, she could always turn it down if she didn't want it. She said she didn't, and was shocked and annoyed by what he'd done, although she knew he meant well. But she didn't like his presumption.

'If you're so hot for me to come here,' she snapped at him, 'why don't you move to Boston?' But the big difference between them was that he had a job, and she didn't, which made her considerably more mobile. She had very little to anchor her in Boston, and he had much more here. He was still teaching at the Sorbonne and had obligations that Brigitte didn't.

'Are you very angry at me?' He looked apologetic, and was aware that it was a pretty gutsy thing to do, but he liked her so much, she seemed at loose ends, and he would have loved it if she moved to Paris, even for a year. If nothing else, they would be good friends. Of that he was sure, and so was she. But she wasn't about to move to Paris for a friend, or a job at AUP. She was going back to Boston to find a job there in the academic community she was familiar with.

'I'm not angry,' she explained. 'Maybe just surprised . . . flattered . . . it's nice to know someone cares that much to try so hard to get me to stay. I'm just not used to people lining up interviews for me, or making my decisions.' Ted never had, and she preferred it that way. She was an independent person, even if she was currently out of a job, and she was perfectly capable of finding one herself. He had offended her a little by setting up the interview for her, but she knew his intentions were good, and she forgave him because of that.

'The decision is yours, Brigitte,' he said firmly. 'I just wanted to give you the opportunity if you want it.' She didn't, but now she didn't want to be rude.

'What did you tell them at AUP?' She was curious

now, even though she wasn't going to interview for a job.

'That you're brilliant and charming and a terrific person and I'm sure you're very good at what you do, and you worked for ten years at Boston University and are looking for a change.'

'Well, that sounds about right,' she conceded, 'especially the brilliant, charming, terrific part.' And she was ready for a change. She just didn't know to what, and the admissions office at another school would be all too similar to what she used to do. It hadn't been a very exciting job, and she realized now that she had been bored a lot of the time. She had done a lot of very tedious work, which was the downside of never having wanted too much responsibility. So she did a lot of menial things. That was the trade-off.

'It's a very small school, and may be more fun for you than a big school. You'd probably have a lot more contact with the students, and more influence. I think it's less than a thousand students.' BU had been thirty-two thousand, both graduate and undergraduate, it was huge, and he had a point.

'I suppose I could talk to them, to not put you in an awkward position, and then go home and interview. And if nothing great turns up there, I could always think of the job here as a fallback position.' It seemed funny to use a job in Paris as backup. She knew that to others it would have been top of the list, but she wanted to go home. She told herself she had a life in Boston. But did she, with no boyfriend and no job? She didn't here either though, and Marc was her only friend. It was something, but not enough, and he was very new in her life, even though he had been very kind. She had a real life, and real friends, somewhere else. But she wasn't entirely opposed to talking to AUP, since he had set it up. Marc was pleased. He gave her all the details that night before he dropped her off at her hotel, and he said he'd call the next day to see how it went.

And much to Brigitte's surprise, it went extremely well. The man she met with in the admissions office was personable, easy to talk to, and loved the school. He was the best PR agent they could have had, and by the time she finished listening to him, she was ready to enlist. Almost. She liked everything he said about the department, but they had no job at the moment, and she still wanted to find a job in Boston. Other than that, it was great. And she reported all of it to Marc when he called her. He'd already had an enthusiastic call from his friend, who thought Brigitte would be terrific for them, and had told Marc, as he did Brigitte, that if anything opened up, he'd let her know. It had been something of an exercise in futility, but it was good practice. She hadn't been on an interview in a while, and it warmed her up for job hunting in Boston.

'Well, I tried,' Marc said, sounding forlorn for a moment. 'I guess it would have been too perfect if they offered you a job.'

'I didn't expect that,' she said kindly. 'It was nice of you to set it up. A little pushy maybe,' she teased him, 'but nice.' She had decided to accept it in the spirit it had been given, with a warm heart.

'So when are you leaving?' he asked, sounding worried.

'Day after tomorrow,' she said matter-of-factly. She had done almost everything she wanted to do, and she was ready to go. It was time to get on with her life. The interview at AUP had been interesting, but it didn't change her course. They hadn't made her an offer, and her sails were set for home.

'I have to have dinner with my publisher tonight. I'm late with the book, and I have to be nice to him, or I'd cancel. And tomorrow I teach a class. Will you have dinner with me tomorrow night?' It was her last night in Paris.

'I'd love to.' He had been nothing but nice and generous with her, and she couldn't think of a more pleasant way to spend her last night in Paris, with a new friend. And hopefully at some point he'd visit Boston, or she'd come to Paris again for a vacation. It was nice knowing people around the world. And Marc was a special person. He really was a lovely man.

He told her he'd pick her up at eight the next day, and she spent the day racing around, tying up loose ends. By the time he came to pick her up, her bags were packed, everything was ready for her to leave the next morning, and she could spend the evening with him and relax. She was wearing a red dress she had bought that afternoon, and he admired it as soon as she came downstairs.

'You look terrific!'

'I saw it in a shop window today, and I couldn't resist. I figured I should bring something home from Paris.' She had bought a beautiful scarf for her mother, toys for Amy's kids, and a pretty sweater for Amy. The red dress had been a final splurge.

He took her to another cozy restaurant, and as usual conversation during dinner was lively. They each expressed a thousand opinions, traded experiences, and laughed a lot. And for the first time neither of them mentioned Tristan and Wachiwi, tonight was only about them. Brigitte had a perfect time, and Marc looked genuinely sad when they left the restaurant and took a walk near Notre Dame, which was all lit up.

'How can you leave a city like this?' he asked her, spreading his hands and looking very French again. He had one of those wonderful expressive faces, with a thousand expressions. He always looked very French, and she liked his looks. Ted had been very Anglo-Saxon. He was handsome but not sexy. There was something sensual about Marc's lips, although she always pretended not to notice.

'I'll have to admit, it's not an easy city to leave.' She looked sad too and she had enjoyed her time with him. But she couldn't stay here forever, particularly once she finished what she had come here to do. She didn't want her Indian ancestor to become an obsession. She was going to turn her notes over to her mother to do with as she wished. It was her mother's project after all, not her own, even if she had fallen in love with Wachiwi.

They walked for quite a while and looked down at the Seine, and then he drove her out of the way, to the Trocadero on the way home. It was the perfect image of Paris, as the Eiffel Tower stood before her in all its splendor, and as though on cue, as he parked his car, the tower began to sparkle, shooting lights in all directions. It was the perfect final night in Paris, and unable to resist the beauty of it, they both got out of the car. She stood looking up at the tower, like a child, mesmerized by the dazzling lights, and the exquisite view of Paris stretching before them, all the way to Sacré Coeur, and as she stood looking at the scene in silence, Mark put his arms around her and kissed her. She was too shocked to pull away or move, and realized she didn't want to. Instead she put her arms around him and kissed him back. It was a moment not to waste, and a night she knew she would never forget. And whatever he was to her, or wasn't, she liked him a lot, and would have been open to more than that if she was staying in Paris. But she wasn't. So all this could ever be was one glorious romantic night kissing someone she truly liked in front of the Eiffel Tower. It didn't get better than that, except maybe if you were madly in love. But she didn't need that now, or want it, it would have complicated everything between them. This was simple and clean and fun. She smiled at him when they pulled apart, and he kissed her again, as a young boy came up and tried to sell them a model of the Eiffel Tower. Marc took his wallet out and bought her one. He handed it to her, and said it was in memory of one of the best nights of his life, and she thanked him and agreed.

They said very little to each other on the drive back to her hotel. There was nothing left to say. They both knew she wasn't going to sleep with him before she left, and he didn't ask. She was going home, and they might never see each other again, or not for a long time, if ever. The times they had shared had been perfect. They enjoyed each other's company, respected each other, liked each other immensely, had a good time, and he had helped her a lot with her research. She knew she would cherish the memory of him and this night forever. And when she said goodnight to him, she was holding the little glass souvenir in her hand.

'Thank you for everything,' she said warmly. 'I had a wonderful time. Again.' She had enjoyed Brittany with him. And the Bibliothèque Nationale, all the restaurants he'd taken her to, their serious discussions, their laughter, the things he had taught her about the history of France, their walks along the Seine. They had done a lot in a short time.

'I hope you come back soon,' Marc said with a wistful look, and then he grinned. 'If not, maybe I'll come to Boston sometime to visit you. It's not so far,' he said, as though trying to convince himself. But it was. Their lives were worlds apart. 'I hope you find a job,' he said, and she smiled at him.

'So do I. I'll have to start beating the bushes seriously when I go home. I'm sure something will turn up soon.'

'I'm sure it will,' he reassured her, and then without saying anything more, he kissed her again. They kissed for a long time, and for a crazy instant she wished that she wasn't leaving Paris and was staying here with him.

'Take care of yourself, Marc,' she said sadly, as she left him. 'Thank you for everything.'

'*A bientôt*,' he said softly, brushing her lips with his own, and then she walked back into the hotel, and he went back to his car.

When she got upstairs, she set the little Eiffel Tower down on the desk and looked at it, and wondered why she hadn't gone to bed with him. What was there to lose? Her heart, she reminded herself, which didn't sound like a good idea to her. It was better like this. She felt a tear roll down her cheek, brushed it away, went to brush her teeth, put on her ancient flannel nightgown, and went to bed. But when she fell asleep that night, for her last night in Paris, she dreamed of him.

Chapter 20

Marc called her on her BlackBerry when she was on the way to the airport. He said that he just wanted to say goodbye to her again. He was trying to sound cheerful about it, but she could tell that he was sad, and so was she. It really was rotten luck in a way, she thought to herself, she had met a man she really liked, and he lived three thousand miles away. It happened that way sometimes, but it would have been nice if they lived in the same city. Instead she had had a great time with him, and she was taking home a souvenir of the Eiffel Tower. Maybe that was good enough. She thanked him again for everything, and dinner the night before, and he thanked her for the time she had spent with him. He was no longer trying to convince her to stay. He had understood.

She said goodbye to him, and checked her bags in when she got to the airport. She was flying to New York, to see her mother first, and give her the notes on everything she'd learned in France. Brigitte wanted to hand them over to her, so Marguerite could get on with her genealogy, and Brigitte would keep a copy for herself. It was nice to have, in memory of an extraordinary time and their remarkable Indian relative.

She went through security. The flight was on time, and once they were in the air, she laid her head back against the seat and closed her eyes. Marc had said he would e-mail her from time to time, and she had promised to do the same. And now, she had to concentrate on finding a job. She had had a great time in Paris, but she had to get on with her life. She was looking forward to seeing her mother and telling her about the trip.

Brigitte watched two movies, had a meal, and slept for two hours on the flight. She woke up just as the captain announced that they were landing in New York. It had gone very fast. And once she was in the airport, picking up her bags, she felt as though she had been shot out of a cannon. All the gentility of Paris had vanished. People jostled her, all the porters were somewhere else as she struggled with her bag. There was an endless line of people waiting for a taxi, it was raining, people were shouting at each other, and she wanted to run back into the terminal and catch the first plane back to Paris. Welcome to New York.

She finally managed to get a cab, gave him her mother's address, and called to tell her she was on her way. They were going out to dinner together, and when Brigitte got to the apartment, she ceremoniously handed over the folder full of meticulous notes about their ancestors, before she did anything else. Her mother hugged her gratefully, and thought Brigitte looked very well. She seemed relaxed and happier and more at ease in her own skin than she had in a long time. Her mother looked at her through narrowed eyes and told her she appeared more 'confident.' Brigitte was amused at her choice of words, and then realized she was right. That was how she felt. All her anxiety about what would happen to her next seemed to have vanished. She was still childless, unmarried, and unemployed, but she felt good about herself. The time in Paris had done her good, and so had Marc.

They chatted for about an hour in the apartment, about Wachiwi, the court diaries, the marquis, his brother, the château, and the Bibliothèque Nationale. And her mother was impressed. Brigitte had learned so much in such a short time. It was the most efficient, thorough job of research Marguerite had ever seen, and she was astounded that Brigitte had navigated the National Archives by herself.

'Well, I have to admit, I had some help,' Brigitte confessed. 'I met a writer at the library, and he gave me a hand. He's a historian, and a professor, and he knew the place like the back of his hand, and he showed me around. I probably couldn't have done it without him.'

'That's interesting.' Her mother was curious, but didn't want to press her, but Brigitte volunteered the rest. Or most of it anyway. Not the kiss on the last night. Some things were better left unsaid.

'He came to Brittany with me, and told me all about the Chouans, the aristocrats who resisted the revolutionaries and fought to keep their châteaux. It's very interesting stuff.' Apparently. And so was the fact that Brigitte had gone to Brittany with him. Marguerite wondered if anything else had happened there, but didn't ask. Her daughter was looking very well, and had a new light in her eyes. Her mother wondered if it was love, or even passion. Whatever it was, it was very becoming. Brigitte was looking terrific, and she was full of excitement as they talked about everything she'd found. She told her mother it was all in the folder she had given her.

'I can't wait to read it.'

'Marc thinks I should write a book about it,' she

volunteered as they left for dinner. They were going to a neighborhood restaurant on Madison Avenue that her mother liked.

'Marc?' Her mother looked quizzical as the doorman hailed a cab for them. This was getting more interesting by the minute.

'He's the writer I mentioned. He thought I could fictionalize it, or do it as a historical. The story is so good, I don't think fiction would add anything to it.' Her mother wanted to hear more about the man she kept mentioning, and finally at the end of dinner, she couldn't restrain herself any longer. His name had come up several times.

'Did anything happen with this Frenchman you met?' She wondered if Brigitte had fallen in love, but she didn't look it. She looked peaceful and happy. She didn't have the anguished look of someone who had left a man she loved in Paris. But her mother sensed that she was different.

'No, I didn't let it. There's no point starting something, and then leaving. It would have been a mess. Long-distance relationships never work. I just had a good time with him. That's all it was. But I'll admit, it's too bad he doesn't live in Boston. You don't meet guys like him too often. He tried to talk me into coming to Paris for a year to write the book. I'm not going to do that. I doubt I'll ever do it. I have a book to finish. And I have to find a job in Boston, that's where I live.' Her mother nodded and thought that everything Brigitte was saying was so pat and sensible that she wondered if it was real. She was beginning to wonder if Brigitte had fallen in love with this man and didn't even know it. But she didn't say that to her daughter. She just nodded, and listened, and watched her, and pretended to believe her, since Brigitte appeared to have convinced herself of everything she was saying.

'Do you think he'll come to visit you in Boston?'

'He said he might. Although I'll probably never see him again. It just doesn't make sense.'

'Not everything makes sense, sweetheart. Or not always,' her mother said gently. 'Feelings aren't sensible. Sometimes you fall in love with people who don't make sense. And the ones who do make sense turn out to be the wrong ones.' Like Ted, where their six-year affair went nowhere. 'Is he in love with you?' Marguerite asked, curious about him.

'He doesn't know me well enough to be,' Brigitte insisted, and she had told herself the same thing. 'He likes me. Maybe even a lot.' Marguerite sensed that there was more to it than that, on both sides, but she didn't push. And for the rest of the evening they talked about Wachiwi, who was an inexhaustible subject. And Brigitte's mother agreed with Marc, although she didn't know him. She thought Brigitte should write a book about her in some form. She obviously had a deep attachment to the subject. Far more than she did for her book about suffrage, which seemed to have died on the vine, or in the research years before. Her mother thought she should shelve it for the time being and do this one, and she said as much to her daughter when they went back to the apartment. Brigitte still didn't look convinced, any more than she was when she and Marc talked about it. She was scared.

And then both women went to bed at a decent hour. It was six hours later for Brigitte, but she seemed to be in good form and great spirits. They both lay in bed that night, thinking, Marguerite about the Frenchman her daughter had met, wishing she knew more about him. And Brigitte about the book everyone thought she should write and was afraid to. It was such a big subject that she was frightened to tackle it and not do it justice. She didn't want to write a bad book about such an extraordinary woman, or to take the risk that she would. It would have been a sacrilege to screw it up and botch the story of Wachiwi. It seemed much safer to her to continue working on the book about women's voting rights, and let someone else write the book about Wachiwi. She didn't feel capable of it, no matter what Marc and her mother said. She was going to stick with her book about suffrage and write the definitive book about it she always said she would. Wachiwi was far too big, complex, and volatile a subject. It was a book she felt she couldn't control, and much scarier than the vote.

Brigitte spent two days in New York with her mother, and they had a great time together. At some point Marguerite asked if Brigitte had heard from Ted, and she said she hadn't. It seemed strange to both of them that six years had ended in one night, fizzled into nothing and died in silence. It showed how little had been there, and they both agreed that it was disappointing.

She flew back to Boston on Saturday night, and took a cab to her apartment. She hadn't heard from Marc either since she got back, and she didn't expect to. She reminded herself that he owed her nothing. And she hadn't contacted him either, nor would she. It would just confuse them. She told herself that the romantic moments that had happened in front of the Eiffel Tower on the last night were a pleasant interlude and an aberration. She convinced herself that it meant nothing to either of them. And it was nice to know that even at her age, you could do something silly and romantic.

When she unpacked that night she put the little souvenir of the Eiffel Tower on her dressing table, and

smiled at it for a minute, and then finished unpacking. She
had half a dozen messages on her machine, none of them
important. The dry cleaner had found her lost skirt. The
library at BU said she had failed to return two books and
was being charged for it. Amy had phoned to remind her
to call the minute she got home and that she loved
her. Two telemarketers. And a call offering to renew the
guarantee on her oven. They were not exactly the kind of
calls that anyone wanted to come home to, with the
exception of Amy's. And when she looked around, she
could see that the apartment was looking dusty and
forlorn. She realized that she needed to spruce it up a little
and throw some things away, maybe move some furniture
around before it got seriously depressing. With Ted gone,
now was a good time to do it. She needed to do something
to spice up her life. And she tried not to panic over the fact
that not one of the places she had sent her résumé to had
responded. Neither by phone nor e-mail. They were probably still busy processing the applicants that had accepted.
Things wouldn't lighten up for them till June. And this
was only the end of April. And the deadline for
acceptance was mid-May. She told herself it was too early
to hear anything.

She called Amy when she finished unpacking. She was
putting the boys to bed but invited Brigitte to spend the

afternoon the next day. She was delighted to do it. She promised to come at noon, and when she did, she could hear screaming in the kitchen. It sounded like someone was being murdered. Before she could ring the doorbell, Amy had yanked open the door, tossed Brigitte the car keys, and told her to drive them to the emergency room. Her three-year-old had bumped his head on the corner of the table, and it was bleeding profusely through a wet towel she was using to apply pressure to it. She had been holding her one-year-old under one arm, and all he had on was a T-shirt, diaper, and sneakers, and he was crying now too. She got them both into the car seats in her backseat, and was sitting between them as Brigitte drove them to the university hospital. The screaming was so loud it eliminated all possibility of conversation. All she said was, 'Thanks!' as she shouted it to Brigitte from the backseat and then, 'Welcome home!' as they both laughed. It was a good thing Brigitte had shown up at that moment – it would have been an even bigger mess if she hadn't.

They waited two hours in the emergency room, while her injured son sucked his thumb on her lap and Amy was covered with blood. And the younger boy fell asleep on Brigitte's lap as the two women had a conversation in whispers.

'So how was Paris?' Amy asked her.

'Terrific. I got some fantastic information for my mother.' Amy nodded. She hoped she did more than that.

'Did you have a fabulous time?' she asked pointedly.

'Yes,' Brigitte reassured her.

'Any guys?' Amy always went right to the point, and for a minute Brigitte didn't answer, which her friend found suspicious.

'Not really. I met a writer at the library who helped me with my research.'

'How boring.' Amy looked disappointed to hear it.

'No, he wasn't. He's a very bright, interesting guy. He wrote a book I read in English a few years ago. He's a writer and teaches literature at the Sorbonne.'

'Still boring.' It didn't sound to her like he made the cut. She was hoping Brigitte would have had a wild affair in Paris. It would help her get over Ted. Spending her vacation in the library doing research didn't sound good to her.

'He came to Brittany with me for the weekend. It was great.'

Amy looked hopeful again. 'Did you sleep with him?'

'Of course not. I'm not going to be some guy's one-night stand and never see him again. How depressing.'

'Not getting laid in Paris sounds even more depressing to me,' Amy said bluntly. 'Of course, sitting in the emergency room for two hours on a Sunday afternoon isn't high on my list of fun activities either.' She went to see what was happening then, complained about the long wait, and a half hour later they took them in. Her son had to have four stitches, and he was exhausted from screaming when they left. It had been a stressful afternoon. Amy put both of them down for a nap when they got home, and she and Brigitte sat down for a glass of wine in the kitchen. Amy said she needed it, and Brigitte sipped hers to keep her company. She never liked drinking in the afternoon, and hardly drank at dinner.

'Okay, so tell me again,' Amy continued. 'No mad passionate affairs in Paris, just some schoolteacher you spent the weekend with. What a waste of a ticket to Paris! You couldn't do better than that?'

Brigitte laughed at how she said it. 'He's a nice guy, and I like him. He's just geographically undesirable. He lives in Paris. I live here.'

'So move. There's nothing special about Boston.'

'I live here. I like it. I'm looking for a job here.'

'Anything new on that score, by the way?' Brigitte decided not to tell her about the interview at AUP. They didn't have anything for her anyway. And Amy would have pounced on it. She was desperate for Brigitte to have a life, a guy, a baby. It was too much pressure for Brigitte.

'I'm going to start calling around tomorrow. This is a busy time of year. They probably haven't had time to get back to me.' Amy nodded agreement, but she also knew that her friend didn't have much to show for her ten years in the admissions office at BU. Being number three after ten years was hardly impressive. But it had been what Brigitte wanted. And it was going to hurt her now, looking for a new job. What it would show any prospective employer was either a lack of ability, or a lack of ambition. In her case, it was the latter, but how were they supposed to know?

They talked until the boys woke up, and then Brigitte left and went back to her own apartment. And once she got there, she didn't know what to do. She thought about going to a movie, but she hated to go alone. There were people she could have called, but she didn't want to explain what had happened with Ted or that they had broken up. It made her feel like such a loser. Uh, yeah . . . after six years, he dumped me and went off to do a dig. Wouldn't he have taken her along if he loved her? The way it had ended would tell everyone that he didn't really care about her, and what did that say about her? Lately her ego was more wounded than her heart. But either way, she didn't want to call anyone and have to explain.

She wandered around the apartment, got out the

vacuum cleaner, and did her laundry. It made her think of the comfortable Sunday nights she had spent with him for six years, at the end of the weekends. They usually cooked dinner together. Just as she had feared, the reality of her solitude was beginning to hit her now that she was home. It reminded her of what Marc had said, that if she had loved Ted, she would have missed him when she was in Paris, not just when she went back to Boston. This was about what she didn't have in her life, not about whom she was missing. Reminding herself of that helped, and she cleaned the apartment thoroughly before she went to bed. It had been an uneventful day, and a far cry from the weekend before, when she'd been in Brittany with Marc, going to fish restaurants, visiting the château, and staying at the cozy little inn. She laughed to herself as she put her flannel nightgown in the dryer. There was certainly nothing exotic about her life. She thought about calling Marc just to say hello, but she didn't want to do that either. She needed to let go of that connection and not hang on too tightly, and by then it was four in the morning for him. And he hadn't called her since she left. He was doing the right thing. She was just lonely and bored on a Sunday night.

She went to bed early and called all the universities she had sent résumés to, the next morning. Everyone was pleasant and polite. Yes, they had gotten her CV, they had no openings at the moment, but they would keep it on file. Some suggested she call back in June, others in September. It seemed incredible that at nine universities, there wasn't a single opening. But there was nothing remarkable on her CV. She'd had a very standard job for ten years, and had done nothing to distinguish herself. She had published no articles, taught no classes, had organized no special programs. She had done no volunteer work. She had worked in the office, spent weekends with Ted, and researched her book. She was embarrassed now when she thought about it. How could she have challenged herself so little, and asked so little of herself?

It made her sit down at her desk with real determination and get back to her book about the women's vote. She reorganized all her research, weeded through it, and took some things out, and by Tuesday, she started to write again. She had written a whole chapter by the end of the week. And then she read it. When she had finished reading it, she burst into tears. It was the most boring thing she'd ever written. Even academics wouldn't want to read the book. She didn't know what to do.

She was sitting at her desk with her head in her hands, when her mother called her on Friday night. She sounded excited. She'd been reading everything in the folder Brigitte had brought back from the trip.

'The material on our little Sioux relative is incredible. And the marquis sounds like quite a guy too. The stuff on her is riveting, and she was barely more than a girl.'

'Yes, it is.' Brigitte sounded lackluster, and her mother could hear it.

'Something wrong?'

'I've been working on my suffrage book all week, and it stinks. I don't know what made me think anyone would care about this. It's like reading cereal boxes, or tax forms, or prune juice labels. I hate it, and everyone else will too. And I've invested seven years of my life in it. I should just throw it away.' Her mother had never thought it an interesting subject, but Brigitte had always argued hotly for it, as an anthropologist and a woman. As a reader, and a retired editor, Marguerite had always thought it sounded pretty dull, but she didn't want to be rude. 'What do I do now?'

'Maybe your friend in Paris is right. Maybe you should write about Wachiwi. I agree with you. I don't think you need to fictionalize it. It's terrific the way it is. What about doing something with that?' Her mother was trying to be helpful.

'Maybe,' Brigitte said, sounding depressed.

'Have you heard from him, by the way?' her mother asked her with interest.

'No.'

'Then why don't you write to him? You can send him an e-mail.'

'I don't want to muddy the waters, Mom. We left things pretty much the way they should be. Friends who would get in touch from time to time. If I start writing to him, it'll confuse us both.'

'What's with all the *shoulds*? And what's wrong with a little confusion between friends?' Her saying that reminded Brigitte instantly of the night they had kissed under the Eiffel Tower. The confusion had felt good that night. But that was then, this was now. And she was home. Paris was like a distant dream. And so was he.

'I guess I'm just feeling sorry for myself. It's kind of a letdown to come back from Paris. What I need is a job. No one seems to be hiring right now.' She had enough to live on until the end of summer, or longer if she was careful, but more than anything she was bored. And her mother could hear it in her voice.

'Well, come back to New York anytime. We can play. I'm in a bridge tournament next week, but after that I'm free.' At least her mother had bridge. She didn't have that. She had nothing to keep her busy right now. And every time she thought about the material on Wachiwi, it scared her to death. And she didn't want to tell Amy how she was feeling, or she'd tell her to go back to therapy. Amy suggested that when Ted left, and Brigitte didn't want to do that right now either. She didn't know what she wanted, or who.

She watched old movies on TV until late that night, and then, for lack of anything better to do, she sat down at her computer and wrote Marc an e-mail. She wasn't sure what to say. Hi, I'm so bored I could scream . . . I still don't have a job, my social life seems to have gone down the tubes . . . my book is the most boring piece of crap on the planet . . . and I'm thinking of burning it, and how are you?

Instead, she wrote him a short e-mail, saying that she was thinking about him, that she'd had a wonderful time with him in Paris and Brittany, and the little souvenir of the Eiffel Tower was sitting on her dressing table. And she said that her mother was thrilled with the material she brought back, and thanked him again for his help. She said she hoped everything was fine with him. And then she sat staring at it, wondering how to sign off . . . 'Bye' sounded juvenile, 'All the best' too businesslike, 'Warm regards' ridiculous, 'Fondly' pathetic, 'Love' misleading. Finally she came up with 'Thinking of you. Take care,' which sounded honest and real. She read it about six times to make sure it didn't sound mushy, romantic, or whiny.

And then she hit the send button, and it went. She gulped when she sent it, and was sorry instantly. There it was. The risk thing again. What was she doing? The guy lived three thousand miles away. What was she thinking? She finally told herself that she was sending an e-mail to a nice guy she had met in Paris, to say hello.

'Okay. I can live with that,' she said out loud, trying not to feel stupid or anxious. She read it again, even though it was too late to do anything about it. And then she went to bed. And for a second as she climbed into bed, she decided she was glad she'd sent it, and hoped he'd write back.

Chapter 21

When Brigitte woke up in the morning, her heart pounded when she saw she had an e-mail from Marc. She felt like a kid, when a boy slipped her a note in class. She felt excited, and guilty, and scared, and she wasn't sure why. She hadn't felt like that in Paris. But this was different. It seemed strange writing to him from here, and a bigger commitment, or a bigger statement. But she had written to him, so she had to deal with the consequences now. She opened his e-mail, and took a breath, and then sighed with relief when she read his. It was fine. Friendly and nice.

Dear Brigitte,
    What a nice surprise to hear from you. How is Boston? Paris seems very quiet without you. I've had very little to

do. My students have spring fever and keep cutting class.
And I want to too!

  The book is going well, my editor has been very helpful,
and I hope to turn it in soon. My publisher seems to have
calmed down a little and is not threatening my life.

  I miss Wachiwi, and you. I'm glad your mother liked the
material you found. I still hope you will write the book
about Wachiwi, sooner rather than later. I hope that all is
well with you. Stay in touch.

And he signed it '*Je t'embrasse*,' which she knew was French
for 'I kiss you' (as in on both cheeks, not on the mouth).
It was a harmless greeting, and he had signed it Marc, and
then added a P.S. 'Each time I see the Eiffel Tower now, I
think of you. I feel now as though it belongs to you,
especially when it sparkles because you like that so much.
Good thoughts to you from Paris. Come back soon.'

It seemed like a totally benign, friendly, warm e-mail,
and she thought the 'Good thoughts to you from Paris'
was sweet. He had hit just the right tone. It wasn't scary,
overly personal, or uncomfortable, it was just warm and
nice and open enough, like him. She was glad she'd
written to him. Her mother had had a good idea.

She had nothing to do after that. And the next few
weeks seemed like the most boring and unproductive of

her life. She finally called a few friends and went out to dinner with them. They didn't make a big deal about Ted, and just said they were sorry they had broken up, but she felt like the odd man out now. They were all couples. The only unattached person she knew was Amy, and she was busy with her kids. One or the other of them had had a cold for the past two weeks so she couldn't get out, and Brigitte didn't want to catch whatever they had. Kids that age were always sick.

It was spring, and Boston was in full bloom. She spent Memorial Day in Martha's Vineyard, which was fun, and then she came back to Boston, and her life stalled again. It was hard keeping busy without a job, and she had shelved her book for now.

She heard from Marc a few times, and she kept her e-mails to him light. She didn't tell him that she was freaked out about not having a job and her life felt like a wasteland right now.

And finally, when she got back from the Vineyard, she took her notes out one night about Wachiwi, and read them, and fell in love with her all over again. More so than ever, with a little distance now. It was an amazing story, and she could see why her mother and Marc thought she should write a book about it.

She thought about it for days after she read it, and just

to see what would happen, she tried to write a first chapter, starting with Wachiwi in her own village. She read up on the Sioux on the Internet, so she could describe them properly, and what she wrote about the young Sioux girl seemed to write itself. It was effortless, and when she finished after three long days of working on it, it seemed beautiful and mystical. It was a story she wanted to tell, and suddenly she wasn't afraid of it anymore. It was beckoning her, and she threw herself into it wholeheartedly. The days flew after that. She had never enjoyed writing anything so much in her life. She thought about sending an e-mail to tell Marc she had started it, but she didn't want to jinx it. She decided to wait for a while, until she had written a few more chapters. It was still very rough, but she really liked what she had.

She had been writing for ten days, and she was hard at it late one night, when her computer told her she had an e-mail, but she didn't want to interrupt what she was doing, so she kept going for several hours. It was like flying, and she didn't want to stop. She was shocked to realize it was almost five in the morning when she sat back with a satisfied look. She saved what she had written. And then she remembered the e-mail she had heard come in. She went to her e-mail and saw it was from the AUP in Paris. She opened it, and discovered it was from the man she had interviewed with. She wasn't particularly interested in it, but she read it, and then stared at it and read it again. They were offering her a job, part time, at a decent salary, that she could live on, three days a week. And they told her that they had studio apartments available for students and faculty, for a nominal fee. The job had opened up because the number-two person in the admissions office had announced that she was pregnant and wanted to take maternity leave for a year. He said she was forty-two, it was her first pregnancy, she was having twins, and they had just put her on bed rest, very early in the pregnancy. So they could offer Brigitte the position for a year. And he made a point of telling her that the head of the admissions office was retiring in a year, so there might be other possibilities for her at AUP, if the current job they were offering her didn't turn out to be permanent, which he thought was a possibility too. In any case, they could promise her a year. And it was also clear to her that if she wanted the job, this time she'd have to take more responsibility and step up to the plate. It was a small school and they needed everyone to pitch in and be flexible, and she was willing to do that. She had learned her lesson. By taking so little responsibility at BU, she had been the first to become obsolete. She wanted this to be different, if she took it. But did she want a job in Paris? She wasn't sure.

They were offering her everything she needed – a job, decent pay, a part-time schedule that would allow her to write the book about Wachiwi if she wanted to, and an apartment for little money if she wanted that. It was all right there, if she took it. She didn't know what to do. She stared at the e-mail and then walked around her apartment.

She never went to bed that night, and she saw the sun come up from her living-room window. She wanted to ask someone's advice, like Amy or her mother, but she was afraid they'd tell her to take it. And what did they know? It was easy for them to say. What if it was a terrible mistake? If she hated it? If she was lonely? If she got sick in Paris? If she missed a great job in Boston because she was in Paris? She had a thousand worst-case scenarios ready. But she also knew that no one was offering her a job in Boston, or hadn't yet. Her CV hadn't shaken the world, and no one had responded. And what if they didn't, and she had no job here either? What if . . . what if . . . what if . . . She had worn herself out totally by ten o'clock that morning, worrying about it. And they had asked her to respond soon because they had to fill the position. They said that the woman taking maternity leave was leaving immediately, and they wanted Brigitte to be there in two weeks. Two weeks to wrap up her life in Boston. What life? she asked herself. She had no life. She had an apartment she had never really liked, she wasn't dating anyone, and she had been out of work for four months. She had started a book, maybe, which she could write anywhere, and maybe better in Paris. But what about Amy? Her mother? She was crying by noon, and by late afternoon she was panicked. The phone rang at six o'clock, and she was terrified it was her mother. She didn't want her to hear how upset she was or have to tell her why. She felt like a four-year-old, and she wanted to hide in the closet. The phone went on ringing. She went to check caller ID and didn't recognize the number, so she answered, and she was even more stunned when she did. It was Ted. She hadn't heard from him since he left. She was shocked to hear him on the phone, and couldn't imagine what he wanted. Maybe he was sorry he'd left her. Then maybe she wouldn't have to go to Paris. It was just too scary.

'Hi,' she said, trying to sound casual, and feeling stupid as she did it. They knew each other too well to play games or at least they used to.

'How are you, Brig?' He sounded happy and in good spirits. She had no idea what time it was for him, or exactly where he was.

'I'm fine. Is something wrong?' Maybe he was in a hospital and needed her. Or had too much to drink, and drunk-dialed. Anything was possible after four months of silence.

'No, everything's great here. I was wondering how you are. I'm sorry things got so botched up when I left. It was hard.'

'Yeah, it was. I'm okay,' she said, but her voice sounded small. He didn't seem to notice. 'I went to Paris and did some research for my mother.' She realized that he'd never known she got laid off. She hadn't wanted him to know.

'Did you take some time off?' he sounded puzzled.

'Uh . . . actually . . . I took a break from work. I'm writing.'

She had been writing for ten days, but she didn't say that. At least she was doing something. He was running a dig for a major university, and she didn't want to sound pathetic.

'That's great.' He didn't ask her what she was writing.

'How's the dig?'

'Fantastic. We're pulling out stuff every day. It was a little slow in the beginning, but it's been really good for the last month. So what else are you up to?'

'Not much.' She hated sounding like such a loser, and then before she could stop herself, she wasn't sure if she said it to impress him, or to ask his advice, she blurted out,

'I just got offered a job in Paris. Ted, I don't know what to do.' She was crying again, but he couldn't hear it. 'I just found out last night.'

'What kind of job?'

'Admissions office at American University of Paris. Part time, with an apartment.'

'Are you kidding? That's right up your alley. Take it.' She was afraid he would say that.

'Why? What if I hate it?'

'How bad can it be in Paris? We don't even have indoor plumbing here.' She was suddenly glad she wasn't with him. 'If you hate it,' he added, 'you can quit and come home. You need a change, Brig. I think we both kind of outgrew Boston, and didn't want to face it.'

'And each other,' she said honestly.

'Yeah, and that too. It's hard to make changes. Things get so comfortable and you don't want to move. Maybe it would do you good to be a little uncomfortable for a while, and do something different. You can learn French.'

'It's an American school,' she reminded him.

'In a French city. I don't know, Brig. It's up to you, but it sounds like an answer to a prayer to me. You've done Boston, you're good at what you do. And if they're offering you part time, it'll give you time to write the book you're working on. What the hell, give it a shot. Sometimes I think "what the hell" is the right answer. You've got nothing to lose. Nothing is irreversible except dying. And moving to Paris for a while sure won't kill you. You might love it.' She had been so busy thinking about everything that could go wrong that she hadn't thought of that. But he was right. What if she loved it? It was the one scenario she hadn't considered.

'I know you get scared, Brig,' he went on. 'We all do. I was scared shitless when I came here, but I wouldn't have missed it for anything. I know what happened with your father really shook you. But sometimes you've got to take a chance. You're too young not to, and you'll probably regret it forever if you don't take it. That's what I was afraid would happen here. If I had passed up this dig for us, I'd have resented it forever. I didn't want that to happen.' She understood, but it had hurt anyway.

'You could have taken me.' She had never said that to him before he left, and it felt good to get it out now.

'No, I couldn't. You'd hate it here. Believe me, it's not Paris. It's hot and dusty and dirty. I love it, but the living conditions are squalid. I knew that from the digs I'd visited. You would have been out of here in ten minutes,' he said, and she smiled thinking about it.

'Yeah, you're probably right. It sounds awful.'

'But it's what I love to do. Now you've got to do what

you love to do. Write the book, go to Paris, change careers, find a guy you're crazy about, who's not going to run off to Egypt after six years. I miss you, Brig, but I'm happy. I hope this winds up being right for both of us in the end. That's why I called you. I've been worrying about you, and feeling guilty. I know it was a shit thing to do, dumping everything after six years. But I had to do this. I want you to find what you have to do. Maybe it's Paris. I hope it is.'

'Maybe so,' she said pensively. It was good to hear him, but he didn't sound like hers anymore. And probably never was. He was someone she had known, but they had never really been connected. She knew that now. And maybe they never would have been right for each other. Maybe she would never find the right guy. But Ted made sense. She couldn't just sit there forever in Boston, waiting for life to happen. She had to grab it by the horns, no matter how scary it was or what the risks were. And how risky could Paris be? He was right about that too. What if she loved it? And if she didn't, she'd come home. She was suddenly glad he had called her. He had given her courage when she needed it. His call had turned out to be a gift.

'Let me know what you decide. E-mail me sometime.'

'I will,' she said softly. 'Thanks for calling, Ted. You really helped me.'

'No, I didn't,' he said honestly. 'You know what you

want to do. Just do it. Take a chance, Brig. It won't be as scary as you think. It never is.'

She thanked him again, and they hung up a minute later, and she sat staring at the phone, thinking about it. It felt strange having heard from him, but good in a way too. It was closure of some kind. They had needed that, and never had it until he called. He had been too chicken to do it before. But at least he had now.

She still wanted to think about the AUP offer. She didn't want to make any hasty decisions. She needed a couple of days. She wondered if maybe she should talk to her mother, or Amy. She went back to her computer and read the e-mail again. It was simple and clear, and a nice clean offer, in a city that she loved. And she had one friend there, Marc. He was more than a friend, she knew, but she hadn't wanted to take a chance on that either. And then, before she could change her mind, she hit the reply button. She thanked them for their very kind offer. She said that she knew it was an excellent school, and she had very much enjoyed her interview with them. She realized then that the letter she was writing was setting it up for her to decline. She sucked in her breath then, and wrote the next line. She almost wanted to scream while she did it. 'I accept your offer. I would like to have one of the apartments you mentioned. Thank you very much. See you in two weeks.' And she signed it and hit the send button. She thought she was going to faint when she did it. But she had done it! And if she hated it, she could quit and come home. A whole new life had just begun.

Chapter 22

Brigitte thought about e-mailing Marc after she sent the one to AUP, but she decided not to. It seemed like too much pressure on both of them, and too much anticipation about what would happen, or might not. She was nervous enough about the job, without worrying how he felt about her for the next two weeks. So she said nothing. He wrote her an e-mail a few days later, and she acted as though everything were normal in Boston. She said she was doing some writing, the weather was beautiful, and asked about his book. Their e-mail exchange was casual and friendly, which was all she wanted right now, until she got there at least.

It took her two days to get up the guts to tell her mother, and another day to tell Amy after that.

Her mother was startled but not entirely surprised. She wanted to know if it had anything to do with the writer who had helped her at the archives, and Brigitte said it didn't, which wasn't entirely true, but she didn't want to admit that to her just yet, or even to herself. And whatever the reason, her mother thought it was a great idea. She said she hated to have her so far away, but she thought it would be a wonderful change for Brigitte and just what she needed. Her mother was aware too that her life had been in a stall for a while. Paris was going to be a wonderful change for her. Her mother promised to come over and visit her in the fall, and after reading all of the material Brigitte had gathered for her, she wanted to visit the château now too.

For some reason, it was harder for her to tell Amy. She felt guilty for leaving Boston, as though she were abandoning her, leaving her alone to cope with her two kids. But it was a choice Amy had made when she decided to have them, and she never complained.

'You're doing *what?*' Amy said, staring at her, when Brigitte told her, sitting in her kitchen. She had mumbled it, and had asked Amy if she could come over for a few minutes. Amy could see that something was up the minute she walked in. Brigitte looked uncomfortable and nervous, and she had a sudden feeling that she was going to follow

Ted to Egypt, and she hoped she wouldn't. She was totally unprepared for the announcement about Paris, and was blindsided by it.

'I'm taking a job at AUP and moving to Paris,' Brigitte repeated, looking miserable. It had been harder to tell her than she feared, but she had to. She was leaving in ten days.

'Holy shit, girl!' Amy exploded, beaming at her. 'That's fantastic! How did that happen, or when? You never told me you applied there.'

'I didn't . . . well, I did . . . but I didn't mean it. Marc set it up with a friend of his when I was there. I just went to humor him. They e-mailed me three days ago. I was too scared to tell you. I thought you'd be upset.' She smiled at her jubilant friend in relief. Amy was the most generous person she knew, and always happy for other people's victories and successes, instead of rejoicing in their defeats as so many others did. It was easy to see that she was thrilled for her friend.

'Of course I'm upset. I'm going to miss you. But there's nothing for you here. You've done it. It was right for a while, but Ted's gone, your job disappeared, you might as well get your ass out of Dodge and try something new. And Paris is about as good as it gets. What does that guy think? Marc, whatever his name is?'

'I didn't tell him. And I sent the man who hired me an e-mail asking him not to tell him either. That's too much pressure for me right now. I can't deal with his expectations and a new job too.'

Amy looked surprised. She thought he had more to do with it than he apparently did. Brigitte looked nervous about him too, not just the job. 'Are you going to tell him when you get there?' It would have seemed strange to Amy if not, except that she knew her well, that she hated change and had an aversion to risk. And right now Brigitte was dealing with both. She was scared shitless. But she was doing it anyway. For once she wasn't taking the easy way, she was facing things head on, and throwing caution to the winds. The writing she'd been doing about Wachiwi was helping her. It was a constant reminder of how brave some people were, and how well things turned out sometimes. Wachiwi's story had had a happy ending. Brigitte was beginning to think that hers could too. And she couldn't hide in her rabbit hole forever, afraid to take chances.

'Yes, I'm going to tell Marc when I get there,' she answered Amy's question. 'Just not yet.' And then she admitted, 'I'm too scared. What am I going to do if I get a good offer from a school here before I go?' She'd been worrying about that for days. It would create a real dilemma for her if that happened.

'Turn it down, silly. Paris or Boston? Now there's an easy decision.' For Amy maybe, not for Brigitte. She would never have had the courage to make the choices Amy had, and she wouldn't have wanted to. She wanted children, but not the way Amy had done it, at a sperm bank. It seemed too uncertain to her, and children seemed like too much responsibility to her to take on alone. If she never married or found the right man, she was prepared not to have children. She and Amy were just very different people, with different needs.

The two women talked for a while, and Amy was startled to realize she was leaving in ten days. It was so soon, and Brigitte had a mountain of things to do before she left. She had decided to get rid of a lot of her things, and put the rest in storage. The studio apartment they were offering her in Paris was furnished, and she didn't want to take too much with her. She asked Amy if there was anything she wanted, and she said she'd come and look that week before they got taken away.

'So when are you going to tell this guy?' she asked, curious about Brigitte's relationship with Marc. She kept saying they were just friends, but Amy didn't believe her. There was a light in her eyes every time she mentioned him, and she insisted on their 'just friendship' much too often.

'I'll tell him when I'm in Paris. Maybe after I get settled.'

'Don't wait too long,' Amy warned. 'If he's a good one, someone else will grab him.'

'If that happens, then he's not meant for me,' Brigitte said coolly. She was thinking of Wachiwi, who had fallen in love with Jean and left for France with him, and ended up marrying his brother. You could never predict what would happen. There was an element of destiny in everything that one could never account for. And it applied to her relationship with Marc too. Whatever it turned out to be would be the right thing in the end. She was convinced of that now. And she wasn't going to rush it.

She told Amy then that Ted had called her, and she looked surprised again.

'What did he want?'

'Some kind of closure, I think. It was okay. It was weird hearing from him at first. He called right after I got the e-mail from AUP, and I was hysterical. He actually helped me. He thought I should do it.'

'Of course he did. Because if you go off to Paris and have a new life, then he doesn't have to feel so guilty for dumping you here in a hot New York minute, and on Valentine's night yet.' Amy had never approved of how brutally he had left her. She had lost all respect for him when he did, and she felt very sorry for Brigitte.

'Maybe it was for the best in the end. I could have wasted another five or six years. It was never right,' she admitted to her friend. 'I just didn't want to see it.'

'He could have been nicer about it,' Amy said sternly.

'Yes he could,' Brigitte conceded. 'I'm not even mad at him anymore. It was strange talking to him though, it felt so disconnected. It was like talking to a stranger. Maybe we always were.' Amy nodded and didn't comment. She had never thought much of the relationship or him. He seemed so totally without passion, except about his work. She hoped the new man in Paris was better, if Brigitte decided to get involved with him. She wondered if she would, but it was beginning to seem likely. And she could no longer use the geographic excuse to avoid it. Maybe that was why she was being cautious about telling him. She wanted to give herself options, or at least that was what Amy thought. All Amy wanted for Brigitte was for her to find a good man. She hoped this one was.

Brigitte spent the rest of the week putting the things she wanted to keep in boxes, and stacking the rest to give away. She got rid of books, mementoes that no longer meant anything to her, sports equipment Ted had left and never reclaimed. She was amazed at much of the stuff she had collected. And she made a small pile of things she wanted to send to Paris for her apartment there, photographs of her mother, some reference books and research papers, and a few sentimental things she knew she'd miss too much if she put them in storage. There were photographs of her with her parents when she was small, a nice one of Amy with her kids. And she put away all the photos of her with Ted. She didn't need them anymore, and had meant to put them away months before. This was a good time for her to sort through everything and get rid of what she didn't need, and all the things that had become obsolete in her life. She put all her mementoes with Ted in a box and sent them to storage. She couldn't bring herself to throw them away.

And then finally, it was over. The apartment was empty, her bags were packed, the furniture had been stored. Amy had taken a few things, and she'd given her the couch she bought with Ted. She didn't need it anymore, and if she came back, she wanted to start fresh. But for now her fresh start was in Paris.

Her last evening with Amy was one of laughter and tears. They reminisced about silly things they'd done together, jokes they'd played on each other and friends. Brigitte remembered the births of both her babies and had been there, and now she was going three thousand miles away, but she was feeling calmer about it than she had at first.

'I know it sounds stupid,' she said to Amy as they sat in her kitchen, 'but I feel like I've finally grown up. I guess I've been coasting for a long time and didn't know it. I think this is the first time I've made a big decision, and didn't just back into it, or slide into home base.'

'I think you hit a home run on this one,' Amy praised her. She totally approved of her decision to go to Paris. And even if it wasn't the right job in the end, it was a great idea to try it, and it might open a door to something else. She had said as much to Brigitte. 'I hope it works out with Marc too.'

'I'm not expecting anything except friendship,' Brigitte said simply, and she almost meant it. Not totally.

'That's what you're expecting. But what do you want, Brig? If you had a magic wand, what would you wish for? A life with this guy, or someone else?' It was an important question, and Brigitte thought about it before she answered. And when she did, she spoke softly.

'I don't know him well enough to be sure. But maybe a life with him. He's a good person, and I really like him. We get along, and I think we respect each other and we have a lot in common. That's a good beginning.'

'Sounds like it to me,' Amy said, smiling at her friend. 'Then I'll keep my fingers crossed for you that it works out. I'm going to miss you like crazy though if you stay there.'

'Boston's not so far. I'll come to visit. I'll come to see my mom in New York anyway.'

'And if I ever get these wild Indians of mine tamed, I'll come to Europe.' But they both knew it wouldn't be anytime soon. And Amy needed every penny she made to support them. No one helped her, which made her decision to have them even more courageous.

'I'll call you,' Brigitte promised when she left. And they had e-mail. They e-mailed each other frequently anyway, even right in Boston. Being three thousand miles away from Amy was going to leave a huge void in her life. She was used to having her right down the hall at work, or a few minutes away.

They both shed a few tears as they hugged each other, and then Brigitte ran down the steps, waving, and walked home. She had sold her car the week before and had gotten a decent price for it. She had disbanded a whole life in ten days. Twelve years in Boston were over.

None of the schools she had sent her résumé to made her a last-minute offer. So the decision to take the job in Paris had been a good one. Brigitte couldn't help wondering if it was the only offer she would get at all. And she had texted Ted a few days before that she was going and thanked him for his input. He really had helped her. It had been just the push she needed to jump off the diving board into the water. And she was waiting to see now if her arrival would be a big splash or a small one. She had to see what happened when she got to AUP, and then saw Marc.

The morning after she said goodbye to Amy, Brigitte rented a car and drove to New York. She didn't want to take her two big suitcases on a commuter flight, and the drive down was pleasant. It was a beautiful June day and the sun was shining, and she found herself singing as she drove. She was feeling good about her decision.

She spent three days with her mother. They went to the theater, and out to dinner. Her mother showed her how she had organized the information Brigitte had given her, and it fit in with the rest. Everything was in order, and they could track their family easily now to 1750. Her mother still wanted to pursue their ancestors before that, all the way to the time the château had been built in the twelfth century, but she was on the right track now and thought she could do the rest of it herself.

'How's your book coming?' she asked Brigitte over dinner.

'I haven't had time to work on it, I've been too busy packing. I'll get back to it in Paris.'

'This is very exciting,' Marguerite said, smiling at her proudly. 'A new job, a new city, a new book, maybe a new man.' She hoped so for her sake. Either Marc or another, just so she was happy. But Brigitte looked very content these days. She had ever since she came back from France the last time. When her mother last saw her, she was still high from her trip and all that she had discovered. There had been some nasty slumps since then, which led to her decision to leave Boston. She had no regrets at all now, and only a few fears. Day by day it felt more right to her than ever. She was feeling confident about the job. The big question in her mind was Marc.

They had exchanged several e-mails, all very friendly. School was almost out for the summer, and he was delighted. He said he was going to the mountains for a vacation in August, to visit some distant cousins. And he said he was going to be in Paris in July. He had asked what she was doing, and she said she didn't have plans yet, which was true. She wanted to settle into her job, and get used to living in the city. She had told him she had a new job, but she didn't say where. And he had forgotten to ask her which school, so she didn't have to dodge the question. She didn't lie, she just didn't tell him. A sin of omission, not commission. And eventually she would thank him for the introduction to his friend at AUP, but not yet. She wanted to see him again first before she told him anything, and see how they both felt. There had been contradictions in their relationship before, the easy friendship that they had both enjoyed, and the kisses beneath the Eiffel Tower on her last night. She didn't know which route they would take, or which one she wanted, the friend or the man. And she wasn't just passing through town now. She would be living there full time, so a relationship between them would have to make sense, to both of them, and not just be an accident of chance. She didn't want to make the same mistakes she had with Ted, of falling into something easy, and never asking the right questions, of him or herself. This time she wanted answers before she took any leaps. She didn't want to be lazy or scared, she wanted to be wise, and have her eyes wide open, not just her heart.

The night that she left New York, she and her mother had an early dinner. They talked until she left for the airport, and her mother hugged her tight before she left. 'Take care of yourself, sweetheart. Have a wonderful time, and I hope you meet lots of good people there, and have a great time.' They promised to call each other, and Brigitte knew they would. They called each other often, and worried about each other. There were tears in Marguerite's eyes when she kissed her. All she wanted was for her daughter to be happy. It was what Brigitte wanted for herself too, and she hoped she would be in Paris.

Legacy

As she went down in the elevator with her bags, it was exciting to know that in exactly nine hours she'd be there. She could hardly wait.

Chapter 23

She was flying Air France on the midnight flight. It would land her in Paris at noon, local time. And the human resource office had told her that her keys would be waiting with the concierge of her building, and they had e-mailed her the address. It was on the rue du Bac, right near Tristan and Wachiwi's house, which felt like a good omen to her.

It was a six-hour flight, with a six-hour time difference from New York. The service on the plane was excellent, and it wasn't too crowded. The two seats next to her were empty, so she could lie down, and she covered herself with a blanket and slept. She felt refreshed when she woke up, and she had breakfast before they landed. Croissants, yogurt, fruit, and coffee. And the next thing she knew, they had touched down.

She went through immigration and customs without problem, and found a luggage cart for her bags, and they just managed to fit in the Parisian taxi. She gave him the address in French. He nodded and they were off in the heavy traffic from Roissy to the city. It took them almost an hour to get there. And she looked at everything once they arrived in the city. The streets on the Left Bank already looked somewhat familiar to her from her recent stay in April, and she was thrilled when they drove past Tristan's house on the rue du Bac on the way to her new address. Tristan and Wachiwi were part of her life now, and they would be increasingly so while she wrote the book, which brought them to life for her. She felt as though they were her best friends now, or much-loved relatives she couldn't wait to see again. She could see them on the pages that she was writing.

She paid the cab driver, pressed the code on the outer door, pushed it open, walked through a narrow passage to a courtyard, and pressed the buzzer marked 'concierge.' It was the apartment where the woman lived who ran the building. The building itself looked charming and ancient, but everything looked well tended and clean. And the concierge knew immediately who she was, handed her the keys, pointed to the sky, and said, '*Troisième étage.*' Third floor. Brigitte thanked her and saw that there was a tiny cagelike elevator that looked barely bigger than a bread-basket. She put her bags in one on top of the other, and then ran up the stairs herself. There was no room for her and the bags. She already knew that the third floor in France was the equivalent of the fourth in the States, and she was out of breath when she got there, and then pulled her bags out of the narrow cage.

She used the keys to enter the apartment, and had already been warned by the school that it was tiny, but it was much better than she had expected. It had an unobstructed view over the rooftops, and at a little distance looked down into a convent garden full of trees, and then her breath caught as she looked straight ahead. She had a perfect view of the Eiffel Tower, and at night when it was all lit up, it would be a light show just for her. It was the perfect apartment. From now on the hourly fireworks and sparks of the Eiffel Tower in the dark would be right outside her window. She could hardly wait. She sat down and smiled as she looked around her for a minute and then explored the apartment. She was smiling from ear to ear. There was a tiny mouse-sized kitchen, with a miniature oven, a microwave, and a fridge barely big enough to keep the makings of a meal in. But everything was clean and neat. And there was no bedroom, just the one good-sized room where she would sleep and live, and then she realized that she could see the Eiffel Tower from her bed. There was a round dining table in front of the window and four chairs. The furniture was worn but pretty. The upholstery was oatmeal color, and the curtains were old pink satin. There were two big leather chairs in front of a fireplace, and a small couch across from her bed. There was ample room to entertain in, live, and have a life in, and best of all she had the view. And when she checked, the bathroom was marble and the tub was a decent size. She had everything she needed, and sat down on the bed and grinned.

'Welcome home,' she said out loud, and felt that way. She still had to unpack, but she didn't want to get started. There was something she had to do first. She had put it off long enough.

She dialed Marc's number on her BlackBerry, and he sounded surprised. She had only called him once since April, normally they e-mailed each other. He seemed genuinely startled to hear her, but very pleased.

'Is this a bad time?' she asked cautiously. She could hear noise around him, and he sounded busy.

'Not at all. I'm being very lazy. I'm sitting in a café. The one we went to across from your hotel, the first time we had coffee. I come here a lot now.' He loved going there because it reminded him of her. And she knew exactly where it was. She picked up her sweater as she talked to him, left her apartment and locked the door, and kept talking to him on her BlackBerry as she hurried down the stairs. He was only a few blocks away, which made it so easy for her.

'And where are you?' he wanted to visualize her where she was. He was reveling in the sound of her voice, and she was smiling as she ran, trying not to sound out of breath. She had crossed the courtyard by then, and gone through the outer doors, and had just reached the rue du Bac.

'I'm just leaving my apartment. I'm walking down the street,' she said to explain the noise around her. 'I just thought I'd call to say hi.'

'That was nice of you,' he sounded happy. He wanted to tell her he missed her, but he didn't dare. She had been so clear with him about being only friends because they lived so far apart. But even if he didn't say it, he had missed her ever since she left. For a short time she had filled his days and evenings, and ever since his life seemed bleak without her. He was thinking of going to Boston one of these days to see her, but he hadn't broached the subject to her yet. He was planning to soon and see how she reacted to the suggestion. 'How's the book coming?'

'I haven't had time to work on it for a couple of weeks. I've been too busy.'

'How's your new job?'

'I haven't started yet. I start next week.' He was still disappointed that she hadn't taken one in Paris, but he didn't say that to her either. And by then she was standing across the street from him, and saw him at the café. He was sitting at a small table, and he looked just the way he had before. His hair was a little shorter, and he was wearing one of the jackets she had seen him in and liked. Her heart skipped a beat as she watched him, unseen by him. This was more than a friend. She had known that it would be clear to her when she saw him again, and it was. She had suspected it the night she kissed him, and now she knew for sure. She fell silent as she stood there, smiling, so happy that she had come back. She wondered if Wachiwi had felt that way when she first saw Jean, or later her husband. Something in Brigitte's gut flipped over, and she felt sure it was her heart. She had forgotten to say anything to him for several minutes, she was so engrossed in what she was seeing, and she saw him look concerned.

'Are you there?' He thought they had been cut off, and she laughed. As she did, she saw him smile. It was funny watching him, without his knowing she was there.

'No, I'm not there, I'm here,' she said, teasing him.

'Where? What do you mean?' They were both laughing, and as though sensing her near him, he turned, and saw her across the street, walking slowly toward him. Without thinking he stood up and just stared at her, and then he walked toward her too. They met on the sidewalk, and he looked down at her with the gentlest look of love she'd ever seen.

'What are you doing here?' he asked her, utterly confused. She was like a vision, as though his wish had been granted and she appeared.

'A lot of things, I think,' she answered cryptically. 'I took a job here . . . the one you found me at AUP. I was going to thank you but I wanted to surprise you when I arrived.'

'When did you get here?' He wanted to know everything, and he was beaming as people walked around them, as they stood facing each other holding hands. Paris was used to lovers, and no one complained or cared that they were blocking the sidewalk, and neither did they. All they could see was each other.

'About three hours ago,' she said in answer to his question. 'They gave me an apartment on the rue du Bac. I have a perfect view of the Eiffel Tower from my window. The place is the size of a postage stamp, but I already love it.' And she hoped he would too. The big leather chairs would be just right for him when he came to visit.

'And you're going to be working here?' He looked ecstatic. It was Christmas in June for him, and hopefully for her too. He wanted both of them to make this decision, consciously, not just him, and so did she.

'Three days a week, and the book.'

'For how long?' He already looked worried, he didn't want her to leave.

'They offered me a year. We'll see after that.' He nodded. Maybe by then she'd be writing full time and living with him. He hoped so. Now that she was here, he had myriad plans for them, if she agreed. And then she looked at him shyly. She wanted him to know the rest. He had been very patient with her last time, and she thought it was only fair to tell him. She had said it to no one else. She wanted to see him first. 'I didn't just come for the job,' she said softly as he moved closer to her, and touched her face with the long gentle fingers she remembered from when he had kissed her last time. He had touched her that way then too.

'What did you come for then?' he asked her. They had both forgotten their phones and still held them in their hands, connected to each other, as they were. A connection never to be broken, hopefully lasting forever.

'I came for you . . . for us . . . to see what would happen if we live in the same city . . .'

'That was very brave of you,' he said as he kissed her, and then looked at her again.

'Wachiwi helped me do it. I figured that if she could be so brave, so could I. I wanted to take the chance.' For the first time in her life.

'And what do you want to happen?' he asked her then.

'Whatever is meant to be. I had to find out what this is, and what we are to each other.'

'I think we know.' She nodded, and he walked over to leave some money on the table he had abandoned, and then he came back to put an arm around her and walk her home. He had his briefcase with him, and he swung it as they walked down the rue du Bac. They both noticed Tristan's house as they passed it and smiled, and a minute later they were at her new address, and she invited him upstairs. They bounded up the stairs like puppies, teasing each other and laughing. She took her keys out, opened her door, and he followed her inside. As she had, he liked what he saw. It was warm and welcoming, and even though it was only one room, it wasn't too small. Even with the two of them there, it was very livable. He stood at the window with her, admiring the view. They looked down at the convent garden below, and then straight in front of them at the Eiffel Tower. It was the perfect Paris apartment. And as he put his arms around her, he kissed her with all the longing of the past two months without her. It had seemed endless to him, and in fact hadn't been very long. He never wanted her to leave again. He wanted her to stay with him in Paris, to discover the wonders of it with him, just as Tristan had when he brought Wachiwi to Paris and took her to court.

'I love you, Brigitte,' he said into her neck, and then kissed her again, and suddenly worried that he had frightened her and gone too far, but she didn't look worried when he looked into her eyes. She was smiling at him and looked totally comfortable and at peace.

'I love you too.' She was sure of it this time. She had no doubts or fears. This time she knew it was right. Her search for her Sioux ancestor had led her to him, and he had found her just as he was meant to. A miracle had happened to them. Destiny. The perfect plan. And they both knew she was here to stay. Just like the little Sioux two hundred years before.

Turn the page
for a sneak preview of
Danielle Steel's
wonderful new novel,

HOTEL
VENDÔME

Chapter 1

The scene in the lobby of the Hotel Vendôme on East 69th Street in New York was one of impeccable elegance and meticulous precision. The black-and-white-checked marble floors were immaculate, red runners were rolled out the instant there was a drop of rain outside, the moldings on the walls were exquisite, and the enormous crystal chandelier that hung in the lobby was reminiscent of the finest palaces in Europe. The hotel was much smaller than the one that had inspired its decor, but for practiced travelers, it was remarkably similar to the Ritz in Paris, where the Hotel Vendôme's owner had worked as an assistant manager for two years, during his training in the finest hotels in Europe.

Hugues Martin was forty years old, a graduate of the

illustrious and respected Ecole Hôtelière de Lausanne in Switzerland, and the hotel on Manhattan's Upper East Side was his dream. He still couldn't believe how lucky he had been, how perfectly it had all come together five years before. His Swiss banker father and equally conservative mother had been devastated when he announced that he wanted to go to hotel school. He came from a family of bankers, and they thought that running a hotel, or working in one, had a seamy quality to it, of which they strongly disapproved. They had done everything they could to talk him out of it, to no avail. After four years at the school in Lausanne, he trained and eventually had respected positions at the Hotel du Cap in Cap d'Antibes, the Ritz in Paris, and Claridge's in London, and even did a brief stint at the famed Peninsula Hotel in Hong Kong. He figured out during that time that if he ever had his own hotel, he wanted it to be somewhere in the States.

Hugues worked at the Plaza in New York before it closed for extensive renovations, and he assumed that he was still light-years away from his dream. Then it happened. The Hotel Mulberry was put up for sale, a small tired hotel that had been run-down for years and had never been considered chic, despite its perfect location. When he heard about it, Hugues put together every penny of his savings, took out every loan he could get in both New York and

Switzerland, and used all of the modest inheritance his parents had left him, which he had carefully put aside and invested. And the combination made the purchase of the hotel possible. He just managed to do it, with a mortgage on the building. And suddenly Hugues was able to buy the Mulberry and do the necessary renovations, which took two years, and at the end of it the Hotel Vendôme was born, to the amazement of New Yorkers, most of whom said they had never even realized that there was a hotel in that location.

The building had been a small private hospital in the 1920s and was turned into a hotel in the 1940s, with abysmally bad decor. In contrast, in its transformed state, every inch of the Vendôme was magnificent, and the service was superb. Hugues had brought chefs from all over the world for their now extremely popular restaurant. His catering manager was one of the best in the business, and everyone agreed that even the food from room service was fantastic. In its first year it had become an overnight success and was booked months in advance now, with reservations made by visitors to the city from around the world. The presidential suite was one of the finest in the city. The Hotel Vendôme was an absolute gem, with beautifully decorated suites, and rooms with fireplaces, moldings, and high ceilings. The hotel faced south, so most of the rooms were sunny, and Hugues had chosen the finest china, crystal, and linens, and as many antiques as he could afford, like the chandelier in the lobby, which he had bought in Geneva at a Christie's auction. It had come out of a French château near Bordeaux and was in perfect condition.

Hugues ran his 120-room hotel with Swiss precision, a warm smile, and an iron hand. His employees were discreet and experienced, had a remarkable memory for every guest, and kept detailed files on each important client's needs and requests while they were there. It had made the Vendôme the most popular small hotel in New York for the past three years. And the moment one entered the lobby, one knew it was a special place. A young bellboy stood at the revolving door, in a uniform inspired by those the *chasseurs* wore at the Ritz: navy pants, a short jacket, a small amount of gold braid on the collar, and a little round hat with a strap under the chin, tilted at an angle. To meet the clients' needs, there was a fleet of willing bellmen, a crew of brilliantly capable concierges. Everyone moved rapidly to serve the guests, and the entire staff was ready to service large requests and small ones. Hugues knew that impeccable service was essential.

The assistant managers wore black tailcoats and striped trousers, once again inspired by the Ritz. And Hugues himself was on hand night and day, in a dark blue suit, always with a white shirt and dark Hermès tie, and he had an extraordinary memory for everyone who had stayed with them and, whenever possible, greeted important guests himself. He was the consummate hotel owner, and no detail missed his practiced eye. And he expected his department heads to meet the standards that he set. Guests of the hotel came as much for the service as the luxurious decor.

As an added touch, the hotel was always filled with spectacular flowers, and its spa was one of the best. There was almost no service the staff wouldn't provide, as long as it was legal and in relatively good taste. And despite the objections Hugues knew his parents had had, he couldn't help feeling that they would have been proud of him now. He had used their money well, and the hotel had been such a success in its first three years that he was almost out of debt. It wasn't surprising, since Hugues worked day and night himself to make it what it was. And personally, his victory had come at a high price. Owning the hotel had cost him his wife. It had been the subject of considerable gossip among staff and guests.

Nine years before, when Hugues had been working at Claridge's in London, he had met Miriam Vale, the internationally famous and spectacularly beautiful supermodel.

And like everyone else who laid eyes on her, he had been dazzled by her the moment they met. He had been infinitely proper and professional, as he had always been with guests of the hotels he worked in, but she was a twenty-three-year-old girl, and she had made it clear that she wanted him, and he fell head over heels in love with her overnight. She was American, and eventually he had followed her back to New York. It had been an exciting time for him, and he took a lesser position at the Plaza to be in the same city with her and continue their romance. And much to his own amazement, she was just as much in love with him, and they were married within six months. He had never been happier in his life than in their early years together.

Eighteen months later their daughter Heloise was born, and Hugues was madly in love with his wife and child. He trembled when he said it, for fear of angering the gods, but he always said then that he had the perfect life. And he was a dedicated man. Despite whatever temptations came his way in the hotel business, he was totally in love with and faithful to his wife. She continued her modeling career after Heloise was born, and everyone at the Plaza had fawned over his little girl and indulged her, and teased them about her name. Hugues assured them honestly that she had been named after his great-grandmother and he didn't expect to stay at the Plaza forever, so there was no reason not to use the name. Heloise was two years old when he bought the Mulberry and turned it into the Vendôme. He had everything he wanted then, a wife and child he loved, and his own hotel. Miriam had been far less enthused about the project and had complained bitterly that it would take too much of his time, but owning his own hotel, and one of the sort he was creating, had always been his dream.

His parents had been even less pleased about Miriam than they had been about his working in the hotel business. They had serious doubts that a spoiled, twenty-three-year-old, spectacularly beautiful, internationally known supermodel would make him a good wife. But Hugues loved her profoundly and had no doubts.

As Hugues had expected, it took two years to renovate the hotel.

It came in only slightly over budget, and the end result was everything he had hoped.

He and Miriam had been married for six years, and Heloise was four, when the Hotel Vendôme opened, and Miriam had obligingly posed for some of their ads. It added a distinctive cachet that the owner was married to Miriam Vale, and male guests in particular always hoped they'd catch a glimpse of her in the lobby or at the bar.

What they saw far more frequently than her mother was four-year-old Heloise following after her father, with one of the maids holding her hand, and she enchanted everyone she met. She had gone from being Heloise at the Plaza to being Heloise at the Vendôme, and became something of a mascot for the hotel, and was clearly the pride and joy of her father's life.

Greg Bones, the famous and notoriously badly behaved rock star, was one of the first guests in one of the penthouse suites, and fell in love with the hotel. Hugues was uneasy about it, because Bones was well known for trashing hotel rooms and causing chaos wherever he stayed, but he behaved surprisingly well at the Vendôme, much to Hugues's relief. And they were fully prepared to meet celebrity needs and requests.

On Greg's second day there, he met Miriam Vale Martin at the bar, surrounded by assistants, magazine editors, stylists, and a famous photographer after a shoot. They had just finished a twelve-page spread for Vogue that afternoon, and as soon as they recognized Greg Bones, they invited him to join them. And what happened afterward hadn't taken long. Miriam spent most of the following night in Greg's suite with him, while Hugues thought she was out when he was working. The maids were all aware of where she was and what had happened – the room service waiters discovered it when Greg ordered champagne and caviar for them at midnight. And it rapidly became the backstairs talk of the hotel and spread like a forest fire. By the end of the week Hugues had heard about it too. He didn't know whether to confront her or to hope it would pass.

Hugues, Miriam, and Heloise had their own private apartment one floor below the two penthouse suites, and the hotel security were well aware that Miriam was constantly slipping up the back stairs to join Greg in his suite, whenever Hugues was in his office. It was an extremely awkward situation for Hugues, who didn't want to ask the famous rock star to leave the hotel. It would cause a public scandal. Instead he begged his wife to come to her senses and behave. He suggested she go away for a few days, to stop the madness of what she was doing. But when Bones checked out, she flew to Los Angeles with him on his private plane. She left Heloise with Hugues and promised she'd be back in a few weeks, and said this was something she had to get out of her system, and begged him to understand. It was a heartbreak and humiliation for Hugues, but he didn't want to lose his wife. He hoped that if he let her do it, she'd get over her infatuation quickly. She was twenty-nine years old, and he thought she'd come to her senses. He loved her, and they had a child. But it was all over the tabloids by then, and on Page Six of the *New York Post*. It was a crushing humiliation for Hugues, in front of all of his employees and an entire city.

Hugues told Heloise that her mother had to go away to work, which was something that the little girl already understood at four. The story became harder to maintain when Miriam didn't come home. And three months later, back in London with Greg Bones, Miriam told him she was filing for divorce. It had been the most devastating moment of his life, and although his demeanor with the guests was unchanged, and he was ever smiling and attentive to them, in the three years since, those who knew him well were aware that he had never been the same again. He was far more aloof, serious, deeply hurt, and withdrawn in his private moments, although he put a good face on it for his staff and guests.

Hugues had been the soul of discretion since the divorce. His assistant and some of his department heads were aware of quiet affairs he had had, occasionally with hotel guests or with well-bred or accomplished women around the city. He was one of the most sought-after bachelors in New York, invited to everything, although he rarely accepted. He preferred to keep a low profile, and keep his personal life to himself. And most of the time he was working at the hotel. The hotel came before all else for him, except for his daughter, who came first. He hadn't had a serious relationship since Miriam left and didn't want one. He believed that to run a hotel properly, you had to sacrifice your own life. He was always there, keeping an eye on everything, and working incredible hours, most of the time behind the scenes to ensure the smooth running of the hotel.

A month after her divorce from Hugues was final, Miriam married Greg Bones, and they had been married now for two years and had just had a baby girl six months before. Heloise had only seen her mother a few times since she left. Heloise was sad about it. And Hugues was angry at Miriam. She was too busy in her new life, too obsessed with Greg, and now their child, to tend to their daughter or even see her. Heloise and Hugues had become relics of her past. It left Hugues no other choice but to be both mother and father to their child. He never commented on it to Heloise, but he considered it a painful circumstance for them both.

At the hotel Heloise was constantly surrounded by doting surrogate mothers, at the concierge desk, in room service, the maids, the florist, the hairdresser, and the girls who worked in the spa. Everyone loved Heloise. They were no substitute for a real mother, but at least she had a happy life, adored her father, and at seven she was the princess of the Hotel Vendôme. Their regular guests knew her, and once in a while brought her little gifts, and thanks to her father's attention to her education and manners, she was both adorable and extremely polite. She wore pretty little smocked dresses, and the hairdresser did her long red hair in braids with ribbons every day before she went to school at the Lycee Français nearby. Her father walked her to school every morning before he started work. Her mother called her once every month or two, if she remembered.

Read the complete novel – available now

Big Girl

Danielle Steel

'Watch out, world. Here I come!'

FOR VICTORIA DAWSON, growing up isn't a happy experience. Born to picture-perfect parents, she never feels pretty enough to meet their expectations. But when her parents have a second child, Victoria is thrilled – she can't help but adore her new baby sister Gracie. And since Gracie is the image of them, her parents finally have the perfect daughter they always wanted. Meanwhile Victoria still never seems to get it quite right – she battles with her weight, she's told she'll never find a man if she's too clever, and the one career she feels passionate about her parents don't approve of.

And so Victoria decides to move to New York to fulfil her dreams and escape her family. Though her new life is exciting, the old temptations remain, and she continues to wage war with the scales.

Victoria struggles to find a life far from the hurt and neglect of her childhood, the damage created by her parents, the courage to find freedom, and become who she really is at last.

9780552159005

Happy Birthday

Danielle Steel

Time to blow out the candles, say goodbye to the past, and make a wish for the future . . .

For April Wyatt, turning thirty is not what she had expected. She's single, with no interest in changing that in the foreseeable future. Her popular, successful restaurant in downtown New York – where she is chef and owner – consumes every ounce of her passion, attention and energy. Ready or not, though, April's life is about to change, in a tumultuous discovery on the morning of her milestone birthday.

April's mother Valerie is a popular TV personality and the queen of gracious living. Since her divorce long-ago, she has worked tirelessly to reach the pinnacle of her career and to create a camera-ready life in her Fifth Avenue penthouse. But she's having trouble equating her age with how she feels, and all the hours with her personal trainer, the careful work of top hairdressers and her natural good looks can't hide the fact that she is turning sixty, and the whole world discovers it on her birthday.

It is also Jack Adams' birthday – the most charismatic sports personality on TV, a man who has his pick of desirable younger women. But he fears his age may finally be catching up with him when he wakes up on his fiftieth birthday needing an emergency visit to the chiropractor . . .

A terrifying act of violence, an out-of-the-blue blessing, and two very unlikely love affairs soon turn lives inside out and upside down. As these three very different people celebrate their birthdays, they discover that life itself is a celebration – and that its greatest gifts are always a surprise . . .

9780593056851

44 Charles Street

Danielle Steel

What makes a house . . . a home?

Everything is falling to pieces for **Francesca Thayer**. Her beautiful, old house is full of leaks and in need of total restoration. Then her relationship with lawyer Todd collapses and he moves out. As the owner of a struggling art gallery she can't possibly manage the mortgage alone, so she is forced to do the one thing she never imagined she would: she advertises for lodgers.

First arrives **Eileen** – a young, attractive schoolteacher who has just moved from LA.

Then comes **Chris**, a newly-divorced father struggling with a difficult ex-wife and the challenges of parenting his seven-year-old son who visits every other weekend.

Last to arrive is **Marya** – a famous cookery author who is hoping to rebuild her life after the death of her husband.

And so Francesca finds that her house has become a whole new world – and as things begin to turn around, she realises that her accidental tenants have become the most important people in her life. Over their year together, the house at 44 Charles Street fills with laughter, hope and heartbreak.

And Francesca discovers that she might be able to open her heart again after all . . .

9780593063040